EN

F Wal

Walls of fear

DISCARD
THIS BOOK IS NO LONGER
THE PROPERTY OF THE
WILLIAM F. LAMAN PUBLIC LIBRARY

William F. Laman Public Library
2801 Orange Street
North Little Rock, Arkansas 72114,

William F. Laman Public Library
2801 Orange Street
North Little Rock, Arkansas 72114

Walls
of
Fear

Also edited by Kathryn Cramer:

Christmas Ghosts
The Architecture of Fear
Spirits of Christmas

Walls
of
Fear

Edited by
Kathryn Cramer

William F. Laman Public Library
2801 Orange Street
North Little Rock, Arkansas 72114

William Morrow and Company, Inc., New York
213232

Copyright © 1990 by Kathryn Cramer

Introduction copyright © 1990 by Kathryn Cramer
"Out of Sight, Out of Mind" copyright © 1990 by Jack Womack
"Tales from a New England Telephone Directory" copyright © 1990 by James Morrow
"Firetrap" copyright © 1990 by Greg Cox
"The Art of Falling Down" copyright © 1990 by Jonathan Carroll
"The Cairnwell Horror" copyright © 1990 by Chet Williamson
"Erosion" copyright © 1990 by Susan Palwick
"Happy Hour" copyright © 1990 by Ian Watson
"The Haunted Boardinghouse" copyright © 1990 by Gene Wolfe
"Inside the Walled City" copyright © 1990 by Garry Kilworth
"Grandmother's Footsteps" copyright © 1990 by Gwyneth Jones
"Madame Enchantia and the Maze of Dream" copyright © 1990 by Jessica Amanda
    Salmonson
"Slippage" copyright © 1990 by Edward Bryant
"The House on Rue Chartres" copyright © 1990 by Richard A. Lupoff
"House Hunter" copyright © 1990 by Sharon Baker
"Penelope Comes Home" copyright © 1990 by M. J. Engh
"Cedar Lane" copyright © 1990 by Karl Edward Wagner

All rights reserved. No part of this book may be reproduced or utilized in any form, or
by any means, electronic or mechanical, including photocopying, recording or by any
information storage and retrieval system, without permission in writing from the Publisher. Inquiries should be addressed to Permissions Department, William Morrow and
Company, Inc., 105 Madison Avenue, New York, N.Y. 10016.

Recognizing the importance of preserving what has been written, it is the policy of
William Morrow and Company, Inc., and its imprints and affiliates to have the books
it publishes printed on acid-free paper, and we exert our best efforts to that end.

Library of Congress Cataloging-in-Publication Data

Walls of fear / edited by Kathryn Cramer.
     p.   cm.
     ISBN 0-688-08967-4
     1. Horror tales, American.   2. Horror tales, English.
3. Buildings—Fiction.   I. Cramer, Kathryn, 1962–   .
PS648.H6W35   1990
813'.0873808—dc20   90-5728
                                                                      CIP

Printed in the United States of America

First Edition

1 2 3 4 5 6 7 8 9 10

BOOK DESIGN BY KARIN BATTEN

For Lloyd Currey, James Allen, Virginia Kidd, and David Hartwell, without whom I would not have learned to drive, without which this book would not have been possible

The editor wishes to acknowledge the help of the following people in the preparation of this book:

Susan Anne Protter, Jim Young, Jeff Yang, Scott Baker, Virginia Kidd, Jack Womack, Chris Miller, and most of all, my editor

David G. Hartwell

Contents

9

10 *Contents*

Introduction
Literary Architecture

KATHRYN CRAMER

And when a farmer has got his house, he may not be the richer but the poorer for it, and it be that the house has got him. . . . I know of two families in this town, who, for nearly a generation, have been trying to sell their houses in the outskirts and move into the village, but have not been able to accomplish it, and only death will set them free.

—Henry David Thoreau, "Economy," *Walden*

This is a companion volume to *The Architecture of Fear*, edited by Kathryn Cramer and Peter D. Pautz (Arbor House, 1987). That book came out of a horror discussion group composed of Peter Pautz, David Hartwell, and me—other books being *The Dark Descent*, edited by David G. Hartwell (Tor Books, 1987) and *Christmas Ghosts*, edited by Kathryn Cramer and David G. Hartwell (Arbor House, 1987). In 1985 and 1986, we met to discuss horror fiction once or twice a week in a coffee shop across the street from Arbor House, where David and Peter both worked.

We developed a theory of horror fiction, most of which is expressed in the introduction of *The Dark Descent*. Briefly, there are three modes in horror fiction: (1) moral allegory, about the colorful special effects of evil and focusing on the conflict between good and evil, for example, a story like Nathaniel Hawthorne's "Young Goodman Brown"; (2) psychological metaphor, in which internal

11

psychological states are externalized, like Edgar Allan Poe's "The Fall of the House of Usher"; and (3) nature-of-reality horror, in which the primary effect is derived from throwing the nature of our world into radical doubt; my favorite example is Gene Wolfe's story "Seven American Nights." Having worked with this terminology for three years, I have also come to recognize that there are stories that play these modes against one another. Examples that come to mind are "The Turn of the Screw" by Henry James and in this volume, "Cedar Lane" by Karl Edward Wagner.

David, Peter, and I had initially thought about writing a book of criticism. However, we were facing a major problem with the examples we wanted to use. Most of the stories were not part of the literary canon, and therefore we couldn't expect anyone else to have read them. One day David came in and said, "We should do anthologies."

We decided that there should be an original anthology and a historical reprint anthology, and divided up the territory: David, being the most authoritative, should do the historical anthology—thus was born *The Dark Descent*. Peter and I, combining complementary skills and youthful enthusiasm, would collaborate on an original anthology. It would be a theme anthology so as to have a simple marketing hook (theory, it was explained to me, is not a marketing hook). Since 1983, when I took a course in Women and Technology at the University of Washington, I had been pushing around my plate ideas about the psychological meaning of architecture. (I also took a writing course from Joanna Russ at that time. I talked with her about houses in horror fiction, and she told me I ought to write an essay.) So I argued that our original theme anthology should be about houses, and suggested the title *The Architecture of Fear*.

In the Afterword to *The Architecture of Fear*, entitled "Houses of the Mind," I argued for the metaphor of house as mind, and made a political argument for understanding architectural horror as a way toward understanding systemic evil. By invoking the fantastic, horror allows us access to hordes of dreadful things that are too painful to perceive directly. The architecture of fear is the central horror of life in the twentieth century, an Escheresque castle in which evil has been loosed repeatedly, unconstrained, has invaded our secure places and left us emotionally deadened and in doubt of both the nature of reality and the nature of actual horrors. Horror fiction can provide insight into nonfictional horrors, and, more important perhaps, awaken emotional response through the mirror of art.

Architectural horror uses architecture explicitly. The Jonathan Carroll story in this volume, "The Art of Falling Down," can be read as a literalization of Ellen Eve Frank's concept of literary architecture, "the habit of comparison between architecture and literature." To be called architectural horror, a story must contain at least one building of some sort. In this book, there are houses, a boarding-house, an apartment, a dollhouse, an ancient walled city transformed by time into a block of fused tenements, a pub, a phone booth, and more. There are three kinds of literary architecture: literal architecture, explicit architectural metaphor, and submerged architectural metaphor. Since there are three of these, I am unable to resist the temptation to pair them with the three modes of horror: literal architecture paired with moral allegory; explicit architectural metaphor paired with psychological metaphor; and submerged architectural metaphor paired with nature-of-reality horror. This is a bit too pat. All stories in this book contain literal architecture, and most contain some explicit and submerged architectural metaphor. But if we ponder these linkings in terms of the most important emotional function of the architecture in a story, they are useful toward understanding the relation of the three modes of horror to architectural horror.

In moral allegory, the architecture tends to be metaphorically related to other architecture: Your house is your fortress, keeping the bad things out. Or it is your prison, and you are locked in with *them,* and must throw them out.

In psychological metaphor, a house tends to be described in psychological terms, as in the famous opening paragraph of *The Haunting of Hill House:*

> No live organism can continue for long to exist under conditions of absolute reality; even larks and katydids are supposed, by some, to dream. Hill House, not sane, stood by itself against its hills, holding darkness within; it had stood so for eighty years and might stand for eighty more. Within, walls continued upright, bricks met neatly, floors were firm, and doors were sensibly shut; silence lay steadily against the wood and stone of Hill House, and whatever walked there, walked alone.

Also, Barnard Levi St. Armand published a wonderful Jungian analysis of the house Exham Priory in H. P. Lovecraft's "The Rats in the Walls," entitled *The Roots of Horror in the Fiction of H. P. Lovecraft.* (The structure of Exham Priory is psychologically similar to the house that Richard A. Lupoff's fictionalized H. P. Lovecraft visits in "The House on Rue Chartres" in this volume.)

In nature-of-reality horror, the structure of the house and characters' relationships to it have implications that undermine our confidence that we know the world. One such example is Robert Aickman's story "The Hospice," in which curtains conceal not windows but blank walls, and all the clues that we cling to in order to orient ourselves only serve to further disorient us.

As Julia Kristeva has argued in her book *Powers of Horror,* the emotional subject matter of horror is material on the edge of repression. If the material were completely repressed, we would have no access to it. So the borderland on the edge of repression is horror's natural territory. There are various ways to define horror *fiction,* but one of the most useful is that horror fiction is fiction whose emotional territory is horror.

Thus, the occupation of the horror writer is not to exceed all limits, but to dance around them, now stepping out, now stepping back, gracefully pulling us along while making us acutely aware of where the lines are. Some have recently argued that it is a horror writer's job to go too far, to break all taboos, exceed all limits. And while this spatial metaphor has some merit, its application has some problems. Once one goes too far beyond the edge of repression, the symbols cease to signify, cease to mean. The result seems unnecessarily gross, or silly, or—worse still—boring. Excess drains and devalues the psychological language of violence.

It is easy to equate limits with parental requirements that you be home before ten o'clock or else you're grounded for a week. But this is a very limited concept of limits. Myself, I subscribe to the mathematical concept of limits. Limits restrict, but limits can also give a sense of inevitability—the kind of inevitability that produces mind-expanding terror.

In architectural horror, the structure of the house becomes an embodiment of the limits—both limits on what can get inside, but also limits on the tensile strength of the beams holding up the ceiling. Our understanding of architecture forces a deadpan rationality onto our formless fears:

> The pentagon, the pentagram, like all patterns, they are defined by their limits. Incorporated in the harmonious patterns of fruits and flowers, they exemplify an epigram attributed to Pythagoras, that *limits give form to the limitless*. This is the power of limits (György Doczi, *The Power of Limits*).

This is the terrifying beauty of literary architecture and of architecture as literature.

And even the art of going too far becomes, itself, a game of limits. In 1984, when I was still a student at the University of Washington, I had some time between classes. So I decided to spend a pleasant, leisurely hour in the Henry

Art Gallery, which at the time was showing an exhibition called "Confrontations," which I knew nothing about.

I wandered, without reading, past a warning sign that said something to the effect that some viewers may find this stuff offensive, over to a well-composed photograph of a sleeping woman in a jumper. It slowly dawned upon me that the woman was not sleeping: she was dead. And those were not the buttons and straps of her jumper, that was a cross-section of her rib cage and those were strips of flesh peeled back during autopsy. The title was "Heroin O.D., age 26" (or something like that). I went from photograph to photograph—many of which involved dead people, ranging in age from the prenatal to the elderly—staring in disbelief, trying to convince myself that this was faked, airbrushed, or that these were drawings, something, anything but that these were artfully arranged corpses. I went back three times that day, and brought a friend in as a witness, just to make sure the pictures were still there and that I was not mistaken.

I bought a book of Witkin's photography, which bore the label: DUE TO PRESENT CENSORSHIP FACTORS, THE PUBLISHER AND I HAVE NOT INCLUDED SEVERAL IMPORTANT PHOTOGRAPHS IN THIS PRESENTATION OF MY WORK.— JOEL-PETER WITKIN. The photograph that made such a deep impression upon me was not among those in the book.

This was not combat photography, not forensics. This was clearly art. But while people donate their bodies to science, nobody that I know of has ever donated his or her body to art. Someone had to give Witkin those bodies to fool with. Who? How? What laws permitted this?

The worst thing about the photographs was that they were beautiful. The issue of unacceptable content posed an artistic challenge to Witkin—a challenge that he tried to meet. The feeling of horrific wonder one gets from the pictures is derived from the interaction of style and content, not from content alone.

Witkin challenges his critics' self-image by placing two

limits in opposition to one another: On the one hand, he has gone far outside the bounds of morality and taste through his choice of material and subject matter; on the other hand, he employs classical standards of beauty on classical images. Postmortem Postmodernism, I suppose. He leaves very little room to criticize him on aesthetic grounds, requiring that we admit the role morality plays in "pure" aesthetics. This effect cannot be achieved in prose any more than it can be achieved in painting, and it is the result of the maddening contrast of his respect for aesthetic limits with his disregard of moral limits.

At the 1986 World Fantasy Convention in Providence, Rhode Island, among the various things being given away were buttons promoting *Hellraiser*, Clive Barker's first movie, that read THERE ARE NO LIMITS. More recently, in their rhetorical introduction to *The Book of the Dead*, John Skipp and Craig Spector discussed the "progress" that can be made by "going too far":

> There is always, as they say, the next frontier.
> The function of the pioneer is to penetrate the unknown; to delve into those culturally uncharted places and report back on what they've found. All progress is based on the willingness of a few to venture into uncharted territory, check it out, come to terms with it, and make it a place where we all can dwell.
> If there is any hope for the future, it surely must rest upon the ability to stare unflinchingly into the heart of darkness.
> Then set our sights on a better place.
> And prepare ourselves.
> To go too far.

This passage oozes male sexuality—implicitly equivocating the writing of overt, graphic horror with sexual intercourse—and Skipp and Spector seem to have a very American notion of progress. But these superficial characteristics distract us from the real thrust, as it were, of their argument. What they mean by limits, boundaries, taboos, addresses issues of content while remaining entirely mute on the question of style.

Limits are not merely essential to horror, they are exciting. It is the existence of the edge of repression that allows the tale of terror to exist at all. It is rationality and physical law that gives Edgar Allan Poe's "Descent into the Maelstrom" its effect. It is the tension between inside and outside that makes the house story.

The scariest movie I ever saw was *The Shining*. It is not the same as Stephen King's novel. The book is primarily psychological metaphor horror, whereas the movie is nature-of-reality horror. And the movie is a careful study of limits. Kubrick repeatedly sets up implied limits: Only Danny can see the ghosts; Jack and Danny can see the ghosts, but Wendy can't; the whole family can see the ghosts, but the ghosts can't actually do anything—and then Grady the Ghost opens the food locker and lets out crazy Jack . . . the scariest moment in the movie, much more so than the ax murder, or the chase scenes, because of its implications—that every time we think something absolutely cannot happen, it does. The architecture of the Overlook Hotel and its grounds is crucial to a number of major scenes: to the food-locker scene; to the most famous scene in the movie, when Jack chops through the door and then sticks in his head and says, "Here's Johnny!," and to the scene in which Jack pursues Danny with an ax through the hedge maze. In fact, the concept of limits is crucial to the setup of the whole story: The family will be snowbound for the winter and will have to stay in the Overlook Hotel.

I saw the movie in 70-millimeter on a great big curved screen, sitting in the front row with my friend Klay. I had just come back a few days earlier from a year in Germany, and was eighteen but looked about fourteen. I had not brought my purse, but brought along my passport for ID (I didn't have a driver's license) in case the ticket seller questioned whether or not I should be allowed into an

R-rated movie. The pants I was wearing had only front pockets, so I gave my passport to Klay to put in his back pocket for the duration of the movie.

After the movie was over and the credits were running over Jack's frozen, crazy grin, I walked to the end of the aisle with Klay and asked him for my passport back. I was feeling very smug. I knew that the passport had probably fallen out of his back pocket and was now sitting under his seat. I knew because it had happened to me before. He felt his back pocket. My passport was gone. He looked under his seat. He found it. He handed it back to me. I felt very self-satisfied . . . until I was crossing my parents' front lawn and realized that I had never, ever, kept my passport in my back pocket. Then the message of the movie came right out of the screen at me. *So you think it's just a movie? Haven't I been telling you all along that every time you think something can't happen, you are wrong?* I didn't sleep for the rest of the night. I kept myself facing away from the door to my room for fear of seeing two little girls in the doorway, saying, "Come play with us for ever and ever and ever," and when I went to the bathroom during the night, I kept my head turned away from the bathtub, to avoid encounters with old ladies who'd passed their sell-by date.

It took me a week to realize that I'd lost money out of my back pocket and that that's what I'd been thinking of. In a letter to Gene Wolfe, I told this story. He wrote back, saying that the part about the money was just an after-the-fact rationalization. Being from a family where we explain such things, I have a ready explanation. But I suppose he's right. It is simply impossible and I should preserve it in all its beautiful impossibility.

There are many stories in this book that are impossible, that cannot have happened, stories of the fantastic, the supernatural: a story of a prehistoric, subterranean intelligence, a fantastically altered America that bears a resemblance to Ancient Greece as portrayed in Greek mythology, a nine-hundred-year-old woman, and, of course, haunted houses. I have, above, defined horror fiction in relation to the emotion of horror. There is another useful definition of the genre we are attempting to know. Let us call it supernatural fiction instead of horror, and require that supernatural fiction involve an element of the supernatural: ghosts, witches, vampires, werewolves, zombies, mummies, the Frankenstein monster—the usual Halloween night crew. The difference between the supernatural and just plain fantasy is mostly tradition and partly a sense of the uncanny.

While in principle horror and fantasy are separable and distinct, at this historical moment, the cutting edge of fantasy is in horror and the cutting edge of horror is in fantasy: Most of us think we know what fantasy is. It comes in three volumes, it's got elves and dwarves and gnomes and unicorns in it. Usually a beautiful princess, and probably a teenage boy who starts out rather ordinary, but goes on a quest and through the quest discovers his true power and becomes king by the end of the third volume. Overproduction of fluffy fantasy novels has degraded many of the more cheerful forms of fantasy. And as the supernatural motifs are strip-mined, the best work in horror is increasingly being done in fantasy. Thus, in this book, there are a disproportionate number of writers primarily known for their fantasy and science fiction. St. Martin's Press has recently begun publishing a combined volume of the year's best fantasy and horror, which is appropriate, given the category overlap in the best work.

In his essay on "The Impossible," M. C. Escher discusses how he uses rationality and limits to give his images plausibility, then introduces an element of the impossible to give his viewer a kind of shock, the same kind of shock, he claims, that the writers of fairy tales achieve. The essence of fantasy is inextricably bound up in the oxymoronic linkage of logic and illogic, rationality and irrationality, the real and the unreal. And horror combined with fantasy potentially has much the same effect as

Kubrick's version of *The Shining* did on me: It casts doubts upon what we think we know about the world, undermines our smug confidence that we know how things are and that things will continue as they are. Fantasy takes a reader by surprise just as real life does. Real-life horror can be sudden and overwhelming. Late at night on CNN, about six hours after the October 17, 1989, California earthquake, the anchorman updated the Bay Area death toll, which was by then estimated to be in the hundreds, and then went to a commercial break. About three commercials in, there was an ad for Rice-a-Roni (remember "the San Francisco Treat"?) in which a potato dances with a box of Rice-a-Roni and sings "Stayin' Alive." At the end, a tiny cable car appears and rings its little bell. The sales pitch? You can save the lives of poor innocent potatoes by eating Rice-a-Roni. But the architectural horrors of the night—the collapse of a one-mile segment of I-880 and a piece of the Bay Bridge, the fire in the Marina District, the building collapses at the Santa Cruz Pacific Garden Mall—gave the Rice-a-Roni commercial a bizarre, macabre cast. The earthquake had changed the rules. It was overwhelming.

Richard A. Lupoff, whose "The House on Rue Chartres" appears in this volume, was sitting at his word processor in Berkeley, not far from the Cypress section of I-880, at the time of the quake. He said that when the room began to shake, he thought that this one was just like the other hundred earthquakes he'd been through. As the shaking got stronger, he realized that, in fact, this one was *not* like the other hundred. This was bigger.

Nature has her limits, but *we* cannot see them. When characters take off in a spaceship, the ship is not supposed to explode in front of a hundred thousand schoolchildren. When characters take a bus from Oakland to San Francisco, the upper deck of the freeway is not supposed to collapse on top of them. The drama of nature can easily, in seconds, exceed the excess of human melodrama. The

William F. Laman Public Library
2801 Orange Street
North Little Rock, Arkansas 72114

213232

fantastic allows us to recapture that element of surprise that reality has but that the rules of realism forbid.

Landscape and architecture define much of what we think we know. They take on a permanence, an inevitability that is both comforting and imprisoning. When they change unexpectedly, the change is both terrifying and liberating.

Last night East Germany announced that it was going to loosen travel restrictions, and opened the border with West Berlin. As I write this, CNN is running footage of people standing and walking on the top of the Wall. And there is much discussion of tearing down the Wall—architectural alteration inevitably following political change and political dialogue conducted in architectural metaphor. Architecture is simultaneously the most personal and political of metaphors.

By consenting to write a house story, the authors in this book are submitting themselves to an inherently psychological process—even more so than the simple act of writing fiction, because houses directly address issues of identity. I'm told that there is a psychological test in which the subject draws a house and then talks about it. Writing a house story makes authors confront the problem of what to expose and what to conceal about themselves. Because the stories herein are house stories, they are to some extent psychological.

Both Sharon Baker and Karl Edward Wagner set their stories in the houses of their childhood. And a number of other stories are set in buildings that really exist: Richard A. Lupoff's, Susan Palwick's, Garry Kilworth's, Ian Watson's, and Edward Bryant's. The very essence of the house story is the balance between the literal and the metaphorical. The very literalness of these houses hints at their metaphorical nature. Have these authors "recognized their houses"? Or have they recognized some other metaphorical truth? The issue of psychology is inescapable. Houses are inescapable.

William F. Laman Public Library
2801 Orange Street
North Little Rock, Arkansas 72114

J ack Womack is the author of *Ambient, Terraplane,* and *Heathern.* In his first two novels, Jack Womack reinvented cyberpunk, giving its mean, slick surfaces a wryness and a political acuity not found in the original C-word fiction. Originally from Lexington, Kentucky, he lives in New York City. This is his first published short story.

Here, lovingly told, is an account of the remnants of a wildly dysfunctional family living out their last in a New York brownstone. The sensibility of this story might be described as a smooth blend of William Gibson and Robert Aickman—New York Southern Gothic.

Out of Sight, Out of Mind

JACK WOMACK

When he said he'd meet us at our office, we had our doubts he'd show," said Sherman, the lawyer for a branch of Lang's family Lang had never known. The blood trapped in his face by his tightly knotted tie appeared yellow beneath his muddy skin. "One of the bank officers claimed your cousin hadn't been in midtown for thirty years."

"Folklore," said Wenzel, Sherman's partner-in-law. Lang thought if you were to take a troll from beneath a bridge and dress him in a thousand-dollar suit, you could provide a twin for Wenzel.

"You expect a degree of elaboration, hearing these situations retold at distance. We offered to meet him at his house, but he demurred, telling us he'd have to dust." The three stepped from the cab onto Central Park West. "A small man, a deep voice. You'd have thought he was the size of a refrigerator to have heard him over the phone. He wore a zoot suit that looked almost new."

"Unexpected haberdashery for an eighty-year-old man," said Wenzel.

"He hadn't bathed since V-E Day, or so we believed. The windows in our office can be opened only in event of fire."

"Such awful weather lately," said Wenzel. "It gets this hot in Kentucky?"

"Tennessee," said Lang, glancing behind him to see what might be bounding toward them from the park's humid jungle. "Hotter. This a dangerous neighborhood?"

"Aren't they all?"

"The police usually get so involved in estate settlements up here?" Lang asked.

"If they're so inclined," said Wenzel, "dependent upon complications."

"He died in your office?"

"My office, actually," Sherman said. "I'd stepped out to get the agreement—"

"I got up to breathe," said Wenzel.

"When we returned, he was peaceful as life."

"Heart," said Wenzel. "You don't have your health, what've you got?"

They crossed the avenue when the light changed. Sirens wailed through the park, sounding as trapped animals. "In appearing and disappearing with such élan, he would have left an indelible impression in any event," Sherman continued. "While he sat in our waiting room, he stacked all the journals lying about into mathematically even piles. When we called him into our office, he pointed to our reference library and told us he read fifty thousand books a week."

"We leaned forward in our chairs," said Wenzel. They walked west down Ninety-fifth; spring breezes glued yellowed newspapers to their ankles. Two weather-worn cats padded by en route to the park.

"Why did the police want us to come up here?" Lang asked. "I'm afraid I didn't quite understand."

"That's the way they like it, Mr. Lang," said Wenzel. "We'll handle whatever they've uncovered."

"There're always problems when one dies intestate," said Sherman. "There're so many complications involved with the property—"

"In what way?" Lang asked.

"You'll see," said Wenzel. "We'd hoped not to involve you in this so directly. You said you never met him?"

"Dad told me he met him once, when they were tads," said Lang. "Thought he seemed a might touched."

"You could say that," Wenzel said. "A shame your father couldn't come up. Everyone should see New York before they die."

"Dad's in no rush."

"Your cousin was from the South originally as well?" asked Sherman, straightening his mustache with a tiny gold comb. Lang marveled at how closely he resembled the little man in the Monopoly game.

"Oh, yes." The lawyers nodded, and kept walking. Tree branches entwined above the street's thin green artery. Lang imagined himself strolling down an arbor through which a sewer ran, so overpowering was the smell of the street. The windows of the four-story brownstones lining the block held no more life than the eyes of subway passengers. As if through a bathroom window Lang saw, down the block, orange figures floating back and forth, seeming to hover above the pavement, contained within their own hazy world. Seven trash containers were stationed along the street's southern curb; countless cats prowled over their loads.

"He clutched a shopping bag from Peck and Peck, which went out of business when I was your age," Sherman went on. "The bag was stuffed with newspapers, sticks, several smaller bags, and a length of pipe. You saw the bowl of matchbooks on my desk, the ones imprinted with the name of our firm? He asked if he could have some, and emptied the bowl into his bag."

"Dad said he never met the sister," said Lang. "She was younger, I gather."

"By twenty years," said Wenzel. "An unexpected birth, probably. Their mother was nearly fifty and died not long after. Their father performed the delivery, it seems. He was an obstetrician, but family planning was so perfunctory in those days."

"Where is she?"

"We're not completely sure of her whereabouts," said Sherman. "Until we saw her name on the first mortgage, we were frankly unaware of her existence. No one at the bank remembered her, but then only one or two remembered *him,* so—"

"We told him we needed her signature as well. He quickly referred us to a court decision of eighteen years ago, appointing him her guardian. That was the last time he'd used a lawyer, he said, explaining that they never dealt with lawyers as their father had been a doctor," said Wenzel. "He said that when he listened, he heard her, but he only infrequently saw her."

The workers drifted through the fog, bouncing between house and dumpsters. Policepeople standing silently by slapped colorless powder from their dark blue uniforms as if tidying themselves after a drug raid. Lang grew cognizant of the fog's origin, approaching its grit; sparkling motes of dust billowed from the house, melding briefly into the air, settling again in layers upon the surroundings. Gray streaks highlighted the brown ivy smothering the facade. Sprayed across the front door were the faded words ROCK THIS HOUSE. Three workmen hauled a wooden pallet out the basement door; tied onto the pallet were five old cabinet radios and a car's front fender. A contraption resembling a children's slide ran from an attic window to the closet dumpster. Cats scattered whenever fresh wreckage poured onto them. Lang considered the dull glint in the house's unpierced eyes. "What did he cover the windows with?"

"Aluminum foil," said Wenzel. "Superfluous, considering."

"They're tearing the place down already?"

"Not yet."

A large blue truck blocked the sidewalk; hoses so thick as a heavy man's waist ran from the rear of its trailer through the basement windows. It was the largest vacuum cleaner Lang had ever seen; it screamed with a hurricane's roar, sucking up the cloud within, spewing it into the air without.

"So much about this case is atypical of our métier," said Wenzel. "There's the sergeant. Let me try to work my charms before we introduce you. We might be able to keep you out of it, Mr. Lang—"

"I'd like to go in—"

The sergeant was a slender woman half Lang's size wearing welder's goggles and gloves resembling those of a falconer. Wenzel sidled up to her as might any informant wishing for a deal. "He smiled, showing no teeth," Sherman continued. "We tried to hustle things along before we could be asphyxiated. To open, I remarked upon the bank's consideration in not having foreclosed upon the mortgage after seven years of nonpayment—"

"Seven years," Lang said. "Why hadn't they been evicted?"

"At the original time of foreclosure several notices went out. All were ignored. Bank representatives visited the house but couldn't get in."

"He kept them out?"

"In his fashion," said Sherman. "After so long the bank essentially gave up on attempting to seize their property. It must not have seemed worth the effort."

"Mighty nice banks you have up here," said Lang.

"On occasion. It could have been nothing more than the usual bureaucratic fumble. Time passed, people left, not even the computers cared after a while, and your cousin was left again to his devices. Late last year the developers of those adjacent lots notified the bank of their wish to purchase your cousin's property. By adding this lot to theirs, you see, twelve more floors of condominiums may be legally added to the tower they proposed. Your relatives' welfare became at once a matter of utmost concern."

As the sergeant spoke with Wenzel, she gestured at the house as if the architecture drove her to jubilation. The black hair she wore knotted up beneath her cap came loose and a skein unraveled beneath her visor. Their words disappeared within the shouts of workmen, the vacuum's howl, the rumble of debris descending the slide. "Their father built the house," said Sherman. "The family owned it outright, once. Your cousin took out a first mortgage, then a second."

"What did they need the money for?" asked Lang.

"He started collecting things," said Sherman.

Tabbies and marmalades slinked over the wreckage, pausing at moments to lick dirt from reddened muzzles. "Dad never mentioned this side of the family until you got in touch," said Lang. "He said his parents never talked about them."

"Most families live as if certain of their members exist in separate rooms, seen only if something's left ajar," said Sherman, staring at the house's gray ivy. "They must have had it hard. For ten years they lived without electricity, for five years without heat, for three years without water." He drew from his pocket a silk handkerchief and daubed the sweat from his forehead. "No record of when the phone was cut off. So, the bank sent letters. Messengers came around, but no one answered. At some point he realized his isolation needed interrupting, and so he called us from a pay phone, having seen our ad in the *Voice*—"

"*Yo!*" shouted the sergeant, waving them over. "Come here." When they traversed the fog, Lang coughed until he feared he'd spit blood; he imagined his lungs filling with sand, so granular grew the air's grain. Wenzel looked to have lost a case upon whose outcome his income depended. "You're the relative?" the sergeant asked Lang, who gasped for breath. "Do something about that cough. What's in your pocket? Take it out."

"I believe he's unarmed, Sergeant—" said Sherman.

"Out."

Lang withdrew the bulge she'd spotted and offered his holdings in his outstretched hand. "Matches," he said. Grimacing as she pulled off her goggles, she squinted against the dust with unshelled eyes. Cleaning the lenses on her shirtfront, she was careful not to scratch them on buttons or badge. As she rubbed them clean, they filmed over anew.

"Like father, like son," she said.

"They were cousins," said Lang. "I never met them."

"You were lucky," she said. "These two tell you anything about what we've got in here?"

"Until his presence was requested, our client's direct involvement in these details seemed nonessential," said Sherman.

"It's all right," Wenzel interrupted. "Mr. Lang doesn't have to come in if he doesn't want to. We do—"

"Thought you'd want to see for yourself," she said.

"Let's get on with it, Sergeant."

"You know my vacation should've started yesterday?" she asked. "Now they're telling me it'll be two weeks before they can get everything emptied out—"

"We're all middlemen here, Sergeant," said Wenzel.

"Somebody oughta suffer besides me," she said. "All right, get suited. I got to call in, be right back. Just hang." As she walked away, she stopped long enough to corner a workman and give him his assignment. He removed three orange coveralls from the cab of the vacuum truck and tossed them to Lang and his lawyers.

"You're sure you want to go in, Mr. Lang?" asked Wenzel.

"Why not? What are these for?" he asked, startled by the weight of the coverall he held.

"Precautions," said Sherman. As they tugged the work

wear over their suits, he continued telling his tale. "From what we'd heard and from what we could discover, we were prepared to work around his personal eccentricities. Once he came in, we both began to believe that the roof wasn't quite on the house." Lang noticed that the material in the sleeves and legs of the suit was several times thicker than that in the body. "His beliefs made a certain sense. He might have reexamined his premises, but I have to admit there was a consistency to his logic—"

"Sounds like he was crazy to me," said Lang. "Nobody'd ever noticed before this?"

"When did anyone see him, Mr. Lang?" Wenzel asked. Lang yanked the suit's hood over his head, fitting the built-in goggles across his eyes and the filter insert into his mouth, grateful that it stole smell so well as dust from the air.

"We told him of the offer the bank made." Donning the coveralls effected metamorphosis; they appeared transformed into bright-hued roaches. "A onetime payment of two hundred thousand dollars to cover resettlement costs. They'll resell it for ten times that, certainly, but considering that they had the legal right to seize the property that day if they chose, it seemed quite fair to us. He didn't bite. The house fit them too well, he said."

The hood's filters made them hear one another's voices as if over a cheap telephone. "We suggested he look upon their offer as a gift and not as a demand," said Wenzel, "but he said a demand by any name still demanded. He couldn't lose what he'd saved, he said, not now—"

A workman shouted. A wooden hogshead rolled off the overhead track and exploded upon the pavement below in a shrapnel-burst of shattered crockery. The foreman, seeing that no one was hurt, spoke. "Break for lunch," he said. "Pass the word up."

A lump of kittens stirred in the nearest dumpster, crying for their mothers. "Were these their cats?" Lang asked.

"I suspect they're after the rats," said Wenzel. "Shoppers rushing to a holiday sale."

"Mr. Lang," Sherman asked, his eyes unreadable beneath the goggles, "are you by any chance claustrophobic?"

"Never before." The workmen shook free of the house's grip, filing off to lunch, each carrying away as they left some scrap of the accumulation: webs of string pitched into boxes, heaps of stained cloth, odd volumes of encyclopedias, treadless tires, headless dolls, skinned taxidermist's trophies, clocks without hands, typewriters without keys, televisions without tubes—archaeological *chotchkes* too quickly rediscovered to hold value.

"There's a certain disarray to the place," said Sherman.

"How can the house be big enough to hold so much?" Lang asked, looking again at the glutted dumpsters.

"They built these old brownstones with families in mind," said Sherman. "This one's standard, with additions. Four large rooms per floor, a kitchen and several bathrooms, small rooms serving as closets, servants' quarters in the attic and a full basement—"

"Less full," said Wenzel.

"The kitchen's split in half, they tell me. Part of it seems to have once been their father's office. There's much more space than it would appear, and he was adept at making things fit."

"Showtime," said the sergeant as she reappeared, tying a surgeon's mask around her face. "You two haven't been back here since the cleanup began, right?"

"There seemed no reason to return," said Sherman.

"And I'm guessing you've never been in New York?" she asked Lang; before he could answer, she continued to speak, as if he hadn't even been there to ask. "We'll go in through the basement," she said. "If it was good enough for him, it'll be good enough for us. The access's easier now. I can't make any guarantees at this point as to how much longer we can keep the papers out of this."

"We'll see to that," said Wenzel.

"It gets pretty bad in there. Don't make sudden movements. Watch your elbows. Keep an eye out for rats, in case. You can hear 'em all over the place, but the bastards hide. Don't get sick in your suits, you'll be sorry. If you feel the floor settling under you, be prepared to—" She paused. "Well, be prepared. If it starts getting to you, say something quick. Let's go."

They ducked, crossing the threshold beneath the stoop. Their filters didn't entirely subdue the house's miasma; a hallucinogenic blend of mildew, excrement, rat, rot, stale water and dust permeated the fine-lined mesh. Excavations laid bare the basement's front half. New growth stood among the virgin forest of floor supports.

"As they started taking the shit out, the floor began to sag," said the sergeant. "They put in all these extra beams. Solid oak," she said, striking one with her fist. She switched on her flash; the sound of animals scampering from the light came as the noise of a brush being drawn across sandpaper. Beyond the stairs lay an inpenetrable canebrake of magazine stacks, columns of bound newspapers, pillars of books and journals. The lowest depths had been soaked for so long that they'd transmuted into black peat; the higher, drier ranges glistened all the same in the brief flickers of light. Lang, coming nearer, saw thousands of silverfish scurrying over the paper, busy converting their country into mulch.

"Goddamn—" he started to say, but couldn't think of what might follow.

"The drawbacks," said Wenzel, "of forever saving for that rainy day."

"Keep moving," said the sergeant, her voice powerful for one of her petite size. "No telling what we'll catch down here. I oughta be in Cuernavaca by now."

"Some remnant of socialization within his being prodded him to attempt explaining his efforts," Sherman said, continuing as they climbed the wet stairs. "At first we thought we rambled only to distract us, but soon we gathered it was something more, though it was hard to say what. He said the aborigines, the Indians, primitives of all lands, once possessed senses and abilities that we lost as civilization grew more oppressive. Being able to hear across vast distances, for example."

"To see the stars in daylight, he said," Wenzel picked up. "To smell the sun. He had an ear for phrasing. As we moderns became postmoderns—he didn't put it that way, but I don't remember everything like some people do—there were awarenesses that our parents took for granted that we had lost as well. In one generation history seemed to have been eliminated from the fabric of society, or at least the knowledge of history."

"To lose the past," Sherman said, "was to lose the soul."

Floodlamps put up by the workmen hung from a thick electric cord attached to the hall ceiling, sharpening shadows into knife-edges. Passageways ran between stacks of *National Geographic* and *Life,* around newspapers bundled into groups of thirty held fast with square knots. The rope nearest the floor was generally chewed through. Lang misstepped, bumped against a paper wall; a flare of pulp streamed outward in a sudden corona. The newspapers appeared hand-tinted; from top to bottom the colors deepened, from cream to lemon, to canary to mustard, to amber, then brown, then black.

"Tunnels and paths run all through the place," said the sergeant. "Turnarounds, false trails, dead ends. Don't see how he kept from getting lost in here himself."

"He remembered where everything was," said Wenzel. "He knew his labyrinth."

"This way first," she said. "Toward the kitchen. Watch your step, floor's a little loose through here. They told me the estimated weight load in here must be like sixty thousand pounds. Couldn't do this in a new place."

"One day he and his sister were cleaning the basement for what I suspect was the last time," said Sherman. "He made a joke about Fibber McGee's closet, and she didn't get the reference. It was a radio show. One of the characters had a closet, and every time he opened it, a ton of junk fell out—"

"Closets?" said the sergeant, "I'll show you closets. They're the neatest places in here. Look." Enough had been removed where they stood that she was able to open the nearest door, and they peered inside. Therein were a dozen shelves lined with pairs of men's shoes, the laces of each neatly knotted, the toes of each pair curling upward at an 80-degree angle. A chirping sound came from all around them, as if upon entering a pet shop they'd awakened all the birds.

"Bastards," she said. "There's poison all through here, hasn't done any good."

"At first, he said, he thought nothing more of his sister's incomprehension. It was no more than discovering that cultural baggage had been lost in transit," Sherman continued. "But the moment kept recurring to him, and so over the next few weeks, thinking that perhaps only his sister was unaware of a program he'd never missed, he tried dropping the reference into his conversation with others as young or younger than she, for in those days he hadn't yet climbed into his bottle and pulled the stopper in after him. He perceived, he said, that no one seemed to know what he was talking about. The more he thought about it, the more it disturbed him, until he grew so preoccupied with the ramifications as he understood them that he lay awake nights, unable to sweep his head clear."

Six refrigerators, each of a different decade's vintage, stood just inside the kitchen. As if to protect children, the doors of each were removed. Pots and pans buried the stove; dishware of a hundred patterns filled the sink. Space within had been made that they could move unhindered into the next room, the doctor's old office; it was almost empty. A long counter ran along one wall; a high cabinet was attached to the wall behind the countertop. An enormous nineteenth-century lock once sealed the cupboard, but someone had pried it away.

"Heredity makes the person before birth, he said," Sherman said, "but environment makes the person afterward. If the environment disappears, what happens to the person? It came to him as he lay there one night that life was so inessential that it might fade away as you watched. Sometimes, he said, he spent hours staring into the mirror, making sure he was still there."

"The notion of a Polaroid reversing itself," said Wenzel. "He wasn't an unintelligent man, but he discovered existentialism too late in life to deal with it so easily as might a freshman."

Foil covered the window above the counter, next to the cabinet; the sergeant ripped the shade away, pushing it aside with her glove. A trail of sunlight burned a path across the room; dust crystals shimmered in its beams.

"Theories need proof, and he sought proof," said Sherman, "throwing references into his conversation to see what might rise to the top with enough stirring. Bickford's cafeterias. The *Squalus*. Sapphire. Martin Dies. Grover Whalen. The Sea Beach Express. He said that, naturally, the youngest were the furthest gone. They didn't remember Reagan, and couldn't find their street on a map."

"He took it so personally," said Wenzel. "That's always bad to do. No one remembered anything he remembered, or so it struck him. Now, as we listened to him speak, we'd already been made aware of why he was so deeply affected as he set about exploring this problem, though we didn't make the connection until later."

"What do you mean?" asked Lang.

"Early on, in referring to the decision appointing him his sister's guardian, he quoted it, word for word, so near as we ourselves could recall, later reading it. He possessed, I believe, an eidetic memory. Whatever flew into its web forever stuck there."

"Take a look at this, now," said the sergeant, prying open the cabinet door, jerking away her hand before the roaches within could race up her arm. There were jars inside: pints arrayed along the top shelves, quarts upon the middle, half-gallons and larger on the bottom.

, "No one cared anymore, he said," Sherman continued. "No one cared that so much was being lost, and the more that he realized was lost, the more he felt himself slipping away. Then one day he walked by a small shop over on Amsterdam—"

"Columbus," Wenzel corrected.

"An avenue. His agoraphobia hadn't become so pronounced yet," said Sherman. "In the window was something he hadn't seen for years. Log Cabin maple syrup, he said, came in tin cans resembling log cabins before the war, and now, years after Pearl Harbor, he found himself looking at one again. He bought it. When he brought it home, he put it on a table and stared at it for hours, allowing its image to resonate throughout his mind. His sister laughed, thinking it was a silly thing to buy, and even sillier to stare at; he said she asked him if he could see the future in it."

The sergeant lithely pulled herself onto the countertop, stirring loose clouds from its surface, and took down one of the pint jars as she descended. Her uniform was almost white with dust.

"For a time they were able to live off their inherited capital after he quit his job," said Sherman, "but in seeking new madeleines, he soon sent his money on its way, going to flea markets, weekend sales, apartment liquidations, wandering the streets window-shopping until something caught his eye."

From her back pocket the sergeant drew a rag and began removing the years from the jar. "Once he got started, it was hard to stop, he admitted," said Wenzel. "The mortgage money came and went, and came and went again. Luxuries fell by the wayside, then necessities, then all that remained was the need to continually rewrap with fresh bandages." The sergeant dropped her muddied rag onto the floor, having brought the jar from opacity into translucence. The jar bore a still-illegible label. Taking his handkerchief from his pocket, Sherman handed it to her, and with it she scrubbed harder, massaging the glass as if to warm it.

"What did it matter to preserve the past if in so doing you lost the present? I asked, dabbling in advocacy," said Sherman. "He said the present didn't trouble him so much as the fact he'd started too late to keep from losing his sister."

"Then she left?" Lang asked, expecting an answer, receiving none. "What is it? You believe she's dead, don't you? You said you weren't completely sure of her whereabouts?"

"Not completely," said the sergeant, pushing the cleaned jar into the sun's path. The rays hit the glass obliquely, forming a prism, throwing a blur of rainbow onto the gray wall opposite.

"Over time I gather he allowed the demands of collecting to supercede all other relationships," said Sherman. "It was too late to save her, he said; her sense of history had so atrophied, she didn't remember being his sister anymore."

Lang stared at the baby floating within its liquid fog. He couldn't read the spidery handwriting on the label from where he stood. Leaning into the light, Wenzel spoke the words aloud. " 'Janiceps. Gladys Murphy, 110 West 100th Street. Aborted June 16, 1904.' " Babies, truly; two squeezed into one body, as if they'd been pressed together to save space. Wenzel looked up at the shelves, the rows of jars. "The doctor had his own hobbies, it seems."

"Why would they have kept them?" Lang said, unable to keep his eye off the swimmers.

"After so long they might have been looked on as members of the family," said Wenzel.

"What do you mean, she didn't remember being his sister?" Lang asked.

"We've since examined the court ruling, as we said, and the attendant medical reports. He was appointed her guardian because she had Alzheimer's, and the disease had so progressed, it's possible she never noticed anything out of the ordinary here at home."

The sergeant placed one of the quart jars in the light, one previously swept free of its surface crust. This jar's occupant was large enough to have been born. Seeing the splayed limbs, the face rising directly from the nape of the neck, Lang thought, and tried not to think, of bullfrogs he'd once, as a boy, gigged in ponds.

"They were surely close, once," said Sherman. "They never went far from the house, even when they could. That surely intensified the situation, over time."

" 'Roger,' " Wenzel read, studying this house's specifications. " 'Ancephalic. January 8''— he coughed— " '1956.' "

"Then he fell silent, having seemed to run out of things to say," Sherman said. "He agreed to take home the proposal and think it over. That was good enough for us. When we left the room, he was just sitting there smiling, as if recalling a pleasant memory."

The sergeant removed a large jar from the bottom shelf, one seeming recently cleaned. "Cecily," she said, reading the label. "They reached the bedroom this morning, right before I called. Let's go." The quartet stepped out of the room, leaving the jars where they'd left them. The workmen were returning from lunch; Lang heard above the perpetual chirp their cries and shouts. They inched down the hall until they reached the stairwell; as they mounted the stairs, the wood cried beneath their feet. "People," the sergeant sighed, shrugging.

"He tried to save her," said Wenzel.

James Morrow is a winner of the Nebula Award. He is the author of *The Continent of Lies, The Wine of Violence, This is the Way the World Ends,* and *Only Begotten Daughter.* He has also written several books about creativity in education. He lives in State College, Pennsylvania. Morrow's fiction tends to combine high-concept satire, moral and political allegory, and probing psychological metaphor. He exhibits all three traits in this tale of a man trapped in a haunted phone booth.

Regarding this story, Morrow says that he intended it as an homage to *Sorry, Wrong Number* and that he wanted to try the horror equivalent of minimalism—how little architecture does it take to make a haunted house? He also says that this story was inspired by a recurring dream he had: He tries to dial a somewhat complicated phone number and keeps getting one digit wrong—a Sisyphean process that captures the trepidation we feel when we go to use the telephone.

Tales from a New England Telephone Directory

JAMES MORROW

B etween two dreary and obscure hamlets in the Berkshire mountains of Massachusetts, on a road that
seemed to exist primarily to carry lost travelers even
further from where they wished to be, a telephone booth
sat on a grassy hill beside an ancient, moldering cemetery.

Unlike the cemetery, whose limestone markers were so
badly eroded they had come to resemble blurry photographs of themselves, the Housatonic Lane telephone booth
was in fine condition. Its phone worked perfectly. The local directory was bound in leather, up-to-date—February
1992–January 1993—and not missing a single page. The
graffiti scratched into the writing table were erotic but
not vile.

One of the names in the February 1992–January 1993
edition of the Berkshire County Directory was Henry
Waxman of 117 Melville Avenue in West Stockbridge.
Henry Waxman had committed suicide in the winter of 1992
at the age of thirty-eight.

The directory also listed Belinda Markson of Lenox and
Paulie Fisher of Van Duesenville, both of whom had died

recently, and with an abruptness that left their survivors feeling guilty and numb. Paulie Fisher was only nine years old when he was molested and murdered barely thirty yards from the Housatonic Lane phone booth.

Another name in the directory was that of Terry Yarber, a New York City salesman who had spent most of his adult life distributing cap guns, water pistols, air rifles, and plastic hand grenades to toy stores as far north as Montpelier and as far south as Philadelphia. Terry Yarber was not dead. In fact, he was in ideal physical health when, on the evening of August 12, 1992, he came walking toward the Housatonic Lane phone booth.

Such a friendly and inviting place, Terry mused as he folded the glass door back upon itself. The booth was a miniature inn, a steel oasis, a landlocked lighthouse—and in such good shape. The floor was immaculate, not a single chewing-gum wrapper in sight. Instead of the usual four-letter words, a delightful image of a nude young woman fellating a goat was etched into the gray paint of the little metal table. The installation itself looked fine, not at all the typical Manhattan telephone, no mouthpiece hanging out like dentures sprung from the jaw of somebody Terry had just slugged to save a woman's self-esteem.

He was a latter-day knight, or so ran Terry Yarber's image of himself. Set Terry down in a working-class bar in Jersey or Connecticut, and he would instantly find the lady most in trouble—the one who needed the fifty-dollar loan, or the ear in which to pour the particulars of her rotten marriage, or the drunken jerk pried off her body and beaten senseless in the alley. Terry Yarber loved women. He did not understand them, but he worshiped them as devoutly as a pagan bowing before his jujus.

The phone was an antique, a classic—it operated on mere dimes. Terry reached into his polyester slacks, grasped his change, and, withdrawing his hand, unfurled his fingers. Two dimes, one nickel, and five pennies lay on his palm like alms.

Night pressed down upon New England, bringing chill

breezes and drizzle. Gloom suffused the phone booth. The grave markers became dull, pale blobs of stone lit by an orange crescent moon hanging in the western sky like a slice of cantaloupe.

Terry dumped the change on the metal table, fished out his AAA Motor Club card and, closing the door behind him, dropped in a dime, half expecting it to spill with a mocking jangle into the coin-return chamber, but somehow it found its way into the bowels of the phone. Punching up the Triple-A service number, he got a young woman with a dry, husky voice. He told her his troubles: flat tire, frozen lugs. She advised him to call Gary's 24-Hour Texaco in Great Barrington. Terry made her say Gary's number three times, enough to fix it in his memory. For a moment he considered striking up a conversation with her—with her sexy voice. He'd tell her about his job. Terry liked telling women he sold guns for a living. He never mentioned that his biggest customer was Toys 'Я' Us.

He hung up, deposited the second dime, and called Gary's Texaco.

Overhead, a light bulb clicked on—sixty soothing watts cutting through the Massachusetts dark. Terry loved the light; he could feel its warmth on his face.

"Yeah?" snorted whichever alienated adolescent was in charge of Gary's after six. "Whatcha want?"

"Is this Gary's Texaco?" asked Terry.

"Gary's not here."

"I've got a flat, and the lugs are stuck really bad. I'm on Housatonic Lane below Williamsville, about a mile east of Route 41."

"Housatonic? What the hell are you doing out there?"

"Taking the scenic route to Hartford. I got lost."

"Way it works is, I radio our truck, and this guy Warren comes out, and he's got loads of muscles and this big mother wrench that could open Wonder Woman's chastity belt. What's he lookin' for?"

"Eighty-seven Plymouth Voyager, blue."

"Go wait there."

"How long?"

"Till Warren shows up."

"When will that be?"

"Depends."

"On what?"

"On where Warren is, whether he's got another job, whether he's with his girlfriend—factors like that."

"So it could be an hour?"

"Could be," said the kid. " 'Bye."

Terry returned the handset to its cradle and grunted. The twentieth century: videocassettes, heart transplants, men walking on the moon—but when your tire blew, it all came down to whether some guy named Warren was getting laid.

He scooped up his remaining coins, grabbed the handle of the door, and tugged.

Except it wouldn't move. "Huh?" he said aloud. He tried again, curling his taut fingers around the handle, pulling as hard as he could.

Nothing.

Both hands this time, all his strength, every muscle of his upper torso—the same muscles that had saved so many women from dishonor at the hands of barroom louts. Hopeless. The door was as tight as the frozen lugs on his Voyager. It was as tight as Wonder Woman's chastity belt.

Trapped in a phone booth? Stupid, crazy—it didn't even have a lock.

Trapped, but not for long, he decided, not while he wore the cowhide boots with which he'd once stomped a Gila monster to death in Alamogordo. He rested his back against the south wall and let fly with his right foot, *crash,* boot leather on glass. His heel caromed off the door. Again he kicked: left foot this time—*crash*—no effect. Now the right—ricochet. Now the left—zip.

His shins ached. His feet burned. The dark glass reflected him—the sweat on his brow, the anger and frustration in his eyes.

He grimaced, spat on the floor, counted to ten—and let his demons loose. He heaved his shoulder against the south wall, pummeled the north with his fists; he flailed and pounded and kicked. Buried alive, he thought. Like a child locked in a discarded refrigerator. Like a bum caught in the defective elevator of a fleabag hotel. Like a minor-league Houdini suffocating to death in a steamer trunk under the East River.

Panting, he leaned against the directory rack, an aluminum cowl in which a leatherbound book hung on a gold chain. Don't panic, he told himself. You're in control. Outside, the storm thickened, peppering the glass with raindrops.

He fixed on the phone. *Dial 911 For Emergency Help,* the instruction card said. *No Coin Needed.*

His pitch would sound ridiculous, of course. Listen, I'm entombed in a phone booth off Route 41. Would you mind popping over with a couple of crowbars and maybe a jack hammer? And bring a peanut-butter sandwich to slip under the door, in case it's a long night. . . .

911, that's all it would take. He placed the handset to his head. The receiver suckled his ear.

There was no dial tone. He moved the plunger up and down, jiggling it with the frenzy of a telegraph operator sending a distress call from a sinking ship. Still no tone. He jabbed the push buttons: 9-1-1. Nothing. 9-1-1, 9-1-1, 9-1-1, 9-1-1. *Nada.* He dropped in his other dime, as if money might resurrect the moribund machine. He dialed 9-1-1. Silence. Rock talk, corpse talk, jokes by giraffes. He hung up.

Overhead, the light bulb blew.

The darkness that descended seemed exaggerated, grotesque: a heavy, swampy darkness, as if far more than sixty watts of illumination had been lost, as if the sun itself had died. Terry couldn't see the road . . . the cemetery . . . the door . . . the telephone. Only the radium-coated hands of his wristwatch, two luminescent splinters, assured him that he'd not gone blind.

Eight-thirty, they said.

By 8:32, he realized he was quite terrified. His teeth

chattered, his bones shook, gooseflesh grew along his limbs like barnacles.

Headlights swung into view, two high beams flying down Housatonic Lane, and then came an '82 Volkswagen camper, hissing through the storm. "Stop! Hey, there! Stop!" Terry hopped up and down, waving his arms like an island castaway signaling an ocean liner. "Stop! Please stop!"

The beams hit him squarely in the face, forcing his eyes closed, but the camper simply rolled on, uncomprehending, indifferent, rainwater shooting upward from its tires like seaspray.

Moaning, Terry slumped to the floor, the soupy night flowing all around him. He stared at the watch hands, allowing them to numb his mind as they made their excruciating crawl around the invisible dial.

Eight-thirty-five, eight-forty, eight-forty-five, eight-fifty . . .

The phone rang.

He started, gasped. A second ring—harsh, serrated. A third. Standing, he fumbled through the opaque air. Fourth ring. His fingers collided with the handset, and he pulled it to his mouth.

"Hello?"

"Good evening, friend." A male voice, coarse and asthmatic.

"You have the wrong number—but listen, don't hang up. I'm in trouble here, and I need—"

"I have the *right* number, Terry Yarber."

An icy wind moved through Terry's bowels. "You . . . you *know* me?" Never before had his own name frightened him.

"I know *everybody* in the local directory." A heavy, wheezing voice. A voice with bits of broken glass embedded in it. A voice wrapped in barbed wire.

"Are you the operator?"

"No," said the barbed-wire voice.

"Who are you?"

"A better question would be, '*Where* am I?' I'm everywhere at once, Terry Yarber. Like the angels, like pollen, like pain. An even better question would be, 'Where are *you*?' "

"I told you—a phone booth."

"You're in a haunted house."

"I'm in a phone booth."

"Do you know who's haunting it?"

"You don't understand—a *phone booth*."

"Who's haunting it?"

"You, evidently."

"No, you. You're a ghost, Terry Yarber." The voice laughed, a sound like a ball bearing rolling around in a porcelain pitcher. "No, not a dead man's spirit, nothing so vulgar and melodramatic. But you're a ghost all the same. You're barely in the world, Terry. You don't register. Your own child can't picture your face. A ghost."

"There are two sides to that story."

"I want to give you some phone numbers."

"So long, clown." Groping, Terry found the cradle and slammed down the handset. "Screw you!" he called into the damp, clotted darkness.

He thought, Wait. Slow down. Think. He'd just got a phone call—the machine was working again.

He reached out, removed the handset—dial tone!—and caressed the pushbuttons as if reading Braille. He learned the territory. Upper-left button: *1*. He counted: *2, 3*—drop a row—*4, 5, 6*—drop a row—*7, 8 . . . 9*. He pushed it, beep, then two *1*'s, beep, beep.

On the other end: the comforting, muted ring of a functioning phone, *purrr, purrr, purrr*. He would summon the Great Barrington Police, he decided. They would have the proper tools—huge chisels, mammoth drills, shears like the jaws of a tyrannosaur. They'd rip this crazy phone booth apart with the same macho competence they employed when cutting half-dead motorists out of mangled cars.

Click, someone came on the line. "Hello, Terry," said the barbed-wire voice. "As I was saying, I want to give you some phone numbers."

Furiously Terry replaced the handset, smashing it into the cradle as if driving home a nail.

He reached into the gloom and brushed the door handle. He yanked. Still stuck.

The phone rang.

And rang, and rang—ten metallic blasts, notes of a cruel and monotonous melody.

He grabbed the handset.

"Leave me alone!"

"Just a minute," the voice wheezed. "Let's get some light in here." The overhead bulb came on, ten times its former intensity, flooding the booth with an otherworldly phosphorescence. "Ready for those numbers?"

"No, asshole!"

As Terry hung up, the door to the coin-return chamber swung back, creaking like a rusty gate.

A head popped out, tiny, sinister, alien: the head of a cicada. The creature crawled to the rim of the chamber and, leaping into the air, began flying around the booth like a tiny and malicious helicopter.

Other insects followed, dozens, scores, a menagerie of beetles and bugs, some specimens taking immediately to flight, others scuttling across the little metal table under the phone. Pop-eyed locusts hopped onto Terry's cotton shirt and wool tie. Long-feelered cockroaches fell to the ground and ascended his cowhide boots and polyester pants like mountain climbers rappeling up a gorge. Swarms of hornets made tiny black tornadoes in the air.

Terry fought back. This time, at least, his feet worked, everything worked—his feet, knees, bare hands—mashing the horrid thoraxes, squashing the revolting abdomens.

He wrapped his dripping, stinking palm around the handset and pulled it to his ear. "All right!" he wailed. "Give me the damn numbers!"

"You surrender, eh?" said the voice,

"Give me the numbers!"

"Take out your penknife."

"How do you know I have one?"

"Take it out," said the voice. "Open it."

Terry obeyed. He drew his knife from his pants and, fitting his thumbnail into the notch, pulled the shiny stainless-steel blade into the blazing light.

"See that little table by the directory? Scratch down this number . . ."

The voice dictated ten digits. Terry carved them into the gray paint, beside the young woman and her goat-lover. The area code was Philadelphia—215—but the other numerals struck no chords.

"Now this one."

Again the voice reeled off numbers. Area code 301—Maryland, Terry believed—followed by an unfamiliar seven-digit string. Terry copied them down.

"Call collect," said the voice. "*0* for Operator. 'Bye."

Click.

Terry jiggled the plunger and, hearing the dial tone, pushed the *0*, then *2-1-5*, then the Philadelphia number.

"Thank you for using Bell of Pennsylvania." Nasal and snotty, the operator's voice suggested a poodle blessed with speech. "May I help you?"

"This is a collect call."

"For who?"

"Whoever's there."

"Your name?"

"Terry Yarber."

On the third ring, a man answered.

"Hello?"

"I have a collect call from Terry Yarber. Will you accept the charges?"

"From Terry? *Terry*? Jesus . . . all right."

Terry's heart descended. His father's voice, no question. Benjamin Yarber: captain of industry, right-wing idealogue, debaucher of the environment.

Terry hung up.

Like a crow taking suddenly to flight, the handset jumped from the cradle and, trailing its metal cord, looped around Terry's neck. The sheathing broke his skin. His tongue shot forward, his arms rowed madly through the glowing air. The cord was a segmented worm, an armored tentacle, a garrote of corrugated steel. He tried to cry out. The cord constricted like a python killing a mongoose, pinching Terry's throat, sealing his windpipe. Pain blazed through his starved lungs, his darkening brain.

He reached out with his index finger. *0* for Operator . . . *2-1-5* for Philadelphia . . . seven digits for his father.

The cord relaxed its stranglehold.

The old man accepted the charges.

"Hi, Dad." Terry coughed; he rubbed his bleeding neck.

"Terry? That really you?"

"It's me, Dad. How are you? How's Mom?"

"How are we? Since when is that a topic *you* care about?"

"I care."

"Yeah, you care so much we get a phone call about every twenty years. That's really caring, that's terrific caring. How'd you know we moved?"

"Somebody gave me your number. I care, Dad." He cared? Life with Father: arguments, insults, put-downs, grudges. But this too: a Labrador retriever, an HO train set, dozens of perch pulled triumphantly from the Chesapeake River, model rockets that sailed into the stratosphere above Jefferson Elementary and landed in the trees. Terry cared, and never so much as now. "Why'd you move?"

"People get old, Son. They don't want to mow their grass anymore. They go someplace without lawns."

"I'm glad you don't have to mow the lawn."

"Let me guess—you need money. That's why you're calling, right? You're broke."

"I've got a problem, Dad, but it's not money. I seem to be stuck in this—"

"Your mother's had a mastectomy."

A malign jolt of electricity zagged through Terry. "God, that's terrible. When?"

"Week ago. She's still in the hospital."

"Is she all right?"

"No, she's not all right. Since when is a mastectomy all right?"

"She getting chemotherapy?"

"Not necessary, they say."

"Then she's all right."

"Listen to him," his father sneered. "Listen to the doctor. The doctor who sells toys for a living and runs out on his wife."

"I'm trying to square things," Terry moaned. "Dad, I want to come visit. Could I visit? I want to see Mom. You and I could go to a Phillies game."

"Since when do I like baseball? You can't remember a damn thing about me, can you?"

"We'll go to a movie. I want to square things, Dad."

"They haven't made a good movie since *Gone With the Wind*. You had your chance with us, Terry, I'm going to hang up now."

"No! Please!"

Click.

Instantly Terry's index finger shot forward, *0* for Operator, *2-1-5* for Philadelphia, seven digits for Dad.

"A collect call for Benjamin Yarber from Terry. Will you accept the charges?"

"No, I won't."

"Dad, please!" Tears flooded Terry's eyes. He hadn't cried since junior high.

"I wouldn't accept the charges if you paid me," his father told the operator. "I wouldn't accept them if you paid me a million dollars."

"Please!"

Click.

Through the saltwater blur Terry punched up the second number; through the pain in his throat he spoke with the operator—collect call from Terry—and of course it was Nancy who came on the line, reluctantly agreeing to accept the charges.

"I want to see the baby," he haltingly told his wife. "I want to see Nicky."

"He's not a baby." When angry, she always became cool and aloof. "He's four. How'd you track me down?"

"Wasn't easy. You're in Maryland, right?"

"Don't come around, Terry. You aren't welcome."

"I want to see Nicky. I want to square things."

"That wouldn't be a good idea."

"Listen, I've got all these toy guns in the car. I'll bet Nicky likes guns."

"Forget it, Terry. Leave us alone."

"He can have any gun he wants."

"Randy and I aren't looking to raise a fascist."

"Randy? Who the hell is Randy?"

"He's Nicky's father."

"*I'm* Nicky's father."

"A father stays home. A father is *there*. Randy's there. He's faithful. I wish you hadn't called, Terry. I think it's time we said good-bye."

Terry wept. He felt torn apart and inaccurately pieced together, heart where spleen should be, lungs where liver belonged. "I want to see my son. Please, Nancy . . ."

Click.

He tried calling her back. The line was busy. His tears kept coming, and coming.

Three minutes later he tried again. Busy.

Nausea spread through him like a hemorrhage.

The phone rang.

He reached for the handset—he grasped at straws. Somehow—oh, please, God, *somehow* it would be his father, *somehow* it would be Nancy. Oh, yes . . .

"Hello?"

"I was right, wasn't I?" said the barbed-wire voice. "You might as well be dead."

"Dead," mumbled Terry, dizzy with confusion, numb with self-loathing.

"You may leave now," wheezed the voice.

"I want my father," snapped Terry. "I want my boy."

"Leave!"

"The door's stuck."

"Not anymore," said the voice. "Look . . ."

The door opened automatically, soundlessly, bending itself in half and sliding against the jamb. The sweet August air rushed against Terry's face, but the sensation was lost on him.

He hung up, took a step forward, and stopped. He felt rooted, glued, as if his heels had become magnets holding him fast to the steel floor. A cryptic remark the voice had made was still with him; it lay impacted in his mind like a tumor, a hard little nugget of ambiguity. "I know *everybody* in the local directory," the voice had said.

Terry lived in Manhattan: 59 West 81st Street, 3-Rear. There was no reason for him to be listed in a western Massachusetts telephone directory—no reason on earth.

A tractor trailer rolled by, smoke gushing from its stacks, diesel engine snorting and belching like a colicky rhinoceros.

Terry pivoted. He grasped the gold chain and, swinging the directory onto the writing table, studied the cover. A cryptic inscription—*Autobiography of a Phone Booth*—was stamped into the thick, glossy leather.

The first several pages were orderly and normal. A bright red page labeled EMERGENCY listed the numbers to call for Fire, Police, and Ambulance. A lucid diagram explained how to read your phone bill. The book devoted two pages to the procedure for calling internationally, and another two pages to the topic of Consumer Rights and Responsibilities. Then came the section titled White Pages, wherein lay a bizarre anomaly, for sprinkled among the expected columns of names, addresses, and phone numbers were boxes filled with small, dense print.

Yagel . . . Yakich . . . Yanak . . . Yapa . . . Yarasavage . . . Yarber.

Yarber, Terrence. 59 West 81st St. (212) 877-0289.

Footloose and alone, Terrence W. Yarber was a man about whom it could truly be said, "His welfare concerned not a single person on earth." This stark fact confronted Terry when, on the evening of August 12, 1992, he used the Housatonic Lane telephone booth in a futile attempt at reconciliation with his father, whom he did not like but whom he deeply loved. His father hung up on him. Longing to speak with his estranged son Nicky, Terry next called his ex-wife and was similarly rebuffed. Sinking into a quicksand of despair, oblivious to the outside world, he left the booth, wandered into the path of an oncoming tractor trailer, and was subsequently smeared all over the grillwork like batter on a waffle iron. He died instantly, mourned by the wind and the rain.

Gripped by the profound unease any man would experience upon reading his own obituary, Terry pawed aimlessly through the pages.

On the chilly afternoon of September 18, 1991, nine-year-old Paulie Fisher somehow managed to wriggle free of the depraved eighth-grade civics teacher who was systematically defiling him in the high weeds of the Housatonic Lane cemetery. The resourceful boy made his way to the adjacent phone booth. Thinking fast, he dialed 911. "Don't worry, Paulie," said the operator, a caring and considerate young woman of twenty-three. "It's perfectly okay what that man's doing to you, and afterward he'll give you candy and toys and lots of money." And so little Paulie returned to his surprised and grateful tormenter, who, after completing the rape, bludgeoned Paulie to death with a crescent wrench.

Terry groaned and trembled. *Perfectly okay?* The operator had called child molestation *perfectly okay?* Impossible. The boy, obviously, had not reached a real operator. The boy had reached an imposter.

On October 12, 1990, Belinda Markson's favorite son, an imperially honest stockbroker named George, pulled his Toyota Celica over beside the Housatonic Lane telephone booth, jammed a dime into the slot, and punched up the emergency medical number so lucidly listed in the directory. Back in the car, Belinda Markson, age seventy-two, shivered in silent terror, her windpipe clogged with a Kentucky Fried Chicken bone. George said, "My mother . . . chicken bone . . . I know there's this movement you make . . ." To which the kindly old physician on the other end replied, "You must reach into

her mouth and push the bone deeper into her esophagus."
George Markson immediately dashed back to the car and performed the suggested maneuver. Five minutes later, his mother
died when her brain, starved for oxygen, ceased to impress
her heart with the necessity of continuous pumping.

A low, soft moan left Terry's lips. Oh, George Markson,
you poor fool. You didn't get a kindly old physician. . . .

For Henry Waxman, a discontented and underrated insurance
agent, the Housatonic Lane telephone booth was in its seclusion and obscurity a godsend. At 8:14 P.M. on January 18,
1992, Henry stopped by the booth as usual on his way home
from work and called his mistress, a landscape designer named
Lilly Templeton. He learned that Lilly was in love. Not with
him—with her boss. "It's all over, Hank. Sorry, honey. We
had some good times, huh?" That night Henry bought a fifth
of scotch, got very drunk, and borrowed his brother-in-law's
Smith & Wesson revolver, forthwith employing it in a manner
that distributed his cerebral cortex throughout the bathroom
of his modest offices overlooking the Great Barrington town
square.

So talented, that voice, thought Terry. The bastard could
impersonate anyone—a telephone operator, a doctor, a
landscape designer. . . .
Terry snatched up the handset. "Hey, clown, I've got
your number. I never talked to my father tonight. I never
talked to Nancy. You're a fucking mimic. I've beaten
you, clown."
"Beaten me?" said the voice. "No, you've merely put
me in a position where I'll have to destroy you more directly."
"I'm not afraid of you."
"You should be."
And then the rain started.
Quite so: rain. It was an interior hurricane, a miniature
monsoon, torrents gushing down from the ceiling and
soaking Terry's shirt, saturating his polyester pants,
drenching his socks and boots. It accumulated mockingly,

relentlessly, blocked by the concrete dams that had mysteriously appeared under the walls and door. The frigid tide rose, moving past his calves, burying his thighs.

"Stop it!" Terry screamed into the handset. "Stop this water!"

The flood kept climbing. Terry pounded on the ungiving glass, flaying his knuckles. This couldn't be happening, couldn't be. Higher, higher: chest, neck, mouth, nose. He dropped the handset, floated to the top of the booth, and, frantically treading water, maneuvered his mouth into the tiny pouch of air near the light fixture. Higher, higher: The water lapped over his lips, spilled into his throat.

So this is what it's like, he thought. This is what it's like to drown.

His lungs convulsed, his esophagus twitched, his blood screamed for air. Bright red comets shot though his skull. He sensed his mind leaking away, drop by drop, drip, drip. . . .

Although his ears were buried by water, Terry could still discern the sweet, holy sound of forged steel cracking glass. The south wall disintegrated, ragged fragments flying into the air, and the water rushed out in one glorious wave, sweeping him into the New England night like a daredevil navigating Niagara Falls. He hit the earth facedown, rolled over, and filled his lungs with God's good air.

A potbellied man stood over him, gripping a lug wrench.

"What *happened*?" Warren asked. He was exactly as Terry imagined he'd be, large and oafish, his bulky chest stuffed into a grimy T-shirt, a John Deere cap perched on his head. "Are you all right?" The cross-shaped wrench was gigantic. You could have crucified a cat on it. "Where'd all that water come from?"

Terry rose from his bed of mud and sopping leaves. "You're Warren?"

"Uh-huh."

"Warren, you've saved my life."

"It appears I have, mister. I've never done anything like that before. You're lucky I heard you screaming."

Terry's dripping clothes hung on his body like gobs of wet moss. His battered knuckles throbbed. "You got any kids?" he asked, spitting out rain.

"Two boys. Tell me about that crazy water."

"From now on, Warren, your two boys are going to get all the cap pistols they want."

"Kindly explain this water business."

"We've got to kill it," said Terry, glancing south down Housatonic Lane. The tow truck lay barely ten yards away, a rusting conglomeration of winches, chains, and ratchets suggesting a traveling torture rack. GARY'S TEXACO, 24-HOUR TOWING SERVICE, said the door.

"Kill what?"

"The booth," Terry explained as he started toward the truck. "It's evil!" he added, opening the driver's door.

"Hey—what are you doing?" called Warren. "What the Christ-in-hell are you doing?"

The key dangled from the ignition. A simple twist, and Terry became the man he wanted to be: exorcist, enemy of haunted houses, scourge of all things supernatural.

An AM radio station popped on: an evangelist talking about the hidden Satanic message of fast food.

"Stop!" screamed Warren, but nothing could stop Terry now—nothing could keep him from sending Gary's Texaco's tow truck straight into the booth.

The evangelist's tonsils shifted registers. He grew raspy and asthmatic. "Do you think you can get rid of me so easily?"

"Bet your ass!" cried Terry.

"I'm everywhere at once, Terry Yarber!" the voice screamed from the radio. "Everywhere at once!"

Contact. The booth flipped over like a tree uprooted by a cyclone and smashed into the gully beside the road. The light bulb exploded. Glass and rivets spurted onto the wet earth. *Autobiography of a Phone Booth* flew into the air and hit the macadam. "Eeiiiii!" screamed the voice as the telephone scudded into the middle of Housatonic Lane, the handset trailing behind it. "Eeyowww!" Such an easy target, Terry mused, as he swerved the wheel and took aim. Such a sitting duck.

Gunning the motor, sailing forward, he pulverized the phone as totally as the dozens of possums and skunks he'd inadvertently run over in his career as a traveling salesman.

On the radio the evangelist warned his listeners about Big Macs.

"Hey, you crazy sucker," blathered Warren as Terry stepped out of the cab, "if there's any damage to my truck, you're going to pay for it."

"Just send me the bill," said Terry, smiling hugely.

"Not to mention that you're probably in all sorts of trouble with New England Telephone now. What sort of beef did you have with that phone, anyway?"

"It took my dime," said Terry, still smiling.

Warren frowned and slung the wrench over his shoulder. "This has definitely been the weirdest call of the day. It began on a much better note, with this lady who needed a jump-start, if you know what I mean."

Terry bent down and lifted the sopping telephone directory off the road. "My van's that way," he said, pointing.

"I know," said Warren. "I already loosened your lugs."

"Then let's go get your boys some water pistols."

An hour later, Terry checked into a Best Western hotel in Hartford. He set the telephone directory on the bureau, right beside a Gideon Bible. It was still too wet to yield any information. When the water finally evaporated, he would begin the arduous process of contacting each man, woman, and child whose obituary still lay in the future, warning them not to believe everything they heard.

He ate dinner, sipped a Miller Lite at the bar, took a satisfying shower, and spent an hour diligently filling out the week's orders from Kiddie City, Kay Bee, and Toys 'Я' Us.

He tossed a nickel into the air. Heads, he'd call his father first. Tails, Nancy.

Heads. He punched up *215*.

reg Cox is a thin young man and a devotee of horror films and *The Weekly World News*. He has had stories published in *Amazing Stories*, *Aboriginal*, and in *Spirits of Christmas*, edited by Kathryn Cramer and David G. Hartwell. His annotated bibliography of vampire fiction is forthcoming from Borgo Press.

Originally from Seattle, he now lives in Brooklyn, New York. He reviews for and is on the staff of *The New York Review of Science Fiction* and works as an assistant editor for a major publisher. In his spare time, he writes cover copy for paperback books.

Most of Cox's fiction is funny. For example, his story "Hana and His Synapses"—in which he casts a Woody Allen–like character as a cyberpunk hero—opens with a scene of the central character trying to snort Orange Tang. In "Firetrap," below the comic surface lurks the quintessential house story.

Firetrap

GREG COX

Moving night, and the house squatted before them like an empty wooden crate waiting to be filled. The chartreuse paint job was mercifully muted by the fading light so that it had merely the sick green look of a possessed child's vomit. Although there were two other homes in the cul-de-sac, one on either side, its location at the end, as well as the wedge-shaped empty spaces between the houses, made theirs seem deceptively alone and apart.

If this is the future, Gordon thought glumly, let's get it over with.

For starters, the doorknob came off in his hand. "Terrific," he muttered as he pocketed the chipped glass knob and pushed the front door open with his foot. Carla and Mick squeezed past him into this, their new communal home. Gordon glanced backward; from the front porch, which was badly in need of repainting, he could see the lights of the campus, less than a mile up the hill. His fingers explored the circular hole where the doorknob had rested all too loosely. For this, he thought, I gave up my cozy room in the dorm? Hell, for this I moved away from home?

The door refused to close behind him, so Gordon left it hanging ajar. Later, after they'd finishing moving their boxes in, maybe he could prop it shut with a rock or something. He found his housemates in the ground-floor living room, which was unfurnished, uncarpeted, and dusty. The floor consisted of worn hardwood planks, separated by as much as half an inch of a dry, black, gummy substance. The bare white walls were whitest in those patches where large holes had obviously been plastered over. The landlord, he recalled, had said something about a rugby team living here before.

Blue eyes beaming, Carla danced around the room as though she'd never seen it before. "Well," she said, throwing out her arms theatrically, "welcome to Altered Estates!"

"Otherwise known as the Amityville Horror, Part Six," Gordon replied.

By any name, their new address was a two-story residence located in the middle of Bellingham's "student slums," within walking distance of the university. The age of the house was given away by its antiquated heating system: a coal-eating furnace in the basement that still needed to be regularly de-ashed by hand and shovel. So, Gordon thought, on top of everything else, we can also look forward to black lung disease.

"Have you seen the bathtub?" Mick asked. "There's enough dirt along the bottom that it could pass for a terrarium." He shrugged his high, stocky shoulders. "Then again, I suppose we can always grow our own food in a pinch."

Carla assumed a threatening pose, elbows out, fists on her hips. Gordon thought she looked like some red-haired Irish Amazon out of an old John Ford movie—even if she was from Hawaii. "That's enough, both of you. This is *our* house now—for just three hundred dollars a month, mind you—and all it needs is a little work to make it perfect. Don't tell me you want to go back to dorm food, not to mention all those stupid regulations."

"It'll look better," Mick conceded, "once we get all our stuff unpacked, I guess."

The eternal stoic, Gordon thought. What admirable unflappability in the face of disaster. Or maybe Mick simply didn't realize yet what a dreadful mistake this was.

"I want you both to remember that this wasn't my idea."

"No," said Carla, grinning, "but you agreed to it quick enough."

Under false pretenses, Gordon almost shot back, but caught himself in time. True, when Carla had first called him up over Christmas break to tell him about this wonderful old house she'd discovered, he had thought that she was talking about the two of them, well, living together; only after five or six glorious minutes had he realized that she was proposing instead a more innocent three-way arrangement involving Mick as well. He had covered himself hastily, but still wasn't sure if Carla had picked up on his initial misconception.

God, that would be embarrassing.

Unwilling to meet Carla's eyes at this particular moment, Gordon leaned casually against the lower pane of the window facing their weed-infested front yard. Almost immediately, the wooden ledge gave way beneath his elbow, and he found himself sprawling on the floor. His glasses skated across the floor, coming to rest in the crack between two planks. His throbbing funny bone pulsed in rhythm to the fervent chorus in his head: This is a terrible, terrible, terrible mistake.

Mick and Carla laughed as he scrambled to his feet and wiped the dust and tar off his hands. Probably got splinters too, he guessed. "That's right, gang up on me, see if I care. I know what's going on here: You two and the house are in cahoots to kill me."

"I'm sorry," Carla said. She still looked like she was

watching an unusually funny sketch on Monty Python. "Are you all right, Gordon?"

His injured elbow was already forgetting the fall. "I seem to be intact, despite the best efforts of this residential death trap."

I suppose, he thought, I should be glad that Mick and Carla get along so well. My best friend and sort-of girl-friend. He remembered the first time he'd brought Carla back to the dorm to meet his roommate, after a marathon study session at the college library; for a while he'd been afraid that Carla would take Mick's dour silence as some sort of snub, even if that was the way he always was. Not to worry. Pretty soon, Carla had practically moved in with them, and was suggesting they make the household official. Granted, the fact that she hated her own roommate didn't hurt.

They were so different, though. Carla: ebullient, moody, temperamental. Unable to pick out any one major or field of study, but the self-appointed cheerleader and social director of their own little troika. The Irish Amazon from Honolulu. And Mick, who *was* Irish but acted as though he'd stepped out of one of Ingmar Bergman's slower-moving pictures; Gordon half expected to find him playing chess with Death one day. Even when Mick was drunk (which Gordon had seen more than once), he still made Norman Bates look like Buster Keaton. The only difference between Mick sober and Mick plastered was the shit-eating grin that spread across his wide, jaw-heavy face as he slowly faded into oblivion. Carla and Mick. Fire and earth. Dorothy and the Tin Man (sans heart). The only thing they had in common, as far as Gordon could see, was that they both kept their hidden depths hidden.

And where did he, the ever-fluid Scarecrow, fit into this cosmology? Witty, sardonic, the future whiz-kid of American film studies? Well, self-analysis was best left to the vain and idle. He had more important things to worry about.

Like this wreck of a house, for instance.

*   *   *

The first part of moving in, carrying their boxes and sleeping bags in from Mick's van, went easily enough. Gordon estimated they had unloaded two dozen cartons of books alone, but at least the night sky, although cloudy, had declined to snow. By nine o'clock, they were already in the kitchen, washing the newsprint off cups and plates that, mere moments before, had been protectively swaddled in back issues of *The Bellingham Herald*. Then Carla plugged in the toaster, and all the lights went out.

The kitchen was totally black. Gordon heard a plate or something shatter against the floor, followed by Mick's muttered curse, but he couldn't see a thing. Great, he thought. Suddenly we've gone from a visual medium to starring in an old-time radio show. *Inner Sanctum*, probably, or *Light's Out*.

GORDON: Who knows what evil lurks in the hearts of men . . . ?

MICK: Must have blown a fuse.

GORDON: Just by plugging in one appliance? Boy, cooking is going to be an adventure in this place.

CARLA: Careful. I think there's broken glass on the floor.

MICK: Sorry about that.

GORDON: No problem. But now what are we going to do?

MICK: The fuse box is in the basement, I think. I'm not sure how we're going to find it in the dark, though.

CARLA: Anybody pack a flashlight? Wait, hang on a second. . . .

A match flared to life a few feet away from Gordon, and for once he was glad Carla was a smoker. She held the match up in front of her so that it cast a dim orange glow over her face. The flame, and the shadows it threw beneath her nose and brow, made her look like a jack-o'-lantern's bride. Behind her, Mick was visible only as a looming gray shadow.

"Gordon, look in that box over by the cupboard. No, the other one. There should be some candles in there, with the rest of my decorations." The match sputtered dangerously close to her fingertips, and Carla flicked it into the sink, where the light drowned instantly in soapy water. Gordon groped through ribbons and greeting cards until he grabbed onto something round and waxy. Carla lighted another match; the something turned out to be a large yellow skull. Or rather, judging from the wick in the cranium, a candle shaped like a skull.

"Leftover from Halloween," she said, lighting the skull, then blowing out the match. "There should be a Santa in there too."

Gordon found the jolly red candle and handed it to Mick. The kitchen still looked creepy in the flickering candlelight, but at least they could navigate again. "Let's try the basement," Mick said.

The door to the basement was at the far end of the kitchen, next to the fridge. Gordon unbolted the door and looked down a steep set of stairs into darkness. "Careful with the candle going down the steps," Carla warned. "We don't want to burn the place down on our first night here."

"Only if we're lucky."

"What?"

"Never mind."

Mick led the way down the stairs, from the bottom of which their candles revealed all but the furthest corners of the cavelike basement. The ceiling was braced with wooden beams, and was low enough that Mick, the tallest of them, had to stoop slightly as he stepped past the narrow archway at the foot of the steps. Their coal-eating dragon, already christened "Smog," chugged noisily just beyond intersecting rings of candlelight. Wispy cobwebs hung from the beams and brushed against their faces, much to the annoyance of Mick, who hated spiders with a passion he seldom displayed over anything else.

"Jesus Christ," Gordon whispered as he looked around.

They had been here before, of course. In the daylight. With the landlord. That had been some weeks ago though, and things had obviously changed since then. A tattered mattress occupied the center of the basement floor, surrounded by garbage: bottles, pop cans, candy wrappers, old newspapers, cereal boxes, and bones. A small window located just above eye-level was conspicuously broken; the missing glass piled in a heap by Gordon's feet. The basement smelled of urine and recent habitation.

"Someone's been living here."

"Obviously," Gordon said, then regretted it. Carla looked upset enough. To be honest, he wasn't exactly thrilled with this development himself.

"Who do you think it is?" Carla wondered aloud.

"Just a vagrant," Mick said. "Nobody we'd know."

Gordon kicked the scattered debris aside. "I don't know," he said. "Remember that weirdo who used to hang out on campus? The one who claimed to be a 'professor' of black magic?"

"You mean Dmitri the Dark?"

"Yeah. That's the one."

"I never figured out how Geraldo missed him," Mick commented. "What a flake."

"Creepy, though," Carla said. "I remember, once, he crashed a party at Higginson, back when it was an all-girls dorm, and started showing off this Nazi dagger of his, which he told us he had—get this—'sanctified in a ceremony of blood and sperm.' Ugh!" Her pale face grimaced, as though she were digesting a rancid memory. "Gordon, you don't really think this is him?"

He examined the trash with an imaginary magnifying glass. "It's a possibility. He used to sleep in the library, until Security finally ran him off campus." Should I go on? Gordon wondered. Why was he trying to spook everybody like this anyway? Then again, when you're standing in the dark holding a burning skull, what else are you supposed to do? "I heard he attacked someone."

"That was just a rumor," Mick said. "Besides, Dmitri was hardly the only transient in town."

"Or the only psycho," observed Carla, obviously getting into the spirit of the thing. "There was that guy who used to perch on the roof of the dining hall, pretending to be a gargoyle."

"Only during finals," Mick said. "He was just a harmless, stressed-out chem major."

Party pooper, Gordon thought. "Don't forget the Hillside Strangler. He eventually ended up in Bellingham."

"And the Green River Killer . . . damn, now you've got me doing it!" Mick's large fingers sank into the warm wax Santa in his fist. Claws into Claus. He trudged into the web-strewn shadows, searching for the fuse box. "What are you trying to do, Gordon? Fill us full of nightmares?"

There are three possible answers, Gordon thought. One, I'm putting on a hell of a show for my own amusement, and maybe Carla's. Two, I'm getting totally paranoid in my old age. Three, there really is a homicidal maniac living here, and we'll all be dead by morning.

The circuit breakers proving inscrutable and intractable, the three sophomores decided to call it quits for the night. Electrical repairs and further unpacking seemed better suited to daylight, so they carefully navigated the stairs to the second floor, where—oh, uncollegiate luxury!—they each had a bedroom of their own. Gordon's was at the end of the hall, farthest from the stairs: a bare, rectangular chamber, about one-fourth as spacious as the basement, lacking both furnishings and light. The uncurtained window opposite the bedroom door offered a dim view of the evergreens in the empty lot behind the house, along with the meager comfort of knowing that very few chain-saw cannibals were likely to come smashing through that particular window, not when an interior stairway was so much more convenient.

As he unrolled his sleeping bag in the middle of the floor, Gordon was not looking forward to the first night in his new room. This house is a stranger, he thought. And if everyone knew that you shouldn't talk to a stranger, how much more foolhardy it must be to actually go and *live* in one.

Still, he blew out the skull before undressing and crawling into the sleeping bag like a skinny pink hermit crab retreating into a padded, polyester shell. The best he could hope for, he knew, was an instant descent into dreamless sleep, hopefully to rise again with the dawn. No such luck. For an uncertain, insomniac interval he lay on his back, looking past the foot of the bag at the rustling pines outside his window. A hint of moonlight suffused the cloudy sky beyond, and the trees were silhouetted against a purple background like monster triffids with dozens of vibrating, venomous spikes. He wondered how the campus gargoyle had made it to his rooftop perch, and realized that the would-be Quasimodo must have climbed trees much like these. Harmless, Mick had said? A likely story. Gordon rolled over in his hundredth futile attempt to physically shift himself into unconsciousness. How in the world had he been talked into this? It was all Carla's fault.

His face buried in the bag's insulation, unable to see the twisting trees or empty room, Gordon was betrayed by his ears. Noises, vague and unidentifiable, swirled around his blinded awareness; he "saw" them in his mind as a shifting cloud of ghostly insects—not fireflies, *whisperflies.* Christmas is definitely over, he thought, for this was sure no Silent Night. Noises from outside his window. Noises from above. Noises from the other side of the wall on his right . . .

Wait. Carla was on the other side of that wall. He concentrated on the sounds coming from that direction, pushing the other whispers out of the way so that he could listen more closely to what he now distinctly recognized as the sound of someone moving in the room next door. Not footsteps; the sounds were too irregular for that. Someone crawling, perhaps, or struggling. Could Carla be doing sit-ups at this hour? Or having a bad dream?

Slowly, trying hard not to make any noises of his own, Gordon sat up in his sleeping bag, listening. The cool air chilled his exposed neck and shoulders. Dammit, why couldn't he hear more clearly? Carla could be in trouble. In the dark, he pulled on a ratty pair of jeans and tiptoed to the not-quite soundproof wall between his room and Carla's. Just as he placed his ear against the rough (and surprisingly cold) surface of the wall, Carla suddenly cried out. He heard an unmistakable gasp, then silence.

Jesus Christ, he thought, scrambling for the skull-candle on the floor, searching his pockets for a match. She's being strangled! With shaky fingers he found the wick and lighted it. The skull glowed: a miniature campfire in the icy blackness of the room. Lifting the skull to the level of his chin, Gordon quietly crept into the hallway outside the door. Insanely he found himself afraid to make even the littlest noise necessary to breathe. This is crazy, he thought. If there is a madman in her room, why aren't I charging to the rescue? And if there isn't, who am I afraid will hear me?

If. That was the problem, wasn't it? That was why he wasn't calling to Mick for help. What if he was wrong? Standing outside Carla's door, the hot wax flowing off the skull so that he constantly had to adjust his grip to avoid being burned by the viscous yellow rivulets, Gordon found himself paralyzed by uncertainty. In the slippery light of the candle, it seemed too easy to dismiss what moments before had been a clear, high-resolution image of Carla, and then the rest of them, being stabbed or strangled or smothered in their sleep by Dmitri the Dark or someone even more malignant. By the invader who had taken possession of what was supposed to be their home.

He stood outside her door, listening but hearing nothing.

Either Carla has rolled over and gone back to sleep, he thought, or there's someone else in there, listening to me listening for him. I should knock on the door, get this over with one way or another, but what if I'm wrong? How am I going to explain this to Carla? Against his will, Gordon remembered that other night, a few months back, when, fired up by too many beers and a steamy movie on TV, he had called her up in the middle of the night, waking her from what was no doubt a sound sleep, and then babbled incoherently about how much he wanted to come over right that minute and . . . God, how he'd made a fool of himself! Humiliating was not a strong enough word, and the worst part had been having to face her the next morning at breakfast.

He'd rather meet a psychotic killer than go through that again.

Almost.

He leaned toward her door, straining to hear. The old cliché was true: it was quiet, too quiet. Even if Carla was sleeping peacefully, she should be making more noise than this. There was something terribly *deliberate* about this unnatural, prolonged silence.

The basement, Gordon thought. He would have come from the basement. Had they left the door to the basement unlatched after they'd climbed back up the stairs to the kitchen? Gordon couldn't remember. He was pretty sure he hadn't, but less so about Mick and Carla. It had been really dark in the kitchen, even with the candles.

There was only one way to be sure—about all of it. Stepping cautiously upon the old timber floor, he turned away from Carla's door and headed for the stairs. Scanning the shadows, holding on to the burning skull with one hand and the railing with the other, he descended to the first floor. The empty living room seemed unusually cavernous now that midnight was past. He was afraid to glance at the tall, uncovered windows on his left; it was too easy to imagine that heart-stopping moment when he saw a crazed, wild-eyed figure looking back at him from the other side of the glass. He could see the whole scene in his mind, feel his breath catching in anticipation.

No question about it. He had definitely seen too many slasher movies.

By contrast with the bleak vastness of the living room, the kitchen, with its counters and cupboards and stove, was reassuringly cozy. The light of the candle exposed almost the entire room; there were not as many black corners from which an attacker could come charging. What was he most afraid of, Gordon asked himself, the monsters in shadows, who couldn't be seen, or the monsters in the windows, who could?

From where he was standing, just inside the kitchen, the door to the basement appeared to be closed. But was it locked? It was too dark to tell.

All things considered, he thought, I'd rather not see the monsters.

Still, sliding his feet softly against the spill-proof tile floor, he approached the basement door. He held his candle far in front of him, in hopes of being able to spot something before he got too close. He was glad that the kitchen floor was tiled, for surely his shuffling pace would have filled his bare feet with painful slivers on any of the rougher wooden floors in the house. Finally he was near enough to the door to cast the heart of the candle's glow upon it.

Not only was the door unlatched, it was open by a crack.

Oh God. Gordon expelled a long, slow breath. He experienced a sudden urge to run, to shout, to wake up Mick and (hopefully) Carla, if only just to share this anxiety with someone else. Instead, he pulled the door open and started down the steps.

Descent after descent, he thought. Just like What's-her-name in *Psycho*—the one who stayed out of the shower— when she went down into the fruit cellar to find Norman's mother, even though everyone in the audience is screaming at her to run the other way. Why did she keep going?

Gordon understood now. Momentum. The urge to completion, to see things through to the end, maybe even to wreak
a little mayhem of your own instead of staying perpetually
on the defensive. Who is least likely to survive: the hero
or the monster? Neither, he realized. It's the born victims
who get chewed to death every time. The extras, the can-
non fodder, the romantic lead's best friend . . .

His shadow followed Gordon down the creaky basement
steps, whose peeling paint scratched his feet and lodged
between his toes. Cobwebs fell in strands from the sloping
ceiling above, too thin and insubstantial to cast shadows
of their own but solid enough to sizzle dangerously whenever the candle drew too near. The basement was notice-
ably cooler than the rest of the house; Gordon could feel
the temperature drop a few microdegrees with each step
that took him further down toward the trash-littered lair of
their unwanted visitor. It was the architectural layout,
though, that was really sadistic. The stairway was flanked
by a partial interior wall, so that there was no way to see
the rest of what was down there until you actually reached
the bottom (just like this), turned to the right (just like
this), took a deep breath, and saw . . .

At first, nothing. Just the cramped clutter of mattress
and garbage, wooden beams and heaps of burned-out coal
and ash. And the shadows, of course, who alone knew
what evil lurked, et cetera. Gordon enjoyed a few frantic
heartbeats of relief—until the furnace came noisily to life
with an unexpected clank, startling him and yanking his
attention to the most distant, blackest corner of the basement, where, outlined by the red glow that escaped the
furnace gratings, a dim but definite figure rose up from behind sloping dunes of discarded ash.

Yes! It wasn't his imagination. He could *see* it.

Gordon screamed, an incomprehensible outpouring of
rough, senseless, throat-tearing noises. He stumbled backward, almost falling. The figure lurched toward him, its
face lost in darkness, its arms reaching for Gordon, about

to touch him. No, he thought, stop it! A newspaper head-line flashed through his head: STUDENT MURDERED IN HOME.

"Wait . . ." he began; then the figure slammed vio-lently into him, and the back of Gordon's head collided with the wall. The force and speed of the attack left him stunned and breathless. The smell of dirty hair and skin, like the dry and dusty musk of baked blacktop, filled his nostrils and mouth. A numbing ache spread from a sharp, bright nova of pain at the base of his skull, and his glasses tumbled from his nose as a clenched and bony fist struck his stomach like a missile.

It wasn't like the movies, he discovered. Real violence wasn't something visual, something choreographed and carefully lighted. It was a force that tore at your flesh, smashed into your bones, and reduced you to a mere solid object buffeted by other objects, harder and more re-lentless.

Shoved against the basement wall, his world a blur of shadows and sudden shocks, Gordon didn't even notice the burning skull slip from his fingers.

Then the figure, the opposing force, went away, and he collapsed forward onto his hands and knees. My glasses, he thought. I have to find my glasses so I can see who it is, Dmitri or the gargoyle. First though, he needed just a minute, please, to recover, to let his head stop hurting, to spit the blood and saliva from his mouth and try to breathe again. Just a couple more minutes . . . He shut his eyes. He smelled smoke.

"Jesus, Gordon, the place is on fire!"

He looked up to see Carla standing over him, Mick run-ning past. "My glasses," he whispered, and moments later felt the plastic frames placed in his hand. As his vision came back into focus, so too did he gradually become aware again of where he was and what was happening.

His candle had landed amid a mess of grocery sacks and old newspapers. Not all the trash had ignited yet, but al-ready a small fire was consuming the scattered candy wrappers and cereal boxes and sending red-hot flakes of burning paper adrift on the air. Wearing only a dark blue bathrobe, Mick beat down the flames with an old, skeletal rake; an orange and yellow gout of fire erupted out of an empty paint can only a foot away from his bare leg. "Shit!" he cried, jumping backward. Thick white smoke poured out of much of the soggier trash, transforming the basement into a foggy hell worthy of Jack the Ripper or the Werewolf of London. His head throbbing, Gordon looked for his attacker and saw only his housemates. There are three possibilities, he realized. One, the invader had run off before Mick and Carla arrived. Two, he *became* Mick and Carla. Three, he was still here . . . somewhere.

"Gordon, are you all right?" Carla asked. She crouched beside him, wearing only a nightgown and fog.

"Get some water!" Mick shouted at them. "Hurry, we're going to need some water!"

Gordon stared into the spreading flames. All that from one little skull . . . ?

"Will *somebody* get me some fucking water?"

That snapped him out of it, finally. Lurching to his feet, he followed Carla up the stairs to the kitchen sink.

Bellingham is a damp and moldy town. In the end, it took only four trips, seven pots of tap water, and a pitcher of sacrificed pink lemonade to extinguish the blaze. The bottom half of the wall beneath the broken window was somewhat blackened, but otherwise the structural integrity of Altered Estates had been preserved; ditto for Gordon, whom Carla, in her best Florence Nightingale mode, determined to have received a bump and not a concussion. By dawn, there was even time for explanations.

"Are you sure you saw somebody?" Mick asked.

"No, I hit myself on the back of the head . . . of course I saw somebody!"

"Well, technically," Carla pointed out, "the only thing

that hit your head was a wall. And that was a stationary
object.''

"And Dmitri, or whoever, shoved me into the wall. Same
difference.''

"I know," she said soothingly, checking once more the
bandage behind his ears. In the absence of any other furniture, they were seated in a circle atop the vagrant's
abandoned mattress. Carla had draped a frayed yellow quilt
over the stained surface of the mattress so they wouldn't
be too grossed out. At the same time, she had retrieved a
bathrobe of her own from one of the boxes upstairs, pre-
sumably not, Gordon assumed, for fearing of grossing out
the rest of them. That would be impossible, especially where
he was concerned.

"We found the front door open when we came downstairs," she continued, "and somebody made a lot of noise
down here, even after you screamed.''

"I screamed?''

"You screamed like a gorilla with a rhino up his ass,"
Mick said, with a grin so wide that Gordon wondered if
he'd been drinking.

"Well, it worked for Tarzan. . . .''

"The bum probably just panicked, then decided to get
the hell out of here.''

"Yeah, you can be pretty terrifying in the dark, Gordo.''
Carla reached out and ran her finger along one of his ribs.
"Probably got one look at that skinny bod of yours and
decided the Living Dead had come to get him.''

Gordon wasn't sure if he was being insulted or flirted
with, but he laughed anyway. They all did, even Mick.

It was moments like this, Gordon decided, that would
make this whole "Altered Estates" venture worth-
while.

Maybe.

*   *   *

They boarded up the basement window right away, then put another bolt on the door in the kitchen. By midterms, a few weeks later, the house was filled with secondhand furniture, what Gordon termed "Early American garage sale." He had to admit that there were advantages to living off-campus, like relief from blaring stereos and biweekly fire alarms, and even though he still woke up sometimes in the middle of the night, he wasn't hearing strange noises anymore, from either below or the room next door. In time, he even got up the nerve to ask Carla about the gasps and commotion he'd thought he'd heard that first night.

"Dreams," she said.

"About what?"

She smiled slyly. "I'm not telling."

Ah, Carla! So tantalizing and bewildering. He still didn't know exactly where he stood with her, not that there was much chance to find out with Mick perpetually hanging about. A great housemate, and easy to get along with, but it was undeniably awkward living with the archetypal "third wheel." If only Mick would fall for some alluring coed who lived on the other side of town; these late-night threesomes in front of *David Letterman* were idyllic as such things go, but a night alone with Carla, just the two of them . . . well, if nothing else, the suspense was killing him.

Nor were things always idyllic, for that matter. Despite their proven compatibility, trouble sometimes surfaced in paradise, like the time Gordon came home from a long night at the library to discover that Mick and Carla had fixed themselves an elaborate steak dinner, complete with veggies and dessert, and not even saved him any leftovers!

"We just felt in a cooking sort of mood, Gordo."

"Yeah, and we had no idea when or if you were coming home. I mean, it's not like we have any designated dinnertime."

"Might as well be back in the dorm," Carla said.

"Fine. Sure. I understand. But I am paying a third of the grocery bill around here, you know."

"If it really bothers you, Gordon, we can deduct the cost of the steaks from your share of the rent next month."

"No, don't bother." Gordon realized he sounded like a crabby old man; he felt a headache coming on. "That way madness lies. We don't want to end up rationing the beers and counting our Rice Crispies."

In the end, peace was restored, but he went to bed that night with a belly full of Top Ramen and undigested resentment. He understood now how so many happy marriages had run aground on household bills and budgets.

And then, of course, there was the Great Unicorn Incident. . . .

Gordon was upstairs typing an essay on Brian DePalma when he heard the front door swing shut. He briefly considered calling out to see which of his absent housemates had returned, but, no, he wasn't quite ready to call it quits on this paper yet. Maybe after a few more pages he could wander down and socialize.

Then Carla shouted from the foot of the stairs, "Gordon! Get down here!"

She sounded upset—and a little bit angry. Gordon had no idea what was up, but already he didn't like it. Uninvited, images of Dmitri the Dark astride a burning skull, brandishing a cum-stained knife, played in the multiplex of his mind. "What's the matter?" he asked as he bounced off the bottom step and skidded to a halt beside Carla.

"What happened to my unicorn?"

"Huh?" He looked across the living room, whose gummy black floor was now covered by an ersatz Arabian rug, at the small end table where, as recently as lunchtime, a foot-high crystal unicorn had posed with its glittering hooves raised up to paw the air. Now those hooves, along with the rest of the figurine, lay in pieces beneath the table. Gordon spotted a spiral horn, curiously unbroken, amid the other chips and fragments.

"At least you could have cleaned up the mess afterward," Carla said. "Not that there's any chance of putting it back together. You really did a number on it."

"It was fine the last time I saw it!" Gordon was genuinely appalled at the accusation. "Why the hell would I want to break it? I gave you that unicorn!"

"I'm not saying you did it on purpose, Gordon."

"I didn't do it at all!"

"You were the only person here this afternoon, weren't you? You must have at least heard something. That crystal looks like it's been dropped *and* stomped on."

She had a point, but since when had Carla become such a demon prosecutor? And of him, no less. "Maybe I was flushing the toilet when it happened."

"When what happened? Even if you didn't hear anything, that still begs the question: How did it get broken?" Carla's tone softened somewhat, and she sat down on the couch beside the unicorn's former perch. "Hey, if it was an accident, that's fine. I'm just trying to figure this thing out."

Gordon barely heard her. The logic of Carla's argument grabbed onto his aching brain and dragged it toward the only possible answer: Someone else, someone destructive, had been in the house today, and maybe still was.

Flames in the basement. A dark figure reaching out . . .

He dashed into the kitchen, cutting off Carla in the middle of a conciliatory sentence. Puzzled and momentarily speechless, she followed him and found Gordon staring at the door to the basement, tugging on the knob.

Both bolts were in place. The door wouldn't budge.

He must have got in some other way, Gordon decided. He turned to face Carla. "Dmitri . . . I mean, the man in the basement. He's back."

"Are you serious?"

"Who else could have broken it? You weren't here, Mick wasn't here, I didn't do it . . . who else could it be? It had to be him, right?" he challenged her. "Right?"

"I suppose," she said finally, but there was a doubt, a wariness, in her eyes that Gordon had never seen there before. He saw the same doubt in Mick's eyes later on when their other third came home that evening. Very well, he thought, don't believe me. I guess it's up to me to protect the both of you, whether you like it or not.

The very next day, Gordon bought a gun.

The newly acquired curtains over the windows made the kitchen and living room even darker than before. Flashlight in hand, Gordon stalked noiselessly through the sleeping house; his other hand held tightly onto the heavy gray pistol thrust deep into the pocket of his sweatshirt. The flashlight's beam patrolled before him, darting over the walls and furniture, scouting out the shadows where who-knows-what may hide. So far, Gordon had surprised nothing more than a small army of ghostly white silverfish who put on a convincing simulation of Brownian motion before disappearing back into the cracks along the kitchen counter. Still, he felt ready for anything.

Except maybe the sound, a few yards behind him, of floorboards creaking beneath a heavy tread.

His throat dried so fast he thought he was choking. The cold that raced over him, freezing him from inside out, shocked him in its intensity; he would have thrown up if he had had the strength or the time. Executing a graceless half-turn, he banged his elbow on the kitchen doorframe, barked an incoherent command at the approaching footsteps, and raised up the flashlight instead of the gun.

The beam caught Mick directly in the face. "Hey, watch the light, will you," he whispered, raising a hand against the glare. "And keep it down. Carla's been sound asleep for hours."

"Jesus Christ!" Gordon said hoarsely. His hand jerked away from the gun in his pocket. Mick would never know how close he came to being blown away. "You scared me to death. When you came up behind me . . . my heart is still racing!" And not just from the shock of Mick's sudden appearance. *God, what would I have done if I had shot him?*

Thankfully neither Mick nor Carla knew about the gun.

"I heard noises downstairs and thought I'd check them out," Mick said. "Tell you the truth, for a while there I even thought it might be that bogeyman of yours, Dmitri."

Since when did Dmitri become exclusively *my* bogeyman? Gordon wondered. Now that the panic and adrenaline were wearing off, he felt a little annoyed by Mick's attitude. Hey, there were lots of things he'd rather be doing than worrying about protecting the house from Dmitri. He was doing this for Mick, and Carla too.

"What are you doing down here anyway, Gordon? An attack of the midnight munchies?"

If I'm smart, he thought, I'll let it go at that. Instead, he held the flashlight between them so he could look Mick in the eye and said, "What am I doing? I'm doing the hard work of making sure that Dmitri, or whoever it is that is sharing this house with us, doesn't get away with anything too terrible while the rest of you are getting a good night's sleep."

"You're joking, right? Since when did we need a security guard around here?"

"Remember the unicorn?"

"That was over a week ago. Anyway, it was just some dumb accident. I know why I'm standing here in the middle of the night. I heard a strange noise, which turned out to be you. Have you heard anything . . . besides me?"

"Not yet. I mean, not really. But that doesn't mean we don't have a major problem here. I didn't make up that lair in the cellar. I was there when that weirdo attacked me!"

"Ssshh, keep it down." Mick adopted a more sympathetic tone. "That was a shitty thing to happen to you on our first night here, but you can't let it make you crazy. We've checked out the basement several times since then without finding a trace of him. The bum's probably selling his blood in Spokane now, or hiding out in somebody else's basement."

"The unicorn . . ."

Mick peered at Gordon over the glowing, upturned lens of the flashlight. Feeling unaccountably exposed, Gordon was tempted to flick off the light. "How long have you been doing this nightly patrol shtick?"

"Since last Friday. On and off."

"Mostly on, I'll bet. You look like hell, Gordon."

"Thanks a lot."

"No, I'm serious. You're shaking, you've got bags under your eyes . . . look, did I ever tell you about my brother?"

"What about him?"

Mick leaned against the nearest wall; Gordon hoped this wasn't going to be a long story. His head was starting to hurt again.

"My older brother, James, drives trucks for a living. Long-distance hauls. Sometimes he'll drive for days at a time on little or no sleep. After a while, he told me, on the really long trips, he starts to hallucinate behind the wheel. He says he sees people, mostly friends and family, standing in the center of the road. He runs them down, too."

"Wonderful." Gordon yawned. "But aside from giving me serious second thoughts about driving on the highway, at least when your brother's on the road, I'm not sure what this has to do with the Dmitri situation."

"The moral is," Mick said, with too much emphasis, "sleep deprivation is a terrible thing."

So is getting murdered in your bed, Gordon thought.

The next day in class though, he had to admit he was feeling the strain. He felt dull, logy; his eyes burned with the effort it took to keep them open, but whenever he closed them, just for a second, he seemed to lose minutes at a time. That today's "lab" consisted of sitting in the dark during a screening of the old, silent version of *The Phantom of the Opera,* minus musical accompaniment, did not make it any easier to stay awake. When he dozed off during the Masque of the Red Death (his favorite part!) and then snapped to attention to discover the Phantom dead, the lovers reunited, and the lights in the lecture hall coming up, he decided to call it a day.

Too bad he couldn't sleep through the walk home. With spring only weeks away, Bellingham remained cold and uncomfortable. The noxious smell of the paper plant down by the harbor permeated the air, leaving a bad taste in Gordon's mouth. His right eye began to throb, a sure sign of a migraine on the way. Hands tucked within the sleeves of his jacket, he staggered downhill to Altered Estates. The run-down house, with its yard full of brown, dying weeds, had seldom seemed so inviting.

Be it ever so desolate, he thought, there's no place like home.

Fatigue made him clumsy, and he dropped his keys three times before finally getting the front door open. He pushed it quietly shut behind him, too exhausted to close it with any more noise or enthusiasm. I will be unconscious, he promised, within five seconds of hitting the bed. First, however, a couple of aspirin.

Procuring tablets in the bathroom, he wandered slowly into the kitchen for a glass of water. When he spotted the basement door, his aching, reddened eyes grew wider than they had been all day.

The door to Dmitri's den was unlocked and propped open with a brick.

Oh God, he thought. Not again. He considered calling out, but, no, there was no reason to alert the intruder until he, Gordon, was good and ready.

Slipping off his shoes, he tiptoed upstairs as quickly as he could and retrieved the pistol from a shoe box at the bottom of his closet. Then he checked both Mick and Carla's rooms. They weren't home. Probably just as well, he concluded.

Gordon returned to the kitchen and approached the half-opened door. Gently he eased it open the rest of the way, until he could look down the entire length of the stairs ahead. The basement lights were dark, but a red, flickering glow came from the interior of the cellar, just out of sight. *Flames. Fire. Fists, and falls, and pain.*

Gordon started down the steps. Partway down, he heard a series of harsh, breathy moans. Like a nonsilent phantom, he thought. Or a housemate in distress. Holy rerun, Batman; here we go again. This time, however, he was armed and dangerous.

The gun in his hand was the center of his being, as if he were holding on to his heart and not a loaded weapon. He placed a finger against his temple and felt the veins pulsing under the skin. The angry pounding within his skull beat over and over until he felt sick to his stomach. Trembling despite the comfort of the pistol, he stealthily rounded the corner at the foot of the stairs and gazed at the tableau before him.

The dim, dancing light came from Carla's other holiday candle: a miniature wax Santa Claus poised atop a stack of wooden cartons at the far end of the basement. Candlelight shone down upon the fresh black sheets that now covered Dmitri's mattress. Gordon noticed an empty bottle of disinfectant lying abandoned in a corner.

Mick was lying on his back upon the mattress, his head pointed toward the furnace against the opposite wall. He was nude except for the silky black blindfold over his eyes. His arms were tucked under him, almost hidden from view, as though they were tied (handcuffed?) together behind his back. Carla sat astride his legs, her back to Gordon, her lush red hair falling over her shoulders, as white and bare and delectably smooth as her back and buttocks. Her fingers stroked Mick's straining erection and coyly ambled across his stocky chest, around his nipples, across his ribs, and down to tangle themselves in the wiry brown hair above his testicles.

The veins in Mick's biceps and neck stood out as he rocked and groaned beneath her.

I knew it, Gordon thought. No, that's not true. I didn't know anything. . . .

Carla's unclothed body was even more stunning than he had imagined. She held Mick's torso down with both hands and laughed in a way that both tortured and provoked. "At last, good sir, I have you in my power! How fare you, gentle knight, in this, my Dungeon of Delight?"

"Fuck, Carla, enough with the games already," Mick pleaded. Sweat ran from his forehead to soak the blindfold beneath.

"What's that, milord? Do you yield already to my dark designs?" She spit upon her palm and rubbed the moistened flesh over the red, engorged head of Mick's penis.

"I yield! I yield!" Mick struggled visibly to free his hands. "For Chrissakes, Carla, hurry up before I come!"

"Very well, then. I shall grant you your last request."

Carla shifted forward, and Gordon had a glimpse of her breasts, taut and oh-so-touchable, before she lowered herself onto his best friend and onetime roommate. The impassioned gasp that escaped her lips was all the worse for being unmistakably out of character.

He had to look away, at the incongruous Christmas candle, at the wavering fingertip of flame above Santa's cap, at anything but the sight of Carla and Mick screwing away on those freshly purchased ebony sheets. And so *tacky,* he tried to tell himself: junior league S & M by way of D & D. A couple of college kids playing at decadence. It was embarrassing, really.

Oh Jesus, he thought, his eyes tearing. Why him? Why not me?

He stared at the candleflame. He wouldn't, couldn't, look at them, but he could still hear them: breathing hard, whispering I-love-you's and indecent requests. The sound of sticky, sweaty bodies pulling apart and coming together again. His head felt as if it were going to explode. He almost wished it would. Where, he wondered, is Dmitri now that I need him? The cold metal gun hung heavy in his hand.

The burning Santa filled his vision, bright and beautiful and inescapable. He knows if you've been bad or good, Gordon remembered. He knows what evil lurks in the hearts of men.

Flames. Shadows. Candlelight. Fire.

Gordon raised the gun. He thought he heard footsteps on the steps behind him. He felt Dmitri take hold of his hand.

Fire.

"No, I'm sorry. You have the wrong number. Mick and Carla don't live here anymore."

Gordon hung up the phone. When were people going to get the message? Carla and Mick were gone. They had eloped to Alaska. That's what he had told everyone. That's what had happened.

He had new housemates now. Like Dmitri over there on the couch, polishing his Hitlerian blade and singing Christmas carols in April. And the gargoyle, bounding about on the roof or swinging in the trees outside Gordon's window every night. Even the Phantom, who he had thought was dead but who was looking much better now that he had finally had the last laugh on those smug, selfish, deceitful lovers.

This wasn't such a bad house, Gordon realized. True, as the weather grew warmer, there was an increasingly unpleasant smell coming from the basement, but that was okay. Nobody ever went down there. Nobody must ever go down there.

There were still three possibilities, he thought. One, he could move on someday and leave all this behind him, but wait, that wouldn't work. Other people would move in then. New tenants would unlock the basement door. Two, he could try to explain to someone about Dmitri and what he had done, but the only person who understood about Dmitri was Dmitri. Three, he could find another housemate, maybe a woman, to move in with them. Except . . .

There were no more possibilities. He had to like it here. These were his housemates, and Altered Estates was his home.

From now on.

J onathan Carroll is a winner of the World Fantasy Award and the author of *Land of Laughs, Voice of Our Shadow, Bones of the Moon, Sleeping in Flame,* and *Child Across the Sky.* He lives in Vienna, Austria.

As with much of Jonathan Carroll's work, this story can be seen as belonging to three different categories simultaneously: judging from its prose style and tone, this tale of mortality and meaning appears to be a work of historical American fiction in much the same mode as E. L. Doctorow's *Ragtime*; beneath this surface is a level of fantasy; and beneath the fantasy resides horror. This story will appear as part of Carroll's next novel.

The Art of Falling Down

JONATHAN CARROLL

Thehere is an art to falling down, you know."

I continued looking at the camera, afraid to let my eyes click over to him as he got up off the floor. His assistant stood nearby, but obviously knew he wanted to get up alone: to achieve the small victory of rising after the large defeat of falling down for the third time since I'd entered his studio with my father.

Robert Layne-Dyer was the first homosexual I had ever recognized, if that is the correct word. Since I was only eight, I had no idea what was "with" him, other than that his gestures were more theatrical than what I was accustomed to in other men and his speech was overly precise, his voice too sweet. I knew my father's southern accent and elbows on the dinner table. I was used to my dad's friends who talked about money, women, politics, and other things with the same appreciative deep-chested chuckles and rumbling growls of indignation or anger.

Layne-Dyer was a flit. That is not a nice word to use these days, because it's like calling a woman a "bimbo," but let's face it—there *are* flits and bimbos in this world. However, the flit who had me posing for him was one of the most famous photographers in the world. Thus he was allowed, back in those dark Republican days of the 1950s, to wave his homosexuality like a mile-long banner at the world. When I think now how much courage it must have taken for a man to behave like that in 1957, it's awe-inspiring.

My father, who was even then rich and influential, had decided it was time I had my picture taken. A devoted and voracious reader of magazines, he leafed through Mother's *Vogue* and *Harper's Bazaar* almost as carefully as she did. On the basis of photographs he'd seen there, he chose Layne-Dyer to immortalize me.

After due inquiry and negotiation. Dad and I arrived one July morning at the door of a handsome brownstone house in Gramercy Park. On the cab ride over, I was told the photographer was probably a "fag," but that I shouldn't let it bother me.

"What's a fag, Dad?"

"A guy, backward."

" 'Guy' backward is 'yug.' Fag is 'gaf.' "

"You'll see what I mean when we get there."

What I saw was a very sick man. He answered the door and, smiling, shook hands with both of us. But there was so little light left in him. He reminded me of a lantern with only a very small flame inside.

He was about thirty-five, middle height and build, with a blond wave of hair sweeping down over his forehead like a comma. His eyes were green and large, but rather sunken in his face, diminishing their size until you looked carefully. Which of course I did because I kept looking for the "fag" in him. He was also the first person who ever called me "Mr. Harry."

"So, the Radcliffes have arrived. How are you, Mr. Harry?"

"Fine, Mr. Layne. I mean Mr. Dyer."

"You can call me either. Or Bob, if that's more comfortable."

Then he fell down.

Just boom! No warning, no tripping or flailing of arms—one moment up with us, the next down on the floor in a heap. Naturally I laughed. I thought he was doing it for me—a crazy kid's joke. Maybe that's what Dad meant when he said fags were guys backward.

My father gave me a jab in the ribs that hurt so much I cried out.

Layne-Dyer looked up from the floor at him. "It's okay. He doesn't understand. I fall a lot. It's a brain tumor, and it makes me do some strange things."

I looked at my father for explanations. We were pals, and he was usually straight with me, but this time he gave a small head shake that meant "Wait till later." So I turned back to the photographer and waited for what he'd do next.

"Let's go in and get you set up." He pushed himself slowly off the floor and led the way into the house.

To this day I remember the way his rooms were furnished: Dark "Mission" furniture, pieces of ornamental glass everywhere—Steuben, Lalique, Tiffany—that caught and turned light into beautiful, intricate performances for anyone interested.

Some of his more famous photographs were on the walls; Fellini and Giulietta Masina eating picnic lunch together on the set of *La Strada*. Tour de France bicycle racers steaming in a tight pack together down a Paris street with the Eiffel Tower looming behind them like a monstrous metal golem.

"Did you take that picture?"

"Yes."

"It's President Eisenhower!"

"Right. He let me come to the White House to do it."

"You were in the *White House*?"

"Yes. A couple of times."

I didn't know who Fellini was, and anyone could race a

bicycle, but to be invited to President Eisenhower's house to take a picture meant you were big stuff, in my book. I followed Bob closely to his studio.

Later I read in Layne-Dyer's autobiography that he hated being called anything other than "Robert." But "Bob" is a pair of soft, familiar jeans to an eight-year-old boy, rather than "Robert," which is the black wool suit you're forced to wear on Sunday to church, or the name of a distant cousin you instantly hate on meeting for the first time.

"What kind of picture are you going to take of me?"

"Come on in and I'll show you."

The studio was unremarkable. There were lights and reflectors around, but nothing challenging, nothing promising besides many cameras that said only matters are more formal in here, watch your step a little more. But I was eight, and having my picture taken by someone famous seemed only right: a combination of what was due me because I was Harry Radcliffe, third-grader, and because my father, a rich and nice man, wanted it. At eight, you're dead serious about what the world owes you: Civilization starts in your own room and moves out from there.

"Sit here, Harry."

A pretty assistant named Karla started moving around the room, setting up cameras and tripods. She smiled at me sometimes.

"What do you want to be when you grow up, Harry?"

Looking to see if Karla was watching, I said confidently, "Mayor of New York."

Layne-Dyer ran both hands through his hair and said to no one in particular, "Humble fellow, isn't he?"

Which made my father laugh. I didn't know what the word meant, but if Dad laughed, then it must be okay.

"Look at me, Harry. Good. Now look over there, at the picture of the dog on the wall."

"What kind of dog is that?"

"Don't talk for a minute, Boss. Let me get this right and then we'll chat."

I tried to watch what he was doing out of the corner of my eye, but couldn't make my eyeball go back that far. I started to turn.

"Don't move! Stay like that! Don't move!" *Flash. Flash. Flash.* "Great, Harry. Now you can turn. It's a 'Great Vendean Griffon.' " *Flash. Flash.*

"What is?"

"The dog on the wall."

"Oh. Are you finished taking my picture now?"

"Not yet. A little while longer."

Halfway through the session he collapsed again, as I've described.

"There's an art to falling down, you know. When you go like I do, with no warning, just *plotz,* you learn after a few times to watch and take as much with you as you can before you hit. The design on the drapes, whatever you can grab with your eye, a hand . . . Don't go empty-handed, don't just go down scared. Do you understand what I'm talking about, Harry?"

"No, sir. Not really."

"That's okay. Look at me."

The dying have a quality that even a child senses. Not because they are already removed, but because even young hearts sense their inability to stay longer. Behind the looks of sickness or fear is also the look of the long-distance traveler, bags on the floor, eyes tired but nervous for any change that may come. They are the ones going on the twenty-hour flights, and although we don't envy their coming discomfort or time-zone skips, tomorrow they will be *there*—a place that both terrifies and thrills us. We peek at the ticket they hold, the inconceivably far destination written there, impossible yet monstrously alluring. What will it smell like for them tomorrow? What is it like to sleep there?

"Are you sick?"

Karla stopped walking across the room and looked away. My father started to say something, but Bob cut him off.

"Yes, Harry. That's what makes me fall down."

"Something's wrong with your feet?"

"No, my head. It's called a brain tumor. Like a bump inside there that makes you do odd things. And ends up killing you."

I am convinced he didn't say it to spook or scare me. Only because it was the truth. Now I was entirely impressed by him.

"You're going to *die*?"

"Yes."

"That's weird. What does it feel like?"

The camera flashgun in his hand went off, making us all jump. "Like that."

When we'd shivered back to earth, he put the flashgun on a table and gestured with his head. "Come with me a minute, Harry. I want to show you something."

All three of us would have followed at that moment if he'd asked. I looked at my father to see if it was okay to go but couldn't catch his eye because he was watching Layne-Dyer so intently.

"Come on, Harry, we'll be back soon."

He took my hand and led me further back into the studio, through a large woody kitchen with silver pots of different sizes hanging from the walls like drops of frozen mercury, a big bunch of red onions and one of ivory garlic.

"Does your wife like to cook?"

"*I* like to cook, Harry. What's your favorite food?"

"Spare ribs, I guess," I said disapprovingly. Men weren't supposed to cook. I was not happy with his disclosure, but he *was* dying, and that was thrilling. At my age, I'd heard a lot about death and even seen my grandfather in his coffin, looking rested. But being near a death actually taking place was something else. Years later in a biology class, I watched a snake devour a live mouse bit by wriggling bit. That is what it was like to be with Layne-Dyer that single day, knowing something was killing him even as we stood there looking at his red onions.

"Come on." We left the kitchen and came to one last

room that was quite dark and empty but for something that made me gasp: a house. A house the size of a sofa. From the first moment, it was clear this was no rinky-dink girl's dollhouse full of pink curtains and little fringed Barbie beds. This was big, serious stuff.

"Wow! What's that?" I didn't wait for an answer before going over.

"Have a look before I tell you."

I was a kid who loved to talk unless something was so fascinating that it shut me up without my knowing it. Stunned me into silence or so glutted me with its presence that I'd lose all appetite for talking.

The photographer's house did it. Later, when I studied architecture and learned all the formal terms, I realized the house was Postmodern long before the term ever existed. Its lines, columns, and color combinations pre-dated the work of Michael Graves and Hans Hollein by at least a decade.

But eight-year-olds aren't silenced by Postmodernism. They are silenced by wonder, the orange flame and thunder crack of the miraculous right in front of them. What, then, was so completely absorbing about Layne-Dyer's model? The perfect details, at first. Carved brass door-knobs the size of corn kernels, stained or bottle glass in most windows, a copper weather vane shaped like the dog in the photograph in the other room. The more complete something is, the more it reassures us. Time was spent here, someone's world stopped for a while—hours? days?— while he worked to get it right. The result tells us it is possible to do things till the end, till *we*—not God, not fate—decide it is finished.

I couldn't stop touching the house, and everything I touched was beautifully or solidly made. The only odd part was that on one side of the building, a portion of the roof had been removed and one of the upstairs rooms seemed to be under construction. It looked like a cutaway diagram in a do-it-yourself repair magazine.

After the initial delight passed and I'd run my hands over

it like a blind man, pausing everywhere for little detours and hidden wonders, a second level of awareness set in. It eventually struck me that things actually went *on* in this house: Homework was finished, bread was baked, checks written, dogs ran across wooden floors when a doorbell rang.

I watched *Twilight Zone* and *Alfred Hitchcock Presents* on television, and had seen shows where dollhouses were malevolent, dangerous things full of toys from hell, or worse. But despite the very strong sense of motion and real life around Layne-Dyer's model, I felt no danger; I didn't feel frightened or threatened by it.

"I'll show you something." Coming around me, he went to the section where the roof had been taken off and put his hand down into the exposed room. When it reappeared, it was holding a bed the size of a small loaf of bread.

"Did you ever eat a bed?" He broke off a piece of it and put it in his mouth.

"Cool! Can I have some?"

"You can try, but I don't think you'll be able to eat it."

"Oh yeah? Give me some!" I took the piece he offered and put it in my mouth. It tasted like salty plaster. It tasted like model.

"Yecch!" I spit and spit to get it all out. Bob smiled and continued to chew and then swallow his piece.

"Listen to me, Harry. You can't eat it because it's not your house. Sooner or later in everyone's life a moment comes when their house appears like this. Sometimes it's when you're young, sometimes when you're sick like me. But most people's problem is they can't see the house, so they die confused. They *say* they want to understand what it's all about, but given the chance, given the *house,* they either look away or get scared and blind. Because when the house is there and you know it, you don't have any more excuses, Boss."

Once again I was baffled by what he was saying, but the

tone of his voice was so intense that it seemed imperative I at least try to understand what he was so passionate about.

"I'm scared at what you're saying. I don't get what you mean."

He nodded, stopped, nodded again. "I'm telling you this now, Harry, so maybe you'll remember it later on. No one ever told *me*.

"Everyone has a house inside them. It defines who they are. A specific style and form, a certain number of rooms. You think about it all your life—what does mine really look like? How many floors are there? What is the view from the different windows? . . . But only once do you get a chance to actually see it. If you miss that chance, or avoid it 'cause it scares you, then it goes away and you'll never see it again."

"*Where* is this house?"

He pointed to his head and mine. "In here. If you recognize it when it comes, then it'll stay. But accepting it and making it stay is only the first part. Then you've got to try understanding it. You've got to take it apart and understand every piece. Why it's there, why it's made like that . . . Most of all, how each piece fits in the whole."

I sort of got it. I asked the right question. "What happens when you understand?"

He held up a finger, as if I'd made a good point. "It lets you eat it."

"Like you just did?"

"Exactly. It lets you take it back inside. Here, look where the roof is gone. It's the only section of the house I've been able to understand so far. The only part I've been allowed to eat." He broke off another piece and popped it into his mouth. "The fuck of the thing is, I don't have enough time now to do it. You can't imagine how long it takes. How many hours you sit there and look or try to work it out . . . But nothing happens. It's so exciting and frustrating at the same time."

Whatever he'd said after "fuck" didn't go anywhere in

my head because he'd said *that word!* Even my father didn't say it, and he was a pretty big curser. I'd said it once and got one of the only smacks in my life. Whenever I'd heard it since, it was like someone flashing an illegal weapon at me or a pack of dirty playing cards. You were dying to look, but knew it might get you in a hell of a lot of trouble if you did.

Fuck. You don't hear that much when you're an eight-year-old. It's an adult's word, forbidden and dirty and owning a dangerous gleam of its own. You don't really know what it means, but if you've ever used it, then it sure gets fast results.

The whole wonder and awe of Layne-Dyer's model house—what it was, what he *said* it was—fell from the horizon the moment this big orange *FUCK* roared up. The magic of death, the magic of great mysteries, lost to the magic of one word.

A short time later, both Karla and my father began calling us from the other room. Bob put his arm around my shoulder and asked again if I understood everything he had said. Lying, I nodded in a way I thought was intelligent and mature, but my mind was on other things.

The photo session ended soon after, and that was just as well, because I couldn't wait to get home.

When I was safely in my room and had locked the door, I ran for the bathroom. Locked in there too, I turned on the overhead light and said the word to myself over and over again. Loud, soft, as a plea, an order. I made faces around the word, gestures, I did everything. Hearing it from Layne-Dyer had set something loose in me, and I couldn't let that thing go until I had understood, had exhausted its every possibility.

het Williamson is the vice president of the Horror Writers of America and has been nominated several times for the Bram Stoker Award. He is the author of *Soulstorm, Ash Wednesday, McKaine's Dilemma, Lowland Rider,* and *Dreamthorp.* His fiction has appeared in *Nightvisions 7, Playboy, The New Yorker, The Magazine of Fantasy & Science Fiction, Twilight Zone,* and various anthologies. He lives in Elizabethtown, Pennsylvania.

In this frightening tale of a castle and a curse, the problem is not that there is a ghost—but that there isn't. This is a story about the power of inheritance.

The Cairnwell Horror

CHET WILLIAMSON

A monster, do you suppose? A genetic freak that's remained alive for centuries?"

"Undoubtedly, Michael. With two heads, three sets of genitals, and a curse for those who mock." George McCormack, sole heir to Cairnwell Castle, raised a three-by-five-inch card on which lay a line of cocaine. "I propose a toast—of sorts—to it then. Old beast, old troll, nemesis of my old great-however-many-times-granddad, whom I shall finally meet next week." A quick snort, and the powder was gone.

George smiled, relishing the rush, the coziness of his den, the company, and found himself thinking about asking Michael to spend the night. He was about to make the suggestion when Michael asked, "Why twenty-one, do you suppose? If it's all that important, why not earlier?"

"Coming of age, Michael. As we well know, all males are virgins until that age, and no base liquors or, ahem, controlled substances have passed their pristine lips or nostrils. Other than that, I can't bloody well tell you until

after next week, and even then, according to that same
stifling and weary tradition, I must keep the deep, dark
family secret all to my lonesome.''

"Yes, but if you don't pay any more attention to *that*
tradition than you do to the others, well . . .''

"Ah, will I tell, you're thinking? In all likelihood, if
there's a pound to be made on it, yes, I damned well will.
I've thought the whole thing was asinine ever since I was
a kid. And the five thousand pounds your little rag offers
can pay for an awful lot of raped tradition.''

"So when'll you be leaving London for the bogs?''

"The *bogs*?'' George snorted. "Careful, mate. That's my
castle you're speaking of.''

"I thought it was your father's.''

"Yes, well.'' George frowned. "It doesn't appear he'll
be around much longer to take care of things.''

"You've asked him what the secret is, I suppose.''

"Christ, dozens of times. Always the same answer—
'You're better off not knowing until the time comes.' Yeah.
Pardon me while I tremble with fear. Bunch of shit any-
way. When I was a kid, I spent hours looking for secret
panels, hidden crypts, all that rubbish, and not a thing did
I find. After a while, I just got bored with it.''

"Ever see any ghosts?''

George gave Michael a withering glare. "No,'' he said
flatly. "Whatever plagues the McCormacks, it's not
ghosts.'' He hurled a sofa pillow at his friend. "*Jesus,* will
you stop jotting down those notes—it's driving me mad!''

"George, this *is* an interview, and you *are* being paid.''

"I'm just not used to being grilled.''

"You knew I was a journalist when we became . . .
friends.''

"You were about to say lovers.'' George smiled cheek-
ily. "And why not?''

"We haven't been lovers for months.''

"No fault of mine.''

Michael shook his head. "I'm here to do a job, not . . .

rekindle memories. I didn't suggest your bogey story to David because I wanted to start things up again."

"And I didn't agree to talk to you because I wanted to start things up either," George lied. "I agreed to it because of the money. We're having a lovely little hundred-pound chat. And if I decide to spill the beans after next week, we'll have an even lovelier five-thousand-pound chat." George stood and stretched, bending his neck back and around in a gesture that he hoped Michael would find erotic.

"And I'm happy to keep it on those terms," Michael said.

George stopped twisting his neck. "Bully for you. Do you want to go up to Cairnwell with me next week?"

"I didn't know I was invited."

"Of course you are." George grinned. "And I'll tell them exactly what you're there for—to expose the secret of Cairnwell Castle, should I care to reveal it to the whole drooling world. That should make old Maxwell shit his britches. You'll come?"

"Wouldn't miss it. Thank you."

"I assume then you'll foot my traveling expenses? My taste for the finer things has laid me low financially once again, and that damned Maxwell won't send a penny. Once I'm laird of the manor, let me tell you the first thing I'm doing is finding a new solicitor."

Cairnwell Castle was as ungainly a pile of stones as was ever raised. Even though George had grown up there, he always felt intimidated by the formidable gray block that heaved itself out of the low Scottish landscape like a megalithic frowning head. Often when he was a child, he awoke in the middle of the night and, realizing what it was that he was within, would cry until his mother came and held him and sang to him until he fell asleep. His father had not approved of his behavior, but his mother always came when he cried, right up until the week that she died, and was no longer able. From then on, he cried himself back to sleep.

"Dear God, that's an ugly building," Michael remarked.

"Isn't it. You see why I came down to London as quickly as my little adolescent legs would carry me."

As they drove into the massive court, charmlessly formed by two blocky wings of dirty stone, they saw an older man dressed in tweeds standing at the front door. "Maxwell," George said. "Richard Maxwell."

The man looked every day of his sixty-odd years, and wore the constant look of mild disapproval with which George had always associated him. His eyebrows raised as he observed George's spiky blond hair and the small diamond twinkling in his left ear. They raised even higher when he learned Michael Spencer's profession, and he asked to speak to George alone.

Leaving Michael in the entryway, Maxwell led George into a huge, starkly furnished antechamber, and closed the massive door behind them. "What do you think you're doing bringing a journalist with you?" he said.

"I think I'm doing the world a favor by sharing the secret of the lairds of Cairnwell, so we can stop living in some Gothic storybook, Maxwell, *that's* what I'm doing."

Maxwell's ruddy complexion turned pale. "You'd expose the secret?"

"If it turns out to be as absurd as I think it will."

"You cannot. You *dare* not."

"Spare me the histrionics, Maxwell. I'm sure you've been practicing your lines for months now, looking forward to my birthday tomorrow, but it's really getting a bit thick."

"You don't understand, George. It's not the nature of the secret itself that will keep you from exposing it—though I daresay you'll want to keep it as quiet as all your ancestors have. Rather, it's the terms of the inheritance that will insure your silence." Maxwell smiled smugly. "If you ever reveal what you see tomorrow, you lose Cairnwell and all your family's holdings. All told, it comes to half a million.''

"Lose it! How the hell can I lose it? I'm sole heir.''

"You can lose it to charity, as is stipulated in the document written and signed by the seventeenth laird of Cairnwell and extending into perpetuity. I've made you a copy, which you'll receive tomorrow. It further states that you're to spend nine months out of every year at Cairnwell, and, *if* you have a male heir''—here Maxwell curled his lip—"the secret's to be revealed to him on his twenty-first birthday. Any departure from these stipulations means that you forfeit the estate. Understood?''

George smiled grimly. "Thought of everything, haven't you?''

"Not me. Your four-times great-grandfather.''

"Sly old bastard.''

"Now,'' Maxwell went on, ignoring the comment, "I would like you to dismiss that journalist and come see your father. He's been waiting for you.''

George walked slowly out to the entryway, where Michael was waiting. "I'm afraid I've rather bad news,'' he said, and watched Michael's lips tighten. "You can't stay. I'm sorry.''

"I can't *stay*?'' The last word leapt, George thought, at least an octave.

"No. It's part of the . . . tradition, you see.''

"Oh, for Christ's sake, George, you mean I motored all the way up to this godforsaken pile for nothing?''

"I'll be in touch as soon as it's over,'' George said quietly, fearing that Maxwell would overhear.

"Christ . . .''

"I didn't *know*. But I'll call you, I swear. I said I was sorry.''

Michael gave him the same look as when he had told George that he didn't think they should see each other anymore. "All right then. Come and get your bloody bags.''

Michael opened the boot, roughly handed George his luggage, and drove away with no words of farewell. George watched the car disappear over the fields, then went to visit his father in the largest bedchamber of the castle.

The twenty-second laird of Cairnwell was propped up on an overstuffed chaise, and George was shocked at the change in his father since his last visit over six months before.

The cancer had been progressing merrily along. At least another thirty pounds had been sucked off the old man's frame. What was left of the muscles hung like doughy pouches on the massive skeleton. The skin was a wrapping of faded parchment, a lesion all its own. There was no hope in the eyes, and the smell of death—of sour vomit and diseased bowels, of bloody mucus coughed from riddled lungs—was everywhere.

His father was the castle. What the man had become was nothing less than Cairnwell itself, a massive tumor of the soul that grew and festered like the lichen on the gray stone.

Then, for just a moment, trapped within the rotting hulk, George glimpsed his father as he had been when George was a boy and his father was young. But the moment passed, and, expressionless, he walked to his father's side, leaned over, and kissed the leathery cheek, nearly choking at the smell that rose from the fresh stains on the velvet dressing gown.

They talked, shortly and uncomfortably, saying nothing of the revelation of the secret the next day except for setting the time when the three of them should meet in the morning. Eight thirty-five was the appointed hour, the time of George's birth.

That night, George could not sleep, so he sat by the fireplace long past midnight, thinking about Cairnwell and its hold on his father, its unhealthy, even cancerous hold on all the McCormacks. He thought about the way the castle had sapped his father's strength, and, years before, his mother's. Although she had never known the secret, she nonetheless had shared the burden of it with her husband, and, being far weaker than he, she had been quickly consumed by it, just after George's eighth birthday.

Then he thought about his debts, about nine months of every year spent at Cairnwell, about the horror that he was to see tomorrow.

When sleep finally came, it was dreamless.

The next morning dawned gray and misty, with no sunlight to banish the shadows that hung in every cold, high-ceilinged room. George rose, showered, and put on a jacket and tie rather than one of the sweaters he usually wore. In spite of his anger over the hereditary charade, he felt the situation demanded a touch of formality. He even removed the diamond from his ear.

His father and Maxwell were already breakfasting when George arrived in the dining hall, Maxwell on rashers and eggs, his father on weak tea and toast cubes. George took the vacant chair.

"Good morning, George," his father said in a thin, reedy tone. The old man wore a black suit that hung on him like a blanket on a scarecrow. The white shirtfront was already stained in several places. "Have some breakfast?"

George shook his head. "A cup of coffee, that's all," he said, and poured himself some from a silver teapot.

Maxwell smiled. "Off your feed today? Can't say I blame you. It's a difficult thing."

"Enough, Richard," said George's father. "No need to upset him. He'll see soon enough."

"I'm not upset, Father," said George, with a cool glance at Maxwell. "I'll wait to hear Mr. Maxwell's bogey story. I hope he won't disappoint me."

Maxwell flushed, and George hoped that he was about to choke on a rasher, but he cleared his throat and smiled again. "I don't think you'll be disappointed, *Master* George."

"I said enough—both of you." The elder McCormack

looked at the pair with disapproval. "This is not to be treated lightly. Indeed, Richard, this may be the most serious moment of George's life, so please conduct yourself as befits your position. You also, George. You shall soon be laird of Cairnwell, so start behaving as such." The voice was pale and weak, but the underlying tone held a rigid intensity that wiped the sardonic smiles from the other two faces.

"Now," McCormack went on, "I think it's time."

Maxwell rose. "Are you sure you don't want the wheelchair?"

"What'll you do, carry it down the stairs? No, I'll walk today as my father walked in front of me nearly forty years ago."

"But your health . . ."

"Life holds nothing more for me, Richard. If death comes closer as a result of what happens today, so much the better. I'm very tired. It's made me very tired."

At first George thought that his father was referring to the cancer, but something told him this was not the case, and the implications made him shiver.

He rose and followed his father and Maxwell as they left the room, passed down the hall, through a small alcove, and into a little-used study. Maxwell drew back the curtains of the room, allowing a sickly light to enter through grimy beveled panes. Then he dragged a wooden chair over to a high bookcase, stepped up on it, removed several volumes from the top shelf, and turned what George assumed was a hidden knob. Then he descended, flipped back a corner of a faded oriental rug, and scrabbled with his fingers for a near-invisible handhold. Finding it, he pulled the trap door up so easily that George assumed it must be counterweighted.

"Good Christ," said George with a touch of awe. "It's just like a thirties horror film. No wonder I never found it."

"Don't feel stupid," said Maxwell, not unkindly. "No

one has ever discovered it on their own." He then opened a closet, inside of which were three kerosene lamps.

"No flashlights?" asked George.

"Tradition," said Maxwell, lighting the lamps with his Dunhill and handing one each to George and his father, keeping the third for himself. Looking at McCormack, he said in a voice that held just the hint of a tremor, "Shall I lead the way?"

McCormack nodded. "Please. I'll follow, and George, stay behind me." There was no trembling in McCormack's voice, only a rugged tenacity.

Maxwell stepped gently into the abyss, as if fearing the steps would collapse beneath him, but George saw that they were stone, and realized that Maxwell, for all his previous bravado, was actually quite hesitant to confront whatever lay below.

They descended for a long time, and, although he did not count them, George guessed that the steps numbered well over two hundred. The walls of the stairway were stone, and appeared to be quite as old as the castle itself.

Halfway down, Maxwell explained briefly: "This was built during the border wars. If the castle was stormed, the laird and retainers could hide down here with provisions to last six months. It was never used for that purpose, however."

He said no more. By the time they reached the bottom of the stairs, the temperature had fallen 10 degrees. The walls were green with damp mold, and George started as he heard a scuffling somewhere ahead of them.

"Rats," his father said. "Just rats."

For another thirty meters they walked down a long passage that gradually grew in width from two meters to nearly five. George struggled to peer past Maxwell and his father, trying to make forms out of the shadows their lanterns cast. Then he saw the door.

It appeared to be made of one piece of massive oak, crisscrossed with wide iron bands like a giant's chessboard. Directly in the center of its vast expanse was a black-brown blotch of irregular shape, looking, in the dim light, like a huge squashed spider. Maxwell and McCormack stopped five meters away, and turned toward George.

"Now it begins," said McCormack, and his eyes were sad. "Go with your lantern to the door, George, and look at what is mounted there."

George obeyed, walking slowly toward the door, the lantern held high in front of him protectively, almost ceremonially. For a moment he wished he had a crucifix.

At first he could not identify the thing that was nailed to the oaken door. But he suddenly realized that it was a skin of some kind, a deerskin perhaps, that centuries of dampness and decay had darkened to this dried and blackened parody before him.

But deer, he told himself, do not have pairs of breasts that sag like large, decayed mushrooms, or fingers that hang like rotted willow leaves. Or a face with a round, thick-lipped gap for a mouth, a broad flap of bulbous skin for a nose, twin pits of deep midnight in shriveled pouches for eyes. And he knew beyond doubt that mounted on that door with weary, rusting nails was the flayed skin of a woman.

He struggled to hold it back, but the bile came up insistently, and he bent over, closed his eyes, and let it rain down upon the stone floor. When it was over, he spit several times and blew his nose into a handkerchief, then looked at the two older men. "I'm sorry."

"Don't be," his father said. "I did the same thing the first time." He looked at the skin. "Now it's just like a wall hanging."

"What the hell is it?" asked George, repelled yet fascinated, hardly daring to look at the thing again.

"The mortal remains," said Maxwell, "of the first wife of the sixteenth laird of Cairnwell." The words were mechanical, as if he had been practicing them for a long time.

"The wife . . ." George looked at the skin on the door. "Was she a black? Or did the tanning—"

Maxwell interrupted, "Yes, she was an African native the Laird met as a young man on a trading voyage, the daughter of a priest of one of the tribes of Gambia. The ship traded with the tribe, and the laird, Brian Mc-Cormack, saw the woman dance. Apparently she was a great beauty as blacks go, and he became infatuated with her. Later he claimed she had put a spell on him."

George was shaking his head in disbelief. "A spell?" he asked, a confused and erratic half-smile on his lips. "Are you serious, Maxwell? Father, is this for real?"

McCormack nodded. "It's real. And under the circumstances, I believe that she *did* bewitch him. Let Maxwell continue."

"Spell or no," Maxwell went on smoothly, "he brought her back with him, she posing as a servant he'd taken on. The captain of the ship—and Brian's employee—had secretly married them on board, and by the time they docked in Leith, she was, technically, Lady Cairnwell."

A low, rich laugh of relief started to bubble out of George. "My God," he said, while his father and Maxwell stared at him like priests at a defiler of the Host. "That's the secret then? That's what's kept this family shamed for over three hundred years, that we've some black blood in the line?" His laughter slowly faded. "Back then I can understand. But now? This is the 1990s—no one cares about that anymore. Besides, whatever genetic effect she would have had is long gone, and this 'Cairnwell Horror' isn't anything more than racial paranoia."

"You're wrong, George," said Maxwell. "I've not yet told you of the horror. That was still to come. Will you simply listen while I finish?" His voice was angry, yet controlled, and George, taken aback, nodded acquiescence.

"Brian McCormack," Maxwell went on, "once back in Scotland, quickly realized his mistake. Whether through diminished lust or the failure of the spell, we can't know. At any rate, he wanted a quiet divorce, and the woman returned to Gambia. She refused to be divorced, but he made arrangements to have her transported back to Africa anyway. She overheard his plan and told him that if she was forced to leave him, she would expose their marriage to the world. Why he didn't have her killed immediately is a mystery, as it was well within his power. Perhaps he still felt a warped affection for her.

"So he locked her away down here, entrusting the secret to only one servant. The others, who had thought her Brian's mistress, were told she had been sent away, and were greatly relieved by the fact.

"Brian then wooed and married an earl's daughter, Fiona McTavish, and the world had no reason to suspect that it was his second wedding. There was a problem with the match, however. Fiona was barren, and no doctor could rectify the situation. After several years of trying to sire a son, Brian asked his first wife to help with her magic. She offered to do so with an eagerness that made him suspicious, and he warned her that if Fiona should suffer any ill consequences from the magic, he would not hesitate to painfully kill the woman. Then he brought her the things she asked for, and secretly gave Fiona the resulting potion.

"Within two months she was pregnant, and the laird was delirious with joy. But his happiness soured when Fiona became deathly ill in her fifth month. It was only then he realized that the black woman had increased his hopes so that they should be dashed all the harder by losing both mother and child.

"In a fury he beat the woman, demanding that she use her powers to reverse the magic and bring Fiona back to health. She told him that the magic had gone too far to save both—that he could have either the mother or the child. Brian continued to beat her, but she was adamant—one or the other.

"It must have been a hard choice, but he finally chose to let the child live." Maxwell cleared his throat. "There was a great deal of pressure on him, as on any nobleman, to leave an heir, so we can't criticize him too harshly for his decision. At any rate, the witch was true to her word. The child was born, but under rather . . . bizarre circumstances."

Maxwell paused and looked at McCormack, as if for permission to proceed.

"Well?" said George, angry with himself for the way his voice shook in the sudden silence. "Don't stop now, Maxwell, you're coming to the exciting part." He had wanted the forced levity to relax him, but instead it made him feel impatient and foolish. He tried in vain to keep his gaze from the pelt fixed to the door. It had been difficult enough when it was simply the skin of a nonentity. But now that it had an identity, it was twice as horrifying, twice as fascinating. He wondered what her name was.

Maxwell went on, ignoring George's comment. "Fiona McCormack died in her seventh month of pregnancy. But the child lived."

"Born prematurely then? Convenient."

"No," answered the solicitor quietly. "The child came to term. He was born in the ninth month."

"But . . ." George felt disoriented, as if all the world was a step ahead of him. "How?"

"The black woman. She kept Fiona alive."

"I thought you said she was dead."

"She was. It was an artificial life, preserved by sorcery, or, we would prefer to think today, by some primitive form of science civilization has not yet discovered. Call it what you will, no heart beat, no breath stirred, but Fiona McCormack lived, and was somehow able to nourish her child *in utero*."

"But that's *absurd*! A fetus needs . . . *life*, its respiratory and circulatory system depends on its mother's!" He laughed, a sharp, quick bark. "You're having me on."

"God damn you, George, shut *up!*" The old man's words exploded like a shell, and sent him into a fit of coughing blood-black phlegm, which he spat on the floor. He rested for a moment, breathing heavily, then raised his massive head to look into George's eyes. "You be silent. And at the end of the story, at the *end*, then you laugh if you wish."

"I don't know how it occurred, George," said Maxwell, "but it has been sworn to by the sixteenth laird and his servant, as has everything I've told you. You shall see further evidence later." He took a deep breath and plunged on.

"She gave birth to the child, and it suckled at his dead mother's breast for nearly a year, drawing sustenance from a cup that was never filled. A short time after the birth, Brian McCormack, with his own hands, flayed his first wife alive, and tanned the hide himself. He must have been quite mad by then. As you can see, he worked with extreme care."

He was right, George thought. For all of the abomination's hideousness, it was extraordinarily done, as if a surgeon had cut the body from head to toe in a neat cross-section, like a plastic anatomical kit he had once seen. George looked at Maxwell and his father, who were both staring quietly at the mortal tapestry on the door. It seemed that the story was ended.

"That's it then," George said, with only a trace of mockery. "That's the legend." He turned to his father with pleading eyes. "Is that all that's kept us in a state of fear from cradle to grave? That's become as legendary as the silkie or the banshee? Dear God, is the Cairnwell Horror only a black skin nailed to a cellar door?"

The expressions of the two men in the lantern light added years to their faces. For a second George thought his father was already dead, a living corpse like the sixteenth Lady Cairnwell, doomed to an eternity of haunting the dreams of McCormack children.

"There's more," said Maxwell in such a way that George knew immediately that they had not been looking at the door as much as what was behind it.

Maxwell fumbled in the pocket of his suit coat and withdrew a large iron key, which he handed to McCormack. The old man hobbled to the massive door and fitted the key into a keyhole barely visible in the dim light. It rattled, then turned slowly, and McCormack pressed against the iron-and-oak panel. The door did not move, and the dying man leaned tiredly against it. Maxwell added his weight to the task. Though George knew he should have helped, he could not bring himself to touch the tarry carcass the older men seemed to be obscenely caressing. The door began to move with a shriek of angry hinges, and George thought of a wide and hungry mouth with teeth of iron straps, and wondered what it had eaten and how long ago. Then the smell hit him, and he reeled back.

It was the worst smell he had ever known, worse than the sour tang of open sewers, the sulfur-rich fumes of rotten eggs, worse even than when he had been a boy and found that long-dead stag, swarming with maggots. He would have vomited, but there was nothing left in his stomach to bring up.

His father and Maxwell picked up their lanterns. "Do you want to come with us," Maxwell asked, "or would you rather watch from here at first?"

George was impressed by Maxwell's objectivity. It was as if the man were viewing the situation from far outside, watching a shocker on the telly. George wished he could have felt the same way. "I'll come," he said, and jutted his weak chin forth like a brittle lance.

Holding the lanterns high, the three entered the chamber. It was a small room six meters square. A rough-hewn round table with a single straight-backed chair was to their right as they entered, another chair, less stern in design, to their left. It was the bed, however, that dominated the room, a massive oaken piece with a huge carved headboard and high footboard, over which George could not see from the door. Maxwell and McCormack moved to either side of the bed, and the old man beckoned for his son to join him.

The woman in the bed reminded George of the mummies he had seen in the British Museum. The skin was the yellow of dirty chalk, furrowed with wrinkles so deep they would always remain in darkness. The same sickly shade sullied the hair, which spread over the pillow fanlike, a faded invitation to a lover now dust. She wore a nightgown of white lace, and her clawed fingers interlocked over her flattened breasts, bony pencils clad in gloves of the sheerest skin. She had been dead a long, long time.

"The Lady Fiona," whispered McCormack huskily. "Your five-times great-grandmother, George."

Again George felt relief. If this was the ultimate, if this dried and preserved corpse was the final horror, then he could still laugh and walk in the world without bearing the invisible curse all McCormacks before him bore. He held his lantern higher to study the centuries-old face more closely. Then he saw the eyes.

He had expected to see either wrinkled flaps of skin that had once been eyelids, or shriveled gray raisins nesting loosely in open sockets. What he had not expected was two blue eyes that gazed at the smoke-blackened ceiling, insentient but alive.

"She's . . . alive," he said half-wittedly, so overcome by horror that he no longer cared what impression he gave.

"Yes," said his father. "So she has been since the spell was put on her." George felt the old man's arm drape itself around his shoulder. "The sixteenth laird wanted her undead misery ended when the son was weaned, but the witch said it could not be done. He tortured her—in this very room—but she would not, possibly could not, relent. It was then that he killed her by skinning. He kept his wife upstairs as long as he could, but the . . . odor grew too strong, and the servants started to whisper. So he brought her down here, and here she has been ever since, caught in a prison between life and death.

"She neither speaks nor moves, nor has she since she died. Giving birth and feeding her child were her only acts, and even then, records the document, she was like an automaton.''

George's head felt stuffed with water, and his words came out as thick as a midnight dream. "What . . . document?''

"The record Brian McCormack left,'' answered his father, "and that the servant signed as witness. The history of the event and the charge put on every laird of Cairnwell since—to preserve the tale from outside ears and to care for his poor wife 'until such time as God sees fit to take her unto Him.' It is the duty of the eldest son, such as I was, and such as you are, George.''

The liquid in his brain was nearly at a boil. "Me?'' He lurched away from his father's cloying embrace. "You want me to mind *that* the rest of my life?''

"There is little to care for,'' Maxwell said soothingly. "She requires no food, only . . .''

"What? *What* does she require?''

"Care. A wash now and again . . .''

George laughed desperately, and knew he was approaching hysteria. "A wash! Good Christ, and perhaps a permanent and some nail clipping! . . .''

"Care!'' bellowed McCormack. "What you would do for *anyone* like this!''

"There *is* no one *like this*! She is . . . she is *dead*.'' The word had stuck in his throat. "I'm not going to have any part of this, nor of Cairnwell. *You* chose this, not me! I won't rot here like the rest of you did. *Keep* Cairnwell— give it away, burn it, *bury* it, for Christ's sake—that's what suits the dead!''

"No! She is *not* dead! She is alive, and she *needs* us! She needs . . .'' McCormack paused, as if something had stolen his words. A pained look grasped his features, and before George or Maxwell could leap to his side, he toppled like a tree, and his head struck the stone floor with a leaden thud.

Maxwell swept around the bed, pushed George aside, and knelt by McCormack. "The lantern!'' he said, and

George moved the flickering light so that he and Maxwell could see that his father's face wore the gray softness of death.

Much later, in the study, Maxwell poured George another glass of sherry. "I shouldn't have let him go down there," the older man said, almost to himself. He turned back to the cold fireplace. "After the last operation . . . it left his heart so weak. . . ."

"It was better," George said quietly. "Better that way than for the cancer to finish him."

"I suppose."

They sat, sipping sherry and saying nothing. George rose and walked to the window. The sun, setting over the ridge of the western fields, slashed a thin blade of orange-red through the beveled panes. He looked at a flock of black-birds pecking in the damp earth for grain.

"I shouldn't have upset him," said George.

"He hadn't been down there for quite a while," Maxwell said. "I shouldn't've let him go."

"You couldn't have stopped him," George said, still gazing out the window.

"I suppose not. He felt it . . ."

"His duty," said George.

"Yes." Maxwell turned from the dead fire toward George's tall figure, outlined in the sun's flame. "Will you go then? Leave Cairnwell?"

George kept watching the birds.

"It's not . . . there's really very little to it," said Maxwell, with the slightest trace of urgency. "You don't have to see her at all, you know, not ever, if you wish it. Just so long as you stay here."

In the field, the blackbirds rose in formation, turned in the wind like leaves, and settled once more. George looked at Maxwell. "May I have the key?"

*   *   *

The door opened more easily this time, and George walked into the room, holding the lantern at his side without fear. He knew there were no ghosts. There was no need for ghosts.

His earlier exposure to the smell made it much more palatable, and he thought about fumigants and disinfectants. He pulled the straight-backed chair over to the bedside and looked at the woman's face.

Strange he hadn't noticed before. The resemblance to his father was so strong, particularly about the eyes. They were so sad, so sad and tired, open all these years, staring into darkness.

"Sleep," he whispered. "Sleep for a bit." He hesitated only a moment, then pressed with his index finger upon the cool parchment of the eyelids, first one, then the other, drawing them down like tattered shades over twilight windows.

"There," he said gently, "that's better now, isn't it? Sleep a bit." He started to hum a tune he had not thought of for years, an old cradle song his mother had crooned to him on the nights when the terrors of Cairnwell made sleep come hard. When the last notes died away, caught by the smooth fissures of the chamber walls, he rose, laid a hand of benediction on the wizened forehead, and started upstairs where his brandy waited.

The twenty-third laird of Cairnwell had come home.

S usan Palwick's work has appeared in *Amazing Stories* and *Isaac Asimov's Science Fiction Magazine* and various anthologies. She is a winner of the Rhysling Award for science fiction poetry, and her story "Ever After" was selected for several Best-of-the-Year volumes. She is a reviewer and critic and was a founding editor of *The New York Review of Science Fiction*, and was on the editorial board of *The Little Magazine* for several years. She lives in New York City, where she works for an executive-search firm.

Palwick's stories work the fertile territory in the borderland between fantasy and horror, as in this story of a seaside house and a mermaid. The story was inspired by the airlifting of a friend's Montauk, Long Island, summer cottage from a deteriorating cliff to a safer location.

Erosion

SUSAN PALWICK

One windy October dawn when Marina was thirteen, her mother jumped from the cliff in their backyard into the sea. Marina had been expecting as much ever since Mother stopped walking. Daddy and the neighbors said something was wrong with her nervous system; the doctors blamed it on stress, and Daddy blamed it on Mother's genes, but Marina knew better than all of them. Mother had certainly dropped enough hints during the tedious weeks of her confinement. You'd have to be crazy not to figure it out.

"Fishwife," she'd told Marina with a tight smile, as she lay in bed with blankets draped over her legs. It was September then, a rainy evening threatening thunder, and the numbness that had started in Mother's toes in June had reached her knees. Every morning she pinched herself to see how much she could still feel, but she'd never let anyone watch. "Haven't you wondered why the people in town always call me that?"

"Because you have webbed toes," said Marina, who also

had webbed toes and had been called Fishy Feet and La-
goon Legs and many other, less pleasant things. "And because you always yell at Daddy about how close the house
is to the water."

Marina's parents had been fighting about the house for
as long as she could remember. When she was born, there
had been twenty feet between the back door and the edge
of the cliff, but the distance lessened every year. Each set
of September storms swept more clay and sand into the
ocean, and each June's surf sounded louder in the attic
room where Marina slept. Her father had cursed the water
and drawn up plans for seawalls, which the waves brought
down in ruins, but he refused to relocate. The house was
where he'd grown up; he couldn't imagine living anywhere
else. Nearly every night of her childhood, as she lay in bed
and listened to the ocean, Marina had stretched her long
webbed toes and dreamt of growing a tail.

And now it was September again, and a mere three feet
separated them from the precipice. "Soon the goddamn
house will be *in* the water," Marina's mother said. "This
is the sixth storm this month, and the cliff's disappearing.
The neighbors know that, even if your father doesn't. He
won't leave the house and I can't leave him, and we're
falling into the ocean. The people in town would call me a
fishwife even if I never raised my voice. Oh, Marina, we'd
be safer already underwater than we are here!"

There was a brilliant flash of lightning outside, and then
an earsplitting crash and the smell of ozone. Marina's
mother clutched her blankets with white-knuckled hands,
and glanced up at the cross-stitched sampler she'd embroidered when Marina was a child terrified of wind-borne
ghosts: "Be not afeard. The isle is full of noises, sounds,
and sweet airs, that give delight and hurt not." It had hung
in Marina's attic room for years, but when Mother couldn't
walk anymore Marina had brought it downstairs and hung
it opposite Mother's bed, so that she could see it whenever there was lightning.

Two weeks went by, and another six inches crumbled from the cliff. The numbness now extended halfway up Mother's thighs. Daddy and the doctors wanted her to go into the hospital for an experimental treatment; she refused. "My legs get worse the more dangerous the house is," she said. "If we were in a safer house, I bet I'd be just fine. How about moving us somewhere else, George? That would be an interesting experiment, wouldn't it?"

"It has nothing to do with the house," Daddy said. "You were fine in the house for twenty years. This is what your aunt had, and she lived in Kansas! It's a congenital tendency—"

"Which is triggered by stress," Mother said sweetly. "Now what could possibly be distressing me, George? Think about it."

Daddy stomped out of the room, scowling, and Marina's mother sighed. "You understand why I'm not going to the hospital, Marina, don't you?"

Marina nodded, shuddering. One of the boys in her science class wanted to be a doctor, and had once asked her if he could write a lab report about her feet. "No scalpels," he'd said, rubbing his hands together and licking his lips. "I promise."

Marina hadn't believed him for a minute, and even people with normal toes disliked hospitals. "But, Mother, I though Aunt Eloise drowned in California?"

"She did. She moved from Kansas to California right after she was diagnosed. The doctors said she got sick because she was terrified of tornadoes, but earthquakes were worse. Next thing we knew, she rowed herself out into the Pacific and was never heard from again."

"Really?" said Marina. "Did she have webbed toes?"

"You bet," Mother said with a wink, and patted the blankets covering her legs just as a drumroll of rain began on the roof.

It rained for six days. At dawn on the seventh, Marina awoke from a nightmare of going deaf to realize that the oppressive silence was only the absence of water. Her toes tingled unpleasantly, and she had to go to the bathroom.

She stumbled downstairs, still half-asleep. On her way back up to the attic, she saw that the light was on in her mother's sickroom. A wind had risen, moaning around the house and rattling the windows. Maybe she's afraid, Marina thought. I should comfort her.

But Mother was sitting up against a stack of pillows and intently pounding her legs with her fists. When she looked up and saw Marina she nodded, as if she'd expected her daughter to wake up at this ridiculous hour, and said, "Darling, I can't feel my legs at all anymore. Will you help me into my wheelchair?"

"Of course," Marina said groggily. Her father and the doctors had been very worried that Mother wouldn't get out of bed; now everyone would be happy. "This is really exciting," Marina said, trying to sound enthusiastic even though all she really wanted to do was go back to sleep. "I'm very happy for you."

"I want to go look at the water, sweetheart. Before the rain starts again. I can't stay in this house anymore."

"I should wake Daddy up. He wouldn't want to miss this."

"No, honey. Don't do that."

"But now he'll understand what really happened to your legs," Marina said. "He'll have to, when he sees—"

"No. Your father will never understand. That's why I need your help. Anyway, he kept his eyes closed for twenty years while the cliff got eaten away. He might as well sleep through this too."

So Marina helped Mother into the wheelchair and steered her into the shrunken backyard. It was high tide, the air astringent with salt, and waves leaped up the cliff like large, badly trained dogs eager to be petted. The wind scoured Marina's face and pulled her hair into a tangled streamer, but Mother laughed and said, "Closer, darling. I want to be closer to the edge."

Marina had hoped for a glimpse beneath Mother's blankets, but even in the wheelchair she remained swathed in wool below the waist. Her legs had changed shape. That much was certain, and Marina needed no further proof to know what had happened. Toes tingling, Marina dutifully wheeled her to the very edge of the cliff, bracing the wheelchair as Mother pushed herself into the water below. Fascinated, and slightly revived by the insistent air, Marina watched the waves for a while to see if Mother would surface. Marina imagined her breaking the water like a porpoise, leaping joyously as foam cascaded from her back, but nothing happened.

After a while, it started to rain again. Marina turned around, hunching her shoulders against the wet, and wheeled the chair back inside so it wouldn't rust. They'd need it when Mother came back.

Her father came out of Mother's room, nearly as pale as his white pajamas, and said, "Where's your mother? What—"

He saw the empty wheelchair and stopped. "Marina? Where is she? What's wrong? Why are your feet muddy?"

The warmth inside the house was making Marina drowsy again. "Nothing's wrong," she said, stifling a yawn.

Three weeks later, Mother still hadn't come back. Marina was starting to worry, and the situation wasn't improved by the fact that her father, who had his own notions of logic, had decided to move the house inland. He hired engineers and surveyors and, finally, a gigantic helicopter, which lifted the house away from its foundation toward an enormous flatbed truck parked fifty feet from the edge of the cliff.

The local folk, gathered in the driveway and by the side of the road, stood gaping at the house as it rose into the air. Someone had brought a video camera; someone else had brought popcorn. The small child who lived across the street waved a flag. Marina had seen two of her teachers exchanging money, and suspected that odds were being placed on whether the house would fall and crush her father, who ran about beneath it waving his arms. Although she couldn't hear anything above the whack-whack-whack of the helicopter, she knew from the onlookers' contorted mouths that they were exclaiming in wonder at this latest evidence of her family's eccentricity.

The house didn't fall, but was deposited safely on the truck. Marina and her father followed in their rusting Toyota as the house was carried away from the ocean and delivered to its new location by the salt marshes. Many of the neighbors trooped along on foot, keeping up easily with the slow procession. Most maintained a respectful distance, although the owner of the camera kept trying to film through the car windows, as if Marina and her father were rock musicians or foreign dignitaries. Marina kept waiting for the taunting rhymes that had wound their way through her childhood—*Ugly smelly Fishyfeet, Smells like dead things in the heat, Get some gills and grow some scales, Go eat seaweed with the whales*—but for once, curiosity had replaced cruelty.

The lens of the video camera appeared at her window, and she made the worst face she could muster, sticking her tongue out as far as it would go and wiggling her ears. After the camera had gone away, she said, "You're making more trouble for everybody, you know. Especially Mother."

"You think I killed her," Daddy said morosely. "That's why you're angry."

All this talk about killing! He hadn't even let Marina talk to the police to explain what had happened, because he was afraid they'd think *she'd* killed Mother. "She isn't dead, Daddy."

"The wind must have done it. She wanted to go outside to look at the water, but she got too close to the edge and leaned out too far, and the wind pushed her in." Her father sighed and chewed on his lower lip for a moment, squinting through the streaked windshield. "I should have thought of this years ago. She always wanted us to move." Marina fiddled irritably with the buckle of her seatbelt. The wind theory was hogwash, but she knew there was no point in saying so. "She wanted *us* to move, not the house! Now she won't know where to find us when she comes out of the water. She'll look around and see a big hole where the house used to be, and no sign of us at all."

"You think I killed her."

"If she were dead, there'd be a body," Marina said, making the buckle snap like a pair of miniature metal jaws.

"The tail was a joke, Marina." His voice was flat and toneless. "The neighbors joked about it, and your mother joked about their jokes to try to make you feel better— but, oh, Marina, that's all it was!"

"She's coming back, Daddy. She *told* me she wouldn't leave you. Didn't she say Mrs. Simpson was an idiot for running off with the UPS man? Didn't she get angry at all those divorced fathers who don't pay child support? She wouldn't *do* something like that!"

Daddy just looked at her and shook his head sadly.

Moving the house was clearly a mistake. The roof creaked in places that had always been sound; damp crept in more pervasively than it had when they'd only been feet from the ocean. There seemed to be constant rain, a disconsolate drizzle in which the only enthusiasm was an occasional flash of lightning.

"The house has to settle," Marina's father said, but as it settled, it warped and bulged. The stairway banister was crooked; every other step buckled, and the floors were no longer level. Doors wouldn't close properly, and window panes cracked. The house sang like an organ played by the wind.

All of this made Marina increasingly nervous, and her

father increasingly nostalgic. "This is where your mother and I first kissed," he said, standing on the precarious porch. The dripping pantry prompted tales of his wife's preserves, the mildewed bathroom of her Saturday night bubble baths. In the living room, its dark corners grown Byzantine with patterns of mold, he spent an entire Saturday afternoon reminiscing about the first time he had seen his future bride, at one of his mother's teas for the neighborhood ladies.

Marina didn't know whether to scream or cry. It was obvious that the more dangerous the house became, the less willing her father would be to abandon it. No wonder Mother had jumped into the ocean! But Marina couldn't simply join her, because then Daddy wouldn't have anyone left.

The next morning Marina grimly ventured out on her own. If Daddy wasn't going to find another house for them, she'd have to do it herself. Knowing that owners of risky property might not answer her inquiries honestly, she composed several questions designed to alert her to possible dangers. How do you feel when you wake up in the middle of the night and hear the attic groaning? Do your palms sweat when it's very windy? How often in the past year have you dreamed of avalanches?

Marina visited all of the houses in town that were for sale. She wore her best satin skirt and velvet jacket; she did her hair in a style fifteen years out of date so that she would look older and more responsible, and took care to compliment the homeowners on their pets and children. For all her efforts, the owners only smiled and called her father to fetch her home again. "Your daughter's gotten loose," one of them said, as if Marina were a dog that had slipped its leash.

Marina lay awake a long time that night, fighting tears and flexing her webbed toes. Where was Mother? A short sabbatical would have been understandable; so much to look at down there, and no thunderstorms. But it had been nearly two months! A tail couldn't be that hard to use! Maybe Daddy had been right, and Mother was never coming back.

Marina buried her face in her pillow. No, that couldn't be right. Mother wasn't like that. Even if she didn't love them at all, even if she'd just embroidered the sampler and cooked all those meals and sewed on Daddy's buttons for the sake of appearances—even then, especially then, she'd never let herself act like Mrs. Simpson! Hadn't she told Marina a thousand times not to run away just because of the songs the other children sang about her? Hadn't she always talked about the importance of good examples? She wouldn't run away herself, not for good. She'd just left for a little while, to show them it was possible. . . .

As Marina chewed on a corner of her sheet, it suddenly occurred to her that perhaps, having given herself to the ocean, Mother was incapable of venturing back on land. How easy was it to shed a tail, having grown one? People needed boats or bridges to cross mere miles of water; perhaps Mother couldn't come home, over the few miles they had moved inland, without some similar contrivance.

Marina relaxed and stopped chewing the sheet. Everything was all right: there were plenty of possible reasons why Mother hadn't come back yet. She needed help, that was all. She'd told Marina she needed help. "Your father will never understand," she'd said. "That's why I need your help."

So Marina put letters into old catsup bottles and pickle jars and hurled them off the cliff. "I miss you so much," she wrote, "and my feet tingle with every high tide. I'll meet you on the beach if you can't make your way onto land by yourself, Mother. Daddy saved the wheelchair, even though he doesn't believe that you're coming back, so it won't be any trouble to bring you home. I'll fill the bathtub with fresh seawater every day; I'll bring you crabs and seagrass and bluefish, anything you could possibly want.

"Only come back, Mother. You have to come back before the walls cave in and the roof collapses. Every night I wonder if I'll be buried in my sleep, and I'm worried about Daddy. Mother, you have to come back.''

To the letters, Marina added bribes: she gathered her mother's favorite tortoiseshell comb, and a silver and coral bracelet Marina had bought her once with allowance money, and swam into the surf with them as far as she could, kicking powerfully with her webbed feet. How her toes tingled; how her tail wanted to grow! But she wouldn't let it: had it grown, she might not have been able to tear herself away from the sea, and then there would have been no one left to protect Daddy.

The townsfolk, who watched all of this with intense interest and complete stupidity, thought Marina was the one who needed protection. Local fishermen and athletes kept performing heroic rescues, dragging her back onto shore as inexorably as the truck had dragged the house inland. Daddy misunderstood her as thoroughly as the neighbors did; he was so frightened whenever he saw her leaving the house that she began sneaking away when he was too busy repairing something to notice her.

One chilly April day when Marina was combing the dunes for some sign of Mother's presence, she found a bleached, barnacle-encrusted rowboat with two splintered oars. This time she gathered Mother's favorite food, all the treats she wouldn't have been able to get in the ocean: strawberries and vanilla ice cream, ham and salami sandwiches, green olives stuffed with almonds. On a breezy, cloudless afternoon, Marina packed the boat with homemade bread and rack of lamb and bottles of fragrant herbs, and rowed out a mile or more, until her arms ached, before dropping the feast in the water. Hoping to see her mother surface, she watched the cans and weighted plastic bags and foil-wrapped packages vanish. She saw nothing.

As she rode back, despondent and bone-weary, the boat started to sink. Water seeped through the boards until she might just as well have been in a salty bathtub, but she was too tired to swim. She clung to some bits of wood and prepared to take a nap; she'd have been stronger when she awoke. But she didn't get the chance, because a fiberglass powerboat came along, belching oil.

Daddy was beside himself when the two potbellied yachtsmen from the city, wearing clothing decorated with patterns of tiny mermaids, brought Marina back to the house. Her lips were chapped from salt; her hair hung in clumps, and her toes itched unbearably. She was a troubled and wayward adolescent bent on self-destruction, the sportsmen said. She needed help, they said—why, she hadn't been glad at all when they found her! She'd acted as if she wanted to stay there and drown!

"They don't know what they're talking about," Marina told her father after the sportsmen had left. "I wasn't trying to drown; I was just taking a nap. I only used the boat because I thought it would make you feel better, anyway. I really would have been safer swimming."

"I was afraid of this," her father said grimly. "I've been trying to tell myself it wasn't true, but I should have known. It's those goddamn feet—you and your mother and her aunt, all of you with webbed toes and crazy as loons! It's all genetic! Well, I'm not going to let you drown too! I won't let it happen!"

Marina scowled and scratched the bottom of one foot. "Nobody drowned, and I am not crazy."

Daddy sighed, staring at the latest tendrils of fungus on the porch railing. "Marina, there's someone I want you to see."

He made an appointment for Marina with the local psychiatrist, who sat behind a huge desk and nodded sympathetically at precise intervals. Marina sat in a back-wrenching modern chair, chatting nervously about storm drains, webbed toes, and needlepoint. "The people who live around here make fun of me because of my feet, you know—I'm sure you've heard them yourself—and my father thinks I'm silly for worrying about how safe the house is, because *he*'s too busy reliving his lost youth. But I'm no weirder than anybody else. I mean, some of the people who rented here last summer had purple hair. Everybody made fun of them too, but nobody said they should talk to you."

"I see," said the doctor, nodding as if listening to an invisible metronome. "Let's talk about how your mother died."

"My mother didn't die."

The doctor gazed at her pityingly. "No? But she jumped into the ocean, didn't she? Doesn't that mean she killed herself?"

"She jumped into the ocean to learn how to swim," Marina snapped, wondering if all middle-aged men were obsessed with death. She considered taking off her shoes and showing the doctor her toes, but decided against it. That hadn't convinced Daddy of anything but her insanity, although the connection between the feet and the brain was an attenuated one, at best. "Why would I bring her all that stuff if she were dead?"

"Because you don't know she's dead."

"Neither do you," said Marina.

They went around in circles like that for another forty-five minutes. At last the doctor decided that Marina was suffering post-traumatic grief syndrome, gave her sleeping pills, and explained at wearisome length why bringing Mother gifts was regressive and dysfunctional behavior.

Whatever else her behavior may have been, Marina soon discovered that it was a waste of time; in the following weeks, almost everything she had cast into the water came back to shore. She found the comb among some rocks, and she saw a surfer's moll wearing the bracelet. As for the food and letters, who could tell? Any of the broken bottles and discarded plastic containers on the beach could have been the ones in which Marina had enclosed her offerings; the paper would have dissolved once the bottles were open to the sea, and the food could have been eaten by sharks or crabs or hungry scuba divers.

As the weather grew warmer, Marina took to wandering along the edge of the cliff and yelling angrily, "Mother, cut it out and come back!" She attracted increasingly large crowds of weekend tourists, now that the summer season had begun again; they watched her from cars and boats, drinking beer and honking their horns. If Mother heard any of this, she gave no sign.

Summer wasn't much drier than winter and autumn had been. As rain trickled into the house and wind bled through the chinks in the walls, Marina often came upon Daddy muttering to himself as he worked, as if determined to halt the disintegration of the house by force of will. The rugs and draperies were long beyond salvation; his latest project, involving arcane combinations of furniture polish, was a rear-guard action against the mold sprouting on the dining-room table. Mother still didn't reappear.

Disgusted with both of them, Marina resigned herself to the uncertain comfort of childhood prayers—a ritual she'd found unconvincing at the best of times, and which now seemed even less substantial than the delicate safety net of Daddy's endless anecdotes. Each night she petitioned for the gift of another morning; each morning, as she awoke more acutely aware of the tug of the tides and the unreliability of the roof, she pleaded fervently for Mother's return.

One chilly October morning, almost exactly a year after Mother's disappearance, Marina opened her eyes to find a cluster of three mussel shells resting precariously on her windowsill. There was a tangled clump of strange white seaweed on the front porch, and a small silver fish, still alive, thrashing about in the front yard.

"Seagulls," Daddy said after she had woken him. He sat propped up on a mildewed mound of pillows, blinking groggily. Each day it became more difficult for him to get out of bed. He had developed a permanent limp, and his cough was almost constant, no doubt aggravated by the spores drifting throughout the house. He spent his free time—the few moments he could spare from his labors on the house—visiting specialists who had no idea what was causing his symptoms, although Marina would gladly have told them had anyone asked her.

"Seagulls are greedy, Daddy. A seagull would have eaten that fish."

He tried to stand, wincing when he put weight on his bad foot. Marina, sighing, offered him her shoulder to lean on. It was good they'd kept the wheelchair; soon Daddy would need it, even if Mother never used it again. "Perhaps the bird was ill, Marina. Perhaps the little fish was ill, and the bird knew it. I'm sure it was seagulls, dear."

"Well, what about the seaweed? You don't see white seaweed on the beach, Daddy. That's from someplace so far down they don't even have *chloro*phyll—"

"Some of it obviously floated to the surface."

"Oh, sure," said Marina. She didn't understand how someone who talked about missing Mother so often, and at such great length, could be so deliberately obtuse. The messages Mother had sent were clear.

I'm alive. I've gone deep. The three of us will be together again.

But when, and how? Why had she waited so long to contact them? Why hadn't she shown herself in the flesh? Had she indeed had no choice but to entrust her messages to seagulls, as Marina had been forced to consign hers to the currents?

Marina pondered these things over breakfast while her father listened to the radio. Water dripped from the ceiling, soaking the pancakes and diluting the syrup. Marina's eggs were small yellow islands, her bacon strips nearly submerged reefs. Everything, including the orange juice, tasted of salt.

"Listen," said Daddy, his voice turned strange. "Marina, are you listening to the radio?"

Yawning, she tuned in the background jabber; the weather forecasters were breathlessly discussing Hurricane Canute, currently brewing over the Atlantic, which would soon move ashore, bringing with it torrential rains and coastal flooding. Extensive damages were expected: the ground, already saturated from heavy rains, couldn't absorb any more water. The storm would hit near high tide.

Marina's heart leapt, even as her father paled and began ranting about the heartless cruelty of the sea. Perhaps, she thought in a crystalline moment, he had been right to move the house. Mother wouldn't have been able to swim to the top of the cliff, even in the storm, but she could reach them this way. Marina hugged herself in gratitude; this had been the proper spot for the house after all.

As the day progressed, nearly everyone in town fled inland, joining long convoys of overcrowded cars. Daddy, for once, wanted to join the exodus, and of course Marina had to stop him. Mother had warned her that he'd never understand; the mussel shells outside Marina's bedroom clearly meant that assuring the family's reunion was her responsibility.

"We can leave in the car when we have to," she told him, "but we'd better secure the house, or it won't be here when we get back. After all the work you've done, you don't want the water to win now, do you?"

So all afternoon she ran about the house taping cracked windows, unplugging appliances that had threatened them with electrocution for months, and covering the mildewed furniture with plastic. Her father, who could no longer do anything quickly, laboriously moved his favorite possessions upstairs, where he thought they might escape possible flooding. Marina invented as many extra chores for him as she could think of, as the wind rose and her pulse raced; while Daddy was defrosting the refrigerator, she ran outside and poured a box of sugar into the gas tank of the car.

He spent fifteen minutes trying to start the engine, although by now it was doubtful that any of the local roads were passable. Marina offered to go back into the house to call for help. She pulled the phone cord out of the wall and hid the vandalism behind a chair before running back out and announcing, in what she hoped was a convincing show of concern, that the lines were down.

"What will we do?" he cried, his voice as high and plaintive as a gull's. "How will we get away now?"

"People will come around to evacuate us, Daddy. Police or firemen; the National Guard. Possibly Saint Bernard dogs with miniature casks of rum. We'd better go in and wait."

Giddy with relief at Mother's imminent return, Marina helped her father back inside and made tea on the gas stove. Into his cup she put two of the sleeping pills the psychiatrist had given her. Daddy looked very peaceful, stretched out on the couch, and Marina knew from the rhythmic movements of his lower lip that he was snoring contentedly, although she couldn't hear him because of the storm.

He continued snoring while Marina watched the water fill the marsh, move slowly across the road, and rise in the yard. Scummy froth was lapping at the porch steps as darkness fell. When the evacuation boat arrived in a glare of searchlights Marina shut off her flashlight—which she had thought might serve as a beacon for Mother—and ignored the doorbell and loudspeakers.

She was afraid someone would enter the house to look for survivors, but no one did. At last they left, after bellowing terrible statistics about seaside fatalities during hurricane flooding. Marina was very grateful Daddy wasn't awake for that part. It would have alarmed him.

By the time he awoke, there were five inches of water in the living room; and outside the flood was rapidly rising above the windowsills. He looked dazedly around him, at old magazines and ashtrays and teacups bobbing haphazardly in the weak illumination of Marina's flashlight.

"Marina, did they—Marina, didn't anyone come for us?" She could hardly hear him; his expression pleaded more eloquently than his words. "How could I sleep through this? Why am I so weak?"

"Mother's coming for us now," Marina told him. "She needed the storm to come, Daddy; she needed the water. She'll take us to her house underneath the ocean, where there are never any storms."

Her father stared at her, his pale face streaked with sweat. Outside the wind howled, and the house vibrated around them, humming in a minor key as if performing a requiem for its own destruction. "No," he said, trying to get up. His voice was slurred from the pills; whenever he managed to sit up he'd collapse again. "Marina, you've been dreaming—all those stories of pearls and coral . . . She won't come back, no, not ever. She can't come back!"

He sounded so frightened that Marina took pity on him. What could she say to make him understand? "We'll be safe, Daddy. Don't worry; Mother will be here soon. I'm sure she's found a way to give you a tail too. She'll lead us home."

Marina could feel her own toes beginning to lengthen, the webs between them stretching as she had dreamed so often of their doing. This time she didn't try to stop them.

"No," he said, making another futile effort to sit up. "She's dead. We have to leave. We have to get out like—like everyone else. Or we'll be dead too. Please, Marina. Please. Help me stand up."

"We can't leave, Daddy. It's too late."

As she spoke, one of the taped windows imploded. Within the gush of water that swept toward them, Marina saw a dim shape, cloudy and obscured. "Oh, Daddy, look—she's here!"

Surely those were hands stretched in welcome; surely that white glimmering was a loving smile, those swirling strands the luxurious tendrils of Mother's long dark hair. But Marina's father cried out in a terrible hoarse bellow, raising his hands. It must have been the sea itself from which he cringed; how could he have feared his beloved wife?

Marina wanted to say something comforting, but there was no time. The wave was upon them, and with her last breath of air she reached joyously for her mother's outstretched arms.

Ian Watson is a winner of the BSFA award, the French Prix Apollo and was a nominee for the John W. Campbell Memorial Award. He is the author of the horror novels *The Power, The Fire Worm,* and *Meat.* He is the features editor of the British journal *Foundation.* He lives in Northants, England.

Set in a suburban British pub, this is a story of adult restraint, supernatural desire, and a carnivorous ventilation fan. The British pub is real. But Ian Watson says, with some dismay, that the owners have since removed the fan.

Happy Hour

IAN WATSON

For Michael Coney

With an abrupt loud clatter the steel slats of the ex-
haust fan exploded open, making our hearts lurch.
Martin mimed quick pistol shots at it.

"Pung! Pung! Gotcha."

That fan was set just beneath the bowed, beamed ceiling
of the bar in the Roebuck. The contraption was at least
twenty years out of date. It didn't purr softly like a modern fan. It exploded open, showing its teeth, and gulped at
the atmosphere. One of the historic stones of this pub—
built in the reign of Good Queen Bess, so a sign on the
wall boasted—had been removed so that the thing could
be inserted. The actual mechanism was hidden inside the
wall. When the fan was in repose, all that showed was a
slatted cream panel one foot square lying flush with the
cream plasterwork. You hardly noticed it, forgot all about
it—until suddenly the Xtractall opened its mouth as if by
its own volition; until the flat panel became a dozen razor
lips spaced an inch apart, through which fuggy air was
sucked into its throat.

147

The fan throbbed lustily, sucking Charlotte's cigarette smoke and my own cigar smoke into it.

"Does it have a built-in smoke detector?" I wondered.

"We could ask what's-his-name. Our host." Jenny nodded toward the deserted bar counter.

"Host" was somewhat of a misnomer. The landlord was a quiet, wispy chap with little by way of personality. He smiled amiably, but he was no conversationalist; and frankly we liked it this way. Right now he would be round in the restaurant annex neatening the array of silver and wineglasses on the tables. The Roebuck was one of those few country pubs that opened fairly promptly at six of an evening, but it relied for its main trade on the gourmet menu from about half-past seven till ten. It wasn't much of a hangout for locals and yokels.

To be sure, now that the licensing hours had been liberalized, the place could have stayed open all day long. Yet what rural pub would bother to? We were lucky to have found the Roebuck.

Jenny and I, Charlotte and Martin, and Alice (who was special) all commuted to London and back by way of big, glassy Milton Keynes Station. Charlotte and Martin had bought a sizable thatched cottage in a couple of acres this side of Buckingham. Jenny and I were based in a different little village outside of Stony Stratford, in a barn conversion. Alice lived . . . somewhere in the vicinity. Alone? Or otherwise? Alice was our delicious enigma. Apparently she was in publishing. Webster-Freeman: art and oriental-wisdom volumes, shading into the outright occult. I sometimes fantasized her dancing naked around a bonfire or homemade altar along with other like spirits, firelight or candlelight winking between her legs. If such was the case, she had never tried to recruit us (and, curiously, my fantasies along these lines never provoked an erection). We were merely one slice of her life on Friday evenings: a slice lasting an hour—twice as long when we all dined at the Roebuck once a month.

Why had we been so honored by Alice? Perhaps she was lonely under her capable, gorgeous facade. Perhaps we were neutrals with whom she could be friends without obligations or ties.

I myself worked for an oil company and was in charge of Butadiene, a gas used as fuel and also in the manufacture of synthetic rubbers. Since I was on the contracts rather than the chemistry side, the job called for some foreign travel—quick trips to Eastern Europe, Mexico, Japan, from which I returned tired out—but otherwise my career was ho-hum. I assumed I would be with the same mob for the rest of my working life, slowly advancing. In our company salaries were somewhat pinched to start with (and indeed to continue with!) until the final five years, when suddenly you were rolling in money and could practically write yourself checks. Thus my masters assured staff loyalty.

My wife, Jenny, was office manager for an airline, which gave us free tickets once a year to hot, exotic places where I didn't need to sit haggling in an office. Jenny was a short, trim blonde who wore smartly tailored suits and lavish bows like big silken napkins tucked into her neckline.

Burly, early-balding Martin was an architect, and his spouse, Charlotte, willowy and auburn, was a senior secretary to an export-import firm called, uninventively, Exportim, which managed to sound like some Soviet trade bureau.

And Alice was . . . Alice.

Weekdays (except Fridays) Martin and Charlotte and Jenny and I all drove our own cars to MK Station, since we might need to work late and catch different trains home. Every Friday, however, my wife and I shared a car; so did Martin and his wife. On that day nothing would make us miss the same return train and our wind-down drink with Alice at the Roebuck. Needless to say, our minor contribution toward car-sharing in no way relieved the parking pressure at MK. By seven-fifteen in the morning every weekday the station car parks were full up, and the central reservations and traffic islands were becoming crowded with vehicles. The new city in the Buckinghamshire country-side boasted a fine network of roads, but where parking was concerned, the planners had cocked up. Pressure, pressure. No wonder we looked forward to our Friday evenings. Or our once-a-month dinner.

I screwed my cigar butt into one ashtray at the exact moment when Charlotte stubbed out her Marlboro in an-other—as if she and I had been reproached by the extrac-tor fan for our filthy habits. We glanced at one another and burst out laughing. The fan thumped shut.

"I heard this in Hungary," I said. "There's a new Rus-sian wristwatch on the market, triumph of Soviet technol-ogy. It'll do absolutely everything: time zones, phases of the moon, built-in calculator. It only weighs a few ounces. 'So what's the snag?' asks this fellow. 'Oh,' says his in-formant, 'it's just the two suitcases of batteries you need to carry round with it. . . .' "

Then Alice told a dirty joke.

"This British couple went for a holiday in the States to tour the national parks. Well, in the first park they made friends with a skunk. They adored the skunk so much they took it with them in their trailer to the next park, then the next. Come the end of their holiday, they could hardly bear to be parted from the animal. 'I wish we could take it home,' said the husband, 'but how could we avoid the quarantine laws?' 'I know,' said his wife, 'I'll stick the skunk inside my knickers, and we'll smuggle it in that way.' 'Great idea,' agreed her husband, 'but, um, what about the smell?' The wife shrugged and sighed. 'If it dies, it dies.' "

Alice was good that way. She was incredibly desirable—tall, slim, long legs, wonderful figure, that mass of raven hair, olive skin, dark broody eyes—but she easily defused any sexual tensions that might have undermined our little group. Lust from the men; or jealousy from the ladies. Charlotte had first fallen into conversation with Alice on the homeward train, and introduced her to the rest of us at journey's end. We rarely sat together on the train itself. Such a rush to catch it. Carriages would be crowded; and we all had work to keep us busy.

Alice refrained from letting us know her home address or phone number—perhaps wisely, in case Martin or I tried to see her privately. Nor, in fact, had she ever asked about our own homes. A tacit agreement prevailed, not to know. Meanwhile, she certainly made our Friday evening group react together. She was our catalyst. Without her, we would have been just two everyday couples. With her, we felt special: a new sort of unit, a sparkling fivesome.

Gleefully Martin took over the baton of joke-telling.

"The mother superior of this convent school invited a Battle of Britain hero to address her girls," he said with relish. "The flying ace told them, 'I was at eight thousand feet in my Spitfire. I saw a fokker to the left of me. There was another fokker to the right of me. I looked up, and the sky was full of fokkers.' 'I should explain, girls,' interrupted the mother superior, 'that the Fokker-Wolf was a Second World War German fighter plane.' 'That's quite right, Mother,' said the airman, 'but these fokkers were flying Messerschmidts.' "

Though the jokes themselves might have seemed silly— it's the way they're told, isn't it?—we excelled ourselves in wit and amity that evening . . . until the pub cat came a-calling on us. This mog was a scruffy ginger specimen, which I had seen the landlord shooing outdoors on a couple of occasions. With the unerring instinct of pussies, it made straight for Alice, to rub against her leg. She drew away.

"I loathe cats. I'm allergic."

"Gid away!" Martin flapped and clapped his hands. The mog retreated a little, not particularly deterred.

So much, I thought wryly, for Alice being any kind of spare-time witch; and to my scanty store of information about her I added the knowledge that there were no felines in her home.

She shifted uncomfortably. "I can't bear to touch them. I really don't like them." This was the first sour note in any of our evenings.

"Derrick," Jenny said to me, "for heaven's sake grab it and shove it out of the door."

"It's their hair," murmured Alice. "It would give me a terrible rash. I hope they don't let it sleep in here at night. Sprawling on these seats, rubbing fur off all the time. If they do let it, and I knew that, well . . . ."

The end of our Friday fivesome. Panic. We would never find another suitable pub.

"I'm sure it's an outdoor cat," Martin assured her. I was shoving my chair back quietly prior to attempting to collar the beast, when that fan on the wall went *click-clack*. It simply opened its slats for a moment, then shut them again as if a strong buffet of wind had surged through from outside—though the weather had been clement when we drove up.

The cat skedaddled as if a bucket of water had been dumped on it.

"That's scuttled him. Thanks, fan. Must be turning blowy outside."

"We should go," said Alice.

"Till next week?" Anxious me.

"Oh yes," she promised. We all rose.

But outside the night was perfectly still. Not even a breeze.

The following Friday our trio of vehicles all arrived at almost the same time at the Roebuck. Under the bare chestnut tree standing sentinel by the car park, Charlotte inhaled.

"Is that your perfume, Alice? It's glorious."

It was indeed: rich, musky, wild, yet subtle nevertheless, like some treasure forever unattainable, unownable.

"A friend of mine runs a perfumery down in the Cotswolds," Alice told her. "This is a new creation."

"Could you possibly get me—?" began Charlotte. "No, don't. Never mind. It doesn't matter."

Of course not. If Charlotte wore that ravishing scent, what might Martin imagine? Alice didn't press her.

"I'm trying to give up smoking," added Charlotte as we headed through the November chill toward the door. "Tonight I think I'll do without."

This seeming nonsequitur was actually an intimate confidence between the two women; indeed between all of us. We mustn't pollute Alice's fragrance. The onus now lay on me to refrain from lighting up any of my slim panatelas.

I rechecked our host's name painted over the lintel of the door—John Chalmers, of course—though I needn't have bothered. I had to tinkle the bell on the counter several times before he came, seeming too preoccupied even to greet us beyond a few nods. As soon as I had extracted a couple of pints of Adnam's for Martin and me, a gin for Jenny, and a lowland single malt for Alice, Chalmers withdrew. Alice was a connoisseur of scotches; another grace note in her favor.

"I'd like to sit under the fan tonight," she announced.

So as to minimize her own fragrance diplomatically, symbolically? We sat at a table different from our usual one. Scarcely a couple of minutes passed before—*clunk-clack*—the slats of the fan sprang open, and the machinery sucked air.

"How odd," said Martin. "None of us is smoking, and it switches on."

"Maybe," I said recklessly to Alice, "it's breathing your scent in. Maybe it's in love with you."

Jenny darted me a dubious glance. The fan continued operating without ceasing, throbbing away, never shutting down.

Unaccountably John Chalmers kept wandering into the body of the bar, dusting ashtrays, adjusting the hang of hunting prints on the walls.

"What's up, man?" Martin asked the landlord during his third incursion.

"Tiger's gone missing. Our cat."

"Aaah," breathed Alice. "I meant to ask: Do you let that cat roam these rooms during the night?"

"The whole place gets a thorough vacuuming every morning," said our house-proud host.

Alice pursed her lips. "An old building. Nooks and crannies. Mice?"

"I have never found any dead vermin inside. Outside, I've found Tiger's trophies. What do you expect? Not in here, never. If there's any mice, he scares 'em off."

Alice continued gazing at him till he took umbrage. "Health inspector gave us a pat on the back last month. He's more interested in kitchens, but he said this was the most spick-and-span bar he'd seen in all the county." Chalmers wandered off, restaurantward.

When he had gone off, Martin pointed up at the busy Xtractall. "*There's* a tiny bit that isn't spick." A russet something—barely noticeable—had lodged between the edge of one slat and the housing.

"What is it?" Alice asked, in a need-to-know tone. Martin had to take off his shoes and clamber onto an upholstered chair, handkerchief in hand.

"Just you be careful of those fingers!" Charlotte called.

"S'all right. Safety grille inside. Stops idiots from mincing themselves." He pried with the hanky and stepped down. "Bit of ginger fur. Ugh, skin? Dried blood?" Hastily he folded the hanky over and plunged it deep in his pocket. I glanced anxiously at Alice, but she was smiling up at the fan.

Presently Charlotte started kidding Alice gently about the arty occult books published by Webster-Freeman. Charlotte had popped into a bookshop to buy new pages of her personal organizer, had happened upon a display of those volumes, and had skimmed through a few out of curiosity.

"What's the use of it all nowadays?" she asked. "Is it a spiritual thread in a material world? Gurus, psychedelics . . . But the sixties are gone forever."

Alice mused. "For a while it seemed as if the world would change. As if a new age were coming: of joy, the flesh, the mind, old values in a new incarnation. Instead, what came was plastic people making plastic money."

Was she criticizing us? We got on so *well* together. Yet there was always the edge of wondrous difference, as if Alice came from . . . elsewhere, outside of our ken.

"You could only have been a little girl in the sixties," protested Charlotte.

"Could I?" Alice craned her lovely neck to look at the Xtractall. "I suppose that's a piece of the sixties. Soon it'll be replaced by some silent faceless box controlled by a microchip. . . ."

"High time too," said Martin. "Can't imagine why Chalmers hangs on to the thing."

"He doesn't know why," said Alice. "He's one of the most neutral people I've ever seen. Till the usual restaurant crowd turn up, prattling about barn conversions and BMWs, this place is limbo. Imagine if the past could grow angry—bitter, like a disillusioned parent . . . yet still somehow hopeful and radiant too. In a schizophrenic way! Trying to keep the old faiths alive . . . And what if earlier epochs feel the same way about, say, the whole twentieth century? If those epochs still try to intrude and guide their offspring who have changed out of recognition? To keep the old flames alive. Smilingly, yet bitterly too."

"Er, how can the past keep watch on the present?" Martin asked with a grin. He thought a joke was due, but Alice stared at him quite seriously.

"The collective unconscious, which is timeless. The imprint of memory on material objects. Don't you think this is what angels and devils may be all about? Affirmative vibrations from the past—and negative, angry, twisted ones?"

"Beats me," said Martin. He laughed. "I always design vibrations out of buildings, mount 'em on shock absorbers, that sort of thing. Make sure there are no resonances likely to set people's teeth on edge."

My teeth were on edge. I felt that Alice was on the brink of revealing herself . . . to us, the chosen few. She was the joyous, positive spirit of an older world—and I wondered how old she really was. She liked us. She hoped for us. Yet for the most part the old world hated us?

She said to Charlotte, "I suppose Webster-Freeman's wisdom books must basically be about power, a power that has grown weak but still lingers on." I had the momentary weird impression that Alice herself had only leafed through those volumes, as casually as Charlotte had. "Power today is money, property, investments, plastic. Empty, dead power. Zombie power. Yet so vigorous. The world's soul is dying . . . of hunger. The plastic body thrives. That fan," she added, "may well be a creature of the sixties."

"Time to replace it," Martin said stoutly.

"And what did it replace? An ancient stone, a hungry old stone. Well," and she smiled sweetly, "must dash home in a few minutes and microwave some goodies. Mustn't we all?"

Was that what she would really do at home, wherever home was?

Before departing, Alice told a ridiculous joke about how to circumcise a whale. How? You use four skin divers. After booking a table in the restaurant for the following Friday, to sample the oysters and partridge, we left contented.

"Alice was in an odd mood tonight," Jenny remarked after we got home. "She *was* just kidding, don't you think?"

"I think that was the real Alice. But I don't know if Alice is real, the way we are."

Jenny giggled. "Do we imagine her every Friday? Is she the soul that's missing from our lives?"

"Not exactly. We're her hope . . . for something. Some . . . rekindling." I thought of flames, and a naked woman dancing, leaping the fire, singeing her pubic hair. "And yet . . . we don't matter too much to her. That place matters more. Chalmers's pub. The limbo pub, at that empty hour. That's what binds us together."

"*You* aren't hoping for something from her, are you?" she asked archly.

"No, You know that would ruin—" I had been about to say "the magic." I said instead, "The happy hour. Maybe," I added, "without us it's difficult for her to make contact with the modern world."

"Come off it! Charlotte met her on the train from Euston. Alice is in publishing. In business."

Is she? I wondered. Alice spoke as if she had been at home in the sixties . . . not just a little girl back then, but herself as now. And I suspected, crazily, that she had existed in earlier times too.

Charlotte had met Alice on the train, Had any of us bumped into Alice *again,* either on the London-bound train or the return one? I knew I hadn't. I had glimpsed Alice coming out of MK Station, and also cruising for parking in her Saab; yet I had never seen her anywhere on the platform at Euston. Given the rush and the crowding, that wasn't totally odd in itself—unless none of us had ever coincided with Alice after that first occasion. Certainly Jenny had never mentioned doing so.

I refrained from asking. We microwaved duck *à l'orange,* went to bed, and made love the same way we usually made love on a Friday night. When Jen and I were making love, I never thought about Alice, never visualized her—as if I were forbidden to, as if Alice could reach out and control me. Only afterwards did I lie awake wondering about angels and demons—contrasting values in the same equation—as messages, vibrations from the past intent on charming or savaging the present day, but not widely so, only marginally, except where a magical intersection of persons and places occurred.

On Monday I had some hard talking to do to some visiting Hungarians, though I mustn't be too stringent. I enjoyed the hospitality in Hungary.

*   *   *

Next Friday, in the Roebuck, we had already scrutinized the menu through in the bar, and ordered. Jenny and Charlotte went off together to the ladies' room. I myself was overcome by an urgent need to piss. So, apparently, was Martin. Martin and I both apologized simultaneously to Alice and fled to relieve ourselves, leaving her alone. Until then the fan had remained tight-lipped. *Clunk-clack,* I heard as we retreated.

It was a long, strong piss for both of us. Martin and I left one urinal basin untenanted between us: a kind of ceramic sword laid not between knight and lady but between squire and squire, both of us being chaste, faithful squires of Alice. Let us get up to no monkey business together. It's odd that women can waltz off together to the ladies' as a sort of social event, whereas chaps should do no such thing, as if mutual urination is a queer sign. Have the boys gone off together to compare their organs? In this case, need dictated.

As we were walking back, bladders emptied out, I heard the fan shut off and close itself. The bar proved to be deserted. We assumed that Alice had followed our wives to the powder room. We chatted about the innovative design of a new office block currently soaring near Euston Station. People were christening it "the totem pole." Then our ladies returned without sight of Alice.

In case Chalmers had summoned us and Alice had gone ahead to the restaurant, I checked there, in vain. Chalmers's wife ducked out from the kitchen to remark that I was a little early. I checked the car park, where Alice's Saab sat in darkness.

"Can't find her anywhere, folks!" I spotted Alice's silvery purse lying on the carpet. Before I could go to retrieve it, Martin hurried to my side and gripped my arm.

"Look at the fan," he whispered fiercely.

The slats of the Xtractall were moving in and out gently one by one, top to bottom, in an undulating fashion. I thought of someone sucking their teeth. The edge of each slat was streaked crimson, thin lines that faded, even as I watched, as if being absorbed or licked away atom by atom.

"Are my eyes playing tricks?"

"What do *you* think, Derrick?"

"You aren't suggesting—?"

"I bloody well am. I've been doing some stiff thinking about Alice since her spiel last week—"

"*Stiff* thinking?"

He looked exasperated. "I never get a hard-on thinking about her. Fact is, I can't seem to, whatever Charlotte may imagine."

"Me neither."

"She's an enchantress. Supernatural. I mean it, old son. Haven't you suspected?"

I nodded cautiously. This wasn't *quite* the thing to admit to one another.

"I thought she might be a modern-day witch," I said. "Despite commuting to Euston and driving a Saab. Type of books she publishes, you know?" I was only telling him a quarter of the truth. Since last weekend I had thought ever more about "angels" and "devils"— for want of better names!—about benign and angry vibrations from a past that had been disenfranchised, in a kind of time-crossed disinheritance: the plastic children forsaking the memory of the parent. Alice was more than any latter-day witch— and less, because she wasn't of our time at all, in spite of her modern gear and jokes.

"Not a witch, Derrick. A *lamia*. As in Keats's poem. Had to read that at school. A female spirit who preys on travelers."

"She never preyed on us."

"Just so. She was being a good girl with us. Friday evening was her leisure time, her friendly hour. She *stopped* us from feeling, well, lustful."

"What are you two arguing about?" asked Charlotte. She and Jenny couldn't see the fan without turning. "Did

one of you say something to Alice that you shouldn't?
Something to offend her?''

"No, damn it," swore Martin.

"But something did go wrong," I insisted, "and she
melted away."

"No!" He grabbed and shook me. Jenny started up,
fearing that we were about to have a brawl—about Alice,
right in front of our wives. "You don't get it, do you?"
His face leered into mine. "The fan ate her. It fell in love
with her just like you said—and it consumed her. It sucked
her into itself."

"It—?"

"The bloody fan!"

By now the slats of the Xtractall were quite clean, and
no longer made that munching motion.

Charlotte also leapt up. "You're mad!"

"Get away from under that fan, love," begged Martin.
"Remember the cat that went missing? Remember how
Alice hated cats? The fan ate the cat up for her—we found
that scrap of bloody fur up there, right?—and Alice knew;
she knew."

I recalled Alice's smile, directed at the fan.

"One night last week the fan extracted poor old Tiger,"
he went on. "Remember what Alice said about how the
fan replaced a hungry old stone? Something up there is kin
to her."

A demon, I thought—to her angel. But both of them as-
pects of the past, still wooing the present weakly, in friendly
or venomous guise.

"That thing's much more powerful than Alice guessed,"
insisted Martin. "When we all went off to the toilets—and
who sent us, her or the fan?—it sucked her in because it
wanted her."

What Charlotte did next was either quite stupid or remarkably brave. Of course, she did not see Alice the way
we fellows saw her. Maybe women couldn't. She kicked
off her shoes, burrowed in her own bag for a neglected
pack of cigarettes, lit one, and mounted a chair.

"That's impossible," she said. "Physically impossible—leaving aside the wild idea of an extractor fan falling in love." Charlotte puffed smoke at the blank face of the fan.

"The cat fur," Martin protested.

Clunk-clack: The fan opened up. The mechanism whirred. Smoke disappeared. Charlotte never flinched. She flicked her lighter for illumination. Daringly she teased two long fingernails between the slats and tugged. Several strong black strands of hair came free.

"Oh," she said, and jumped down. "Is this some joke the two of you cooked up with Alice? Is she waiting outside the door stifling her giggles?"

Martin crossed his heart like a child. And Charlotte faltered. I was wrong: Each in our way we must have been thinking along similar lines about Alice. Our ladies had both been resisting such conclusions.

"It's still impossible," Charlotte said, "unless the fan leads somewhere else than just to the ordinary outside. And unless it changes what it takes. Unless it etherializes stuff instead of merely making mincemeat! Maybe it does. What was the landlord saying about never finding any mice? How can that be a magic fan? How?"

By now Jenny was caught up in our conviction. "We can't call the police. They would think we were insane. We don't even know Alice's surname, let alone where she—"

I had remembered the purse and swooped. I emptied it on a table over the beer mats. Car keys. Cosmetics. Tiny bottle of perfume. Ten- and twenty-pound notes, but no loose change. A tarnished old medallion. No driver's license, no check book, no hint of her full name or where she lived.

"At least we have the car keys," said Martin.

"There'll be no clues in her car," I told him. "She isn't any ordinary human being."

"Oh, we know that already, Derrick darling." My wife's tone was somewhat spiced with irony.

"She's a supernatural being. Didn't we know it all along?" I was echoing Martin, but those had been my sentiments anyway.

Charlotte didn't disagree with my assessment, however skeptical she may have seemed before. "And she's our friend," she reminded me. "*Was,* at any rate! So two supernatural forces have collided here—"

"Or come together. Like the poles of a magnet, like anode and cathode."

"What do you suppose our landlord knows about that fan?"

I laughed. "Our Mr. Chalmers doesn't realize the fan's possessed. He thinks Tiger was a demon mouser. I doubt he knows much about the stone that was drilled to dust to make space for the fan. The ancient stone, the sacrifice stone." A hard pain in my left hand alerted me to the fact that I was clutching that medallion from Alice's purse. As I opened my palm, the pain numbed to a cold tingling.

"Carry on." Charlotte eyed the metal disc intently, an amulet from some ancient time.

Words struggled to the surface like flotsam from a shipwreck. Don't hold them down. Relax. Let them bob up.

"The vibrations of the sacred stone imbued that space up there. When the stone was destroyed, the force possessed the fan that replaced it. At least a fan could *do* something, unlike a block of stone. It could open up a channel—to somewhere—a feeding channel. No one had fed the stone for centuries. It lay neglected, inert. Some Elizabethan builder picked it up and used it as part of the pub wall. It stayed inert. It was hungry, weak. It was the demon side of . . . the angry past. But it was kin to Alice."

I was holding Alice's medallion out blatantly, like a compass. The disc was so worn that its face was almost smooth; I could barely make out faint symbols unknown to me. A coin from the realm of magic, I thought, from the domain of lamias and hungry spirits. The inscription was well-nigh erased. How had Alice kept her vitality so long? By connecting with people such as us? Preying on some, befriending others?

Jenny touched the piece of metal and recoiled as if stung. "It's freezing."

"That space up there is dangerous," said Charlotte, who had so boldly shone a light into it. "Still, it didn't bite my fingers off. It only reacts to some stimuli—Alice being the biggest stimulus of all, eh, fellows?"

"It took her by surprise," I said. "It was playing possum till we went to the toilet; till the vibrations tickled our bladders. Or maybe that was Alice's doing. She wanted to be alone with it. It overwhelmed her."

She had been well aware of it, must have sensed its true nature when we first brought her here. She was flesh; it was an object—her malign counterpart, which nevertheless yearned for her. She wanted to commune with a kindred force, but imagined she was stronger.

"We want her back, don't we?" Charlotte went on. "This is the machine age, right? We know machines. That thing's out of synch with the age."

"What are you driving at?" Martin asked his wife.

"You're a dab hand at fixing things, aren't you?" She jerked a thumb at the leaded window behind the bar counter. A NO VACANCIES sign hung facing us. Consequently anyone approaching from outside would read the alternative invitation, VACANCIES. "We'll spend the night here. You have a tool box in the car. When all's completely quiet, we'll sneak down, do a spot of dismantling, and reverse those damned fan blades so that the air blows into this room, not out. Air, and whatever else."

"Cigarette and cigar smoke is like foul incense to it," I found myself saying.

"She'll come back minced," muttered Jenny. "Spread all over the floor, sticking to the walls."

"Why should she? If it can take her apart, it can put her back together! We must try," insisted Charlotte.

We were blunderers. We were the opposite of stone-age man placed cold before the instrument panel of a Saab or Jaguar. We were techno-man faced with the stone and blood controls of some old, alternative world of spirit forces.

Chalmers appeared, and announced, "Your table's ready. If you'd like to come through?"

"I'm afraid there'll only be four of us," said Martin.

"Did the other lady leave? This *is* the time you booked for."

"I know. She was called away. A friend came for her. She had to leave her car. We'll see to that tomorrow."

Chalmers raised an eyebrow.

"Fact is," blustered Martin, "we'd like to enjoy a bit of a celebration. Special occasion! Do you have two double rooms free for the night? Don't want the police stopping us afterward. Breathalyzing us. Can't risk that."

The landlord brightened. "We do, as it happens."

"We'll take them."

"Mr. Chalmers," said Charlotte, "out of curiosity, why did you mount that fan in that particular position?"

"Had to put it somewhere didn't we? That was the first year we came here, oh . . . a long while ago. As I recall, the plaster up there was prone to staining. Dark damp stains. The stone behind was . . ." He wrinkled his nose. "Oozy." Changing the subject, he waved at the counter. "If you get thirsty during the night," he joked, "help yourselves. You're regulars. Guests can drink anytime. Just leave a note for me to tot up."

Charlotte beamed at him. "Thank you very much, Mr. Chalmers."

Yes, I thought, we're all raving insomniacs. We'll certainly be holding a quiet party down here at two in the morning.

"My pleasure. Will you come this way?"

If we were supposed to be celebrating, Chalmers and his wife and the pair of waitresses from the village must have decided that the Roebuck's cuisine wasn't our pleasure that evening, to judge from how we picked at it. Or else we were engaged in a peculiar silent quarrel about the choice of fare. However, we did sink some wine, almost a bottle apiece. As we toyed with our food, the restaurant began to fill up with local subgentry enjoying a night out. When we returned to the other room for coffee, the place was crowded and the fan was busily sucking smoke out. Incense of drugful death, I thought, wondering whether this might be a phrase from Keats.

Jenny and I lay stiffly on top of the bedspread, never quite sinking below the surface of sleep. Eventually our wrist-watch alarms roused us. Soon Charlotte tapped at our door. She had a torch. We tiptoed down creaky though carpet-muffled stairs to rendezvous with Martin, who had switched on the dim wall lamps in the bar and was up on a chair, scrutinizing the surface of the Xtractall with a powerful torch beam. Before we went up to our separate bedrooms, he had fetched his tool kit—nonchalantly, as though the metal box was a suitcase containing our absent pajamas and nighties.

"Charlotte," he said, "nip behind the counter and find the switch for the fan. It's bound to be labeled. Make sure that it's off. Not that being off might make much difference!"

"Why not?"

"How do mice get sucked into it overnight?"

"*If* they do," I said. I should have followed this thought through. I should have pursued this possibility. I should have!

"Fan's off," she stage-whispered.

"Right. Up on a chair, Derrick. Hold the torch."

I complied, and Martin unscrewed the housing, then removed the safety grille.

" 'Course, it mightn't be possible to reverse the action. . . ." Perspiration beaded his brow. He wasn't looking forward to plunging his hands into the works. "Hold the beam steady. Ye-ssss. The mounting unfastens here, and here. Slide it out. Turn it round. Bob's your uncle."

He worked away. Presently he withdrew the inner assembly gingerly, reversed it, slid it back inside.

"I keep imagining Alice walking in," said Jenny. "What silly jokers we would seem. What a studenty sort of prank, gimmicking a fan so that cold and smoke blow *into* the pub!"

Martin unclenched his teeth. "If Alice tried to come through the front door now, she'd probably set off a burglar alarm. . . . There we are! Pass the grille up, Jenny, will you? Now the slats. It's got to be just the way it was before. . . ."

We both stepped down and cleared the chairs away, then hauled a table aside to clear a space, as if Alice would simply float down from that little opening above, her feet coming to rest lightly on the carpet.

"Switch the power on, Charlotte. Got a cigar handy, Derrick?"

When I shook my head, Charlotte brought a pack from behind the counter, stripping the cellophane wrapper with her nails. Lighting a panatela, I didn't merely let the smoke uncurl. I sucked and blew out powerfully.

"Let's all hold hands and wish," suggested Jenny.

We did so. Me, puffing away like a chimney, Jenny, Martin, and Charlotte. What silly jokers.

Clunk-clack. The slat opened and the fan whirred, blowing a dusty breeze down at our faces. The noise of the mechanism altered. Without actually becoming louder, the fan seemed to rev up as if a furious turbine were spinning inside the wall almost beyond the pitch of our ears. Our chorus line retreated. Then it happened.

Matter gushed through the slats of the fan—bubbling, convulsing substances, brown and white and crimson, blobs

of yellow, strands of ginger and black—which all co-
alesced into a surging column of confusion struggling to
reassemble itself before our eyes.

"Alice!" squealed Jenny.

The thing before us was Alice, and it wasn't Alice. It
was her, and it was a cat, and it was mice and iridescent
black beetles and spiders and flies, whatever the fan had
swallowed. The shape was human, and most of the mass
was Alice, but the rest was fur and wings and tiny legs
and all else, melted together, interwoven with scraps of
clothing, black hair growing out at random. I was too appalled to scream.

The Alice-creature jerked brown lips apart as if tearing
a hole in its head, and *it* might have wanted to shriek. The
noise that emerged was a coughing, strangled growl. Fac-
etted eyes ranged the room. And us; and us.

"We're sorry!" babbled Martin. "We're so sorry. Tell
us what to do!"

Unbidden, I knew. Terrified, I snatched from my pocket
the medallion and the keys to the Saab and tossed these
onto the table nearest to the half-human creature.

Her fingers seized the keys. Her legs took her to the
front door. Her hand unlatched and unbolted the door—so
she was still intelligent. Tearing the front door open, she
fled into darkness.

A few moments later an engine roared, headlamps stabbed
the night, tyres gouged gravel. Her Saab slewed its way
onto the road. It was Martin who shut the door and re-
locked it—he had been wrong about burglar alarms. There
were none.

"What have we done?" moaned Jenny.

"Maybe we saved her from something worse," I said.
"Maybe she knows how to heal herself. She left her medallion . . . why would she do that?"

Martin groaned and sat down heavily. "You don't need
fucking jewelry when your body's glistening with bits of
beetles."

I gathered the worn, cryptic medal up. "This is much more than jewelry. We'd better keep it."

"No," mumbled my wife, as I dropped the disc into my jacket pocket.

"It would be terrible not to have it to give to her if she comes back."

"It could *lead* that thing to us, Derrick."

"What's going on?" John Chalmers had come downstairs, attired in a paisley dressing gown and, God help us, a nightcap with dangling tassel. He seemed to be holding something behind his back—a cudgel, a shotgun? He moved in behind the counter and laid down whatever it was.

"Our friend came back for her car," Charlotte attempted to explain. "We're sorry we woke you."

"You're all fully dressed. You weren't intending to . . . depart?"

"You said we could partake of a late drink if we wished, Mr. Chalmers."

"Mm. Screwdrivers?"

For one stupid moment I imagined he was offering to fix cocktails for us. However, he was eyeing Martin's tools, still lying in view.

Charlotte was quick on the uptake. "Our friend's car needed fixing. That's why she had to leave it earlier."

Chalmers shook his head skeptically.

"I'd like a brandy, please," she told him. Her hand was straying automatically to the shoulder bag she had brought down with her, hunting in it . . .

"Don't smoke, love!" Martin said urgently. "If you have any, don't light up! Make that two brandies, will you? Doubles."

"Same for us," I said.

As Chalmers busied himself, Martin nodded significantly at the fan. It was still set to blow, not suck. Could anything else emerge from between those slats? Or was the eerie zone beyond its blades, the zone of the past, empty now? Where the hell had my panatela gone? I was dimly aware of discarding it when the fan began to gush. Ah—it was lying in an ashtray. Gone out, by the look of it. Nevertheless, I crushed the cigar into extinction. How could we put the fan to rights? Chalmers would be on the alert till daybreak. We couldn't. We would have to abandon the Roebuck in the morning, abandon and never come back. We gulped our brandies and trooped upstairs.

Next morning, haggard and exhausted, we ate bacon and eggs in the restaurant, paid our bills, and went out to the two cars. The day was bright and crisp; frost lingered.

"So, no more Fridays for us," Martin said dully. "Get rid of that medallion, will you, Derrick?"

"Alice may need it," I said.

"She may need us, she may need you," said Charlotte, "but not in the same way as before."

We parted and drove off from the Roebuck through the dead, cold countryside.

Jenny worked on me all weekend about that wretched medallion until I did promise to dispose of it. On Monday morning, walking through London to work, I dropped the worn disc down a sewer grating.

That night I dreamed about Alice, the Alice we had known before. This time she beckoned me lasciviously toward a doorway. She dropped her clothing. Naked, she invited me.

On Tuesday, prior to a meeting with some Japanese about supplies of Butadiene, Martin phoned me at the office.

"A car followed me home last night, Derrick. It hung well back, but when I was passing through————"—he mentioned a village with some decent street lighting—"I'm sure it was a Saab. Thought I'd better tip you off, eh? I've been thinking . . ." He sounded furtive. "I've been thinking about Alice. She never knew where we lived, did she?"

"I'm not sure she wanted to know."

"She knows now, so far as I'm concerned." He rang off.

Martin didn't phone again—though I made a call, to Webster-Freeman, publishers. They had never heard of an Alice. I wasn't surprised.

It's Friday night, and I'm driving home on my own, listening to Vivaldi's *Four Seasons*. It's the time that should be the happy hour. Jenny and I both took our cars to MK today. Headlights are following me, always keeping the same distance behind whether I speed up or slow down. If Alice comes calling, what do I give to her now?

Since Monday I've been increasingly haunted by mental snapshots of the old Alice. The other day I heard on the radio how the average male thinks about sex eight times an hour; that's how often Alice crosses my mind.

I realize that I've fallen in love—or in lust—with her. Does Martin secretly feel the same way—for his "lamia"? These feelings overpower me as surely as I was possessed in the pub that night by an urge to piss, the need to release myself. Even after what happened, maybe Alice left that medallion behind to protect us—from the altered lamia? Now that token no longer does so.

Ahead there's a lay-by where a caravan is parked permanently: Sally's Café, serving breakfast to truck drivers all day long—but not by night, when it's locked up, shuttered, abandoned.

I'm pulling in, and braking fifty yards past the caravan. Will the car in my mirror overshoot, pass by? No. It pulls in too. It parks abreast of Sally's Café, douses its lights. A Saab, I'd say.

The driver's door swings open. Soon I may understand all about Alice and her domain, which we first denied, then stupidly desecrated. Has the past's love of us all turned sour now? Grown vicious?

A dark, amorphous figure emerges from the Saab, and rushes toward me. I'll let her in. The Alice we knew always appreciated jokes. The final joke is: I've become an almighty fan of hers. Will I have time to tell her? To hear her laugh—or shriek? I open the door. I can't help myself.

Best known for his four-volume work *The Book of the New Sun,* and the novels *The Urth of the New Sun* and *Soldier of the Mist,* Gene Wolfe is a winner of both the Nebula Award and the World Fantasy Award. "In the House of Gingerbread," his house story in *The Architecture of Fear,* was nominated for a World Fantasy Award. His most recent books are the collections *Storeys From the Old Hotel* and *Endangered Species* and the novel *Soldier of Arete.* Gene Wolfe lives in Barrington, Illinois.

This story of a man on an errand in a fantastically altered America merges the bright optimism of such tales as "Leaf by Niggle" by J. R. R. Tolkien with a darker, more horrific sensibility—perhaps that of the Käthe Kollwitz drawing "Death Recognized as a Friend."

The Haunted Boardinghouse

GENE WOLFE

E nan Bambrick had left the university at the close of
his third year. It had been due only to the largess of a
gentleman of his neighborhood, a certain Dr. Foxxe,
that it had been possible for him to attend at all; but the
doctor had married again, and his bride had not approved
of his charity—or indeed of any other expenditure not devoted to her adornment.

The news reached Enan at midwinter. He had saved a
little money; and his college, which professed to cherish
classicists, had permitted him to run up an inconsiderable
debt, to be repaid if his patron's interest should reawaken,
or if Enan should find another, or if ever he was himself
in a position to repay it.

But when spring came and the roads were once more
passable, he was informed that his business with Calpur-
nius Siculus and Pomponius Mela was now ended, for the
time being at least. His fellows urged him strongly to steal
what books he could from the library in order that he might
trade them for food while pursuing his studies in those that

remained. He rejected this well-intended advice, departing the halls of learning with no luggage beyond a clean shirt, a collection of coins begged upon his behalf by his dearest friend, and a tattered, leather-bound *Moralia*—this last wholly his own, the gift of one of his professors, who, having found a better one, no longer wanted it.

Upon reaching his native town, some nine days after setting out and after privations too easily imagined, he discovered that his father, a tailor, had small need of his assistance. Through his father's influence, however, he was at length able to secure a position as a draper's clerk; and a draper's clerk he remained for something in excess of a year. *Alis volat propriis.*

He flies with his own wings—but not too high, for he slept, with two brother clerks, in the loft above the shop. And if he continued to dine at his parents' table once or twice a week, if he read *Moralia* on long summer evenings, if he made for himself a little manual of Latin in a foolscap notebook, the others had peculiarities no less striking; and it was by no means apparent that his eventual end was to be in any way different from theirs.

Spring returned, and it struck Enan with almost unbearable poignancy that a year had passed; many of the faces he had known would soon be gone. There would be much talk of examinations now, and much casting of summer plans. The wealthiest students would issue invitations—though not, of course, to such as he had been. The ancient apple on the common (said to date from the second millennium) would be wreathed in bridal white. '

Even at the draper's, summer was not altogether without its pleasures. The shop closed early on Wednesday and Thursday, and was closed altogether on Monday. Enan discoursed upon Virgil to certain attentive cows and buttercups, and wrestled and fished with two younger brothers. He had very nearly become reconciled to a lifetime of praising, measuring, and selling cotton, linen, and wool when the letter came. It was from the kind friend who had

begged coins for him; and because it was the most important, and very nearly the only, letter he had ever received,
it will be given here in full.

My Dear Enan,

    We have heard nothing of you here, but I trust you are doing
well. Ollie did not matriculate but will be back next term, or
so he says. Jo is married now. I doubt you know him.
    I am writing to tell you about a letter I got from a distant
relation called Seely. He keeps a little school and wants somebody to take charge of the library there and tutor a bit. Putting
it as a favor, he asks me to come. I intend to die an M.A.,
and so I told him I could not, but I might know of someone.
Praised you to the firmament, you may be sure. Seems to be
board, with a trifle of salary. You'd have to help him with this
and that at all hours from what he says, and there might be
tips from parents now and then. If you are interested in it,
write to the Headmaster, New Lake School, Granville.

Your friend always,
Leo R. Pruitt, B.A.

Enan's hands were shaking before he had finished his
first reading of this letter, which he read through a second
time, and a third, before refolding it and laying it aside.

To be master of a library! There would be scores of
books—there might well be hundreds. There would be
funds, perhaps, now and then for the acquisition of more.
He could continue his studies, prepare for an eventual return to the university. It might even be possible to complete his degree in the vicinity of Granville, concerning
which he knew nothing except that it lay some fifty miles
to the east.

Or perhaps in time some wealthy family might desire a
tutor to accompany its heir. Enan had known several such
individuals, half teacher and half servant. A tutor might
attend a class or two himself, might take on an additional
pupil here and there in order to make that possible. And
who could be more suitable? . . . young Arthur's present
tutor . . . known and respected . . . himself.

It says something for Enan's character that he wrote his friend to thank him before writing the headmaster of New Lake School. Then, and only then, with much chewing of the draper's already well-chewed pen, with much scratching of head and much wringing of hands and walking up and down, did he dare address Mr. Seely, modestly and even humbly, expressing *ab imo pectore* his entire willingness to accept the position on whatever terms Mr. Seely might think suitable. With what care this letter was folded and stamped, with what feelings it was committed to the town's post office, need not be described.

The tobacconist around the corner had in his youth been a stoker of coaches, and Enan seized the earliest opportunity to question him regarding Granville.

"You're not figuring on staying very long?" the tobacconist inquired, knocking out his pipe.

"I might." Enan was scrupulous. "A friend of mine's got family there."

The tobacconist shrugged. "Lock your door, lad. And shut your window, too. You know the coach don't run?"

Enan shook his head.

"Not no more—used to be a big place." The tobacconist did not know whether there was a university in Granville or near it, had never heard of New Lake School.

June was nearly spent already. July passed without word. The pupils at New Lake School, Enan told himself, very probably did not attend classes during the summer months; it might well be that Mr. Seely himself had gone afield.

Toward the end of August, in a fever of anxiety, he wrote again.

When the harvest was nearly in, when cartloads of pumpkins were to be seen in every street and the breath of men and horses smoked at two the afternoon, when the bell of the grammar school that had been his own sounded before sunrise, and little troupes of its pupils went from door to door at dusk, habited as witches, tunnel men, and ghouls, the letter arrived.

It was torn and stained, and had been marked by a town

far to the south. When Enan opened it, he discovered that it had been composed in August—by one of those coincidences that seem nearly preternatural, upon the same date that he had penned his second missive. As a precedent has now been established, this tattered letter, too, will be given in full. *Usus magister est.*

Mr. Bambrick:

You appear nicely fitted for the position in question. I should appreciate it if you would come at once; in any event you must arrive before the fifteenth of September, at which time our new term commences. Please consider this urgent.

G. Vincent Seely

Enan wrote immediately, informing Mr. Seely that his letter had miscarried; but he slept very little that night, and in the morning, with every apology he could lay tongue to, but with the tenacity of one clinging to his last hope, he resigned his post with the draper. In less than an hour, he had packed his scant belongings and bade his parents farewell.

There was, as the tobacconist had warned him, no coach to Granville. There was, however, a coach to Bradford, which was, Enan was assured, not much over ten miles from it. Noon found him aboard, having secured a half-price ticket by his promise to help fire and carry water, and to push if necessary. Vast and clumsy, streaming brownish-black smoke, it departed at a pace no horse could have maintained for more than half a mile; and Enan knew for the first time (and the last) the exhilaration of rapid, tireless motion. The night's hard frost had left every twig of every bush and every blade of grass in every meadow traced with white. White, too, were the plumes of spent steam leaking from the coach's cylinders; white still, they froze upon the rattling window panes until the interior was left in milky twilight, and Enan was forced to lay his book aside.

The man in the seat across the aisle asked whether he

was going to Bradford. He shook his head. "No, to Granville."

"Hello . . . To Granville? Is that your home?"

Enan shook his head again.

"Know the place?"

"No," Enan said truthfully. "I've never been there. Where are you from?"

"Bradford." The man paused, sucking his teeth. "You have a care, hear me?"

"I'll surely try to," Enan said. "It's a dangerous place, I take it?"

The man turned to look at the sheeted ice on his own window for a moment, and Enan feared he had offended him.

"Granville's an odd sort of place, that's all," his fellow passenger told him at last. "Know anything about its history?"

Enan shook his head.

"It's old, that's all. They say it goes back to the first settlers hereabouts. Older than that, maybe."

Enan ventured to ask how that was possible.

"Oh, there was people here before. We just don't like to talk about them is all. And then Granville wasn't left empty in the war like most places. There was more boats on the river then, and Granville had something to do with them—I don't know what. Anyhow, walls got put up all around, and they're still there. There's fever and worse in the swamps, too. Things left over from the wars, just like the walls, they say."

"Perhaps you could put me on the road to Granville when we get to Bradford," Enan suggested. "That is, if you would be so good."

His fellow passenger cocked an eyebrow. "How you going to get across the river?"

That was what Enan himself wondered as he studied it from a pier of the ruined bridge. The ice near the shore seemed solid enough; but a winding snake of dark water showed near the center of the wide channel, vagrant and threatening. The most sensible thing to do, he realized, would be to stay the night in Bradford and hope for a cold one that would make for stronger ice in the morning; but he commanded only scant funds, and he was far too diffident to beg a lodging from the traveler he had talked with on the coach, even if he were able to locate his house.

Yet the short autumn day was nearly spent. Something would have to be done soon, if he was not to undergo a freezing night in the open air.

After a few moments of indecision, he decided to work his way upstream along the bank. It might well be (he told himself) that at some point sound ice stretched across the entire river; or if there was no such crossing place, he might come upon some riverside cottage whose occupants would take him in.

It was in this way that he was granted his first sight of Granville, after three weary miles. The sun was setting behind him, and its level rays illuminated the squat gray battlements as well as the venerable spires and skeletal towers overlooking them. Granville had been, as he now saw, built upon a low hill. The flooding of a century ago had turned the fertile bottomlands around it to marsh, among whose myriad shallows and tussocks the bewildered river lost its way. Isolated though this sunset town was, and decayed as Enan felt it must certainly be, it seemed to him to breathe promises as well as threats, to sparkle as well as to glower. Possibly some untimely recollection of the enchanted isles mentioned by Philostratus colored his thinking.

He blinked, and then Granville seemed enchanted indeed, for he realized that a complete path might be traced across the ice from the point from which he viewed it to the high ground that had preserved the moated town—not a direct path, but a path all the same, one that would skirt every dark reach of open water by a margin that appeared safe; the distance would be, he imagined, hardly greater than a mile.

He had a mile yet to go when the treacherous ice splintered beneath his feet, and icy water closed over his head.

Enan dreamed of cold, of riding forever in a jolting cart,
and of monstrous shadows that accompanied and pursued
him; but always chiefly of cold, and once that he lay in his
grave. His father stood at the graveside, threading a needle
in the murky twilight; his mother wept, her tears cutting
his cheeks and lips like sleet.

He was thrown into hell, and there burned for all eternity, the sport of demons; and though he cried aloud to
God and to his mother, they could not hear him, or perhaps would not. A fiend wrapped him in a sheet of flame;
he cast it aside, and for whole ages roamed hell's contorted corridors, moaning in his agony and igniting all that
he touched. There he met an angel; and though he could
not voice his strangled pleas, he fell prostrate at her feet.
And she, for one moment only, laid her cool hand upon
his burning head.

Chill winter sunlight streamed from a small, high window of many panes. For a long time it seemed to Enan
that it dyed the quilt, as sunshine through the windows of
a church may dye the faces of the congregation; when he
looked again, a little wooden tray had grown there, and
sprouted a bowl and a tall and narrow cup, each one a
cylinder of the lumbering coach. Something hot pressed
his lips, and after a while he decided that it must be a rose
aflame, because its fragrance filled his nostrils.

"Eat. This is very good. That's right, open your mouth."

A heavy-armed, wide-faced woman dipped her spoon into
the soup again. She had blue eyes and white hair. "I died,"
Enan told her.

She smiled, studying him. "You will, if you don't eat."

In some remote fashion Enan felt he should question her,
though he did not know which questions to ask.

When he woke again, the window was dark, his throat aflame. His groping hands found a ewer beside his bed; he drank from it, and was as before. *Nobis cum semel occidit brevis lux, nox est perpetua una dormienda.*

A long sleep indeed, but not in fact a perpetual one. He sat up and saw a shadow fly the room.

Standing, he nearly fell. He clutched the bedpost, leaned against the chill, plaster wall, and at length managed a step, then another. The window was too high to let him look out. The gray light beyond might have been dawn or dusk, or merely that of a dark winter's day. The room held the narrow bed in which he had lain, a washstand with a mirror half spoiled by damp, a chest of drawers, and a plain wooden cane-bottomed chair. The ceiling was much lower on the side of the room that held the bed—low enough that he might knock his head against it, though he was not tall.

He went to the door through which the shadow had run, half afraid he would find it locked. It opened with a squeak. The shadow had neither opened it nor closed it, he felt certain; the shadow had not been real, then. Too-loose clothing hung limply from nails beside the door. Bracing his back against it, he put on his trousers, then added his shirt while seated on the chair.

Beyond the door lay a contracted hall. A cramped stairway ended almost at his feet; his was the first door of three. The second opened onto an even smaller room, much like his. The bed was made (though not very neatly), and a clean shirt reclined at ease upon it. There were tattered books—*A Modern Geography of America* and *English Composition*—on a folding table. Enan left, shutting the door carefully behind him.

The third door, two steps higher than the others, opened on a wide, shingled roof, not in the best repair. Here a fresh wind greeted him; upon it, sailing like some swift sloop of war, rode a peregrine falcon. It passed him at eye-level, perhaps twenty feet away, and he succumbed to the urge to wave. If it saw him, it gave no sign.

After testing the latch to make certain the door could not lock him out by swinging shut, he stepped out onto the shingles. A thaw had come, surely; the wind held that watery renewal that signals that winter is on holiday. The confused sounds of play drifted up to him from some trampled spot he felt must be very far below—this though a half-naked tower at no great distance rose much higher.

Turning to look back at the place from which he had come, he found it an octagonal turret. One narrow window showed the ill-made bed with its occupant shirt.

He advanced, climbing the slope toward the ridgeline. An irregular clump of wilting feathers recalled the corsair falcon. Melting snow slumped in the shadow of a dormer. A second turret sprang into view, and a third. Chimneys he had assumed belonged to other buildings were, it now appeared, parts of this one; for although a whole jumble of roofs—shingled, leaded, and tiled—lay between them and himself, there was no gap to indicate that the monstrous house had ended.

From the ridge he saw it whole, four-faced, a beast without a back. The decayed wall, an earthenwork battlemented with wood and stone, lay only a street away; beyond it stretched the marsh he remembered, sheathed in ice. The breeze whipping his hair was pleasant and cool, sparkling with dancing snowflakes. He filled his lungs. How good he felt! How free now from sickness and pain!

The shadow of the falcon raced toward him across the roof; for a moment it seemed that a second shadow raced with it, that (perhaps) of a girl or slender woman. Then both were gone, and there was only the falcon, wheeling above the boys who romped in the street below, then darting away.

Though he told himself that there was nothing left for him to do, he was reluctant to return to the narrow bed in which he had lain. Was it possible to reach the ground from this roof? Or to reenter this strange house by another door? He wandered aimlessly until he stood before a garret window and peered into a bare room in which a pale maiden in black sat weeping before a second window. When he tapped on the glass, she lifted the sash for him.

"What were you doing out there?"

"Looking," he told her, and hoped she would not ask at what.

"That's good." She hesitated. "You're Enan Brambrick. Do you remember me?"

Embarrassed, he shook his head.

"I came to see you several times while you were so ill."

"That was certainly very kind of you." He groped. "What's the matter?"

"Nothing's the matter." She wiped her eyes on her sleeve.

"Why were you crying?"

"For a boy who fell from this window."

"I've been looking at that," he said. "It—it doesn't go outside, not like the one I came through. There's another room over there."

She nodded. "Another boy sleeps in that room now."

"Then this boy couldn't have fallen—" He did not want to contradict her, and realized he already had. "Or at least," he finished weakly, "that's how it seems to me."

She rose. "You don't know this house. Come. I think you should go back." She opened the door and took his hand.

The corridor seemed warmer, though it was not until he felt its warmth that he knew he had been cold. With a key she took from her sleeve, she opened the protesting door of a storeroom that was practically empty. Daylight stole faintly through the slanted roof overhead.

"Is this your house?" he asked her.

"Not yet."

A ladder led to the floor below. She went down it first, without hesitation, and as far as he could see, without effort. He felt tired by the time he reached the bottom.

The corridor was wider here, the ceiling higher, the walls prickly with nails and pegs. "This was a fine house once," Enan said.

"Don't let him hear you." The pale maiden favored him with a sad smile. "He thinks it a fine house still."

"Who does?" he asked, but she did not reply. An open door revealed a wide room holding half a dozen cots. Beyond another, a gray-haired man sat writing at a desk; he did not look up as they passed. A second corridor was less spacious, the stair at its termination nearly as steep as the ladder. "This isn't the best part," the maiden told him.

He nodded.

"Go up. I'll follow you."

There was an open door at the top of the steep stair. In the little room beyond, a white-haired woman bent over something shapeless. The small room was his own; his clothing hung there. "Lie down," the maiden whispered. "Hurry!"

He did, and the woman shook his shoulder. "Yes?" he said. "What is it?"

"Thanks be!" She laid a plump red hand over her heart. "I thought—never mind. We ought to have somebody to sit with you, truly we ought."

Enan wanted to suggest the maiden, but she had gone. He sat up.

"How're you feeling?"

"Weak."

"No wonder, when you won't eat." She laid a tray on his lap. "That's good stew. I made it myself, and the boys loved it. I've saved the bottom of the kettle for you—that's where the best meat goes. Can you hold the spoon?"

He could. The stew was delicious.

"That's it. You shouldn't give an old lady such a fright."

"Where is this?" Enan asked. "This house?"

"Corner of Gate and Prescott. That's what I always tell people—what the headmaster tells when he writes them, too."

Enan's spoon rattled against the side of the bowl. "Is this the New Lake School?"

" 'Course it is. Eat your stew."

To mollify her, he took another bite.

"They found his letter in your pocket—them that saved you did. So naturally they brought you here."

Enan's heart pounded as though his ribs were the bars of a prison. "Is the post filled?"

"You," the white-haired woman told him, "aren't going to be filling any post, young fellow, not for a while. First, you're going to get better. Then you're going home to your poor mother, that's worried to death about you. We get a letter from her in every mail."

"Mrs.— Are you Mrs. Seely?"

The white-haired woman laughed. "Wish I was that young and pretty again, dear. I'm Mrs. Boyle."

"Mrs. Boyle, is the post filled? I really must know."

"Yes, it is, and don't you bother your head about that anymore. You drink your tea."

Hours passed before his next visitor arrived; and though Enan was awake, they flew swiftly in utter idleness. *Temporis ars medicina fere est.*

This second visitor was a boy of twelve or thirteen, who peeped around the door with wondering eyes. "Hello," Enan said.

"Hello."

"Come in, if you want. What's your name?"

"Wade."

"Do you go to school here, Wade? To the New Lake School?" He might, Enan thought, have punned upon the name of the school and that of the boy; but it did not seem worth the effort, and was probably inadvisable.

The boy nodded. "I'm finished—my last class. I came up to put my books away."

"May I see them?"

They seemed very heavy; Enan nearly dropped them. "Do you like any of these?"

The boy hesitated and fidgeted, struggling almost openly with the cultural demand that he express nothing but contempt for learning. Eventually he triumphed. "That one, sir."

It was *A Modern Geography of North America*.

"Because it has colored maps?"

"Yes, sir. Where people used to live, the islands and all that stuff."

Enan quoted, " 'My boyhood saw Greek islands floating over Harvard Square.' "

"Yes, sir. I guess so. And this one."

English Composition. "They've got you reading Hemingway, of course. And—let's see—Kipling, Parker, Thurber, Crowley . . . no modern writers. My, my, W. H. Hudson. Do you like him?"

"Yes, sir. But there's only this one little bit."

Enan let the book fall to his quilt. "You have a library, don't you, Wade? Here at the school? Perhaps you could find more."

Bitterly the boy said, "He always says they haven't got it."

"I see."

"I just came to leave off my books, sir. They said for me to help you if you called or get somebody, so I thought it would be all right for me to look in."

"It was," Enan told him. "It was very kind of you."

"Thank you, sir."

"I do call, Wade. I need your help now." As decisively as he could, Enan pushed aside quilt and sheet. "I don't think I'm going to be very steady, Wade. Would you bring my shirt? There it is."

The little room whirled when he stood, but with the boy's help he stood again, and this time it was steadier.

"These are steep steps, sir. You better let me go down first."

"If I fall, I'll knock you down them."

"I won't *let* you fall, sir."

"Are there more stairs?" Enan asked when they reached the bottom. "Where is the library? What kind of house is this?" A streak of naked wood down the middle of the corridor betrayed a vanished carpet.

"Two more flights, sir. It's across the street."

"I'll be all right," Enan told him, "I'm feeling stronger."

"It's Headmaster Seely's house, sir. The town boys go home after class, but the rest of us board with him."

Enan nodded to show he understood. The second flight was wider than the first, and less steep; he clung to the banister while the boy braced his free arm.

"The teachers board here, too, except for Master Burke— he's married. And we rent rooms to travelers, too. It helps pay for the school."

"But is the school worth paying for, Wade? Do you learn?"

Clearly the boy had not thought about that; he did so now, although he sighed with relief when they reached the foot of the stairs safely. "It's supposed to be the best on this side of the river, sir. My folks sent me here, and it takes all day to get here from Gilman."

"That merely indicates it enjoys a good reputation," Enan explained patiently. "Do you consider it deserves it? Do you study rhetoric? What is personification?"

"Yes, sir. It's when you pretend something's a real person. Like, 'Nature will have her due.'"

"But isn't there a Nature, really? A blond lady who plans for the animals and so on?"

"No, sir. They have to do that themselves."

"Very good." Enan smiled. "Euphemism?"

"It's when Master Snyder says that Headmaster Seely's sick, sir."

"And he isn't?" Here, large bedchambers had been combined to make apartments; a ramp sought to smooth a change in levels. "These used to be separate houses, didn't they, Wade?"

"Yes, sir. No, sir. You're sick—he's drunk. They grew

together, like, because you couldn't build new houses inside the walls. But most of the people left when they had the siege."

"Classics? Who were the Eumenides? Euphemism's named for them."

The boy's face fell. "I don't know, sir."

"They were spirits of revenge, Wade. You see, the Greeks feared them so much that they called them the 'Gracious Ones,' which is what *Eumenides* means. Ancient pictures show them with wings and claws, and snakes in their hair."

"Really?"

"Yes, really. Most people say the Classics are a waste of time and effort, Wade; but once you know even a little, you find it illuminates a hundred other matters, making them both clearer and much more interesting. What's the largest city on the Great Lake?"

"West Chicago, sir."

"Excellent. The Pythagorean Theorem?"

" 'The sum of the areas of squares constructed on the sides of a right triangle will be found equal to the area of a square constructed on the hypotenuse.' We had to make a diagram that proved it."

"Proved it or illustrated it?"

"Illustrated it, sir."

"Very good. But you don't know who Pythagoras was, do you? Do you know anything about his other discoveries?"

"No, sir."

They had come to the final stair, broad enough for a coach. "You don't have to hold my arm here, Wade. Some of them are quite interesting; that concordant musical intervals correspond to numerical ratios, for example. . . ."

A maidservant in a long black dress with a white collar was lighting lamps on the floor below.

"You should have a coat, sir."

"But I have none, and so must do without."

The street was twilit, its ancient lamps darkened or half-destroyed, one lying (as it had for many years) parallel to the cracked walk, where it had gathered a trifling soil; the grasses and weeds that had sprouted from this had perished in the first frost, and lay limply beside their corroded parent pole, so many slaughtered children.

When its heavy doors had shut behind them, the school felt colder than the wind-sad street, perhaps simply because they had hurried across it, shoulders hunched, hugging themselves against its freezing sob. Here, in the two-hundred-year-old school, the atmosphere hung motionless, ripe with dust and chalk; their feet upon the naked planks evoked a cacophonous music of squeakings, squeals, and moans, as though they had brought in their train a goblin orchestra.

"Is the library on the first floor, Wade?"

"Yes, sir."

"That's well, I think."

The door was locked. Enan rapped on it, and when there was no response, pounded.

"Maybe he's gone, sir. There aren't any more classes."

"He is inside, smoking a cigarette." Enan thumped the door once more. It was opened by a man half a head taller than he, his senior by perhaps a decade; untidy heaps of disordered books formed a backdrop. The librarian said nothing, glaring at Enan and staring at the boy.

"*Green Mansions*," Enan told him. At this critical juncture his mind refused the name of the author. "Do you have it? Wade needs it."

The librarian withdrew and attempted to slam the door, an attempt that would have succeeded had it not been for Enan's foot. "Let us in! I'll look for it myself."

This provoked only a muttered curse.

Enan thrust an arm through the narrow opening. "That is my library, and you know it!" He threw his weight against the door.

"Don't, sir!"

"Before I fell sick"— Enan gasped for breath —"I was no weakling." It was a lie, but one the moment demanded. The door flew back, taking Enan with it. He had just time enough to see the librarian's clenched fist before it crashed into his face. He staggered, collided with a stack of books, and sent them flying as he fell.

Strangely the librarian's blows did not hurt, though each rocked his face like a boat. If he had known that fighting was thus painless, Enan reflected, he would have been less timid as a child. *Pax in bello.*

They found him sitting up, two books beside him, trying to stanch the gush of blood from his nose with his shirt.

"Good God," the gray-haired man said, and knelt beside him.

"I'm all right. A little weak."

"Tilt your head back," the boy urged him.

"You're right. I had forgotten. Are you Headmaster Seely, sir?"

"I'm Snyder, chemistry and biology. This is awful, young man. Intolerable!"

Enan nodded. "I shouldn't have. But I wanted to find . . ." The blood-soaked shirt muffled his voice. "Here's *The Book of a Naturalist,* Wade. It's Hudson's, too. And one that I chose for you myself, Hawthorne's *Wonder Book.* Take them, will you? I don't want to get them dirty."

The boy opened the latter at random. The bright old plate showed Bellerophon astride winged Pegasus, diving from the sky at the Chimera. Seeing the boy's eyes at that moment, Enan knew he had won, and that whatever might come afterward did not matter. *Nos exaequat victoria caelo.*

*   *   *

Headmaster Seely was burly, red-faced, and bald. He entered Enan's room somewhat diffidently, bringing with him the faint, heady aroma of corn whiskey. "Well, Enan, what did the doctor have to say?"

Enan, who could recollect no doctor and was innocent of the identity of his caller, replied, "He said I was making progress, sir." It seemed safe.

"And said the same to me. Indeed, indeed. Enan, I want to show you a letter I've written. Master Snyder speaks highly of you, by the way. I won't mail it unless you approve."

It was thus that Enan ascertained his visitor's identity, for he recognized the hand long before reaching the signature.

Mrs. Bambrick:

Although your son continues to mend, another month must pass before you have the pleasure of beholding him again, radiant with health as of old. After due consideration, my bride and I have resolved to proffer to him the post of School Librarian, which post he has consented to accept. At the Christmas holidays, Enan will return (as I suppose) to the bosom of his family. His family must, however, bear in mind that his duties will require his presence here before the fifteenth of January.

G. Vincent Seely

"You must compose yourself, my boy. Do you have a chill?"

"Yes, sir," Enan said humbly, returning the paper. "It will pass off. Mail that, please, sir. Today."

Headmaster Seely nodded. "I will."

"And—and accept my thanks. My very sincere thanks."

"Think nothing of it, my boy. Had my letter reached you in time . . . Well, no use in that. I'll tell Mrs. Boyle to bring you another blanket."

Enan woke to find it had been spread across his face. The air for which he gasped was hot and stale, his thin pillow damp with sweat. He pushed the blanket aside and sat up. The room was dark and refreshingly cool. Someone wept there, the sound a tiny whimpering; he heard a tear plash on the floor like one single drop of rain. "It's you, isn't it?" he asked.

"Yes, it is I."

"And you're Headmaster Seely's wife, the bride to whom he referred in his letter."

"Yes. I am his bride."

"You thought me dead," Enan said. "It was very good of you, wonderful of you, to mourn for me. But you don't have to sit there in the dark. Isn't there a candle, or a lamp?"

"I have my own."

Later Enan decided that it must have been on the floor, with the flame turned down so far that it had been practically invisible. Now it was in her hand, a small oil lamp with a metal base. He gasped at her beauty.

"Do you wish to walk with me?"

"Very much," Enan said. "That is, if you want me to. I mean, if you're going out, you shouldn't go alone. I've been told that this is a dangerous town."

"It isn't dangerous for me."

"Perhaps I had better take this blanket. I don't have a coat."

She did not reply. He pulled the blanket from the bed, folded it, and laid it across his shoulder.

The walls of the house were transparent to the light of her lamp. It was not that they had in any sense vanished; they were there, and Enan knew he could not walk through them. Yet he saw the sleeping boys; the weary man (small and thin, with graying, thinning hair) who sat before his window staring at the slender crescent moon; Headmaster Seely with his bottle and glass, his candle, and his old-fashioned revolver; the empty rooms; and the rooms that were not empty though no living man or woman or child slept or woke in them.

"This is the house of four faces," Seely's bride told
Enan, "but we must go outside for me to show them
to you."

The first and eldest was neoclassical. "This is a house
for gods," she said, "though the gods will never dwell in
such houses again. Men live in such a house like rats in a
house of men; yet it is possible to live there, and even to
be happy for a time."

"I understand." Enan unfolded the blanket and put it
over his head like a shawl and about his shoulders like a
cloak.

Slowly, hand in hand, she bearing her lamp in her free
hand while he clutched the blanket close with his, they
walked along Water Street.

"If it will not sadden you too much, could you point out
the window from which that poor boy fell to his death?
I'd . . ."

"Yes?" A half-smile played about her lips.

"I'd like to know where we were when we first met.
That's all."

"It is within the structure now," she told him.

"Oh, yes. I'd forgotten."

"But I will show it to you, if you will look closely. We
have a moment still." She raised her lamp, and he saw it—
faint yet distinct, outlined in flaking green paint. Even now
a boy was climbing across the sill.

"It was many years before he died, though he was horribly injured. That was why I wept, Enan."

"I see."

"You must turn quickly. There is a cutthroat behind you.
He raises his knife as I speak."

Enan whirled. The knife rang, falling to the old, cracked
walk; the cutthroat fled.

"He is a coward, as you saw. He could not meet you
face to face, though he tries so hard to win a smile from
me." Stooping, Seely's bride picked up the knife and handed
it to Enan. "This side is Tudor, as I was on the point of

telling you. Do you see the window high up that shows a faint blue light? That is the window of your room."

"What is the light?" he asked her.

"My lamp. Prescott is the next street. It was named for a man long dead, an historian."

"I remember." Enan nodded. "I've read his *History of the Conquest of Mexico.*"

"So had those who renamed this street, at the height of the siege. This face is neo-Victorian, as is your world. If you look closely, you can see the bullet holes."

Enan did not see them. "Some of the windows are broken."

"This part of the house is abandoned, save for a few rooms. Can you guess what the fourth face is, Enan? On Gate street?"

"I shouldn't have to guess. I crossed Gate Street to reach the school."

"Yes."

"But I can't remember—I never looked back. Modern?"

"Contemporary."

Gate Street was narrower than the rest, and darker because of it; yet Enan, looking along it, could make out the wall, the gate itself (open now) and the moonlit marsh beyond.

"The Mexican soldiers rushed down this street when the town fell. Your people fired upon them from this house and from the school, and from other structures along this street; and though many fell, they killed many. Some had only kitchen knives taped to broomsticks. Poisoned winds drove them into the streets, and there they died."

Enan coughed. His right arm stung, and he rubbed it with his left.

"When the Mexicans retreated south of the Ohio, the gates were rebuilt; but they stand open, as you see. Does it give you pleasure, knowing that your nation is so secure?"

He shook his head.

"The children beg that they be shut at night, saying that evil things enter the town by night, but it isn't done."

"Are the children right?" he asked.

"Sometimes."

"He's gone, that librarian," Mrs. Boyle told Enan. "Did you know?"

"I'm going down to the library today."

"No, you're not," she said positively. "You're not well enough yet."

But when she herself had left, he wrapped his blanket about his shoulders as he had when he had toured the four faces of the house; and he carried with him, with a sickly reverence, a dog-eared and water-stained *Moralia*—his contribution to the library that was to be his. Should Headmaster Seely resist the class he would propose, he could point out truthfully that their library already possessed one work in Latin at least. *Nullum est librum tam malum ut non ex aliqua parte prodesset.*

Some exploration proved necessary before he discovered the broad and kindly stairs that he had descended with Wade, for he found that he did not recall the way as well as he had supposed; but he reached the head of it at last, and was about to descend when he glimpsed a young woman in a green silk dress in the act of surrendering her furs to the maid.

The young woman glimpsed him as well, and gave a little shriek.

Enan stumbled backward, covering his face with the blanket.

That evening the boy brought a razor borrowed from Master Snyder, a scrap of soap, and a basin of warm water begged from the cook. He laid a towel across the pillow. "I've done this before," he told Enan. "You don't have to worry."

"I wasn't," Enan said. "Who was it you shaved?"

"My grandfather, after he got so sick. His secretary used to, but then he thought he'd stolen something and sent him away. I don't think he did. He was old, like my grandfather, and you could see how he felt about it."

Enan nodded, getting soapsuds on his nose. *"Omnia fert aetas, animum quoque."* Seeing the boy's incomprehension, he murmured, "All is borne away by age, even the mind."

"Yes, sir. He passed away in the fall, the day the pond froze, but I used to shave him twice a week until then. I was the only one he would let come near him with a razor."

It passed gently down Enan's left cheek, and the boy held it before his eyes to display the collection of curling hairs. "What was it like when you were dead, sir?"

Enan sighed. "Was I dead, Wade?"

"That's what everybody says, sir. What was it like?"

"Chill, while I was still in my body. I remember thinking that I lay in my grave while my mother wept over me. Burning hot, when I was no longer there. Hell was a labyrinth like the Minotaur's. I had no clue to guide me, but I stumbled down the winding corridors until I met Ariadne. She returned me to this life, I suppose."

The boy wiped the razor and began Enan's left cheek. "You were damned, sir?"

"I imagine so. They didn't tell me why, but then I suppose they don't have to. Was I dead for long, Wade?"

"Nobody knows. Mrs. Boyle came with another blanket, and you were dead. They sent for the doctor—that's what you have to do here—and he gave you injections. That's what I heard." The razor slipped. "Oh, I'm sorry, sir!"

"Did you cut me? I don't feel it." Enan touched his cheek and stared at his crimson fingers.

"Wait just a minute, sir. A piece of tissue will stop the bleeding."

"It doesn't matter," Enan told him; he was thinking of his walk, the cutthroat, and many other things.

"I don't want to get blood on the towel, sir."

When he was through, the boy took the old, spotted mirror from the washstand and held it so that Enan could see himself. "You won't frighten Mrs. Seely again, sir."

Enan rolled his head from side to side. "That wasn't Mrs. Seely, Wade."

"Yes, it was, sir."

The school library, when Enan reached it at last, he found to have attained that final stage of disorder in which apparent patterns are purely illusory. Now and again some volume might be discovered keeping company with one upon a similar subject; in the same way, a storm may wash ashore, at times, two objects of like color or size, but follow them with half the wreck of a schooner, or a tangled mat of kelp. The catalog was useless, inaccurate and out of date, prepared some years before (as Enan surmised), when the impossibility of repairing the computer was finally accepted, solely to impress Headmaster Seely. He threw it out and began anew, starting with the *Moralia* and sifting the worn volumes with patient delight. It was nearly a week before his fever returned.

Though she was often away, Mrs. Seely—the boy's Mrs. Seely—visited him at times, seating herself demurely in his rickety chair and watching him from the corners of her sly green eyes as she talked of clothes or gain. "As I've told George," she said, "he ought to move this whole school east of the mountains. The profit from the very first term would cover the relocation. You wouldn't mind packing all these up?" A heavy, sweet perfume and the smooth and almost greasy pallor of her décolletage made her seem a slightly stale confection. "Are any valuable?"

The only gem Enan had unearthed was Augustine's *Confessions*, brass-fitted and bound in decaying calf, with Latin and English on facing pages—the spoil of some pillaged seminary. He hid it after Modesty's first visit.

The difficulties he had anticipated in connection with his class vanished like smoke, as anticipated difficulties so often do. Headmaster Seely was only too happy to add another subject to the list he sent the parents of prospective students, and the boys took fire from Enan's own enthusiasm. When the maiden in black joined the class, as she often did, he was sorely tempted to ask why she had called herself the headmaster's bride—though any such question was surely better asked in private, and indeed it might be impolite to ask it at all. No doubt she had feared his importunities.

"When the ancient world was destroyed," Enan said, "those who sought to regain its knowledge studied Latin and Greek in order that they might read such books as had survived. *Notitia linguarum est prima porta sapientiae*—the knowledge of tongues is the chief door to wisdom. Like them, we seek to learn from the books of a previous age, but they are in our own tongue, for the most part. Why study Latin, then?" He pointed to a fat boy whose grades in other classes indicated he might be far brighter than he appeared.

"If we're ever to rise again," the fat boy said slowly, "it would be good to understand how they did; if we're going to fall further—and that's what I believe myself, Master Bambrick—it will probably be because of all the things we don't understand."

She was among the class, though he had not seen her enter. Softly she said, "Tonight." He turned to the board so that the boys could not watch his face, writing *Doctrina sed vim promovet insitam;* and when he turned back, she was gone.

That evening he carried the day's discovery up to his room. The pages of Ruskin's *Queen of the Air* had darkened to sepia and cracked, many were torn and some were gone altogether; yet what he read so enchanted him that he resolved to make a fair copy at the earliest opportunity. Headmaster Seely had been generous in the provision of paper; those sheets, Enan thought, might make a little book. Folded once and sewn with silk thread, they might bear Ruskin's words down another four centuries, just as Ruskin himself had borne Homer's.

". . . and she gave him strength in his shoulders, and in his limbs, and she gave him the courage"—of what animal, do you suppose? Had it been Neptune or Mars, they would have given him the courage of a bull or a lion; but Athena gives him the courage of the most fearless in attack of all creatures, small or great, and very small it is, but wholly incapable of terror,—she gives him the courage of a fly.

He woke cold, in a dark room. The candle had guttered to the socket, and she had not come—or if she had, had left again, having found him asleep in his chair. He rose, and discovered with some surprise that he was so weak he could hardly stand. The candles rattled in their drawer before he could extract a fresh one, and the hand that grasped the match trembled so much that he was forced to brace it with his left to light the wick.

Someone had thrust something white beneath his door. His first thought was that the maiden had left a note for him, but it was only a stamped letter, postmarked at the southerly town of Gilman the week before. When he unfolded the sheet it held, he discovered to his infinite astonishment several bills of no mean denomination.

Dear Master Bambrick,

Though it is somewhat early for Christmas gifts, we thought it better to send this now, since Wade has told us that you will return to your own home for the holidays.

Our gratitude goes with them. Wade's letters show clearly how much influence you have gained in a very short time, and how well that influence has been employed.

Wade is destined for the university, as you clearly realize. That you will do everything in your power to fit him for a career there, now and at the university itself should you so desire and his progress at New Lake continue satisfactorily, is the grateful wish of—

Charles & Natalie James

Enan smoothed the bills, marveled at the numbers in their corners for a minute or more, and after some thought pinned them inside his shirt, which he decided was fit for a third wearing in the morning.

This accomplished he draped the shirt carefully over the back of his chair, positioned the chair close to the head of his bed, heaped the rest of his clothes on the chair seat, read Mrs. James's letter a second time, and a third, and retired. Lying in the dark with his hands behind his head, he told himself that he had almost certainly misunderstood. She had not said *tonight,* but *tomorrow,* or perhaps *Tuesday*—although it might be that she was delayed. No matter how beautiful she was, or how good, she was still, like every other woman and every man, at the mercy of Fate. What was it Apollo had confided to King Croesus? "Even the gods . . . Not even the gods. . . ."

She woke him with kisses. "May I lie here beside you? How warm you are!" Her hand was a benediction. "Paul Snyder swears you can't infect me."

Enan had kissed a woman, had held her hand and embraced her—had done those things three times precisely beneath the ancient apple that stood at the center of the common. He responded as a boy, half-afraid, half-asleep, and wholly unbelieving. When she left him at last, she left him frightened and unbelieving still. As if in a trance he heard the scratching of the match, and shut his eyes against the flare of light and the steadier radiance of the candle.

"Do you mind? I can't very well get dressed in the dark. Besides, I thought you might want to see me."

Rolling his head on the pillow, he looked. Looked, and saw Modesty Seely wiping herself with one of his handkerchiefs. She posed for him briefly, standing on tiptoes to appear taller, her arms above her head to lift her breasts. "Aren't I beautiful?"

He managed to nod.

"I want to tell George." She smiled. "Let him know where I've been. I want to see his face."

A shadow dashed from the room.

"Can you fasten this for me, Enan? There's a little catch at the back."

When she had gone, he sat for a time on the bed, his bare feet flat upon the freezing floor. At length he stood, washed as well as he could in water from the ewer, and began to dress. The money was still pinned to his shirt; he noted it without interest, as he noted the burnt matchstick on the floor. The first shot came as he was tying his shoes.

For a moment he remained just as he was, the shoelaces in his hands, listening to the echoes and the sounds of running feet. He completed the bow and pulled it tight. Somewhere, on a floor below him, someone was pounding on a door. The second shot came as he stood.

He picked up the candle and looked about the little room. Was there anything here he wanted? He remembered the coat he had worn as far as Bradford and lost when the ice gave way beneath him. It would be nice, he thought, if that coat were returned to him now. But it was not there.

An odd sound had replaced the shouts and the running feet; he thought of some great animal, a fighting bull or a buffalo, rushing through a thicket of thin and very brittle twigs. There was a smell of smoke. He stuffed three letters from his mother in one pocket, *The Queen of the Air* in another.

He opened the door upon a darkling landscape. Sullen fires smoldered far off, and a dead man in bronze armor lay almost at his feet. Dark bowmen on lean and eager horses wheeled like the falcon; one loosed an arrow, missing his head by a scant inch.

"The dead have need of you, Enan."

It was the maiden. "You came!" he said.

"This is their darkest hour. Today ten legions fell at Cannae. Varro escaped to Venusia with seventy horsemen, and those seventy constitute the Army of Rome tonight."

He nodded, resigned yet frightened still. "Marcus Junius Pera will raise a new army. No one can say how."

The maiden smiled, and it was the smile of one who knows a secret. "Some scholars have called that an army of freed slaves and boys."

They had begun to walk over the battlefield. Enan said, "Boys and freed slaves could never defeat Hannibal. Pera will require every man. Take me to him." A gust of smoke made him sneeze. He stepped across a shabbily clothed corpse, and only when it was behind him realized that it had been his own.

Placidaque ibi demum morte quievit. "At last he found rest in peaceful death." For we are ever most at peace where we are most sorely needed.

cott Baker introduced me to Garry Kilworth at the World Fantasy Convention in London, suggesting, as he brought me over, that I might ask Kilworth for a story. Not much later, I received "Inside the Walled City" in the mail.

Garry Kilworth is the author of *Witchwater County*, *Cloudrock and Spiral Winds*, and *The Songbirds of Pain*. He is a winner of the Gollancz/Sunday Times SF Short Story Competition. He lives in Hong Kong.

"Inside the Walled City" is an indoor jungle adventure set in a building several blocks from where Garry Kilworth lives that was due to be torn down a few weeks after the story was written.

Inside the Walled City

GARRY KILWORTH

T hey had been loud-hailing the place for days, and it certainly looked empty, but John said you can't knock down a building that size without being absolutely sure that some terrified Chinese child wasn't trapped in one of the myriad of rooms, or that an abandoned old lady wasn't caught in some blocked passageway, unable to find her way out. There must have been elderly people who had set up home in the center of this huge rotten cheese, and around whom the rest of the slum was raised over the years. Such people would have forgotten there *was* an outside world, let alone be able to find their way to it.

"You ready?" he asked me, and I nodded.

It was John Speakman's job, as a Hong Kong Police inspector, to go into the empty shell of the giant slum to make sure everyone was out, so that the demolition could begin. He had a guide of course, and an armed escort of two locally born policemen, and was accompanied by a newspaper reporter—me. I'm a freelance whose articles appear mainly in the *South China Morning Post*.

You could say the Walled City was many dwellings, as many as seven thousand, but you would be equally right to call it a single structure. It consisted of one solid block of crudely built homes, all fused together. No thought or planning had gone into each tacked-on dwelling, beyond that of providing shelter for a family. The whole building covered the approximate area of a football stadium. There was no quadrangle at its center, nor inner courtyard, no space within the ground it occupied. Every single piece of the ramshackle mass, apart from the occasional fetid air-shaft, had been used to build, up to twelve stories high. Beneath the ground, and through every part of this mon-strous shanty, ran a warren of tunnels and passageways. Above and within it, there were walkways, ladders, cat-walks, streets, and alleys, all welded together as if some junk artist like the man who built the Watts Towers had decided to try his hand at architecture.

Once you got more than ten feet inside, there was no natural light. Those within used to have to send messages to those on the edges to find out if it was day or night, fine or wet. The homemade brick and plaster was apt to rot and crumble in the airless confines inside and had to be constantly patched and shored up. In a land of high tem-peratures and humidity, fungus grew thick on the walls and in the cracks the rats and cockroaches build their own col-onies. The stink was unbelievable. When it was occupied, more than fifty thousand people existed within its walls.

John called his two local cops to his side, and we all slipped into the dark slit in the side of the Walled City, Sang Lau the guide going first. Two *gwailos*—whites—and three Chinese, entering the forbidden place, perhaps for the last time. Even Sang Lau, who knew the building as well as any, seemed anxious to get the job over and done with. The son of an illegal immigrant, he had been raised in this block of hovels, in the muck and darkness of its intestines. His stunted little body was evidence of that fact, and he had only volunteered to show us the way in exchange for a right to Hong Kong citizenship for members of his family still without Hong Kong citizenship. He and his immediate family had taken advantage of the amnesty that had served to empty the city of its inhabitants. They had come out, some of them half-blind through lack of light, some of them sick and crippled from the disease and bad air, and now Sang Lau had been asked to return for one last time. I guessed how he would be feeling: slightly nostalgic (for it was his birthplace), yet wanting to get it over with, so that the many other unsavory remembrances might be razed along with the structure.

The passage inside was narrow, constantly twisting, turning, dipping, and climbing, apparently at random. Its walls ran with slick water and it smelled musty, with pockets of stale-food stink, and worse. I constantly gagged. Then there were writhing coils of hose and cable that tangled our feet if we were not careful: plastic water pipes ran alongside wires that had once carried stolen electricity. When the rotten cables were live and water ran through the leaking hoses, these passageways must have been death traps. Now and again the beam from the lamp in my helmet transfixed a pointed face, with whiskers and small eyes, then the rat would scuttle away, into its own maze of tunnels.

Every so often, we paused at one of the many junctions or shafts, and one of the Chinese policemen, the stocky, square-faced one, would yell through a megaphone. The sound smacked dully into the walls, or echoed along corridors of plasterboard. The atmosphere was leaden, though strangely aware. The massive structure with all its holes, its pits and shafts, was like a beast at the end of its life, waiting for the final breath. It was a shell, but one that had been soaked in the feverish activity of fifty thousand souls. It was once a holy city, but it had been bled, sweated, urinated, and spat on not only by the poor and the destitute, but also by mobsters, hoodlums, renegades, felons, runaways, refugees, and fugitives, until no part of it remained consecrated. It pressed in on us on all sides, as if it wanted to crush us, but lacked the final strength needed to collapse itself. It was a brooding, moody place and terribly alien to a *gwailo* like myself. I could sense spirits clustering in the corners: spirits from a culture that no Westerner has ever fully understood. More than once, as I stumbled along behind the others, I said to myself, *What am I doing here? This is no place for me, in this hole.*

The stocky policeman seemed startled by his own voice, blaring from the megaphone: he visibly twitched every time he had to make his announcement. From his build I guessed his family originally came from the north, from somewhere around the Great Wall. His features and heavy torso were Mongol rather than Cantonese, the southerners having a tendency toward small, delicate statures and moon-shaped faces. He probably made a tough policeman out on the streets, where his build would be of use in knocking heads together, but in here his northern superstitions and obsessive fear of spirits made him a liability. Not for the first time I wondered at John Speakman's judgment in assessing human character.

After about an hour of walking, and sometimes crawling, along tunnels the size of a sewer pipe, John suggested we rest for a while.

I said, "You're not going to eat sandwiches in here, are you?"

It was supposed to be a joke, but I was so tense, it came out quite flat, and John growled, "No, of course not."

We sat cross-legged in circle, in what used to be an apartment: It was a hardboard box about ten-by-ten feet.

"Where are we?" I asked the torchlit faces. "I mean in relation to the outside." The reply could have been "the bowels of the earth" and I would have believed it. It was gloomy, damp, fetid, and reeked of prawn paste, which has an odor reminiscent of dredged sludge.

Sang Lau replied, "Somewhere near east corner. We move soon, toward middle."

His reply made me uneasy.

"*Somewhere* near? Don't you know exactly?"

John snapped, "Don't be silly, Peter. How can he know *exactly*? The important thing is he knows the way out. This isn't an exercise in specific location."

"Right," I said, giving him a mock salute, and he tipped his peaked cap back on his head, a sure sign he was annoyed. If he'd been standing, I don't doubt his hands would have been on his hips in the classic "*gwailo* giving orders" stance.

John hadn't been altogether happy about taking a "civilian" along, despite the fact that I was a close friend. He had a very poor opinion of those who did not wear a uniform of some kind. According to his philosophy, the human race was split into two: There were the protectors (police, army, medical profession, firemen, et al.) and those who needed protection (the rest of the population). Since I apparently came under the second category, I needed looking after. John was one of those crusty bachelors you find in the last outposts of faded empires: a living reminder of the beginning of the century. Sheena, my wife, called him "the fossil," even to his face. I think they both regarded it as a term of endearment.

However, he said he wanted to do me a favor, since he knew that my job was getting tough. Things were getting tight in the free-lance business, especially since Australia had just woken up to the fact that Hong Kong, a thriving place of business where money was to be made hand over fist, was right on its doorstep. The British and American expatriates equaled each other for the top slot, numerically speaking, but Aussie professionals were beginning to enter—if not in droves, in small herds. With them they brought their own parasites, the free lancers, and for the first time I had a lot of competition. It meant I had to consolidate friendships and use contacts that had previously been mostly social. Sheena and I were going through a bit of a rough time too, and one thing she would not put up with was a tame writer who earned less than a poorly paid local clerk. I could sense the words "proper job" in the air, waiting to condense.

Even the darkness in there seemed to have substance. I could see the other young policeman, the thin, sharp Cantonese youth, was uncomfortable too. He kept looking up, into the blackness, smiling nervously. He and his companion cop whispered to each other, and I heard "Bruce Lee" mentioned just before they fell into silence again, their grins fixed. Perhaps they were trying to use the memory of the fabled martial-arts actor to bolster their courage? Possibly the only one of us who was completely oblivious, or perhaps indifferent, to the spiritual ambience of the place was John himself. He was too thick-skinned, too much the old-warrior expat, to be affected by spooky atmospheres. I thought he might reassure his men though, since we both knew that when Chinese smiled under circumstances such as these, it meant they were hiding either acute embarrassment or abject terror. They had nothing to be embarrassed about, so I was left with only one assumption.

John, however, chose to ignore their fear.

"Right, let's go," he said, climbing to his feet.

We continued along the passageways, stumbling after Sang Lau, whose power over us was absolute in this place, since without him we would certainly be lost. It was possible that a search party might find us, but then again, we could wander the interior of this vast wormery for weeks without finding or being found.

A subtle change seemed to come over the place. Its resistance seemed to have evaporated, and it was almost as if it were gently drawing us on. The tunnels were getting wider, more accessible, and there were fewer obstacles to negotiate. I have an active imagination, especially in places of darkness, notorious places that are steeped in recent histories of blood and founded on terror. Far from making me feel better, this alteration in the atmosphere made my stomach knot, but what could I say to John? I wanted to go back? I had no choice but to follow where his guide led us, and hope for an early opportunity to duck out if we saw daylight at any time.

Although I am sensitive to such places, I'm not usually a coward. Old churches and ancient houses bother me, but I normally shrug and put up with any feeling of spiritual discomfort. Here, however, the oppressive atmosphere was so threatening and the feeling of dread so strong, I wanted to run from the building and to hell with the article and the money I needed so much. The closer we got to the center, the more acute became my emotional stress, until I wondered whether I was going to hyperventilate. Finally, I shouted, "John!"

He swung round with an irritated "What is it?"

"I've—I've got to go back. . . ."

One of the policemen grabbed my arm in the dark, and squeezed it. I believed it to be a sign of encouragement. He too wanted to turn round, but he was more terrified of his boss than of any ghost. From the strength of the grip I guessed the owner of the fingers was the Mongol.

"Impossible," John snapped. "What's the matter with you?"

"A pain," I said. "I have a pain in my chest."

He pushed past the other men and pulled me roughly to one side.

"I knew I shouldn't have brought you. I only did it for Sheena—she seemed to think there was still something left in you. Now pull yourself together. I know what's the matter with you, you're getting the jitters. It's claustrophobia, nothing else. Fight it, man. You're scaring my boys with your stupid funk."

"I have a pain," I repeated, but he wasn't buying it.

"Crap. Sheena would be disgusted with you. God knows what she ever saw in you in the first place."

For a moment all fear was driven out of me by an intense fury that flooded my veins. How *dare* this thick-skinned, arrogant cop assume knowledge of my wife's regard for me! It was true that her feelings were not now what they had been in the beginning, but she had once fully loved me, and only a rottenness bred by superficial life in the colony had eaten away that love. The mannequins, the people with plaster faces, had served to corrode us. Sheena had once been a happy woman, full of energy, enthusiasms, color. Now she was pinched and bitter, as I was myself: made so by the shallow *gwailos* we consorted with and had become ourselves. Money, affairs and bugger-thy-neighbor were the priorities in life.

"You leave Sheena's name out of this," I said, my voice catching with the anger that stuck in my throat. "What the *hell* do you know about our beginnings?"

Speakman merely gave me a look of contempt and took up his position in the front once more, with the hunchbacked Lau indicating which way he should go when we came to one of the many junctions and crossroads. Occasionally, the thin one, who now had the megaphone, would call out in Cantonese, the sound quickly swallowed by the denseness of the structure around us. Added to my anxiety problem was now a feeling of misery. I had shown my inner nature to a man who was increasingly becoming detestable to me. Something was nagging at the edge of my brain too, which gradually ate its way inward, toward an area of comprehension.

God knows what she ever saw in you in the first place.

When it came, the full implication of these words stunned me. At first I was too taken aback to do anything more than keep turning the idea over in my mind, in an obsessive way, until it drove out any other thought. I kept going over his words, trying to find another way of interpreting them, but came up with the same answer every time.

Finally, I could keep quiet no longer. I had to get it out. It was beginning to fester. I stopped in my tracks, and despite the presence of the other men, shouted, "You bastard, Speakman, you're having an affair with her, aren't you?"

He turned and regarded me, silently.

"You bastard," I said again. I could hardly get it out, it was choking me. "You're supposed to be a friend."

There was utter contempt in his voice.

"I was never your friend."

"You *wanted* me to know, didn't you? You wanted to tell me in here."

He knew that in this place I would be less than confident of myself. The advantages were all with him. I was out of my environment and less able to handle things than he was. In the past few months he had been in here several times, was more familiar with the darkness and the tight, airless zones of the Walled City's interior. We were in an underworld that terrified me and left him unperturbed.

"You men go on," he ordered the others, not taking his eyes off me. "We'll follow in a moment."

They did as they were told. John Speakman was not a man to be brooked by his Asiatic subordinates. When they were out of earshot, he said, "Yes, Sheena and I had— had some time together."

In the light of my helmet lamp I saw his lips twitch, and I wanted to smash him in the mouth.

"*Had?* You mean it's over?"

"Not completely. But there's still you. You're in the way. Sheena, being the woman she is, still retains some sort of loyalty toward you. Can't see it myself, but there it is."

"We'll sort this out later," I said, "between the three of us."

I made a move to get past him, but he blocked the way.

Then a second, more shocking realization hit me, and again I was not ready for it. He must have seen it in my face, because his lips tightened this time.

I said calmly now, "You're going to lose me in here, aren't you? Sheena said she wouldn't leave me, and you're going to make sure I stay behind."

"Your imagination is running away with you again," he

snapped back. "Try to be a little more level-headed, old chap."

"I am being level-headed."

His hands were on his hips now, in that *gwailo* stance I knew so well. One of them rested on the butt of his revolver. Being a policeman, he of course carried a gun, which I did not. There was little point in my trying force anyway. He was a good four inches taller than I and weighed two stone more, most of it muscle. We stood there, confronting one another, until we heard the scream that turned my guts to milk.

The ear-piercing cry was followed by a scrabbling sound, and eventually one of the two policemen appeared in the light of our lamps.

"Sir, come quick," he gasped. "The guide."

Our quarrel put aside for the moment, we hurried along the tunnel to where the other policeman stood. In front of him, perhaps five yards away, was the guide. His helmet light was out, and he seemed to be standing on tiptoe for some reason, arms hanging loosely by his sides. John stepped forward, and I found myself going with him. He might have wanted *me* out of the way, but I was going to stick closely to him.

What I saw in the light of our lamps made me retch and step backward quickly.

It would seem that a beam had swung down from the ceiling, as the guide had passed beneath it. This had smashed his helmet lamp. Had that been all, the guide might have got away with a broken nose, or black eye, but it was not. In the end of the beam, now holding him on his feet, was a curved nail-spike. It had gone through his right eye, and was no doubt deeply imbedded in the poor man's brain. He dangled from this support loosely, blood running down the side of his nose and dripping onto his white tennis shoes.

"Jesus Christ!" I said at last. It wasn't a profanity, a blasphemy. It was a prayer. I called for us, who were now lost in a dark, hostile world, and I called for Sang Lau. Poor little Sang Lau. Just when he had begun to make it in life, just when he had escaped the Walled City, the bricks and mortar and timber had reached out petulantly for its former child and brained it. Sang Lau had been one of the quiet millions who struggle out of the mire, who evolve from terrible beginnings to a place in the world of light. All in vain, apparently.

John Speakman lifted the man away from the instrument that had impaled him, and laid the body on the floor. He went through the formality of feeling for a pulse, and then shook his head. To give him his due, his voice remained remarkably firm, as if he were still in control of things.

"We'll have to carry him out," he said to his two men. "Take one end each."

There was a reluctant shuffling of feet, as the men moved forward to do as they were told. The smaller of the two was trembling so badly he dropped the legs straight away, and had to retrieve them quickly under Speakman's glare.

I said, "And who the hell is going to lead us out, now he's gone?"

"I am," came the reply.

"And I suppose you know which way to go?"

"We're near the heart of the place, old chap. It doesn't really matter in which direction we go, as long as we keep going straight."

That, I knew, was easier said than done. When passageways curve and turn, run into each other, go up and down, meet forks and crossroads and junctions with choices, how the hell do you keep in a straight line? I said nothing for once. I didn't want the two policemen to panic. If we were to get out, we had to stay calm. And those on the outside wouldn't leave us here. They would send in a search party, once nightfall came.

Nightfall. I suppressed a chill as we moved into the heart of the beast.

Seven months ago Britain agreed with China that Hong

Kong would return to its landlord country in 1997. It was then at last decided to clean up and clean out the Walled City, to pull it down and rehouse the inhabitants. There were plans to build a park on the ground then covered by this ancient city within a city, for the use of the occupants of the surrounding tenement buildings.

It stood in the middle of Kowloon on the mainland. Once upon a time there *was* a wall around it, when it was the home of the Manchus, but Japanese invaders robbed it of its ancient stones to build elsewhere. The area on which it stood is still known as the Walled City. When the Manchus were there, they used it as a fort against the British. Then the British were leased the peninsula, and it became an enclave for China's officials, whose duty it was to report on *gwailo* activities in the area to Peking. Finally, it became an architectural nightmare, a giant slum. An area not recognized by the British, who refused to police it, and abandoned by Peking, it was a lawless labyrinth, sometimes called the Forbidden Place. It was here that unlicensed doctors and dentists practiced, and every kind of vice flourished. It was ruled by gangs of youths, the Triads, who covered its inner walls with blood. It is a place of death, the home of ten thousand ghosts.

For the next two hours we struggled through the rank-smelling tunnels, crawling over filth and across piles of trash, until we were all exhausted. I had cuts on my knees, and my hair felt teeming with insects. I knew there were spiders, possibly even snakes, in these passageways. There were certainly lice, horseflies, mosquitoes and a dozen other nasty biters. Not only that, but there seemed to be projections everywhere: sharp bits of metal, cables hanging like vines from the ceiling and rusty nails. The little Cantonese policeman had trodden on a nail, which had completely pierced his foot. He was now limping and whining in a small voice. He knew that if he did not get treatment soon, blood poisoning would be the least of his troubles. I felt sorry for the young man, who in the normal run of things probably dealt with the tide of human affairs very competently within his range of duties. He was an official of the law in the most densely populated area of the world, and I had seen his type deal cleanly and (more often than not) peacefully with potentially ugly situations daily. In here, however, he was over his head. This situation could not be handled by efficient traffic signals or negotiation, or even prudent use of a weapon. There was something about this man that was familiar. There were scars on his face: shiny patches that might have been the result of plastic surgery. I tried to recall where I had seen the Cantonese policeman before, but my mind was soggy with recent events.

We took turns carrying the body of the guide. Once I had touched him and got over my squeamishness, that part of it didn't bother me too much. What did was the weight of the corpse. I never believed a man could be so heavy. After ten minutes my arms were nearly coming out of their sockets. I began by carrying the legs, and quickly decided that the man at the head, carrying the torso, had the best part of the deal. I suggested a change round, which was effected, only to find that the other end of the man was twice as heavy. I began to hate him.

After four hours I had had enough.

"I'm not humping him around anymore," I stated bluntly to the cop who was trying to take my wife from me. "You want him outside, you carry him by yourselves. You're the bloody boss man. It's your damn show."

"I see," John said. "Laying down some ground rules, are we?"

"Shove it up your arse," I replied. "I've had you up to here. I can't prove you planned to dump me in here, but *I* know, pal, and when we get out of this place, you and I are going to have a little talk."

"*If* we get out," he muttered.

He was sitting away from me, in the darkness, where my lamplight couldn't reach him. I could not see his expression.

"If?"

"Exactly," he sighed. "We don't seem to be getting very far, do we? It's almost as if this place were trying to keep us. I swear it's turning us in on ourselves. We should have reached the outside long ago."

"But they'll send someone in after us," I said.

And one of the policemen added, "Yes. Someone come."

" 'Fraid not. No one knows we're here." It came out almost as if he were pleased with himself. I saw now that I *had* been right. It had been his intention to drop me off in the middle of this godforsaken building, knowing I would never find my own way out. I wondered only briefly what he planned to do with the two men and the guide. I don't doubt they could be bribed. The Hong Kong Police Force has at times been notorious for its corruption. Maybe they were chosen because they could be bought.

"How long have we got?" I asked, trying to stick to practical issues.

"About five more hours. Then the demolition starts. They begin knocking it down at six A.M."

Just then, the smaller of the Chinese made a horrific gargling sound, and we all shone our lights on him instinctively. At first I couldn't understand what was wrong with him, though I could see he was convulsing. He was in a sitting position, and his body kept jerking and flopping. John Speakman bent over him, then straightened, saying, "Christ, not another one . . ."

"What?" I cried. "What is it?"

"Six-inch nail. It's gone in behind his ear. How the hell? I don't understand how he managed to lean all the way back on it."

"Unless the nail came out of the wood?" I said.

"What are you saying?"

"I don't know. All I know is two men have been injured in accidents that seem too freakish to believe. What do you think? Why can't we get out of this place? Shit, it's only the area of a football stadium. We've been in here *hours*."

The other policeman was looking at his colleague with wide, disbelieving eyes. He grabbed John Speakman by the collar, blurting, "We go now. We go outside now," and then a babble of that tonal language, some of which John might have understood. I certainly didn't.

Speakman peeled the man's stubby fingers from his collar and turned away from him, toward the dead cop, as if the incident had not taken place. "He was a good policeman," he said. "Jimmy Wong. You know he saved a boy from a fire last year? Dragged the child out with his teeth, hauling the body along the floor and down the stairs because his hands were burned too badly to clutch the kid. You remember. You covered the story."

I remembered him now. Jimmy Wong. The governor had presented him with a medal. He had saluted proudly, with heavily bandaged hands. Today he was not a hero. Today he was a number. The second victim.

John Speakman said, "Good-bye, Jimmy."

Then he ignored him, saying to me, "We can't carry both bodies out. We'll have to leave them. I . . ." but I heard no more. There was a quick tearing sound, and I was suddenly falling. My heart dropped out of me. I landed heavily on my back. Something entered between my shoulder blades, something sharp and painful, and I had to struggle hard to get free. When I managed to get to my feet and reached down and felt along the floor, I touched a slim projection, probably a large nail. It was sticky with my blood. A voice from above said, "Are you all right?"

"I—I think so. A nail . . ."

"What?"

My light had gone out, and I was feeling disoriented. I must have fallen about fourteen feet, judging from the dis-

tance of the lamps above me. I reached down my back
with my hand. It felt wet and warm, but apart from the
pain I wasn't gasping for air or anything. Obviously, it had
missed my lungs and other vital organs, or I would be
squirming in the dust, coughing my guts up.

I heard John say, "We'll try to reach you," and then
the voice and the lights drifted away.

"*No!*" I shouted. "Don't leave me! Give me your arm."
I reached upward. "Help me up!"

But my hand remained empty. They had gone, leaving
the blackness behind them. I lay still for a long time, afraid
to move. There were nails everywhere. My heart was racing. I was sure that I was going to die. The Walled City
had us in its grip, and we were not going to get out. Once,
it had been teeming with life, but we had robbed it of its
soul, the people that had crowded within its walls. Now
even the shell was threatened with destruction. And we
were the men responsible. We represented the authority
who had ordered its death, and it was determined to take
us with it. Nothing likes to die alone. Nothing wants to
leave this world without, at the very least, obtaining satisfaction in the way of revenge. The ancient black heart of
the Walled City of the Manchus, surrounded by the body
it had been given by later outcasts from society, had enough
life left in it to slaughter these five puny mortals from the
other side, the lawful side. It had tasted *gwailo* blood, and
it would have more.

My wound was beginning to ache, and I climbed stiffly
and carefully to my feet. I felt slowly along the walls, taking each step cautiously. Things scuttled over my feet,
whispered over my face, but I ignored them. A sudden
move and I would find myself impaled on some projection.
The stink of death was in the stale air, filling my nostrils.
It was trying to drive fear into me. The only way I was
going to survive was by remaining calm. Once I panicked,
it would all be over. I had the feeling that the building
could kill me at any time, but it was savoring the moment,

allowing it to be my mistake. It wanted me to dive head-long into insanity, it wanted to experience my terror, then it would deliver the *coup de grace*.

I moved this way along the tunnels for about an hour: Neither of us, it seemed, was short of patience. The Walled City had seen centuries, so what was an hour or two? The legacy of death left by the Manchus and the Triads existed without reference to time. Ancient evils and modern iniquity had joined forces against the foreigner, the *gwailo*, and the malodorous darkness smiled at any attempt to thwart its intention to suck the life from my body.

At one point my forward foot did not touch ground. There was a space, a hole, in front of me.

"Nice try," I whispered, "but not yet."

As I prepared to edge around it, hoping for a small ledge or something, I felt ahead of me, and touched the thing. It was dangling over the hole, like plumb-line weight. I pushed it, and it swung slowly.

By leaning over and feeling carefully, I ascertained it to be the remaining local policeman, the muscled northerner. I knew that by his Sam Browne shoulder strap: Speakman had not been wearing one. I felt up by the corpse's throat and found the skin bulging over some tight electrical cords. The building had hanged him.

Used to death now, I gripped the corpse around the waist and used it as a swing to get myself across the gap. The cords held, and I touched ground. A second later, the body must have dropped, because I heard a crash below.

I continued my journey through the endless tunnels, my throat very parched now. I was thirsty as hell. Eventually, I could stand it no longer and licked some of the moisture that ran down the walls. It tasted like wine. At one point I tongued up a cockroach, cracked it between my teeth, and spit it out in disgust. Really, I no longer cared. All I wanted to do was get out alive. I didn't even care whether John and Sheena told me to go away. I would be happy to do so. There wasn't much left, in any case. Anything I had felt had shriveled away during this ordeal. I just wanted to live. Nothing more, nothing less.

At one point a stake or something plunged downward from the roof and passed through several floors, missing me by an inch. I think I actually laughed. A little while later, I found an airshaft with a rope hanging in it. Trusting that the building would not let me fall, I climbed down this narrow chimney to get to the bottom. I had some idea that if I could reach ground-level, I might find a way to get through the walls. Some of them were no thicker than cardboard.

After reaching the ground safely, I began to feel my way along the corridors and alleys, until I saw a light. I gasped with relief, thinking at first it was daylight, but had to swallow a certain amount of disappointment in finding it was only a helmet with its lamp still on. The owner was nowhere to be seen. I guessed it was John's: he was the only one left, apart from me.

Not long after this, I heard John Speakman's voice for the last time. It seemed to come from very far below me, in the depths of the underground passages that wormholed beneath the Walled City. It was a faint pathetic cry for help. Immediately following this distant shout was the sound of falling masonry. And then, silence. I shuddered, involuntarily, guessing what had happened. The building had lured him into its underworld, its maze below the earth, and had then blocked the exits. John Speakman had been buried alive, immured by the city that held him in contempt.

Now there was only me.

I moved through an inner darkness, the beam of the remaining helmet lamp having faded to a dim glow. I was Theseus in the Labyrinth, except that I had no Ariadne to help me find the way through it. I stumbled through long tunnels where the air was so thick and damp I might have been in a steam bath. I crawled along passages no taller or wider than a cupboard under a kitchen sink, shared them with spiders and rats and came out the other end choking on dust, spitting out cobwebs. I knocked my way through walls so thin and rotten a single blow with my fist was enough to hole them. I climbed over fallen girders, rubble, and piles of filthy rags, collecting unwanted passengers and abrasions on the way.

And all the while I knew the building was laughing at me.

It was leading me round in circles, playing with me like a rat in a maze. I could hear it moving, creaking and shifting as it readjusted itself, changed its inner structure to keep me from finding an outside wall. Once, I trod on something soft. It could have been a hand—John's hand—quickly withdrawn. Or it might have been a creature of the Walled City, a rat or a snake. Whatever it was, it had been live.

There were times when I became so despondent I wanted to lie down and just fade into death, the way a primitive tribesman will give up all hope and turn his face to the wall. There were times when I became angry, and screeched at the structure that had me trapped in its belly, remonstrating with it until my voice was hoarse. Sometimes I was driven to useless violence and picked up the nearest object to smash at my tormentor, even if my actions brought the place down around my ears.

Once, I even whispered to the darkness:

"I'll be your slave. Tell me what to do—any evil thing—and I'll do it. If you let me go, I promise to follow your wishes. Tell me what to do. . . ."

And still it laughed at me, until I knew I was going insane.

Finally, I began singing to myself, not to keep up my spirits like brave men are supposed to, but because I was beginning to slip into that crazy world that rejects reality in favor of fantasy. I thought I was home, in my own house, making coffee. I found myself going through the actions of putting on the kettle, and preparing the coffee, milk and sugar, humming a pleasant tune to myself all the while. One part of me recognized that domestic scene was make-believe, but the other was convinced that I could not possibly be trapped by a malevolent entity and about to die in the dark corridors of its multisectioned shell.

Then something happened, to jerk me into sanity.

The sequence of events covering the next few minutes or so are lost to me. Only by concentrating very hard and surmising can I recall what *might* have happened. Certainly, I believe I remember those first few moments, when a sound deafened me, and the whole building rocked and trembled as if in an earthquake. Then I think I fell to the floor and had the presence of mind to jam the helmet on my head. There followed a second (what I now know to be) explosion. Pieces of building rained around me: bricks were striking my shoulders and bouncing off my hard hat. I think the only reason none of them injured me badly was because the builders, being poor, had used the cheapest materials they could find. These were bricks fashioned out of crushed coke, which are luckily light and airy.

A hole appeared, through which I could see blinding daylight. I was on my feet in an instant, and racing toward it. Nails appeared out of the woodwork, up from the floor, and ripped and tore at my flesh like sharp fangs. Metal posts crashed across my path, struck me on my limbs. I was attacked from all sides by chunks of masonry and debris, until I was bruised and raw, bleeding from dozens of cuts and penetrations.

When I reached the hole in the wall, I threw myself at it, and landed outside in the dust. There, the demolition people saw me, and one risked his life to dash forward and pull me clear of the collapsing building. I was then rushed to hospital. I was found to have a broken arm and multiple lacerations, some of them quite deep.

Mostly, I don't remember what happened at the end. I'm going by what I've been told, and what flashes on and off in my nightmares, and using these have pieced together the above account of my escape from the Walled City. It seems as though it might be reasonably accurate.

I have not, of course, told the true story of what happened inside those walls, except in this account, which will go into a safe place until after my death. Such a tale would only have people clucking their tongues and saying, "It's the shock, you know—the trauma of such an experience," and sending for the psychiatrist. I tried to tell Sheena once, but I could see that it was disturbing her, so I mumbled something about, "Of course, I can see that one's imagination can work overtime in a place like that," and never mentioned it to her again.

I did manage to tell the demolition crew about John. I told them he might still be alive, under all that rubble. They stopped their operations immediately and sent in search parties, but though they found the bodies of the guide and policemen, John was never seen again. The search parties all managed to get out safely, which has me wondering whether perhaps there is something wrong with my head—*except* I have the wounds, and there are the corpses of my traveling companions. I don't know. I can only say now what I *think* happened. I told the police (and stuck rigidly to my story) that I was separated from the others before any deaths occurred. How was I to explain two deaths by sharp instruments, and a subsequent hanging? I let them try to figure it out. All I told them was that I heard John's final cry, and that was the truth. I don't even care whether or not they believe me. I'm outside that damn hellhole, and that's all that concerns me.

And Sheena? It is seven months since the incident. And it was only yesterday that I confronted and accused her of having an affair with John, and she looked so shocked and distressed and denied it so vehemently that I have to admit I believe that nothing of the kind happened between them. I was about to tell her that John had admitted to it, but had second thoughts. I mean, *had* he? He certainly inferred that there had been something between them, but perhaps he was just trying to goad me? Maybe I had filled in the gaps with my own jealous fears? To tell you the truth, I can't honestly remember, and the guilt is going to be hard to live with. You see, when they asked me for the location of John's cry for help, I indicated a spot . . . well, I *think* I told them to dig—I said . . . anyway, they didn't find him, which wasn't surprising, since I . . . well, perhaps this is not the place for full confessions.

John is still under there somewhere, God help him. I have the awful feeling that the underground ruins of the Walled City might keep him alive in some way, with redirected water, and food in the form of rats and cockroaches. A starving man will eat dirt, if it fills his stomach. Perhaps he is still below, in some pocket created by that underworld? Such a slow, terrible torture, keeping a man barely alive in his own grave, would be consistent with that devious, nefarious entity I know as the Walled City of the Manchus.

Some nights when I am feeling especially brave, I go to the park and listen—listen for small cries from a subterranean prison—listen for the faint pleas for help from an *oubliette* far below the ground.

Sometimes I think I hear them.

G wyneth Jones has recently written a number of excellent fantasy stories, and is the author of *Divine Endurance, Escape Plans,* and *Kairos.* She also writes children's books under the pen name of Anne Hallam. She lives in Brighton, England.

It is often said that horror is a conservative form written mostly by men. However, it is also true that some of the best horror has been written by feminists, for example "The Yellow Wallpaper" by Charlotte Perkins Gilman, "My Dear Emily" by Joanna Russ, and *The Vampire Tapestry* by Suzy McKee Charnas. This is a story about the psychology of oppression.

Grandmother's Footsteps

GWYNETH JONES

Pride Comes Before a Fall

The site meeting was intense: the operations so major and the discussion of them so deep I felt as if Don and I ought to be wearing hard hats and carrying clipboards. By the end of it we were exhausted. Donald and Mr. Hann (the house doctor) walked toward the front door, still consulting as they negotiated the scaffolding. Suzy was asleep on Don's back. Dear child, she'd been as good as gold; her little face puckered up seriously as she listened and peered over her daddy's shoulder. I hung back. I muttered something about wanting to take another look downstairs, but I didn't intend to be heard. I wanted to do something that was private—or maybe just too foolish for public attention.

It was mid-February then, and already cold, gloomy dusk at the end of the working day. The plumber and the electrician and all of Mr. Hann's henchpersons had packed up and left while he was giving us the benefit of his really wonderful bedside manner. I climbed down the dark stairs that at present ended in planks laid across a pit, found the power cable that hung over a naked ceiling joist and pressed the switch. Inside a dangling gray bulb, the twisted ribbon bow of incandescence seemed to be struggling against the odds, as if rising damp were a kind of reinforcement of darkness. Our basement looked awful, really awful, like a drained abscess or a drilled-out tooth.

I stepped out into the middle of what had once been a room, and tried to remember it the way I had first seen it. The house was standing empty then, and even with all its problems was almost more than we could afford. There was a fearsome sense of urgency in feeling the developers at our backs and seeing the dry rot and the damp busily working away. I would collect the key from the agent and come down here with Suzy nearly every day, to wait for yet another surveyor, house doctor or rot expert. Suzy practically learned to walk in this basement. She was an early walker: At barely ten months old she began to toddle. It was here, in the shadow, in the musty emptiness, that she had taken some of her first wobbly, triumphant steps.

Now it looked more like an archaeological dig than anywhere people might live. Or like part of a mass-murder inquiry. When our friends (we had to show them—couldn't keep such a spectacle to ourselves) came round to admire, they all said the same thing: "Have they found the body yet?"

But in spite of all the trauma we knew we were doing the right thing. Ever since the baby was born, and before, we'd known that this was coming. It was the house move that marked the actual completion of the change in our lives that she had wrought. And this was the only way that was right for us. We wanted to live in a place that had its roots deep in the past, but cleared out and remodeled entirely to our specification. We needed the old and the new fused together, in our bricks and mortar as in our lives.

I stood and waited for the presence of the old house to come back from wherever it had been driven by blaring pop music and the thunder of power tools. I don't believe in ghosts, but I do believe in atmosphere. I had never owned a house before. I wanted to rediscover the emotional meaning of the step that I was taking: something that had been obscured by the panics and crises of the last weeks. I closed my eyes, with the fugitive feeling that I was taking some kind of risk.

It was peaceful down there, despite the cold and the damp, oozy smell. The burr of traffic far away sounded mild as a lullaby after the way it shouted in the busy street below our flat. When I knew I was calm, when I'd accomplished that subtle but unmistakable transition into undistracted, neutral awareness, I opened my eyes. I saw an old woman sitting by the hearth—in front, that is, of the gaping hole where our restored Victorian fireplace would be. She sat upright in a straight-backed armchair. She was crocheting; a white heap of work lay in her lap. She didn't see me. She was quite absorbed, her face bent with a severe yet half-vacant expression—the expression that goes with the kind of task that occupies the hands and empties the mind. Her skin looked soft as rose petals—the delicate, just faintly crumpled complexion of a placid grandmother; cheeks that you knew would be as soft to the touch as a baby's. I'll never have a face like that. I think too much, argue too much: Sometimes I don't sleep very well.

She looked very sure of herself, this old lady by my hearth—*plantée là,* as the French say—as if she had a perfect right to be there, as if nothing could possibly move her. She had a disquietingly contemporary look, too, for a ghostly emanation. She was no Victorian granny but a nicely preserved old lady of the present day: a collector of recipes from TV cookery shows, a comfortable reader of fat, glossy family sagas. The vision persisted, growing clearer as I stared, feeding on I don't know what scraps of information in the pattern of darkness and shattered brickwork.

The white cobwebs of newly exposed dry rot floated through Granny's head—became the crochet on her lap and the deft, soft hands at work.

Then I began to hear her breathing. That was nasty. The whole basement seemed to echo with it: a heavy, asthmatic gasping, as if somebody were dying. It was a filthy noise. It even occurred to me that maybe someone *was* dying, in the basement next door. After a minute or two it stopped, and I left.

Donald was waiting in the car. The baby—still asleep—was strapped into her chair in the back. He had left the driver's seat for me. I got in, and we sat there holding hands rather helplessly. Don couldn't have looked more depressed if Mr. Hann had been a real geriatrician and we'd been hearing serious news about a beloved relative. But it wasn't *too* serious. We'd known that we were taking on a challenge: We would win through.

"Well? What did you get just then, anyway? What's it like, this character we're going to live with?"

Of course he knew what I'd been up to. He knows me. We are very close, Don and I. Which is something I wouldn't have thought worth saying a few years ago—we're married, aren't we? But I've seen so many relationships turning sour, the bad old stuff coming to the surface under the pressure of two careers and the child-care thing. I know better how to value what we have.

"A bit shattered at the moment," I said. "A little bruised and battered. But structurally sound."

I could have told him I had seen the spirit of our house alive and well and sitting cozily by its own fireside. But I didn't. I don't like petal-cheeked grandmothers: those foot-binding, petrol-pouring pillars of society. If I'd had to have an image of an old woman, I'd much rather it had been a smelly bag lady. And anyway, there was that horrible noise. I didn't think Don wanted to hear about a desperately sick neighbor just now.

He heaved a huge sigh. Money! Where was all the money going to come from?

"We'll survive, Rose."
"Of course we will."

A Woman's Work Is Never Done

We moved in. So much to do, so many layers of dirt, decay and neglect to be stripped away. We were suddenly poor again after years of double-income, low-outgoings prosperity: It was going to have to be mostly our own work. Days were spent camping out on the roughly habitable upper floors. Every evening we plunged into a world of chemicals and power tools and paint, hour by hour.

Far down in the basement our kitchen-to-be was still a disaster. The sunny terrace overlooking the garden, where I imagined perfect alfresco breakfasting, was heaped with rubble: the kitchen walls oozing with a black, tarry bitumen mixture that obstinately refused to "dry out." We had a makeshift arrangement in the room that would be Don's den: the fridge in a corner, the kettle and a microwave sharing his big old desk; we did the washing up in the bathroom. It all seemed like fun at first, a great joke trying to keep the turps substitute out of the butter, and the chili sauce out of the builders' receipts. Don and I hardly saw each other. At night we would bump into each other at the door of the fridge, foraging for beer and chocolate. It was like the hunter and the gatherer meeting briefly to share an underdone chop or two at the firehole. We joked that the house had succeeded where the world had failed for years, in segregating our lives.

Anatomy of a fireplace: Collect the tools, the can of stripper, the gloves, the mask. Shroud the surroundings, set to work. The last layer, the top one, was white paint: before that the green, before that an incredibly sticky blue that clung devotedly to the detail of the molding; first of all there had been the dark brown. Why the devil did anyone want to paint a black cast-iron fireplace dark brown?

There was a lot of buried treasure in this house, things lovable and rich in detail in a way you never see in modern dwellings. There was also an amazing amount of pure willful ugliness.

It was necessary, for these tasks of mindless drudgery, to develop a special state of mind. Without even meaning to, I had trained myself to toil away, thinking of practically nothing, in a positive trance of stripper fumes and burning muscles. In such a state hallucinations are not unlikely. I decided to give the power drill a rest, and put out my hand for the steel wool. I found myself tugging at a hank of human hair. I dropped it in instant revulsion, but not quickly enough. My hand was stinging as if I'd dipped it in paint stripper. I'd forgotten that I'd taken my gloves off: When I looked, I saw that my fingers and palm were stippled with drops of blood. I knelt, staring at my hand, feeling prickles of unease at the back of my neck. The house seemed very quiet now that I'd switched the drill off, and the light looked extra artificial, as it always does in an empty room at night. I put on my gloves and went on. The white, the green, the sticky blue, the ugly brown . . . I plodded patiently on at the endless, endless task, until my wad had become clogged and useless. I reached for the hank of wool again: It was hair. I felt it resist and flinch away as I tugged. In an instant my mind was flooded by another consciousness. I felt the indignity of senile helplessness, when you can't even look after yourself and have to bear the brusque attentions of a careless nurse or a resentful daughter. The feelings of this hated old woman under my hands washed through me, arousing no sympathy, no pity—only fear and disgust. Then the experience was gone, and I was left shuddering . . . freed from the possession. Far away I could hear the radio playing quietly from where Don was at work papering walls on the floor above.

I went and called up the stairwell, "Can we change over? The stripper fumes are beginning to get to me."

Anatomy of a staircase: This old house of ours is tall

and wide. One of its main beauties is the stairway. It sweeps down from the sunny eyrie where the work processor waits patiently for those stolen moments, down and around into the generous hallway with its black-and-white checkered tiles. It was those elegant tiles, I think, and the sight of the graceful stairway, that decided us to buy this place. I knew that these stairs were going to be perfect. I saw the banisters stripped and lightly varnished, the walls painted in washes of delicate sea colors, pale turquoise and lilac and azure, rippling into each other. But what a job it was! At least there were no chemicals involved in the preparation, so I could try to get a little done during the day. At home, at the other place, I used to play with Suzy all the time when she wasn't with the child-minder. Such housework as we considered necessary, Don and I would share evenings and weekends. Now I'd become the "working mother" of my worst nightmares—every day a series of tiny challenges and defeats, intense campaigns to achieve petty little goals. Suzy had become almost my enemy. I kept promising myself I'd make it up to her when the needs of the house had been satisfied. . . .

I was sanding the top-floor stairs, scrubbing away with patient, mindless care at the excrement-colored dado. (Who was it who chose to have walls the color of shit?) Suzy left whatever destruction she was wreaking in my neglected office, and came and took the block from me. Stop, she said (in that proto-English only Don and I can actually understand).

"Please get out of my way. Sue."

"Please stop."

I've told her that that word "please" is like a little kiss, so she kissed me as she tugged at the sanding block with those determined, imperious small hands.

"I'm sorry, honey, but I must get on."

I'm becoming a real mother, I thought in despair. I've no time for my darling, she's part of the drudgery. And I had sworn to myself that *my* baby would never be "work."

But I was hypnotized by the task, it seemed the only way
back to Suzy was to get through this—

I began to scrub again. I found that I was scrubbing flesh.
The old wood was soft, it smelt of talcum powder and
sour age: It shrank away from me as I scoured. I kept
on, stubbornly fighting the stupid illusion of an overtired
brain.

"Please stop! Please stop!"

Insensate cruelty to the helpless flesh. I was kneeling
astride the old spine, flaccid skin falling in loose folds . . .
Get out of my way, you old brute. . . . I jerked away, got
up and ran for the bathroom. I was actually, physically
sick then; I vomited and lay on the floor at the foot of the
toilet. I stared up at the crazed plasterwork of the ceiling,
veined like the rich and ugly marble of a Victorian public
building. But that was decay up there, not riches. Bare
boards under my head, gritty and paint-smeared: rags and
varnish tins heaped in the corners. Our chaste Victorian-
reproduction bathroom suite seemed to float above its surroundings, like a family of swans strayed into a scummy
old canal. Slaving against the encroaching tide of filthy
chaos, all day and every day like a Third World housewife
. . . this can't be my life. I was near to despair. I heard
Suzy come trotting into the room, rolled over, and saw her
standing there in her little green dungarees, holding the
sanding block, her red-gold curly hair a glowing aureole.
She laughed, uncertainly—I was playing a game that she
didn't understand.

It was a few nights after that when I heard the breathing
again. It might have been going on for a long time: I was
putting up shelves and only heard the other noise when I
stopped to rest. The sick person went on gasping, gasping,
gasping until the spasm reached some kind of climax, and
then ceased. Whoever it was, they'd been moved up from
the basement to the first floor (I could hardly imagine
someone who made a noise like that able to climb stairs).
It was only later, when I was putting my tools away and

the stertorous breathing began again, that I noticed the sound had also changed sides. It was coming through the uphill wall of the terrace now; it had been downhill before.

I went up to London for a script meeting, feeling resentful because I'd rather have spent all Suzy's child-minder days on the house at the moment—anything to get the awful task over with. Zak Morgan, the animator, came out to the pub with me afterward and actually bought me a drink. I knew I must be looking terrible if even Zak took pity on me. We were not fond of each other. He smirked at me over the little table, chin on hand as if he were posing for an old-fashioned photo (Zak is always posing for something). "You know, you've really mellowed over the past six months, Rosie. We've all noticed. No more of those porcupine prickles everyone used to dread."

No friend of mine calls me Rosie. Patronizing bastard. But it was true. I used to fight long guerrilla campaigns at these meetings. It was only a kiddies' cartoon, but as far as I could make it so, it was always going to be on the side of the world I wanted for my Suzy. There was the time when they thought I was giving the female toon characters too many strong lines. There was the rain-forest one, when they were worried that my "ecological" bias might offend some people (for heaven's sake!). My strength was that everyone knew that I wanted as much as anybody for our product to be a success. I didn't always get my way, but I often did—just by being humorous and reasonable and yet standing my ground. Which last was way out enough to brand me as a total fanatic ın Zak's eyes.

But that was before the house. It was true, he was right— I wasn't fighting for anything at present. I had no aim in view except to keep on turning in stuff that was good enough so they'd go on paying me. I watched Zak watching me as I digested his unwelcome compliment, and the worst thing he'd told me was that a half-year had gone by. Half a year of my precious life had dropped into that abyss of a house and vanished without a trace. He was smiling as if he could see right into me: the springs of grief and loss that welled up inside. Loss irremediable, grief unassuagable . . .

"Ah, well," I said seriously. "That's because I'm rather preoccupied at the moment. I'm being haunted, Zak. I have become the victim of psychical possession."

Zak was thrilled. Just as he was getting ready to restrain me in some humane but painful fashion until the men in white coats could get here, I laughed.

"I mean the new house, Zak. I'm being haunted by dry rot. It's terrible stuff, you know. You can be riddled with it before you even suspect there's anything wrong. Maybe I should tell you about colloidal cracking, so you can check your place over before it's too late."

But on the train journey back home my joke began to take on an unintended meaning; or perhaps to take the shape of a truth that I had been avoiding. Donald was already home, and had fetched Suzy from the child-minder's. I left them playing together in her room, and went downstairs.

In fact, the dry rot was supposedly totally eradicated, and we had guarantees to prove it. But the idea of that creeping cancer of bricks and timber unnerved me, and I'd developed a bit of a phobia about the basement, where the rot had been so rampant. Though Mr. Hann's team had packed up forever two days before, I was dragging my heels. I said I wanted to wait until the weekend to take possession, when we would have more time.

Down, past the room where the sick person gasped on the other side of the wall; and the other room where I had hallucinated steel wool into an old woman's matted gray hair . . . Through the front hall, where my beautiful dream was just beginning to be realized.

Takeaway cartons still littered the basement stairway. The walls were still dirt and dark brown paint, the air still smelled of empty house—junk mail decaying in a damp hallway. I pushed open the door at the bottom of the stairs, and looked into the place Mr. Hann had elected to call "the family room." There was a wet, acrid smell of new plaster. A mountain of crated furniture and boxes stood in the middle of the new white pine floor. I literally had not been down here alone since the last site meeting before we moved in. There had been plenty to do elsewhere. I hadn't had to explain my reluctance to anyone. But I had been nervous enough about it myself to dream up that phobia about dry rot.

The white cobwebs and bare bricks had gone, but she— it—was still there. It sat exactly as I had seen it before, placidly in possession. Its hands moved constantly, hooking and twiddling away; its soft face was blankly complacent.

You Can't Make a Silk Purse Out of a Sow's Ear

I decided that I wasn't going to tell Don anything. I understood what was happening to me, I could translate the language of this haunting easily enough. But I was afraid of my reputation. Don believed in my "feelings" about places and people. I knew I had to keep quiet and weather my way through this crisis alone, or the house would be poisoned for both of us. I'd have to tolerate the slight damage that ensued to our relationship meanwhile. Once I came back from another business day to find Don rooting through my desk. There were voices downstairs. I'd noticed that we were in for an impromptu social evening and was having to brace myself. I was more anxious than ever to get the decorating and fixing up done, *to bury her.* But I would sound crazy if I said I'd rather scrape paint than relax. Don was throwing up flurries of paper, like a dog digging for a buried bone.

"What are you *doing?*" I shouted.

"Oh, Rose. I was just looking for that photograph. The one of the old Polish lady?"

This photograph we had found at the back of one of the

fitted cupboards that we took out of Suzy's room. It was an old, old sepia print, nothing to do with *my* ghostly grandmother. But I had burned it anyway.

"Why are you making such a mess?" I yelled. "It isn't in there. I don't know where it is!"

I chased him off my territory. He left with that bored, naughty-boy expression he puts on when he thinks he's run up against the incomprehensible feminine in me: Rose seen as a faulty appliance.

This house . . . For me it had its own smell now, no longer masked by damp or tar or raw plaster and wet paint. Whenever I turned my key and opened the front door, the stale perfume enveloped me: lily-of-the-valley, or maybe lavender, with a vaguely antiseptic afternote. It smelled a little of hospitals; or of the powder room of a sedate, old-fashioned department store, where underneath the effortful sweetness of old ladies who like to look nice lies just a whiff of sour, unclean decay.

I dreamed about the first time we came to see the empty house. But it wasn't empty. We were met, in the big, gloomy, cluttered hall, by the old lady from the photograph. She was a long bundle of dark blouse and skirt, like a bag tied in the middle. Her face was yellow as beeswax: her hair, pulled back into a hard bun, still quite black. We looked around. The house was full of furniture and ornaments and curtains. At the back of the big hall, its black-and-white tiles almost obscured by grime, an old gas chandelier dangled, crusted with cobwebs, as if—impossibly—the house had never been wired for electric power. Under the chandelier three doors in frames of intricate wood carving stood in a line. The wood was varnished treacle-thick, and richly freighted with dust. Each door opened onto an awkward angular slip of a room, such a perverse arrangement it was hard to guess at the original use. It was the kind of error that worked like a drug on us, making us desperate to strip out, knock through, open up . . . as if we were the only ones who could discover the *true* house, the one the original architect had failed to realize.

Everywhere there was the gloom that starts with blinds pulled down to preserve the carpets (for whom?) and becomes the murky cave where an old lady living alone hides the fact that she has become unable to cope. It was obvious that she'd just given up on most of the rooms. In an upstairs drawing room velvet curtains hung in rags, their uniform dirt color preserving in the folds odd streaks of vivid purple: the lurid taste of a long-dead age. An upright piano stood rotting on its feet, shards of its backboard scattered on the floor; inside, the dusty hammers fallen and twisted with rust. In one bedroom we lifted a mattress—I can't remember why—and found under it a layer of wriggling white larvae. Don kept looking at me hopefully (the silent communication system of the house hunters); and I was signaling, No, no, no. . . . In the middle of our viewing the men in white coats came and took the old lady away. It was someone else who let us out, and Don—that is, a part of me—was very relieved. She was gone, and we were safe. The Don part of me thought everything would be all right now. But I said, No, no, no . . .

The incident with the larvae never happened. The old Polish lady had gone to a nursing home to die several months before the house went on the market: The house was stripped down to its rotten walls before we ever saw it. We never saw a piano in here or a gas chandelier: Those three strange doors had been in another house. But some dreams become true. They become part of your remembered experience, and can't be banished by reason.

We finally moved into the basement, and at last the whole place was ours. I heated up some coffee in the microwave and stared into the sunny garden, below basement-level here at the back of the house. But I wouldn't let the wilderness out there tempt me. This was going to be a Suzy-free day spent entirely at my desk. I sipped the coffee, which tasted like hot rainwater, and headed for my office. We'd just finished decorating the big room in the front of the basement—which we were helplessly calling "the fam-

ily room,'' although we hated the description. The walls
were a clear, opaline yellow, with a geometric frieze in
black and umber over which I had taken enormous pains.
The windows that we'd had enlarged carried great swaths
of sunlight up and down, echoing my yellow: Curtains of
heavy linen still had to be hung. When the sunlight failed,
there were white-light wall fittings to replace it. I'd insisted on indirect lighting. No overhead lamps to hang down
and cast gloomy shadows: This basement would never be
gloomy, I'd been determined about that. Our old living-
room furniture—some of it looking pretty shabby—stood
about a little awkwardly in its big new home—the chairs
that hadn't yet been recovered, the old coffee table that
would have to be replaced because it just didn't fit in anymore. The art-nouveau fireplace, this one scraped by Don,
not by me, gleamed darkly in its restored beauty, its glossy
iron lilies to be echoed by the baroque yellow lilies on my
new curtains.

No trace of the decay that had conjured up my vision
remained, but I averted my eyes as I passed. I still had to
get to grips with my bad feeling about this room, in spite
of all the changes. If I don't look, then there's nothing
there. . . . I opened the door to the stairs: a narrow boxed-
in flight of steps down here, which would never look particularly lovely. There was someone climbing ahead of me.

My hand had reached automatically for the switch on
the wall; it was in artificial light that I saw the figure. She—
it—was wearing a lilac-colored dress with a white cardigan
over it. I couldn't tell much about the style of the dress,
but it looked the kind of thing any old lady might have
worn, any time in the last thirty years. The figure was
leaning on the banister with one hand, and helping itself
along with the other hand on the wall. It was looking at
me over its shoulder.

I shut the door. There were boxes of our possessions
still piled in the middle of the floor, waiting to be arranged
on polished shelves and hung on the pale walls. I went and

sat on a box of books, my back to the hearth. I was sweating. Ridiculous thoughts rushed through my mind, ridiculous expedients. I would leave a note for Don, leave now
by the basement door, go and fetch Suzy from the child-
minder's and we would run for it. We would never come
back here. We would take to the roads, become nomads.
There was no other hope of escape.

I fought with myself, and conquered. I went back and
heated up my stale coffee over again. The figure on the
stairs was no longer visible; if it was still there I walked
through it. And I did a day's work at my desk: not good
work, but good enough so I'd get paid for it.

One of my grandmothers had died before I was born.
The other, a self-sufficient old lady, hadn't had much time
for our family since her husband died. She lived in Can-
ada, I hadn't seen her since I was a child—but I discovered from my mother that she was alive and well, spry as
ever. Don had no grandparents living. Both of us had parents who were as yet untouched by age. There was no hint
of the ghost grandmother in his mother, bird-boned and
still cut-glass glamorous: or in my own dear vigorous, untidy mama. And yet I was left with the faint certainty that
I'd seen the woman on the stairs somewhere before. I dug
out photograph albums that had been buried for months in
the turmoil of moving and studied them furtively, hunting
for that soft old face. She wasn't there. Where had she
sprung from? I knew the answer of course: from deep inside myself—familiar as a bad dream.

What harm can a ghost do? Fiction apart, in the reports
that come nearest to being believable there never seems to
be purpose or coherence in these things. They just happen, they just are. What is there to be afraid of? The fear
is of the contagion of death. In Chinatown once, in an exotic city far away, I saw a deathhouse: a place to which
the old and very sick were hurried, still breathing, in a
ruthless attempt to quarantine them—exactly as if death
were an infection that could be contained. I was sick with

that infection. Something old that should be dead had used the house as a way into my mind. I knew what was happening. Doing up this house was reducing me to a mindless piece of flesh-and-blood machinery: bludgeoning me into the "housewife" role that I had always fiercely rejected. Some part of me must have been afraid of this consequence of home-ownership all along. I knew that my fear, of all that the complacent granny represented, was taking this hallucinatory form because I was so tired. I would be better soon, as soon as I could throw away my stained, burned work gloves and become Rose again. I knew all this, but I could not stop myself from thinking about that figure on the stairs. Sometimes I saw it when I opened that door, sometimes I didn't. It was always with me.

One day I was at my desk, just dashing off a quick letter or two while Suzy played in her room down below. I had the baby-listener at my side. I could hear her talking. Baby talk always sounds conversational, they always leave pauses for an invisible listener's replies . . . but suddenly I knew that she was not alone. I jumped up and ran down the stairs. There was nobody to be seen, of course. She was surrounded by a strew of colored bricks, some of them piled two and three and four.

"Who were you talking to, Suzy?"

Suzy laughed. "Gone—" she said. Or maybe, "Gran"?

I stared at her, horrified to see no trace of fear or repulsion in my child's face.

"You mustn't talk to that lady. I don't want you to play with her. She's not my friend, or yours!"

I didn't know what I was saying. When I realized the implication of my own words, I was shattered. My knees gave way under me. I crouched down on Suzy's pretty green rug.

"Oh, baby, darling . . . I didn't mean that. I know there was no lady. Mummy's not—Mummy's not well. . . ."

Children are fickle creatures. Suzy didn't cry at my strange behavior, or come to me. She lay down on the

floor instead and stayed there, gazing dreamily at the bricks
and humming a vague little tune.

I sat in the family room that night with Don. He had
demanded that we both take an evening off, to be together. It wasn't being a success. He was slumped in front
of the TV, and I couldn't even rest. My hands were itchy
for occupation.

"I feel so tired," I wailed. "I look in the mirror and I'm
horrified. And the worst is, I keep thinking I'll be all right
when things get back to normal. But they never will, Don.
Do you realize what this house has done? It has dragged
us across the great divide. We're not young anymore. What
I think of as 'normal' was being young. We managed to
hang on to that state even through having Suzy, but now
it's gone forever—"

He looked at me in bitter reproach, like a dog that's
being beaten.

"You always dramatize things, Rose. You'll be fine when
this bloody fixing up and beautifying is finished."

I'd been sitting there fighting with an impulse that really
scared me. I was still *frightened* by what I'd imagined I'd
heard Suzy say that afternoon. I was frightened too by the
way I couldn't stop myself from thinking of strange comments Don had made. He didn't say anything about a
ghost—but he would say, "The basement's awfully dark,
isn't it?" (which it was not), or "The den always seems to
feel chilly, don't you think?" Which it did not. I got up
and opened the door, looked up. It was there. I was beginning to learn what it must feel like to be really insane: to
live, always, in fear of things that no one else can see.

"Don, come here."

He came.

"Do you see anything?"

He peered up the stairwell, which was still uncarpeted:
and still the color of mud or the color of scorched, stripped
wood until two steps from the top. I saw him wince and
shudder. For a moment he terrified me.

"Oh, shit. Rose, you *promised* not to mention the house."
He glared, innocently pragmatic. "I suppose you mean
that we should be painting. Rose, are you aware that this
house is driving you crazy? No wonder you feel exhausted. You're driving us both into the ground, you're
like some kind of megalomaniac. Does it really matter
if the basement stairs don't get painted for another month
or two?"

He stomped away, growling that I had ruined the evening for both of us by nagging. So we sat among the ruins,
and eventually, when we went to bed I walked through the
thing on the stairs as if it wasn't there; and so did he.

There's No Use Crying over Spilled Milk

Suzy wasn't sleeping well. I made no connection with my
haunting; I thought it was her back teeth starting to come
through. We took turns monitoring the baby-listener. I didn't
really mind when it was my night. I lay listening to Suzy's
quiet breath and gentle stirrings, right by my pillow. Night
in this house was no different from day to me, but it was
still a comfort to have her there, exorcising the silence. I
was thinking about my cartoon characters. They were funny
little things—supposedly the denizens of a rock pool, but
they bore no resemblance to any known marine species.
Lucky creatures, they didn't have houses. Any crevice in
the rocks was good enough. I was half dreaming, story-
making, when I realized there was something wrong about
Suzy's breathing. So wrong that I was up—naked—and
down the stairs instantaneously, without even pausing to
grab a dressing gown. I didn't need to put on any lights.
A white three-quarter moon was shining full in through the
stairwell window. We had given her what was perhaps the
best room in the house, a big, sunny place with lovely windows in the front on the first floor. I saw *it* in the moon-

light, on the landing outside. It was walking away from me slowly, breathing in heavy, effortful sighs. It was going back downstairs. It had left the door of Suzy's room a little ajar, the way we always do.

Suzy was still asleep. I stood looking at her, hugging my naked body in my arms. In the blue glow of her mermaid night-light (the only piece of cartoon-merchandizing I would allow in the house) I watched her quiet breath. I could smell the faint hospital smell of talcum powder. I could see an indentation in Suzy's pillow that surely hadn't been there before. I put my own hand down beside it: Those were not the marks of my fingers. An old woman with thickened, knotted finger joints had leaned down over the child. From the corner of the room a pile of helpless eyes watched me: Suzy's toys.

She did not wake, she did not cry. I felt cold, so cold. I went back to our room, and woke Don only to have some company.

"I think I'll keep her away from the child-minder's for a while." I told him. "I'll take some time off work: It won't do me any harm."

He had been deeply asleep; he assumed I'd been dealing with another tearful teething session. He looked a little frightened. We've always been so clear that I must do more than just work for pay, I mustn't fall into the part-time, second-job trap. I must pursue my career.

"All right, Rose, if that's what you want. If you really think it's necessary."

I stayed at home. I shut my office. I worked away like a demon at the restoration of our house. Sometimes it seemed to me that I was trying to placate an evil old goddess, whom I had offended and into whose temple I had then rashly strayed. Now she had my child hostage, and I must pay. So many hours of mindless drudgery, for Suzy's life and freedom. But soon it wasn't just me; everybody noticed the change in Suzy. She had always been such a bold, bouncy little person. It is not easy to tell the gender of a clothed child that age, unless the parents choose to signal "this is a boy"; "this is a girl." Stupid people were always calling my Suzy "a real little boy!" When I corrected them, she'd become a "real little tomboy," the smile of approval visibly diminished . . . Now no more. Suzy was quiet and good. She did not climb on stepladders, she did not climb out of her cot. Suzy became a proper little girl, her movements gentle, her play sedate. In the night, almost every night now, I heard that horrible breathing. And almost every night Suzy woke sobbing, her eyes dilated in terror, her little heart thumping wildly as we held her and rocked her and walked her back to calm.

Suzy was alone with me every day; she saw the struggles that I managed to hide from everyone else. I tried to protect her from my daytime nightmares, I tried to explain to her that there was really nothing wrong with the basement stairs, it was only Mummy being silly. But soon she wanted to be carried if she had to go downstairs or upstairs at all. . . .

I was the only one who knew what was wrong, and I dared not tell. I began to have sympathy with those hysterical females in the horror videos. The woman who goes after the monster in her negligee and her feather mules, alone, because she just can't shake her husband and tell him, "Wake up, there's a . . ." A what? I could not tell. A bogey from my mind, leaning over Suzy's cot at night and whispering terrible secrets, the petal-cheeked granny's secrets that all women have to learn, can't start too soon. . . .

It was a Saturday afternoon, a sunny day in September. I was at work at my desk, and Don was in charge of Suzy. As I had taught myself to think of nothing while I was stripping and sanding and painting the old woman's body, I was now teaching myself to carry on my life with the persistent tingling nausea of anticipatory fear in my belly. Life in a dentist's waiting room, life in the last few moments before the bad news becomes certain. . . . What I was waiting for came; the breathing started.

It was such a disgusting noise. It sounded like an old man masturbating in a filthy public toilet. I could see his gap-toothed, foul-smelling mouth fall open, a little saliva dribbling out as he panted and gasped his way to satisfaction. *It was terrifying.* I went out on the stairs. The sound followed me. I sat clinging to the banisters, looking down into the hall below. Everything that I'd imagined, we had realized. Pearly sea colors lapped me around, foam-white, aquamarine, pale emerald. Souvenirs from far away decorated the walls: sea treasure gathered and arranged on the shore of our new found land. The varnished woodwork was exquisite; down below, the checkered tiles gleamed. But the horrible noise went on. I was thinking, I must tell someone. I'm going crazy, and I'm harming Suzy. And then, as I crouched and watched, the grandmother figure was there. In its styleless, timeless lilac dress and white cardigan, it drifted along the hall. When it came to the door of Donald's den, it disappeared. Fear shuddered through me, the contagion of the deathhouse.

Something moved inside Don's room, a small, natural sound. I realized that he was in there. Instantly, I was on my feet. I ran down the stairs, pushed open his door.

"Don—"

He'd made himself very cozy in there, revealing an unsuspected weakness for bright rugs and soft cushions. One corner was a small jungle of plants in blue-and-white Chinese pots. The new desk that I'd bought for him stood in the window: Two generous armchairs faced each other before the fireplace. The computer workstation lurked apologetically, half-hidden by a Japanese lacquer screen. It was a lovely room, another of our triumphs.

Suzy wasn't with him. That was normal now. She was so quiet and good, you could leave her playing by herself for half an hour or more. Don was sitting by the fine Adam-style fireplace that I had restored, his hands idle in his lap, no book or newspaper in sight. He looked up, guiltily.

The grandmother wasn't visible, but I felt a flash of bitter jealousy, because of his look of guilt surprised. Maybe

to him the spirit of this house was the old motherly type
that men love, who hurries to do them little services, gives
them the kind of attention they can't get from a demanding, liberated modern woman. Maybe she was often in here
with him, massaging his ego with little psychic touches while
he pretended not to know what was happening. . . .

"Don?"

I touched back of his chair and at once drew my hand
away, shuddering. She was here. That hideous, masturba-
tory gasping was in here as well. It filled the air. And I
forgot what I had been going to say, because I looked into
Don's eyes. I saw that he knew. He knew all about the
thing that was in this room with us.

It seemed that should be some kind of relief (I didn't
want to be mad), but instead I found myself plunged into
renewed despair. If the ghost was real, I still had to keep
my secret. There was nothing quaint or exciting about this
experience, it was simply hideous. If I mentioned it to Don
at all, I'd have to say, "We've got to get out of this place."
And we couldn't afford to leave. He must have realized all
that ahead of me.

I imagined my life continuing like this for years; yes,
maybe years. After all, she—it—didn't seem to do any actual physical harm. There are certain things, certain realities to adult life, that mean you have to bear with a few
crumpled rose leaves. And since there was nothing to be
done, I, too, must learn not to see the ghost. I must learn
to be like Don: to brush horror aside, to refuse to think
about the unmentionable pollution of our precious life together. It was hard to think straight, because whatever I
touched in here felt like flaccid warm skin. The dead weight
of a body that could no longer support itself lay in my
empty arms. And such pity for my lover filled me. Poor
Don, poor Rose, what a dismal fate for them.

"Don, I've been thinking. I don't really need an office
at the moment, and we could use another guest room. Why
don't I bring my word processor down here, and we can
work together—the way things used to be. . . ."

He stared at me as if I were mad, as if I were babbling trivialities at a deathbed. I found that I had begun to shake and sweat. No one ever escapes unscathed from these visitations. Evil comes after them. What was I talking about? What did money matter, when my child was hostage? Suzy wakening and screaming at the thing that bent over her . . .

"Don, I'm sorry. I hardly know what I'm saying. I've got to talk to you about Suzy—"

"Yes," he said. "Yes . . . I know."

We went to the door of her room and stood looking in, in the bright sunlight. Suzy was sitting on the floor, playing with a sorting toy she had conquered weeks ago. As we watched, she gave up the unequal struggle and clambered to her feet. She took a few steps across the green rug, then sat down again as carefully as an old lady. The room was neat and tidy: no strew of bricks, no wreckage of overturned racing cars. Suzy sighed—a strangely adult sound of human weariness—and watched the sunlight on the wall. She seemed quite content.

Don took time off from work to take her to the clinic. He said he understood why I didn't want to go along. I waited until they were out of the house, and then I fetched out the dust sheets that had so recently been folded and stored away. I cleared every surface and shrouded the furniture in our "family room." It was important to me that I should set to work with method, not like a crazy woman. I pulled the phone plug and put on my working clothes.

I found destruction amazingly easy at first, such a relief from the tedious drudgery of restoration. The fireplace with the cast-iron lilies, pillars, and mantel was all in one piece. I hauled away the polished fender, dismantled the firebasket that had never yet held a fire in this incarnation. I drilled out the new mortar from all around the iron and pulled it free. The yellow wall of the chimney breast was spatttered with plaster and dirt by now, like gouts of blood.

I was looking for something that was buried, so I ignored the gaping wound of the chimney's throat and set to work on the stone hearth slab below. It wasn't as immovable as it looked; a crowbar lifted it. I did not pause to be amazed at my own strength, I knew where it came from: *hysterical,* they call it. Women have lifted cars. . . .

I climbed down into the pit and began to dig. When I hit rock, I turned on the brick piers that supported the new chimney breast. I knew then that even my fantastic excuse for hope had deserted me: This ghost would not be laid by exhumation. But I went on. Maybe I could never find it, but it was buried somewhere, everywhere, in the bricks and mortar, the body of an evil old woman: the rotted bones of soft complacent age, the decay that was poisoning our air. I hacked away the skin and tore at the red flesh of this, my other body, just as the builders had hacked away at the horrible lesions of rot. The smell of damp and decay came welling out like blood.

I knew all along the place was still rotten under all our paint and polish: the rot still creeping, the old gray lungs still sodden with moisture. I would expose everything this time. I would drain the abscess, scour and burn. . . .

It was engrossing work. I was so absorbed I didn't realize how time was passing. I was still hard at it, plastered red to the elbows with sweat and brick dust, when I heard Don's key turn. Then I woke up. I saw the devastation that surrounded me—shattered brickwork, ruined floor, the gaping pit I stood in: the filthy chaos that I'd made in the heart of our home. I had a moment of blind panic: *He'll have me locked up!*

Don came down the basement stairs with Suzy in his arms. He stood staring at what I had done, neither shocked nor surprised, his face a mirror of my own helpless desperation.

What Can't Be Cured Must Be Endured

Time has passed—oh, eons of time—and to think I once imagined six months was a lot to lose. It is late evening.

I'm sitting in the family room, reading and watching television. The fuel-effect gas fire flickers in our chrome-and-steel firepit: providing a kind of space-age coziness that somehow works very well with the art-nouveau furnishings. Don is in his den. Spending time apart from each other, when we can, has become a habit. I even still do some scriptwriting—well enough that they pay me. I don't really know what Don gets up to. We could go out more often, one at a time. We can get help, it wouldn't be impossible. But somehow neither of us wants to be away from our little old lady for long.

What's it like to live in a haunted house? It's frightening, disturbing, irritating; and finally, you just put up with it. Sometimes I wake in the night and hear that terrible sound, which has now become quite familiar and accustomed to me. I go next door, if it is my turn, into the faint, sour sickroom smell that nothing can quite expunge, and tend the young-old body that grows a little more helpless every day. For a moment I am possessed by an alien consciousness. In my mind a lost Rose shouts and struggles and has violent, ruthless visions of escape for herself and her child. But it doesn't last. We will escape, Don and I, soon enough. Of course, it will be too late (as Rose always feared). I don't suppose we'll ever move, for one thing. There's too much that we love, too many memories buried here. And there is a quietness in this kind of life that takes the edge off you: I don't honestly think I could face the rat race again, even if it would have me.

"It isn't our fault!" That was Don's first cry when he brought her home, on the day that we will remember forever as the most important in our lives. Such anguish strips people naked: He meant that Suzy's illness is not hereditary. No one really understands why children like Suzy suffer and die: not yet. There are some statistics that point accusingly to a pesticide that was in general use when I was pregnant (it's banned in this country now). But nothing's proven. And perhaps Don and I, although at first we used to demand answers like a pair of remorseless Furies,

are happier in ignorance. Too little, too late: The tiny ways in which I tried to save the world for Suzy's sake seem so absurd now. It's better not to think too much. It's better to stay at home, and let the world look after itself.

This house. I should have known that remodeling was not enough. We should have razed it to the ground, burned the foundations out to bedrock. Sometimes I torment myself with thoughts of that kind, with the conviction that there was a chance and I didn't take it: that when we moved in here, I tried to defy something old and utterly implacable, and I have been horribly punished. But more often I accept the other version, the one that hurts less. I understand what it was—who it was—that came to me, to tell me the bad news. . . . There's no more need for a warning now, but I think as long as we live in this house, the figure on the stairs will always be there, looking back at me over its shoulder. I will find myself a little closer, and a little closer, as the years go by, until at last I can recognize the face.

I find it very hard to switch out of my busy mode nowadays. When I force myself to relax, I end up like this, neither watching the TV nor reading my book. In a moment I'll have to fetch myself something to do—it scarcely matters what.

Jessica Amanda Salmonson is a winner of the World Fantasy Award and an expert devotee of nineteenth century supernatural fiction. Her most recent book is *What Did Miss Darrington See?: An Anthology of Feminist Supernatural Fiction*. She lives in Seattle, Washington, where she runs a bookstore, Aunt Violet's Bookbin & Menagerie: A Home for Decayed Gentlewomen. She describes this story as an account of "a descent into a headlong madness." This story is a powerful combination of the horrific, the surreal, and the fantastic.

Madame Enchantia and the Maze of Dream

JESSICA AMANDA SALMONSON

I.

In the maze of dream, we cannot see our human sorrow.

—Anaïs Nin

II.

These have been difficult months for me. After years of a peaceful relationship with a gentle lover, things unexpectedly ended. There was no reason, unless boredom is a reason. We never fought. If we'd hated each other, it might have gone on and on. "Even good things change," I was told; there was no fuller explanation.

I reread *Wuthering Heights*, seeking that belief in soul-partners, and found it, along with assurance they bring each other only pain.

I believe in the pain, at least, and in the horror. What is the supernatural compared to the terrors of our common

259

lives? What is more horrific than an ordinary broken heart? That is why I've come to seek Our Lady of Tattoos. That's why I stand before you now. Will you introduce me to her? I seek nothing save admission to the maze. I know about it from a man who lives and drinks and mumbles in the streets. He has a tattoo on his forehead. Yes, yes, that's right, the tattoo of a coiled serpent, devouring itself, in faded blues and reds. It is like the third eye of the mystics. He saw that I was hurting. His eyes were filled with pity, his three eyes. It is because of the things he told me that I have come all this way.

Oh, thank you. Thank you. I'll sit right here and wait to see the Madame.

III.

You're more beautiful than I imagined, Madame Enchantia! I wish I were as beautiful as thee. Such wonderful black hair! Mine is dirty yellow. Your dark, dark skin! I am far too sallow. I wish I were a gypsy. I wish I were a negress. I wish I were a Jewess. I wish I were Italian. I wish I were anything but pale as a maggot and always sad.

Oh, that's very kind of you, but it isn't so. I'm not at all pretty. Why, I'm almost middle-aged, getting old. I could stand to shed a few pounds, that's certain. Yes, you're right; I do consider myself terribly plain. You can't convince me otherwise, although once I looked fair enough, in the flush of youth. The young are always prettiest, don't you think so? No? Well, I do.

I was told that youth awaits us in the maze. Is it so? Oh, but I was informed . . . well, never mind. Whatever waits, I'm eager. There has to be something more to life than what I see. I'll settle for anything at all outside the bounds of reason. A chaotic universe has got to have more options than such a reasoned one as this.

If there is magic, then there might be a heaven, am I

right? Otherwise, the only thing that happens is we suffer, then we die. What good is there in that? It strikes me as unfair, and not in the least pleasant.

IV.

That's right, it's as your assistant told you. I broke up with someone. I've not been well since. Despair's much more frightful than vampires and ghosts. By comparison, such monsters would be a relief. I was always frightened about such things, afraid they might exist. But now . . . it would be better that they did exist. Oh no, not because I would want them to kill me. At least, I don't think I've come on a suicidal impulse, although it may play some small part; do we ever know ourselves?

When I heard about the maze, I was curious. I hadn't been curious about anything for a while. It was a marvel to be curious. I'm not as afraid as I might have been before I lost security and love. Or perhaps it's only that the fear no longer matters. I think the maze will be interesting, that's all.

It might change my perspective. That's what I think. Just like those people who've had near-death experiences. You've heard about that. They know something the rest of us cannot believe because we've never seen it. They're more at peace with themselves. I just want to know something for a change, something that's not real—really know it, rather than suspecting, doubting, wondering, hoping.

Reality is pain, and I can't stand it. There has to be something else, or it's not worth seeing through. So it could be that my quest is antisuicidal. You don't have to worry about some slier intention on my part.

What are you handing me? A phone number? But I wanted to see the maze. Whose number is this? Won't you say?

Well, as you insist, I'll go home and try it. But I was hoping to go into the maze at once.

V.

Hello? I was told to call this number. Goodness! Madame Enchantia! Why did you send me home to call you? Can I make an appointment for the maze? I—I am? Already? But I haven't seen anything new. I'm still right here in my grubby apartment. Pardon me? What—what should I tell you about it? Well, it's a third-floor flat, entirely ordinary. I have a lot of books. Yes, I read lots. All the time. I guess that's why I'm so boring to people. All I ever do is read. Other people go to movies or watch news on the television, and can share their ideas about things. They have a common knowledge. They're part of the larger world without having to try. When I talk about these books, people look at me like I'm strange.

I don't blame them for being bored, but I like old books so much. I can't give them up. I know it's awful. Maybe I'd still have my lover had I been willing to change. Oh, that's very kind of you, Madame Enchantia, but you'd be bored by it, too, if I said much more about it.

The walls? They're behind bookshelves. You can hardly see the walls. What shows is blue. That's odd, because I would have sworn they were yellow. Funny thing to have forgotten.

It's a wonder the books don't fall on the floor with the shelves at such wild angles. I put them up myself, but only this minute realized what a bad job I made of it. They're every which way. The bed? I keep it in the living room. It's ordinary. About forty-five feet long and four feet wide. It sticks out the front-room window way over the street. I can't use most of it.

There's a carpet. A baby-blue carpet. (But I'd thought it was yellow!) It's crawling with bugs. I used to have a dog, but he died a year ago because a neighbor gave him a poison wienie. It was sad. I've tried ever since to get rid of the parasites he left behind—mostly tiny beetles, but also fleas and spiders. But I'm adverse to chemicals, given that I myself crawl around on the floor a great deal.

The fleas never bite me. There is something in my chemistry they don't like. Whatever it is that's strange about my system, it stops wristwatches, too. If I wear a wristwatch for about two days, it stops, and won't get going for a long time after I take it off. So I never know what time it is. Wristwatches and fleas don't like me. But at night mosquitoes come in the front-room window. I can't shut the window with the foot of the bed sticking so far out.

VI.

The ceiling's vaulted, that's right—how did you know? I hadn't noticed personally, until you mentioned it. It's rather a nice ceiling. I should have paid more attention before. It goes way up there, so I can't see everything. It's all shadowy, but there are paintings between exposed beams. The beams are gold and silver-leafed.

The paintings are of classical subjects in the manner of Michelangelo. I can make out Buddha and Zeus and Smet-Smet the Hippopotamus Goddess, a real jumble of mythology. I could look at it all day.

VII.

I can't imagine why I used to complain about the rent. I have a lot of room for what I pay. Thousands upon thousands of square feet. I need it for the library. The ladders go way, way up and disappear into the shadows. They're on coasters and roll along the fronts of shelves. Everything I ever learned, experienced, or imagined is in those books.

The library takes up only a living room and dining area, but the shelves act as partitions, so there are dozens and dozens of hallways and dark corners and the illusion of innumerable rooms. Rows and rows, stacks and stacks, books everywhere, and I never seem to have enough shelves for everything, so I've piled books in all the corners, teetering heaps eager to topple and bury someone who's not careful.

Vast numbers of books surround me, an infinity of volumes all around, yet I've read nearly everything. It's surprising, but I have. Sometimes two or three times. Now and then something gets hidden before I have the chance to read and ponder it, but it pops out eventually, and I'm happily amazed to find something I'd forgotten I'd obtained.

Golly, it's just lots of fun in here.

VIII.

My kitchen is a marvel. The telephone cord only reaches about halfway down the book-strewn table. There are hundreds of feet of uncoiling phone cord, but it won't reach so far as the candelabrum and the gleaming crystal goblets. Spread amid the books all along the length of the enormous table are fragments of manuscripts for stories I've been working on my entire life but never finished. It doesn't look like much of a filing system, but I know where everything is.

There are numerous copper pots hanging on the wall above the great iron stoves. It takes a telescoping rod to reach the pots hanging nearest the top. The ceiling isn't as high as in the other rooms, but it's still high. I've got all these herbs and peppers and garlics hanging from the ceiling as well as some inverted flowers drying out. It smells good in here. You'd like it.

I've got a lot of stuff in the walk-in box, a regular Arctic Circle in there. You could take a team of dogs and a sled and wander for days admiring the hams, whole sides of beef, scores of fryer hens, and those wonderful ice sculptures left in there by some people from Sapporo.

The walnut doors of the cabinets have etched-glass windows. In the cupboards are row atop row of blue-and-yellow boxes of Kraft macaroni and cheese.

IX.

I don't sleep in the bedroom. I sleep in the living room to be near my books, so I can read whenever I wake up in the night. I only sleep about three hours, then read by lamplight.

Here's a book about Samuel Pepys's clerk. Here's one about Lola Montez in old San Francisco. I'm fond of biographies. People about whom books have been written are ever so much more fascinating than people who write such books. Or read them, for that matter. I read about people of the past, people who are dead, and I get to feel as though they're my friends, that they know me and are glad that I exist. I never feel that way about individuals I meet in my everyday existence. I'd rather be with people in books than with people in real life. I'd rather be with people who are dead.

The bedroom was converted into an artist's studio. My lover was a painter. Now the room is empty. The phone won't reach, but that's okay, as I hate to go in there. It reminds me of things, things that are gone. It's like a desert, too bright because of huge windows along two walls, spectacularly tall leaded-crystal windows; rainbows shine on everything. It's oppressive. I prefer a dark room. I may get dark curtains, curtains of black lace, or just paint the

windows black, then extend my library when I'm feeling
ambitious enough to add extra shelving. As it stands, the
room is useless, horrible. I feel like a vampire trapped in
a greenhouse when I go in there.

X.

Yes, there is something of an attic, though it isn't an attic
per se. The owner of the complex used to live in this unit
and therefore made some extraordinary additions for himself. An iron spiral staircase leads to a Gothic tower. I
rarely go up there because I'm afraid of heights. It's always dark up there, even in the midst of day, even though
it's made of glass.

It's an observatory for the alchemical study of the matter of the universe. The landlord made a fortune extracting
rare ingredients for obscure elixirs, ingredients found only
in the swirling soups of half-formed galaxies. He eventually built a larger observatory elsewhere, and no longer
requires this one.

From that unwholesome loft I've witnessed universes
within universes, but that sort of thing is not for me. It's
dizzyingly incomprehensible to my simple mind. I wouldn't
go up there at all except to replenish the automatic bird-
feeders. In the crisscrossing crystal rafters there are owls
the size of bumblebees, with eyes like gleaming rubies. I
feed them pine nuts, freeze-dried fruit flies, oxblood, and
ground-up trout pellets, in accordance with instructions
posted by the American Ornithological Society.

The tower is not visible from the street except as a ghostly
trick of light, for the glass is of a special kind that scarcely
refracts light and exists, additionally, between dimensions.

Can you hold a minute? There's someone at the door.

XI.

What a surprise! I was just talking to you on the phone.
How did you get here so fast? Do come in, won't you?
You'll have to excuse the mess.

You look so serious, Madame Enchantia. Why don't you
say something? Is your voice still in the phone?

You look so sad, Madame Enchantia. I'm sorry if it up-
sets you so much. She and I got along so well. We were a
perfect couple. Everyone said so. We dressed similarly in
brightly embroidered kimonos. That's before I took to
wearing black. We walked around the rainy city wearing
high wooden geta so our feet wouldn't get wet. We went
arm in arm under a big paper umbrella. Tourists took our
picture all the time. We were local characters, liked by
everyone, and everybody smiled to see us. Then I was left
alone, and everybody asked where she was. They were
surprised when I told them she left me. After so many
years, they had taken us for granted.

I cried and was morose and wandered around the streets
alone, dragging my umbrella upside down. I wailed at the
doors of shops. I was even arrested for making noises with
my eyes and nose and mouth, sounds of pain that no one
liked.

XII.

To tell the truth, I'd had better lovers. She was too pas-
sive, too selfish. But sex isn't everything. I was happy and
wasn't ready for the end.

XIII.

One day I'd been downtown alone, standing on a street
corner, wailing. She unexpectedly pulled up at the curb in

her yellow Volkswagen that's so dirty because she hadn't washed it once in seven years. She threw open the passenger door and shouted, "Don't stand there screaming, get in!" She drove me around to bookstores I'd not been to since she left me. She said, "We're having such a good day together. You see, we can still be friends."

But I was not having a good day, and she didn't know a thing, stupid, unfaithful shitface I'd like to kill. I was polite and said yes to everything. When she went in a grocery store to buy some chocolate-covered marshmallows, which she stupidly liked better than any kind of candy, I stayed in the car. When she was out of sight, I jumped out and removed from my shoulder bag a container of toilet cleaner I'd been carrying for days. I hurried behind the VW and opened the hood to the engine. I dumped half the toilet cleaner into the oil and closed the hood. The other half I added to the gasoline.

When we were on the road, headed toward some outlying bookstore, the car broke down. She got out and looked at the engine, and saw toilet-cleansing crystals spilled around the oil cap. She started shouting, "You bitch! You stupid bitch! We were having a nice day, and you ruined it! You bad, stupid bitch!" I started walking home, and left her there with the car.

That was a thrilling event for me. We'd always got along so well, she just hadn't known how enraged I felt. She hadn't believed such intensity of feeling was possible. She thought she could change all the rules and still have her way, have me as her best friend and to hell with those years of being lovers.

XIV.

The next time I saw her it was in a nearby bookstore. I grabbed the glasses off her face and ran outside. She came shouting behind me and caught up in time to see me grind her glasses into the sidewalk.

The time after that was when I went to the place she worked, a vintage-clothing store. I kicked my foot through the jewelry display case. I had to pay the shop owner, but my ex-lover was fired, so it was worth it.

XV.

She believed in the supernatural, but I was a skeptic. Her mother died the year we met, and she said it was like her mother had sent me to take care of her at a hard time. Sometimes, she said, it was as though her mother's soul had transmigrated into me and I was literally her mother.

I can't imagine what kind of relationship they had.

XVI.

For a long time I went into seclusion because I had become a burden to everyone and couldn't stop. I sat in this apartment all day, all night, staring and sobbing, the walls absorbing my anguish. I couldn't concentrate to read, which is a terrible thing for someone like me.

It felt as though I had become some sort of fixture—an electrical socket or water pipe—with the majority of my inner essence sucked out out of me and hidden in these walls. The walls became my skin. My actual body was weightless and hollow. If I went out into the world, I was in danger of floating away. Most of me was left behind in the walls of my apartment. I would soon return to reclaim the rest of my being, and wallow in an agony of desolation.

My thoughts explored the most appalling convolutions. I felt myself vanishing, vanishing. Not until I learned about your fabulous tattoo parlor did I think to get outside myself, to bring the internal windings to the surface, to absorb more completely my environment before it absorbed what was left of me. We are each of us mazes, Madame Enchantia, and the struggle has always been to escape ourselves. Yet to struggle is useless. If only I could externalize and accept these truths completely, I would be healed. I still pray that you will accept this eager pilgrim.

XVII.

I did have one pleasant interlude from all the horror, but it didn't last. I met a woman on holiday from New Orleans. She was tall and handsome and naïve and an African-American who had never made love with a woman but was attracted to the possibilities. She was attracted to me. She dreamed about opening a bookshop. She thought I was pretty, and she was impressed by all my obscure knowledge of the past. We spent every minute together, and went all over town visiting bookstores. That was her own idea, so I didn't have to feel guilty. We saw three films, one of which made her sick. We talked until late into the night about really sexy stuff. But I wasn't willing to leap into anything after so many monogamous years. It was too strange and distressing to consider a mere weekend romance. When she flew back to Louisiana, I felt abandoned. I cried for hours, and felt numb and foolish for not having gone to bed with her.

I learned from this experience that it was possible to get over certain things. I had thought it likely I would never again be attracted to anyone, that I could never get so much as a crush on somebody, that my trust and ability to love were forever lost.

But as it turns out, nothing really matters. It's all just as pointless as that.

XVIII.

Where are you leading me now, Madame Enchantia? I'm glad enough to follow. It stinks back here in the shadows.

To be near to you, to speak with you, makes me feel as though I've lived my whole life in a maze and only now am free. Gracious, your eyes are sad, Madame Enchantia: beautiful dark pools of sorrow. How I wish that I could ease your pain!

See these Victorian cookbooks? They're hard to use because they give imprecise measurements and no temperatures, but where else can you find recipes for skunk-cabbage stew, roast muskrat, and sugared moss? It's a different world in these old books, I'll let you know.

Never leave me, Madame Enchantia. Please, never leave me.

XIX.

Hello-hello? Oh, thank goodness, you're still on the line. I was talking to you in the living room when suddenly you climbed out the window and used my bed as a bridge to get to the brownstone across the street. When you went down that fire escape, swift as a spider down a web, and vanished through the alley, I feared I'd never see you again. I wasn't sure if I was supposed to follow, as you didn't motion for me to do so. I'm relieved to hear your voice.

Why wouldn't you talk to me while you were here? It's all right. You're forgiven. It was strange, though; almost as though you weren't flesh. If I believed in ghosts . . . but there's nothing unexpected in this world. Life is prosaic and banal. Nothing unexpected ever happens.

I should come where? All right. I'll meet you in the tattoo parlor at midnight.

XX.

How very much I love you, Madame Enchantia. I wish you could love me half as well. But I'll settle for the needles that you're pressing to my skin, the blood you draw, the colors placed just so. I'll stay here in the maze for weeks, for months, forever, however long it takes to disguise this sallow flesh, to cover me with gaudy hues and Aztec convolutions, beasts, landscapes, shadows. The sweet agony of knives! The pretty dyes and dripping crimson; the scabs that last for days, then fall away, revealing artful shapes and shades around my breasts, around my eyes and lips, along my legs and arms and fingers, the winding paths of pretty pigments beautifying me.

Soon no inch of me remains horridly unblemished. Nothing is left vulnerable to mirrors and prying eyes. Here, in the maze of dream, reality is unchanged, but all of it is pleasure.

E dward Bryant is a winner of both the Hugo and Nebula awards. His books include *Cinnabar, Wyoming Sun,* and *Particle Theory.* His fiction has been published in *OMNI, Rolling Stone, Analog, The Magazine of Fantasy & Science Fiction,* and *National Lampoon.* He is a book reviewer for *Mile High Comics* and *LOCUS,* and was formerly a reviewer for *Twilight Zone.* He grew up on a cattle ranch in Wyoming and now lives in Denver, Colorado.

"Slippage" is set in a house that Bryant and his fellow instructor, Joyce Thomsen, lived in during the summer while teaching at the Haystack Arts Conference. It was a house assigned to the faculty, so he had no contact with the person responsible for the interior. But the house's strange interior caused him to ask himself who built it . . . and why? The physical setting invoked the psychological story we see here, which gives us a glimpse of the life and death of a narcissistic couple who have all eternity to reflect upon their life-style.

Slippage

EDWARD BRYANT

Y ou really don't get much practical use out of the mar-
ble-veined mirror squares lining the walls and ceiling
of the upstairs bath. The light from the sixties triple-
globed monstrosity strung along a vertical chain is ren-
dered dim and diffused by the gold veining.

In the downstairs bathroom, the veining is all in blood,
scarlet beginning to dry to black. You were starting to shave
that morning, remember? The straight razor glittered in the
light from the Hollywood makeup bulbs. Too bad you
slipped. It *was* slippage, wasn't it?

You didn't have to use that cold, honed edge. A perfectly good Norelco triple-headed electric nestled in the
right-hand drawer of the under-sink cabinet. But you had
to shave the way you understood men shave. Real men.
The kind of man who reads the magazine you modeled this
whole house after. The sort of man who would lather the
soap in the small ceramic dish and slather it on your throat
with the fine, limp brush that used to belong to your grandfather. The stubble was so pale and soft. You always wanted

275

it to be a little more bristly, the kind of tough abrasive that could make a woman cry out.

No woman cried out when you were finally found. All the housecleaner said when she let herself in a sweltering five August days after the razor slipped was first, Jeez what a stink, and then, Oh, shit, when she saw what lay across the orange-and-green shag. Not much of an epitaph. Ah, love, I'm sorry I was away for that week in San Francisco. I should have known. No one called.

You really love this three-story weathered gray house overlooking the Pacific. The timber's started to warp a little, the Oregon wetness swelling and rotting the boards. At one time—1962, isn't it, when it was first built?—all the rooms look exactly like the backgrounds in the glossy photographic layouts that so enthrall you. All the appointments are precisely right, from the nautical touches such as the hawser railing winding all the way down four flights of stairs to the old schooner wheel bolted to the living-room wall above the bright orange couch. All the furniture is still vintage. You fixed on orange and red, didn't you? You said the colors reminded you of fire and of life.

The master bedroom is the centerpiece, the heart of it all. At first, the mirrored ceiling disoriented us when you woke up in the morning. You looked strange from this angle, not at all the way you imagined yourself, not the way you encountered your face when you closed in on the medicine cabinet mirror in the bathroom. Part of the alienness is the fact that you woke up without glasses. You needed corrective lenses, but were too vain to go to the eye-doctor.

You wondered what it would look like in the ceiling with a beautiful woman cradled in your arms, chin nestled against your shoulder, breasts barely covered with the red velour coverlet. You never found out.

Perhaps you should have. Perhaps I should have allowed you. I didn't believe I was ready. Now, after all these years, I don't recall what I was waiting for.

You used to walk the outside deck, staring west past the towering rocks and the combers to the flat horizon, wondering why so many of the house's interior walls were shake-shingled. You want a clear demarcation of what's in and what is out. I can sympathize. Maybe you shouldn't have handed the decorator what was effectively a blank check.

But you wished something ideal. You've always wanted that. In a way, it's what you finally achieved.

There's no going back.

The blood has never come completely out of the downstairs shag. But then the carpet was supposed to mask just about any spill, to soak up and hide anything. And so it has.

It's such a house for late-blooming adolescents, said the one woman who might eventually, given plenty of time and the right circumstances, have ended up waking in the marshmallow bed in the master bedroom, who might have looked up at the mirrors along with you and smiled at the blur of tangled, naked limbs, who might have basked lazily in the warmth of the carpeted and corkboarded walls and the flocked wallpaper. I could have done that.

But even she finally came right out and said you had more money than maturity or sense, or even love. Then she went away on that trip to San Francisco. She led you to believe it was forever. But as it turned out . . . My good-bye was kind, but distant. Yours was hurt and bewildered.

Grow up, I said. Maybe you'll have the ghost of a chance.

You tried.

Now you'll never grow up, you know. No more than you did. Not ever.

Nor will I. The pills and the vodka—neat—were *my* downfall. I think it was an accident. A slippage . . .

We will be around for a long, long time.

Ah, yes, my love—there's nothing like two consummate

narcissists accompanying each other for eternity in a house of mirrors. Too deeply in love we are, with ourselves as much as with each other.

It really is too bad we cannot see ourselves in all that shining glass.

Richard A. Lupoff is the host of the weekly show *Probabilities* on radio station KPFA in Berkeley, California, and has written more than twenty books, including *Time's End, Circumpolar!, Countersolar!,* and *Lovecraft's Book.* He has worked as a journalist, radio and TV writer, screenwriter, speech writer, critic, and author. He lives in Berkeley, California.

When I first began investigating stories of haunted houses, I discovered that many of them were allegedly nonfiction. Certainly, I had expected this of works from the nineteenth century. But that tradition has been carried forward to the present day. Examples include *The Amityville Horror,* as well as collected accounts of hauntings in such books as *Haunted Houses* by Richard Winer and Nancy Osborn and *Houses of Horror* by Richard Winer. Here, Richard A. Lupoff skillfully blends literary history and fiction in this tale of H. P. Lovecraft's visit to E. Hoffmann Price in New Orleans. Lupoff paid a visit to New Orleans this past summer and says that though the events of the story are speculative, the places (except for the cellar) are authentic.

The House on Rue Chartres

RICHARD A. LUPOFF

alik Tawus's chili party—in later years Lovecraft would always think of it as Malik Tawus's chili party— took place on Lovecraft's last full day in New Orleans. He would be gone before tomorrow's sun disappeared behind the Mississippi, and never again would he set foot in the state of Louisiana.

Lovecraft had treated himself to a gentleman's tour of the Southeast, concluding his travels with the Crescent City. He had been delighted when E. Hoffmann Price had sought him out at his hotel in the Vieux Carré.

Price said, "I had a telegram, no less, from Two-Gun Bob Howard. He told me you were in New Orleans, gave me your hotel and all. Good thing he did, too. Imagine, if we'd been living within a rifleshot of each other and never even got to break bread."

"I didn't know you were here, Malik. Thought you were out West working for some giant corporation."

"Hah! Prestolite! Looked as if we were riding out the Depression in good shape, then one morning—*wham!*—no

job. Maybe it's all for the best." Price smiled ruefully. "It's
sink or swim now, as a writer. I'd long wanted to take the
plunge but I never had the courage. This time the gods
have forced my hand."

Lovecraft nodded in sympathy. "Your stuff is first-rate,
Malik. You've an ideal background for literature. West
Pointer, world traveler, swordsman extraordinaire. Not to
mention your alleged prowess as a chili chef."

"Alleged?" Price snorted. "Is that a dig? Or maybe a
hint. I understand that you like it hot, Abdul. But I think
my recipe is a bit *too* hot for your New England taste."

Lovecraft said, "I find that hard to believe."

Price grinned wolfishly. "There's a pot on my stove now.
It's been simmering for two days. You haven't had your
dinner yet, have you, Abdul?"

"I should be honored to sample your product, Malik."

While Price attended to the cooking, Lovecraft pottered
around the room, picking up gimcracks that bore the mark
of craftsmen's hands around the world. Shortly Price
emerged from the tiny kitchen, aproned and hatted as a
proper chef. The plate he bore contained a concoction of
red beans, yellow rice, and brown meat in a bubbling crimson sauce. He set it before Lovecraft.

One taste brought tears to Lovecraft's eyes. The chili
was delicious, but—

"Are you all right, Howard?"

Lovecraft managed to nod; he did not trust himself
to speak.

He managed to down a bowl of the fiery concoction.
When he was able to catch his breath, he complimented
Price on the excellence of the cuisine. Price followed the
chili with a pot of his personal coffee, thick enough to stand
a spoon in and strong enough to dissolve the metal if it
were left too long.

When Lovecraft had drained his third cup of grainy Java,
the talk turned to other matters, to stories and their authors, to the editors with whom Price and Lovecraft alike
had to deal, to mutual friends and interests, likes and dis-

likes. Price praised Lovecraft's tales, spoke enthusiastically of Lovecraft's brooding, morbid Randolph Carter and the obsessive experimenter Herbert West. Lovecraft returned the encomia, dwelling in particular on Price's peerless medieval swordsman Pierre d'Artois and his faithful aide Jannicot.

"Tomorrow I return to Providence," Lovecraft said. "My purse is empty. 'Tis time to resume my scrivener's crouch."

Price smiled ruefully. "I know I can't induce you to stay in New Orleans longer, Abdul. I've tried! But . . . come along now, my friend. You survived a bowl of chili that would raise blisters on a saddle. I've arranged another treat for your last night in the Vieux Carré."

They left Price's room and made their way through ancient streets illuminated dimly by flickering gaslight. A shower had passed while Lovecraft dined on Price's prize chili; the night had cooled. Ragged clouds, blown by a wind from the Gulf of Mexico, shrouded a faint sliver of pale moon.

At a dim turning of the street, Price and Lovecraft paused to watch as a horse-drawn carriage rattled by. The recent rain, heated by the cobblestones, now rose in a ghostly mist. Through it could be seen the lettering that indicated Rue Chartres.

"Just a bit farther, Abdul." Price led the way. Despite the presence of all-night revelers in the Vieux Carré, the Rue Chartres seemed deserted save for Lovecraft and Price. Price halted before a heavy wooden door.

"Here, my friend, is the very building prepared for the great Bonaparte more than a century ago. The pirate Lafitte and Governor Claiborne of Louisiana had invited the emperor to come to New Orleans. They built this house for him. It would have been his final home in exile. Or—who knows?—he might have had other plans than a peaceful retirement, eh?"

"But Napoleon never visited the New World, Malik. Surely you are aware of that. What are you driving at?"

"You're right. He died before the plan could come to

fruition. But the house was built, and here it stands." Price shrugged. "Still, the emperor was a strong-willed man. If his spirit dwells somewhere beyond the Great Divide, waiting the moment to make its return, might it not cross an ocean as easily, Abdul? The world is full of strange and wondrous things, of which we comprehend but few!"

Lovecraft snorted. "And on the Day of Judgment we shall all rise from our tombs and dance a merry gavotte. Really, Malik!"

Price raised one hand and rapped out a pattern on the ancient wood. The house appeared to be in total darkness, yet Lovecraft thought he detected music from inside.

A panel no larger than a playing card slid open in the door. An eye peered out, a voice said, "Mr. Price!" the panel slid closed once again, and the door swung wide on silent hinges. Price stepped inside, drawing Lovecraft behind him. The door slammed behind them.

Lovecraft recoiled from the sights and sounds and odors that smote his senses. Tables held the glasses, bottles, and dinner dishes of celebrants. Others hosted card games. Stacks of greenbacks and gold and silver coins slid back and forth dizzyingly. Gaslights provided dim illumination. At one end of the room couples jumped and bounced to the music of a crew of sweating black-skinned musicians who blew savage horns and thumped jungle drums on an elevated bandstand.

The person who had admitted Price and Lovecraft led them to a table. Before Lovecraft could speak, they were joined by a female. Price leapt to his feet and kissed her hand, holding her chair. Her perfume swept before her. Her dark hair was done up in the high, graceful coiffure of a bygone day; most of the females in the room wore the modern bob and shingle styles that Lovecraft detested. This woman wore an old-fashioned gown, elegant, of magenta satin and black lace trim, its bodice cut low to reveal an ample, graceful bosom.

Lovecraft averted his eyes. This female looked familiar. Had he encountered her somewhere before? His mind sought out a tour upon which Price had taken him. They had been seated, drinking coffee in the French Market. . . .

Price smiled at a young lady seated alone at a table nearby. The young lady was an attractive, dark-haired wench done up smartly in the latest fashions. Her skin was smooth, with a touch of olive. Was that evidence of Mediterranean blood, Lovecraft wondered, or of Creole?

The young lady returned Price's smile with a definite wink.

Lovecraft asked, "An acquaintance, Malik?"

"Of sorts. Would you care to meet her?"

A frown crossed Lovecraft's lips. "After my unfortunate venture into matrimony . . ."

"One thing we learned in the cavalry, Howard. Once a horseman gets thrown, he'd better climb back on."

"Thank you, Price, but on that subject I am definite. I have had enough of the sex."

"We'll see about that." Price drained the last of his coffee.

The memory slipped back into the dark recess from which it had emerged. Lovecraft was once more in the present. He heard Price address the woman. "This is my friend, the slightly mad Arab Abdul Alhazred."

The female laughed. "Pleased to meet you, Mr. Alhazred." She extended a hand. Lovecraft touched it briefly. "My name is Lily," the woman said. Lovecraft was certain that this was the same woman he and Price had encountered in the French Market.

"Your usual tonight?" Lily asked Price. Lovecraft noticed that Lily's speech was marked distinctly by a flavor of the local patois. Dark hair, dark eyes. Yes, he concluded, there was surely Creole blood in her. He shrank slightly in his seat

Price said, "For me, by all means. As for my friend—" He nodded questioningly at Lovecraft, but Lovecraft merely frowned.

Lily signaled to a waiter. In a moment there was a tall

bottle on the table, and two miniature glasses. The waiter poured a thick fluid. In the tiny glasses it caught the reflected light and gave back a baleful green shimmer, as if some evil worm were looking out from its lair.

"Mr. Alhazred?" Lily laid her fingers on Lovecraft's wrist. He kept from recoiling, realizing to his startlement that her touch was soft and pleasant. It had been more than a half a decade since his divorce, and his contacts with women since the event had been restricted to the company of his two aunts in Providence.

"Just coffee. I cannot abide the taste or smell of alcohol."

Lovecraft detected a look that passed between Lily and Price, then Lily signaled to the waiter. She gestured toward Lovecraft. Shortly the waiter approached their table and placed a silver coffeepot and demitasse before Lovecraft. Even though Lovecraft added his usual generous portion of sugar, the coffee had a strong, bitter flavor. But as Lily refilled Lovecraft's cup, he found the flavor becoming familiar, even pleasant. He relaxed, and his mood improved. The horns of the black musicians blared, and the trumpeter lowered his instrument long enough to mop his sweat-covered brow. In a grating voice he began to deliver a chorus of "That's Why Darkies Were Born." Lovecraft sipped coffee and discovered to his astonishment that the music and even the trumpeter's gravelly voice were blending to form a pleasant, comfortable whole.

Lovecraft was vaguely aware of Price and Lily, their heads close together, whispering and nodding like reeds along the banks of the Mississippi. Again Lily summoned the waiter, spoke to him, and sent him away. Lovecraft sipped at his seemingly inexhaustible cup of coffee and chatted with his companions. He found himself on the small dance floor, the pounding of African drums throbbing through his head, Lily in his arms, her perfume in his nostrils. This time he did not avert his eyes from the bodice of her dress.

Lily's beauty—somehow he had failed to appreciate it before. The nearness of her and the warmth of her flesh, the scent of her hair, the pounding of the music, combined to make Lovecraft dizzy. They collided with other dancers, who seemed to pay them no heed. He was whirling, tasting the strangely bitter coffee, peering into Lily's eyes that seemed to be the same green color he had seen somewhere else.

He was dancing dizzily, and then somehow he was climbing stairs, Lily on one side of him, Price on the other. They supported as much as they guided him. As if from a great distance, he heard his own voice. "A touch of vertigo. Heat and fatigue. Perhaps another cup of coffee . . ."

A door swung open like some cosmic gateway, and he glided into a parlor that might have changed little in a century or longer. Ladies dressed as Lily was, in garments the colors of emeralds, champagne, or roses sat on ornate, brocaded couches. Paintings of satyrs and nymphs cavorting in Elysian fields drew upon him until Lovecraft had to look away lest he be captured by their glamour and pulled bodily through their frames.

Bottles and glasses stood near the couches, a few ancient books lying among them, and a jarring touch of modernity, stacks of ragged-edged and well-read popular magazines. Prominent among them, Lovecraft saw copy after copy of his chief outlet, *Weird Tales*. There was an issue that he recognized—it was the one with his own story "In the Vault." And another, with his "Strange High House in the Mist."

Doors led from the room. He could not remember which one he had come through with Price and Lily. He could hear the music from the hall downstairs, penetrating the masonry and stone of the house. Price was introducing him to the women in their daring yet elegant gowns. He was giving Lovecraft's name, his true name, not the jocularly assumed appellation of Abdul Alhazred or E'ch-Pi-El.

Dizzy, Lovecraft lost track of the time and place.

In the days following their first meeting, Lovecraft had visited Price's apartment several times, and Price had visited Lovecraft at the Hotel Orleans. They had toured outlying townships in Price's Isotta roadster. Price seemed to know New Orleans and its environs as thoroughly as Lovecraft knew his own beloved Providence, and proved an adept tourist guide and tutor.

Between such outings Lovecraft occupied himself with walking tours of the Vieux Carré and adjacent sections of New Orleans. The modern sections of the city distressed him, and he avoided them as much as he could. He doted on the old mansions with their white painted columns and meticulously preserved fanlights. He visited the gardens that blossomed extravagantly in the lush soil and the abundant sunlight and moisture of the city.

Most of all he loved the old cemeteries. The same abundant groundwater that nourished the plant life of New Orleans would flood any newly excavated grave, so the dead were laid to rest in granite crypts above the soil. They had been so interred for centuries, and it pleased Lovecraft to stroll among the mausoleums, stopping to ponder now and again the pathetic faith that they represented.

One tomb in particular struck his liking. It was built to resemble a miniature church, with a cruciform opening in its easternmost wall. On the Day of Judgment the rising sun would carry the joyous news to the dead who lay within those stone walls, as the moment of resurrection called them to rise and stand before their Maker.

"Superstition," Lovecraft chuckled. "Pathetic superstition. As I left the cemetery, a sweating worker saw me. He must have taken me for a mourner visiting a departed relative, for he doffed his straw hat in respect."

He blinked and shook himself. To whom had he been narrating the anecdote? Lovecraft looked around. Where was Price?

A female clutched Lovecraft by the arm. "H. P. Lovecraft!'' she exclaimed. ''I love your stories. All the ladies love them. This is really H. P. Lovecraft!'' She turned, still clutching his sleeve, showing him off to her friends. Lovecraft found himself surrounded by adoring females, their scents mixing with the recollection of the too-bitter coffee, their flesh suffocating him, the jungle drums and blaring horns pounding in his chest so he could not tell which was the drumbeat, which his heartbeat, which the blast of a horn, which the bleat of his own voice as he cried out in terror. Because he knew, now, what kind of house this was.

He knew what kind of house this was!

He managed to break free from the clutching, grasping arms of women and stagger to a doorway. He flung it open and plunged through. He was in a stairwell. The only illumination came from above, from the room he had just escaped. He stumbled down the stairs, dizzy and vaguely aware that Price was behind him, calling his name, striving unsuccessfully to halt his descent.

The stairwell debouched into a room of stone. Here, there was even less light. What little there was seemed to come from a pale moss or fungus that clung to the cold, moist walls where fetid water seeped between dark blocks of basalt. Rough-hewn tables and benches and ancient chests were scattered about. Cobwebs half concealed épées mounted on the walls, their blades dulled with accumulated rust—or something worse.

A tall, dark-haired man sporting a mustache and neatly trimmed beard entered the room. He wore the loose blouse, tight trousers, and floppy-topped boots favored by the buccaneers of an earlier age. He was followed by another man, a stockier, older individual dressed in the frock coat and weskit of a nineteenth-century gentleman.

Torches flared in braziers.

''So you've brought him, Malik?'' the stocky man inquired.

''I've brought E'ch-Pi-El,'' Price answered.

"Let me see, let me see!" The stocky man stared up at Lovecraft. Lovecraft realized that the man was shorter than he by half a head. The man shook his head. "He's the wrong one. I know that I am taller than the right one. *Longer,* he would say. Lafitte, he's brought the wrong one!" The pirate strode forward. Before he could reach Lovecraft, Price stopped him, planting himself in his path. "He is innocent. He knows no better."

"He is wrong!" the pirate snarled.

"Will the right one never come?" the stocky man demanded. His voice seemed almost to plead.

"Never! Never! He is dead!" Price roared.

"Malik Tawus!" The pirate drew a sword from his sash and menaced Price and Lovecraft.

"Lafitte! Claiborne!" Price leaped away, snatched an ancient épée from its cobwebby place, confronted Lafitte.

The pirate lunged.

Malik Tawus, the Peacock Emperor, eluded him and flicked out his needle-tipped épée.

Lafitte avoided the strike of the épée and swung his sword. The sword was sharpened along its curving edge, almost as if it were a cavalryman's sabre. The épée was rounded for its whole length, pointed only at its tip. Lovecraft, observing every move, realized that while Lafitte could slash, Price could only lunge.

The two figures danced back and forth in the eerie light. Lovecraft saw Lafitte slash at Price's arm. Blood sopped into Price's shirt, black rather than red in the pale illumination. But now Malik Tawus scored deep beneath Lafitte's rib cage, drew back, yanking his épée from the wounded flesh. A thin stream of blood gouted forth.

Still Lafitte advanced, slashing at Price, the Peacock Emperor parrying, dodging, lunging. And scoring, scoring again and again.

Lovecraft saw the stocky Claiborne standing to one side. He reached inside his frock coat and drew a pistol, a tiny thing that peered from his fleshy hand like a mouse from a tussock. "Stop!" He pointed the weapon at Price. "Stand back, Lafitte. Stand back, and we shall have done with this Malik Tawus!"

Lafitte drew back, laughing.

Lovecraft saw Price swing his head left and right, looking from Lafitte to Claiborne, from Claiborne to Lafitte. The two were concentrating on Price, ignoring the unmoving Lovecraft.

Lovecraft silently lifted a dust-covered bottle from the table before him. With a supreme effort, as if moving through the syrupy atmosphere of a dream, he brought it crashing onto Claiborne's skull.

Even as Claiborne toppled, the pistol flew from his beefy hand. Without a moment's hesitation the agile Price caught the pistol in midair. Holding his épée as he had, he pointed the pistol at Lafitte. "Enough," he snarled at the pirate. "You are dead. Claiborne is dead. Bonaparte is dead. Your plans all came to naught, nor will they ever succeed. For better or for worse, Lafitte, I command you to return to the land of shades!"

He turned to Lovecraft. "I'll get you home, Abdul. This was a very bad idea of mine."

Lovecraft awakened in his hotel room. The height of the New Orleans sun told him that he had slept half the day away. His head hurt with a fierce, pounding pain. He felt as if the savage band of the previous night were playing its barbaric music inside his skull. His very eyeballs ached as if they had been pierced by a million red-hot needles.

He fell back against his pillow. He shut his eyes.

Today was the day he must depart New Orleans and return to Providence. There was time to pack his meager belongings and travel to the railroad depot.

But en route there, he would call upon Price.

Within an hour he stood in Price's room. "What happened last night, Malik? How did we reach that cellar? Did we see the ghosts of the pirate Lafitte and of Governor Claiborne? Were they really awaiting the arrival of the emperor Bonaparte?"

Price said, "Sit down, Abdul. Let me get you a cup of coffee."

"Yes, thank you." Lovecraft lowered himself gingerly. "But the house on Rue Chartres—I demand an explanation."

"You do look a bit the worse for wear." Price peered into Lovecraft's face, then turned back to his task. "Here, Abdul. This should pick you up. Guaranteed to contain not one hair of the dog that bit you last night."

"What was it that we saw in the cellar? I refuse to accept any tale of ghosts. Were those actors? Were they criminals? Was it all some sort of jape, Price?"

Price handed Lovecraft a cup full of his thick coffee. Lovecraft reached for the sugar bowl and began counting spoonfuls. Price said nothing.

Lovecraft said, "Your silence befits you ill, Malik. You are one of the glibbest of men. Bad enough that you betrayed me into visiting an establishment the likes of which I would never have set foot in, had I but known its true nature. The noise, the liquor, the savage sounds that pass there for music! The women! Had I not fled, heaven knows what would have happened in that upper apartment!"

"Come along, Abdul! You know perfectly well what would have happened. If I offended your sense of morals, I apologize."

Lovecraft sniffed, lifted his cup, tasted the thick liquid. "At least your coffee is still good, Malik. That foul brew last night had an odor and a flavor I hope I never encounter again."

"You probably will have your wish."

"But I demand—I *demand* to be told the truth. What happened in the cellar?"

"Honestly, Lovecraft, you're not making sense."

"Jean Lafitte the pirate—that pompous politician Claiborne—we barely escaped with our lives. Your performance was brilliant—worthy of Pierre d'Artois himself. And I blush to claim for myself the role of the faithful Jannicot, a veritable Sancho to your Quixote, humble but helpful. Still, were we a trifle less lucky, our bones would lie at this very moment in that cellar!"

Price shook his head. "There are no cellars in New Orleans, Lovecraft. The groundwater is too high. If anyone dug a cellar, it would be hopelessly flooded within twenty-four hours. That is the same reason why they bury their dead aboveground in this city."

"You hold to your story, then, do you?"

Price spread his hands.

Lovecraft reached into his pocket and withdrew an Elgin watch. "I must be off. If I miss my train today, I shall have to stay another night in this city. I cannot afford the charges—nor do I wish to remain here any longer. If you will not admit the simple facts of what happened to us, Price, then there is no point in discussing the matter longer."

He placed his coffee cup, now empty, on its saucer, and rose to leave the apartment.

"You really believe we were in a cellar at the Bonaparte House? You really believe we encountered Jean Lafitte and Governor Claiborne?"

"You deny it, sir?"

"It can only have been the absinthe, Lovecraft. Drinkers do experience strange distortions of reality, fantasies that seem as real to them as reality itself."

"Absinthe? I would never—Malik, you know me too well."

"I apologize again, Abdul. You noticed the odor and taste of your coffee. It was heavily spiked with absinthe. You had a lot of it, my friend. Quite a lot. You were a bit woozy toward the end of the evening, but I thought that you handled it well. I seem to have been wrong. I brought you home to the Orleans in my Isotta. But no harm done eh? Save your hangover. And that, too, shall pass—hard though it may be to believe it right now!"

Price smiled sympathetically. He reached for Lovecraft's valise. "The auto is just around the corner. I'll give you a ride to the depot." He winced as he attempted to lift the valise, and Lovecraft heard him emit a grunt of pain. Price dropped the valise and reached with his other hand.

"The truth will out!" Lovecraft exclaimed. "You were slashed by the saber of Jean Lafitte! I can see the bandage now, where it shows through your shirt, Malik!"

"Abdul, don't be foolish. I cut myself slicing beef to make chili. That was days ago. Pirates don't return from the tomb to chop up living men."

"On the shoulder, Malik! You were wounded on the shoulder! You might cut yourself on the finger, slicing chili meat. An exceptionally clumsy chef might even wound his forearm. But the shoulder? No! Confess it now—confess that I am right, and give me the explanation to which I am entitled."

"It's getting late, Lovecraft. Let's start for the depot, or you will miss your train."

Riding in the Isotta, his valise stowed behind him and his fedora held firmly in his lap to keep it from sailing away on the breeze, Lovecraft was unable to get Price to speak further of their visit to the house on Rue Chartres.

AUTHOR'S NOTE—"The House on
Rue Chartres"

Several years ago the late E. Hoffmann Price gave a group interview at his home in Redwood City, California. In a wide-ranging conversation he spoke of many events in his long life and career. He spoke of living in New Orleans in the 1930s, and described H. P. Lovecraft's visit.

Price told his interviewers (I was one of them) about his "hot chili challenge" to Lovecraft, and of their visit to a bordello. Price also served his Redwood City visitors some of the same thick, strong coffee he had served to Lovecraft half a century earlier. I didn't sleep for three nights after drinking it, and to this day I can remember its flavor and its muddy *feel* in my mouth!

In his *Selected Letters* (Volume IV), Lovecraft gives his version of his New Orleans days. By and large, Lovecraft supports Price's story, even mentioning the chili party. Not surprisingly, he makes no mention of any visit to a bordello.

In his definitive biography of Lovecraft, L. Sprague de Camp also describes the Lovecraft/Price encounter, and offers a lengthy quotation from Price, again supporting his version of the story (but alluding only indirectly, if at all, to the visit to the house on Rue Chartres).

Certainly Lovecraft's visit to Price resulted in a collaboration between the two ("Through the Gates of the Silver Key," *Weird Tales*, July 1934). Lovecraft's interest in—not to say his fascination with—the pirate Jean Lafitte antedated his visit to New Orleans by many years. See what is possibly Lovecraft's most famous story, "The Call of Cthulhu" (*Weird Tales*, February 1928).

Still, when an author mixes real personages and real events with imaginary ones, he is sometimes subjected to severe—and not necessarily undeserved—criticism. The truth is a slippery enough thing, without coating it with still more grease! Therefore, lest I be accused of misleading my readers, let me say here and now that "The House on Rue Chartres" *is* a work of fiction, and should not be taken as true.

—Richard A. Lupoff
Rue Chartres, New Orleans
July 1989

S haron Baker is the author of *Quarreling, They Met the Dragon, Journey to Membliar,* and *Burning Tears of Sassurum.* Like Gene Wolfe, she looks much more ordinary than her fiction would lead one to expect. She lives in Seattle, Washington. This is her first published short story.

In this tale of punishment, child abuse, and death, Sharon Baker balances conspiracy theories, the psychological, and the metaphysical. The physical setting for the story is the house where she grew up. She said that originally she had wanted to write a story with an ax-murder in it, and that the only kind of person she could think of that deserved to be killed that way was a child abuser. The image of Mother with a sharp object in her hand appears in Robert Bloch's *Psycho* and elsewhere, but here the resonances are rather different.

House Hunter

SHARON BAKER

he old man twitched his pointed nose in disbelief. Rubbing his hand over his head until the gray tufts stood upright, Martin Aickman stared through a rosy, flickering tunnel at the Spanish-style house he had expected never to see again with corporeal eyes.

Heedless of the pepper trees whispering overhead, their pink seeds crunching underfoot, and the mad guitars at his back, Martin shoved his knotted hands in his raincoat pockets, and hobbled forward. *Stucco walls glowing like gold in the hazy Los Angeles sunshine; pigeons burbling under the red roof tiles; bees droning on either side of the flagstone walk to a black iron gate.* "Hallelujah! It's exactly like . . . It *is* my house!" Martin blinked his dust-colored eyes. "But it can't be."

For he had seen his home demolished for a freeway overpass. He'd had nightmares about it for years.

His father had inherited the place. After he died, Martin and his mother raised a dozen foster children there, and

Martin's two babies after his wife died, until they died, too.

No! I won't remember! Martin halted under the trees, clenched his fists in his pockets, and concentrated on the house. *Behind the gate: a patio and iron-grilled front door. Facing the street: narrow windows barred with iron lace.*

"Isn't it a treasure? I knew you'd love it. Our contemporary traditionals we looked at simply weren't *you*. But you'll have to move fast on this one, Mr. Aickman. It's just been listed. When my associate puts up the signs, it'll be gone like that!" Lois Marshall's snap of her fingers coincided with the crack of her gum. Her carefully charming tones were those of a Hollywood newscaster, starlet, or the professor she was. (Moonlighting in real estate, Lois had confided with her toothpaste smile, paid the rent.) Now she yanked her suede skirt down toward her knees, clicked off the ignition—and the Pink Floyd tape stopped at last. ("Broken switch," Lois had said shortly when Martin plugged his ears against the devil's music.) Now she swung her booted legs from the vintage Thunderbird that had brought them. Martin hardly noticed.

Behind the patio walls, hanging pots of fuchsias; in back of the fuchsias, windows glittering with tiny panes. Home.

How could she guess this is the one place I might actually buy? It's the hand of God. Or a setup. Martin covered a suspicious glance at Lois with his one-sided smile.

But her brown eyes seemed to crackle only with zeal for a sale as she straightened, shook back her dark bob. ". . . all the conveniences. Heritage Properties does well by its clients!"

While Lois described her firm's renovations and liberal loans to practicing Christians, Martin studied the house and its surroundings. (Wasn't the grass unnaturally green for fall?)

On the shady side, an archway . . . No skates or scooters, traps in the shrubbery or bare spots in the lawn. The house was straight out of Martin's dreams: flawless. As it had been before the war, before Daddy died and the foster kids came.

Under the archway, turquoise gates closing off the drive. Beyond the drive in the house's shadow, the roof of the garage . . . Martin stiffened.

He shrugged off Lois's questioning glance as she ducked back into the car for her purse and clipboard.

In the darkness at the side of the house, something stirred. Did it raise an arm, ready—if he didn't answer— to shout at him to get inside and explain himself?

"Coming, Mother!" He moved his lips in a soundless whisper. The old hopeless feeling shortened Martin's breath, melted his knees. He pressed his fist to his faulty heart. Would he never be free of her commandments and quotes, able to do as he liked? Once, in desperation, he had asked.

"When you stop your evil ways!" Smoothing her flowered housedress over her bulk, Mother had quoted the Bible. "Then you can 'Love, and do as ye will.' But not now."

Mother's dead! Martin recalled for the hundredth time. As dead as his babies—crib deaths, Mother had told the doctor when Martin, weeping, led him to their small, still bodies—as dead as this house, the only thing Martin had loved that had never hurt him. Only his illogical dream of its return could have made him answer the *Los Angeles Herald-Examiner*'s ad:

DON'T MAKE HOUSES LIKE THEY USED TO? Seniors: We match older homes to older people. Loans for those who qualify. "In my Father's house are many mansions." (John 14:2) Heritage Properties.

"Do go ahead, let the outside speak to you. I'll be up in a seccy to open the door." Lois rummaged in her leather shoulder bag, held out a white pasteboard rectangle. "If the neighbors stop you, show them this."

Martin palmed her business card. He didn't need to read

it. He'd memorized it in the week since he'd yielded to temptation and called the number in the paper. After looking up John the Apostle's words and being encouraged by their accuracy, he checked on Heritage Properties, then Lois's master's degree in social work from the University of California at Los Angeles, where she taught. And when he met Lois at the real estate office, he matched her to the UCLA secretary's description: slim, dark hair and eyes, pizzazz. Probably Mother would say Lois's heart was a net and snare. Certainly Lois made Martin awkward with shyness. He stole another glance at her, afraid she knew too much about him. As had Mother. And his wife.

Martin trudged up the walk, refusing to remember the dour woman Mother had brought from church to make a man of him. At his protest Mother snapped, "Praise God anyone'll have you with your tricks—and that heart." Instead, Martin looked hopefully at the stucco and ironwork ahead.

If he could own this house, he'd be Somebody. Only homeowners were respectable, Mother and Daddy had said; houses owned for generations almost conferred nobility. To keep theirs after Daddy died, Mother worked ceaselessly. She had little time for Martin. Loneliness had been a hollowness in him for as long as he could remember.

He pushed open the gate, entered the patio, and examined the front door. Solid. Dark-stained mahogany. At eye-level, a window with a grill over it. A key box hung from the latch.

Martin inhaled the smell of damp cement, potting soil, and . . . *gardenias.* He swung around, elbow bumping the door.

Beneath the fuchsias stood thin trunks ending in glossy leaves and flat white petals with furled edges. Just like those Mother required on her birthday! *Always gardenia perfume. And at Christmas, orange, lemon, or lime trees; for Mother's Day, hibiscus . . .* He turned back.

The front door was slowly opening.

The smell of Johnson's Wax drifted outward. A cone of muted light from the patio revealed the entry's hardwood floor.

Breathing quickly, Martin glanced over his shoulder. Lois was in the car, putting up windows. *I have time.* He stepped over the threshold, started to close the door. . . . *Mother's gone to her Reward!* Defying her rule, he left the door open.

The coolness of the house enfolded him. *I've come home again,* Martin thought. *I'd be admired here. Envied. Maybe even have friends. . . . I wonder if any children live nearby?*

Dull light fell from the entry's window—narrow and barred like the one in his memory!

Unbelieving delight almost quenched Martin's anxiety over the answers he'd given Heritage Properties. But not quite. *It's okay,* he repeated now, and ticked off the interviewer's approval of Martin's investments left from Mother's death and the city's payment for his house; his agreeing that Martin's heart was no problem since he avoided exertion, shocks; and when Martin said he wouldn't stir up old trouble for the foster kids by discussing them, he had called Martin "remarkable." But the man had added, Martin's fostering of problem children showed a Christian charity that might qualify him for a loan.

So, hungry for a chance at a home, Martin had grasped the receiver in sweating palms and given names and dates.

Now, behind him, a creak, an oiled click. Martin whirled, heart jolting. The front door, which he had left open, had shut. Locked. *I wasn't frightened. Just startled. Doors often close alone in old houses.* Still, he peered through the door's barred window.

In the empty patio the fuchsias stirred. *It must have been the wind.* Beyond the wall Martin glimpsed Lois still in the car, head bent over her clipboard.

If only he could explore before that Jezebel brought her clumping boots and sales jargon into the waiting silence! With guilty excitement Martin started toward the living

room. Which reminded him. He reached under his raincoat for his bifocals. The coat got in his way. Might as
well hang it up.

He peered through his black plastic frames at the entry
closet's door. It looked as he remembered: The brass knob
was a lion's head, the push plate its body; its paws gripped
a steer whose horns were the lock. With growing elation
Martin shucked off his coat, opened the door. The closet
was deep. Only a little light seeped in.

For an instant he seemed to glimpse black and red rub-
ber boots, a scarred white volley ball, red and blue metal
Slinkys jumbled beneath shadowy coats. Around Mother's
Inverness cape peeked a girl with brown curls, her face
stained with tears, green eyes dark with fury. A foster child,
locked in the closet, awaiting their merciful whip, to save
her from God's chastisement with scorpions.

Martin tried to enter. He couldn't. The child's anger
formed a wall.

He blinked. The coats and Slinkys rearranged themselves into shadows, the vision of the child faded with them.
And the barrier was gone.

"Memory's playing tricks." He hung his coat on the hook
by the door. *His* hook. Martin fizzed with joy. *This is my
house!* Hurrying into the high-ceilinged living room, he
glanced outside.

Lois, tripping up the walk toward the gate. *Hurry!*

Martin's pulse thudded as he dodged the sofa with its
pink chintz roses, made for the fireplace beyond, outlined
with tiles. *Good!* No hatchet leaned against the fire wall
for the foster kids to split tinder from the kindling. Martin
loathed the axes, knives, blades, that filled his dreams—
terrible dreams. He dropped onto the hearth, knees
creaking.

The acrid stench of old fires entered his nostrils. He
pushed up his bifocals. With shaken satisfaction he made
out scratches a couple of feet over the andirons. And a
few bricks above that, the mortar was gone, as if some-

thing had clawed it. A pleasurable chill edged up Martin's spine as he relived the fires he had lighted here, the foster kids he had started climbing. . . . Only occasionally had he been forced to use the hatchet.

But he had never let Mother find him here. Lois shouldn't either, even if she wasn't a virtuous woman like Mother, whose price was above rubies.

Martin scrambled to his feet. Smoothing his hair, he looked casually toward the entry.

It was vacant.

He glanced out the windows, past the spring-green lawn.

On the walkway only a blackbird hopped, a worm in its beak.

Running, Martin tripped, almost bumped Mother's Duncan Phyfe coffee table before pressing his nose to the beveled panes. Funny. From this angle the grass looked properly faded, sere.

At the top of the lawn Lois squatted, copying the meter reading onto her clipboard. If he was quick . . . *To hell with the grass!* Martin dashed toward the hall and the bedrooms.

He meant just to glance into Mother's. Green light filtered through the roof-high poinsettias outside to shimmer on the ivory walls he remembered, and Mother's white satin spread. He sniffed. The faint scent of gardenias. *From outside! Or . . .*

Looking for a perfume vial, he took one forbidden step onto the shining floor. He expected any second to hear, "Mar-*tin!* You'll stay out of my room if you know what's good for you!"

It didn't come. *It can't.* He took another step, his gaze drawn to the white satin pillows.

Against them lay Mother's doll she had cooed over and Martin secretly had wished were him. The doll's stiff blond hair and crocheted skirt spread around her. Her blue glass eyes seemed to stare at the night table and the riding quirt that lay on it.

"Mar-*tin!* Evil spreads in you like a green bay tree, like it did in your father, may he rot in hell. You need discipline!" Mother's husky voice seemed to come again from the empty hall. Once more the house shook with the tread of her orthopedic oxfords as she made him come in, take down his pants. . . . He'd had to kiss the quirt before and after. He had hated her!

Now Martin stood beside her bed, the poinsettias tapping with green and scarlet nails at her windows. The flowers' bitter white sap was poison, Mother had said, and ordered Martin not to pick them.

Over the years he had dripped that sap in her coffee, the bottle of scotch under her bed that she thought he didn't know about; he had milked the cut stems into the cream she poured on her Wheaties. But she had only grown stronger.

With a guttural sound, Martin darted to the night table. He whacked the quirt over his knee, tore at the braided leather handle, bit the thongs, worrying at them until they ripped.

Breathing hard, he wiped his mouth and looked around. Good thing Lois hadn't seen him. She might think he was crazy, lose him his chance at this house, the bitch. Martin scurried about on his knees, shoving pieces of the quirt in his pockets, the tops of his socks.

It was when he snatched a last scrap from under the night table that he saw the two small pallets between it and the wall.

When Martin and Mother had brought home his twin babies, Martin had wanted them in his room to stroke their downy heads, sniff their warm breaths, fondle their round, silken bodies.

But Mother said no, none of him was in them, they were hers to set on the path of righteousness. She took them to her room where gardenias cloyed the air.

As she made up their mattresses along the wall, Martin showed her the girl's pointed nose like his, the boy's blue eyes turning his shade of hazel, the fuzz on its head that looked brown like his; he jiggled the babies until they laughed so she could see how they smiled on one side of their mouths as he did.

"No!" Mother barked. Locking her door on them, she crossed to the kitchen where she started oatmeal boiling.

Martin trailed behind her. "They should learn to honor their father, too," he muttered as he put out bowls.

Mother stopped ladling gruel. She set her hands on her flowered hips, stretching her white ruffled apron over her belly. "With your wife dead and her salary gone—and you not holding a job with your visions and palpitations—*I* support us by feeding and housing these burdens on the state." She waved the ladle at the listening foster children crowded into a booth in the adjoining breakfast room. "With their mother with the worms and their father, corruption, my only grandbabies would never get to Glory. I won't let you contaminate them, Martin, or this house. I'm leaving it to them, not you. Your wicked ways may not be all your fault; I've tried to whip them out of you, God knows; but you're of your father the devil—rotten clean through!"

Now Martin backed from Mother's room to the hall. *She shouldn't have said that, not in front of the foster kids. Those babies were mine. They looked more like me every day. And the house should have been mine, too. She deserved what she got.*

At the end of the connecting passage lay the foster kids' bathroom. After Daddy died, Mother had offered the bathroom to Martin, but he hadn't wanted it. Through the open door, he glanced at the yellow-and-black tiles that made his stomach churn, the white pedestal basin, the tub where he'd had to duck the boys to keep them docile. "He that loveth him chasteneth him," he would hiss in case Mother was near. His palms tingled, recalling the slick, struggling bodies, warm water sloshing over gaping mouths and eyes bulging in panic. He recalled how after, they had obeyed. The memory of God's power kindled in him.

But one night Mother had caught him, stopped his supervising the boys' baths. He didn't go in. Instead, with a flutter of anticipation, Martin pushed open the neighboring door.

Sunlight streamed through windows hung with white ruffled curtains. It lay in bright panels on white chenille spreads. White rag rugs decorated the floor. Martin thought with pleasure of the pretty little girls who had undressed for him on those beds, their slim bodies unencumbered with breasts lying back, surrendering to his fingers; their small hands trembling on his zipper, on him. One little beauty's eyes had been green as a cat's under her brown curls; she'd obviously wanted it as much as he did, she'd fought him so deliciously. He took an invigorating breath. How like God he had felt here! In control, respected . . .

"Yoo-hoo! Mr. Aickman, where are you? Naughty, naughty, stealing into the house without me." Lois's television-land accents wafted down the hall to the bedroom.

Calling me bad. Just like Mother. Martin whirled, God's lightning sizzling in his fingertips. He splayed them, focusing on her throat talking, talking. . . .

Lois fell back into the hall. Over an odd sound like gagging she said, "Oh. So this is where you got to."

Mother was Taken, Martin reminded himself again and, *I want this house.* He forced his arms to his sides, smoothed a smile onto his face. When he could control his breathing, he said humbly, "The door was open. I'm sorry. I'll go now."

Lois's smile looked strained, perhaps a trick of the hall's shadows. For after a deep breath she said in a rush, "It's all *right*, Mr. Aickman. You couldn't resist this gem, and I don't blame you! Did you *see* those hardwood floors? An inch thick or I'll eat them! And coved ceilings, fourteen feet high, I measured—they don't make them like that nowadays, you bet your sweet . . ." She choked and rattled on, patches of rouge showing on her pale face. "Solid mahogany interior trim, all those built-ins, and the space! Bathrooms, bedrooms . . ." She swallowed.

Martin was edging toward her. Surely the Bible said somewhere the Lord hated a chattering woman.

Lois whirled, started out the door. "The kitchen! I must show you the kitchen. You haven't seen it yet?"

"No." Martin dropped his hands, confused. Why would he want to see a kitchen? There were knives there. And sometimes, in spite of his screams about safety, the foster kids would leave the ax by the door instead of in the garage. They knew what scared him. Little bastards. Anyway, he hated to cook. In his room overlooking the endless concrete of Shady Acres Nursing Home, Martin heated TV dinners on a hot plate.

"Oh, good!" Lois was halfway up the hall. "I'll show you the appliances. We even put an intercom in these old walls."

Reluctantly Martin left the virginal bedroom. "That'll be convenient," he said politely as he followed her.

"I hope so, Mr. Aickman." Lois walked into the kitchen. Her voice echoed. ". . . breakfast room. The master station's through here. . . ." A door shut, dimming her voice, still talking.

In the hall Martin glanced from the closed breakfast-room door to the one opposite, leading to the laundry. While Lois praised cabinets and beveled mirrors, he took in the kitchen's familiar white sink, black-and-white tile counters, windows overlooking the shady drive lined with hibiscus. . . . He froze.

Someone stood before those windows, silhouetted by the light. Someone with a knife.

The figure moved, separated from the shadows. Martin guessed at thinning blond hair, tight jeans, cut-off sweat shirt.

". . . kitchen intercom by the hall, Mr. Aickman," Lois called as the man prowled toward Martin, Nikes soundless on the speckled linoleum, blade shining coldly in the dusky light. "Here's a quieter appliance," he whispered.

By Martin's elbow, a panel shot up, revealing a nook with an intercom grill, toaster, and boxy electric can opener with its handle on top. Martin jumped as Lois announced from the grill, ". . . modulates. Yours broadcasts in here, at the front door. . . ." She halted. "Shit. Stuck!" came through, then static.

Martin inched toward the crackling panel. *I'll whisper for help, crank the front door feedback to a howl, call "police!"*

The man prowled closer. "Want to test the edge?"

Martin groped behind him for a knob. His sleeve caught on something. He glanced down. His jacket had slipped over the can-opener handle and round blade beneath. He tried to pull free. Clicks and exclamations came from the intercom grill.

The man was very close now, his whisper harsh as the scrape of leaves outside. ". . . sharp enough to cut skin? An artery?"

Artery. "You're a foster kid!" Martin remembered the boys' shrieks, the scarlet knife. "I didn't want them to die! Just take off a little skin, so while it healed, they'd remember not to sass me. It wasn't my fault they had big veins so near the surface." He reached behind him, pulled. His sleeve tightened.

"Just enjoy the kitchen, Mr. Aickman." Lois's distant tones, muted by the closed door, had an undercurrent of strain. "I'm sure I'll get this going in just half a seccy."

The man hissed, "When the social worker called the police, you made us say they did it themselves. Then, if we changed our stories, we'd hang as accessories to murder. Like this!" He sprang.

Martin flung up an elbow. The can opener came too, as

Lois boomed from the kitchen speaker, "There, Mr. Aick-man!" and Martin jumped again.

The man missed.

The can opener whacked the intercom, rammed into the grill. Frantically Martin pulled as the man once more brought up the knife. A ripping sound. Martin tore free, scraped his arm along the can-opener blade as the knife hummed from the side.

"Fixed! You try." Lois's now-quiet voice sounded smug.

Martin stared at his cut sleeve, the blood oozing from his cuff to the liver spots and blue veins. Thin fire blazed to his knuckles. His heart banged. A vise tightened around his chest.

"Mr. Aickman?" The breakfast-room door jiggled.

The man faded to the shadows by the laundry with its exit to outside. "Next time I'll bring a bigger appliance."

An ax. "No! I never meant . . ." Martin couldn't breathe. The pressure under his shoulders expanded to an ache.

The breakfast-room door smacked open. Lois walked, then ran to him, heels thudding on the gleaming floor as she scrabbled in her purse. "Mr. Aickman, I'm sorry! I've got Band-Aids in here somewhere. Give me your hand." She glanced up at him. A brown rim showed against the white of her eye. Colored contact lenses. Beauty? Disguise? Her absence had been convenient.

Betrayed into the hands of sinners! The scenario flashed behind Martin's eyes. *Kill her. But first: Run!* Martin dashed to the laundry, flung open the door. As Lois stared at him in consternation, he slammed and locked it behind him.

He sped past yellow walls and the panel hiding the ironing board, the washer in front of the door to the basement furnace. . . . Ah! The screen door, just where Martin expected. It clacked shut as he staggered down the back steps, fell to the driveway in the shadow of the house.

From within came quick footsteps, then banging on the laundry door. "Mr. Aickman. Open this at once!"

Martin sped, wheezing, across the drive. He plunged into the tall hibiscus. He hit a cement-block fence. Sweat coursed down his cheeks. To quiet his gasps, he pushed his fist against the swelling agony in his chest.

A splintering sound came from inside. Shouts.

He jumped at the concrete blocks. Couldn't get a toehold, fell back. Twigs and leaves scattered into his collar, scratched his bleeding hand and arms.

Behind him, the screen door clattered.

Martin dropped onto his belly behind the bushes. Yellow and red flowers stared back at him as he listened to Lois call his name. She muttered. *Giving orders?* He couldn't see the young man. He imagined them separating to search around the house.

Next they'd try the drive. Frantically Martin looked toward the arch above the gates and escape. The Thunderbird! Could Lois have left her keys in it? Not likely. He squinted through the tops of his bifocals at the turquoise panels. *Padlock and chain around the center posts . . . too high to climb . . .*

He twisted, glimpsed the garage's turquoise doors at the other end of the drive. Chills inched down his arms. *Inside is the ax from my nightmares . . .* One door stood ajar. A loose board at the back was a way out for the foster kids. He'd never told, in case he had to use it, too. A chance. *I'm afraid! But I can't stay.* Now! While the blond man was gone and Lois had her back turned.

Martin scuttled down the drive, lunged through the door, skidded in painfully on his hip. No cars. At one end Daddy's tool bench gathering dust. Breath sawing in his lungs, he rested his forehead on the cold cement smelling of oil and dust. Outside, the rustle of pigeons, a zephyr sighing around the walls. After a while he rolled over and looked about.

Light sifted through windows blurred with cobwebs, revealing unfinished walls, their silver insulation clogged with shadows. *Lois must be a damned foster kid, too. Another one that stole Mother from me.* Martin raised himself on his elbow, tears sharp behind his lids. But he couldn't cry. He had to think how to get out of this fix. He snuffled, dabbed at his eyes, really looked around him. And froze.

For it wasn't the wind sighing outside the walls. It was breathing. Inside. A shadow parting from its silver background, breath hoarsening, becoming a man.

Light and darkness blew across the windows, melding into faces looking in—black, white, scruffy, tidy, old, young as the day they died. While outside, ghostly footsteps seemed to brush the grass, shrubs rustled as if bodies pressed through them; the pigeons' soft quarrels were secret voices planning. . . .

Lids at the stretch, Martin watched the tall shape solidify. A dusty sunbeam glanced off fair hair, sweatshirt, and cutoffs, bare muscular arms below a wedge-shaped flash. . . . *The ax.* Shivers rolled down Martin's ribs.

"You! From the kitchen." Martin glared at the window where faces bared their teeth, silently laughed, and dodged away. "You're all foster kids!" He cursed the ad and himself for wanting a home so much, he'd come out of hiding. The foster kids had sworn they'd get him. Now they had.

"Martin? *Mar*-tin!" From the drive, Mother's deep tones. "Prepare to meet your Maker!" The garage door crashed open.

Heart galloping, Martin fearfully looked up. A stocky cutout with long, loose hair loomed against a dazzle of sky before the door banged shut. In the dark the shimmer of a lace collar, sturdy oxfords, a whiff of jasmine . . . The figure he'd glimpsed from the street. But she hadn't aged.

She held out her hand.

The man by the door gave her his ax.

Holding it, she stood over Martin, her back to the windows, and rasped, " 'Every man bears his own burden,' says the Good Book. You've been mine too long, Martin."

"You . . . you're alive? The police put you up to this!

Or the kids! They told me you were dead," Martin babbled. "And I saw . . ." He stopped. She didn't seem to
notice his slip.

"Dead like your babies?" Mother was taunting. "Praise
God, they died. I'd never have let you defile them, never."
Her hair swung over the dark pits of her eyes. She lifted a
hand that should have been withered to push back the
strands.

"*You* killed my babies!" Tears poured down Martin's
face as at last he let himself remember the night after his
babies' funeral. Mother had come to his room and awakened him.

She'd seen Martin in his babies, she raved on a blast of
scotch; the Lord told her to hold a pillow over their faces.
Just as, long ago, He'd told her to hold one over Daddy's.

"Because he . . . he . . . You made me remember how
he'd coax me into his bathroom, lock the door, watch me
take off my clothes. . . ."

Martin's voice shook as he relived that dreadful night.
"You dragged me into your room." It reeked of gardenias
and scotch. A Black & White bottle lay by her bed. "You
said my babies were bad seed!"

Then Mother said *Martin* was bad seed. The Lord told
her so.

"You shoved me on your bed, leaned on a pillow so I
couldn't see, couldn't breathe." A sob tore Martin's burning chest. He hurt all over now. But the scene behind his
eyes forced him on.

"I tried to push you off!" His hands stuck in her robe.
Trying to free them, he yanked it down her arms so she
couldn't move. He rolled on top of her to stop her yelling,
biting, writhing toward the quirt. "You shouted you h-hated
me, cursed the day I . . . I was born." To stop the terrible words, he crammed the pillow over her face.

When she was quiet, he tidied up as she'd taught him and went back to bed. A doctor woke him, called by the foster children.

"He told me you'd died in your sleep from overwork, grief." When Martin could only stare, the doctor had shaken his head and given him an injection. "You never, never l-loved m-me. . . ."

In the silence the only sound was of Martin's sobs.

Mother straightened as if recovering from a blow. Her blade glinted in a stray sunbeam as she hoisted it. Her voice shook, gained strength. "You *are* bad seed, Martin. I've returned to make sure this time, you're sterilized from the earth!" She pushed him in the chest.

Behind Martin's ribs, a bomb seemed to explode. He fell to his knees, fists to his breastbone in a parody of prayer.

Horrifyingly tall above him, Mother poised the ax over her head. "Discipline time." The shining blade arced down.

Martin seemed to expand into pain that filled the universe, shoved him through it. The last flickering star on its edge winked out, and he shot into endless night . . . freezing, naked, alone forever. He couldn't bear it, his heart was breaking. . . .

The pain was gone, as if it had never been. Martin felt as if he rode on cushioned tires, even flew; strange music wailed around him, insistently pulsing. . . . Warily he opened his eyes.

He seemed to be floating, light as a helium balloon, against the beams and silver paper of the garage ceiling. Below him, shadows clustered around a pile of rumpled clothes.. No, an old man's face topped them with bristly gray hair, black-framed glasses askew on a pointed nose. . . . Why, the old man was him!

With astonishment and growing indignation Martin watched Mother lower her still-pristine ax, yank off her gray-slashed wig, then a neat black one, and run shaking fingers through her own brown curls. *Lois. In disguise. Just as I thought! But those brown curls remind me of someone.* . . .

"Poor old bastard," Mother-who-was-Lois-who-was-somebody-else said in the flat Valley Girl accents Martin had almost expected. "So he actually did in the old besom, paid her back! I never guessed he had the guts. I went dry, had to ad-lib."

So. It was *a setup.* Raging, Martin also wanted to weep.

"You were awesome! Totally great!" A shadow with a glint of fair hair knelt beside Martin's discarded body, peeled back an eyelid.

While the shadow poked and listened, Martin turned over Lois's words. A match flame of warmth sputtered in him. She was right. He had disobeyed Mother. And gotten away with it!

"Heart attack," the kneeling shadow said, "probably dead before he hit the floor."

"So, I killed him." Brown contacts glinted in Lois's palm. She stared at the body, green eyes darkening with fearful anger.

Martin's own eyes widened. For behind the shadows a silver-papered wall was glowing into faint radiance, forming a passage across the drive to the lawn and the house, beckoning. . . .

Irresistibly drawn, Martin skimmed to the opening, wafted through. Birds shot, screeching, from his path. He saw them no more than he did the blond man nearing the gates with a hammer. For with delight Martin was sinking into the grass, flowing up the furnace ducts and walls, to become one at last with his goal: the timbers, plaster, and shining glass eyes of the house.

Eldritch melodies swirled about him as he lay cradled in his home at last. The illumination around Martin deepened to a glowing pink. Ragged drumbeats joined the unearthly harmonies as through his windows he watched the blond man take a For Sale sign from the Thunderbird's trunk and hammer it into Martin's lawn.

Martin giggled. The stake tickled. And he'd had a thought. *Whoever buys this house may have children. Or if they don't, they may not like it here.* Martin's blissful sigh started the fuchsias swinging, doors closing up and down the halls, and pigeons fluttering from their eggs beneath the red roof tiles. Strange, discordant music echoed up the ducts—calling, promising. As Martin luxuriated in increasingly cozy warmth, the light bathing him hollowed into a luminous tunnel, its furthest reaches shading from rose to magenta to pulsing ruby.

"Mar-*tin*? Martin!" Obscuring the tunnel's end, a stocky shape glided toward him. "I'll teach you not to shut that front door. You'll be trained up in the way you should go or I'll know the reason why."

You can't be here! I can love and do as I will at last! The music grew wild, the light above and below Martin changing in time with the insistent strumming, odd chords and resolutions.

"Devil quoting Scripture, Martin?" Grimly the figure shook its head as it drew closer, its tread—was that the shine of orthopedic oxfords?—shaking the rosy glory.

Defeat shrouded Martin like a miasma, the brief flames of his triumph and happiness turning to candles in a mist, dwindling, guttering. . . .

Soundlessly he whispered, "Coming, Mother."

Then he turned to stare down the rosy, flickering tunnel at the Spanish-style house he expected never to see again.

M J. Engh is the author of *Arslan,* a book that some regard as the best political science-fiction novel of the last twenty years. *Wheel of the Winds* is her most recent science-fiction novel. She has also written books for children.

In 1982, Engh received a National Endowment for the Arts Creative Writing Fellowship and took a year's leave of absence from her job at the Washington State University Library. She spent seven months of her free year poking around Italy and southern France, with a bit of Yugoslavia and a piece of Turkey, on the trail of Galla Placidia, a fifth-century lady who is the heroine of her first historical novel (which has since grown into a trilogy). The following year she quit her job at the WSU Library, and says that ever since then she's lived mostly in the fifth century. She lives in Pullman, Washington.

Penelope Comes Home

M. J. ENGH

What surprised me about Greek temples wasn't the grace, the balance, the refinement, all that stuff the textbooks prepare you for; it was the massiveness, the threat. I stared up at those swelling columns and thought, *Yes, gods could live here.*

That was when I was a graduate student on my first drachma-pinching visit to Greece, wanting to be impressed, preferably by something the books didn't mention. I soon got over it. Fifteen years later, I remembered.

"You'll love the house," I had told Elizabeth. "It's really more your style than ours. All that ground is just wasted on us."

Elizabeth had chuckled knowingly. "I don't believe that, Penny. You love it yourself."

"Oh, I do. We all do, actually. The baby stopped crying

the first time I walked in the door with her. But that doesn't mean we know what to do with it. We just live there.''

That was slightly less than sincere. I had known from the moment I crossed the threshold that the house was our style, *my* style. The outside hadn't impressed us. We'd driven past it time and again—people who live in Pullman, Washington, do drive the eight miles to Moscow, Idaho, time and again, and the airport road is a pleasanter, prettier drive than the main highway—we'd seen the For Sale sign and agreed that it wasn't worth looking at. Only despair of finding anything better, and a reduced asking price, had persuaded us to give it a glance. The front looked, as Roger put it, like an acrocephalic garage—the butt end of a sharply peaked roof set on a featureless white frame face.

"Of course, it's not really the front," I said. "The side is the front."

It was true. What had been intended as the front door faced east, a perfect 90 degrees away from the airport road onto the gravel turnoff that led farther into the surrounding farm country. "This is where somebody meant to put in a circle drive," the real estate agent said, amused. "But you see what they did instead."

What somebody had done instead was plunk down a freestanding garage, its door flush with the end of the house and just enough space between them for a sidewalk bordered with discouraged daylilies. Daylilies are the only flowers in existence that I actively dislike. Behind the garage was a line of other small outbuildings, which the agent identified as a henhouse, a potting shed, and a toolshed. Between the toolshed and the gravel turnoff was the gravelike mound of a fruit cellar.

"You could take all of these out if you wanted to," he added encouragingly. "Or move them farther back on the property. Except the fruit cellar, of course. That's mostly underground."

Roger hunched his shoulders in a philosophical shrug. "Circle drives are effete."

From the daylily sidewalk there were three steps up to a little concrete entrance porch, with a useless gable over the paneled front door. Inside, a proper foyer with hall closet and stains that indicated where the umbrella stand and potted plants had stood, and a door to the kitchen, and a door that opened onto a flight of stairs leading up to the bedrooms. A big living room ran the full length of the north side, with a bow window ("That's going to make it harder to heat," Roger observed) opposite a fireplace. A separate dining room—"Look, a real door," I said; "I like houses with doors"—with west windows, and another real door into the kitchen.

But the natural way to enter the house was by the south door, straight to the kitchen in the first place. That was the way the agent first showed us in, and that was when I knew this was a house where I could be comfortable. Not to look like a pushover, I kept up a stream of objections. "On a gravel road with wheat fields all around—it's going to be dusty. We'll get pesticides blowing into our food. Right off the airport road—planes will be buzzing us. And there's no front yard. Everybody will come to the kitchen door, and I'm not sure I want people seeing our messy kitchen. Look at the view from these east windows—you can't see anything but the garage and all those sheds." But I loved it. I've never been anybody's idea of a cook, but I like kitchens. This kitchen was full of sunshine, and multitudes of cabinets and little drawers, and space—enough for a proper kitchen table that you could sit around and walk around and pile things on. One door into the dining room and one into the foyer.

"Of course, this south door doesn't open exactly *into* the kitchen," the agent said. "It opens into the basement stairwell, and there's this little entrance landing where you can take off your muddy shoes and hang up your coats on these hooks. So it's nice that way. And nice for the kids to be able to run straight downstairs and not mess up your living space."

"When was this built?" Roger asked. We were outside again, squinting up at the house and trying to imagine loving it.

"About nineteen-forty," the agent said. "They still knew how to build houses then." He kicked at a flat stone almost buried in the grass. "Of course, there was an old homestead here before. This was part of the walk, I guess."

There were trees, too—a valuable consideration on the rolling prairie land of the Palouse; not only the little golden willows along the trickle of creek, but the ruins of a poplar windbreak on the west side, a maple behind the house, some weedy mountain-ash trees among the towering lilacs at the back of the yard, and an old apple orchard on the hillside above.

"This used to be part of the Morrisey farm," the agent explained. "The reason this little parcel is for sale is because when the son took over the farming he built himself a house on the other side, and when the old folks died he rented this one out till it got to be too much trouble to bother with. It's nice for somebody that works in town and wants to live in the country. Your five acres includes this whole front side of the hill. Those are pea fields over yonder. Or lentils; hard to tell from here."

Roger nudged me. "You see? It's not all wheat."

"So we get a variety of pesticides," I said. But we were both humming when we headed back to the car. We do that sometimes.

We came back with the children the next day. Melanie was still a baby—it was her arrival that had roused us to looking for a bigger house—and Todd was in his three-year-old glory, not yet chastened by nursery school. He took off immediately on a tour of the outbuildings, Roger behind him for damage control. Melanie was fussing in my arms, upset from being waked at the wrong time. "Wait a minute!" Roger shouted, as Todd struggled to lift the sloping door of the fruit cellar.

"Is that thing safe?" I asked the real estate agent. The

world looked bleaker and more dangerous than it had a few minutes ago. Melanie's cry rose to a squall. Out here in the country, away from doctors and pavements and block parents, who knew what unanticipated hazards might threaten my children?

"The door may need some fixing," the agent said loudly. "But the cellar's as sound as the Rock of Gibraltar. I inspected it myself." I followed him reluctantly to the kitchen door. He held it open for me, and I walked in. Melanie stopped crying.

I was looking into cabinets when Todd burst in a few minutes later, managing the kitchen door as if he'd practiced opening it for weeks. "Mom, come! Come! There were Indians here!"

"Of course there were," I said. "There were Indians all over this country."

"No, I mean in the fruit cellar!"

The real estate agent might have inspected, but it took a three-year-old to find Indian sign. I followed Todd, putting a tranquil Melanie into Roger's arms as we passed in the driveway. "It's dark in there," Roger warned.

"Don't worry, there's a flashlight here," I called back. It sat ready in the grass beside the open cellar door. I clicked it on—the case was faded and cracked, but it worked— and followed Todd down the stone steps. Inside, the wonderful underground smell that always makes me think of fresh mushrooms.

In the back wall, just at Todd height, an oblong niche had been dug into the dark earth. "Wait, wait a minute, Todd!" I pulled his hands back out of the hole. One of them came out clutching an arrowhead, the other a bedraggled and filthy feather. He turned his triumphant grin up to me in the flashlight beam, and I laughed. "Indians, Todd! You were right. Take those and show Daddy."

"And these!" He stopped for more cobwebbed treasures, already tumbled onto the dirt floor. I turned the beam to light his way out, and then bent to examine the niche.

Two feet wide and barely a foot deep, it had been crookedly troweled into the solid soil; a cruder storage place than the board shelves that lined the cellar's long sides. Perhaps a child had hidden this very small and very amateur collection here decades ago—the thankless son who had built his own house on the opposite side of the farm and sold this one, forgetting his treasures, when it became "too much trouble"—or perhaps the old people who had built and lived and died here. Maybe the first homesteaders had personally looted these once-useful curios from the real owners of the land. There were more arrowheads, a scattering of feathers and tiny bones and pebbles and a scrap of fur—remnants, perhaps, of a medicine bag—and toward the back, squatting in my flashlight's beam, a little lump with eyes. It looked so much at home there that I hesitated before I reached in and closed my hand over it.

It was carved stone—or rather, pecked stone. Its great owl eyes were two sets of nested circles, their broad lines formed of many little pockmarks, as if they had been chipped out with a hammer and nail. I carried it with me into the sunshine, where Todd was exhibiting his prizes to Roger and the agent.

"How does he know about Indians?" Roger asked me, impressed by his son's sophistication.

"Didn't he show you that book we've been reading?" I opened my hand, displaying the little figure, and Roger shifted the baby in his arms to pick it off my palm.

"You know what this reminds me of?" He squinted at the shapeless lump, lifting it in the sunlight. "That time I let Clint Golding and his anthropological bunch talk me into going down the Columbia on one of their petroglyph-viewing tours. There's a big one somewhere down by the Dalles that looks just like this—all eyes. Miniaturize that one by a factor of about forty or fifty, and you'd have this." He tilted it back and forth. "She Sees You Come, She Sees You Go. That's what the local Indians call it, or so I was told. I don't know how far you can trust an anthropologist."

"Let's put it back," I said. "Come on, Todd, let's put all of this back where it belongs."

"My mom," Todd confided to the agent, "likes old stuff."

We came back one more time, Roger and I alone. That was our house-hunting strategy: First, check out a possibility; then, if we liked it, try it on the kids ("or try the kids on it," as I told friends); and finally, if it was still holding up, go over it once more without the distractions of children or agent.

"There are so many things wrong with it," I protested, running a hand lovingly over the mantel. "That dinky little bathroom off the dining room! And the one upstairs isn't much better."

"We're lucky to get two baths at all in a house this age," Roger said. "Of course, the whole place faces the wrong way. There's that huge backyard with the absolute minimum of sun, and no room to plant anything in front. What's the use of moving to the country if we can't have a garden?"

"It's five whole acres," I said. "We can do anything we want to with it. And an apple orchard."

"An abandoned apple orchard," Roger amended. "We'll be doing well to get a pound of wormy apples. Basement completely unfinished—"

"But dry," I said. "And if we got rid of those ugly foundation shrubs, there'd be a lot more light in it."

"Plenty of room, certainly," Roger said. "We could install a bathroom and a computer room down there, and separate off the laundry area and the furnace, and still have space for a fair-sized family room. The pipes are all there; plumbing shouldn't be any problem. But I don't know about the wiring."

"And those wood floors will be glorious, once we pull this grungy carpet off and get them refinished. It's too bad the attic isn't high enough to stand up in. I'd love to have a sunny attic room to work in."

"It's high enough in the middle. Eventually we might knock out part of the roof and put in dormers."

"And the cats will love it," I said.

We looked at each other and laughed. "I think," Roger said, "we've just talked each other into a house."

Five years later, we were still congratulating ourselves on the luck or cleverness that had led us to our house. We complained about its defects, but much as we complained about our children's faults or each other's—the ritual complaints of happy people. The prudent have always offered such sacrifices to avoid any appearance of hubris, that excessive self-satisfaction which tempts the gods to set things straight.

By then, I had my own ideas about luck. Your luck shows what sort of terms you're on with the universe. Or, as Roger paraphrased me, "Luck's not accidental.

"I believe it," he added gallantly. "Pasteur was onto the same thing when he said that chance favors the prepared mind."

But Elizabeth objected strenuously. "I don't like that a bit, Penny! The next step is 'luckier than thou.' You know— 'I'm lucky because I deserve it, and you're unlucky because *you* deserve it.' "

"It's more a matter of competence than morality," I said. "It's the same way some people are better at making money than other people. Might doesn't make right, but it works."

I'd liked Elizabeth Bannerman from the first day she turned up in my Ancient Religions course—a big, fresh, jolly, handsome young woman, one of the few I was never tempted to think of as *girl*. She stayed to ask intelligent questions after class, and by the end of the semester we were friends. She was a teaching assistant, slowly writing her dissertation on women in fifth-century B.C.E. Sparta. I was the one who taught her to use "B.C.E." (Before the Common Era) rather than "B.C." (Before Christ) for a world to which Christianity had no relevance. As a reasonably good Catholic, she'd never thought of that.

When Roger put in for his sabbatical, we began thinking about Elizabeth and her family as possible house sitters, and when he got the firm offer from the Université de Montpellier, I called her immediately. They were weary of renting, perishing for a place in the country, and not yet able to afford a house that would fit them. Her husband, George, was a hunter and a would-be farmer (both of them were from midwestern farm families), stuck unproductively in a job as a telephone lineman. They had three children, spread over an age range that secretly horrified me: Mark was twelve, Jane seven, the baby barely a year old. The children had slowed down her academic progress— she was only a few years younger than I—but she took all the hurdles of her life with such vigorous good cheer that I could only stand back and applaud.

It was one of those everybody-wins situations that make you think you must indeed be on pretty good terms with the universe. The Bannermans would take better care of our house than we ever had, be good to the cats, pay the utilities, and give us exactly what they had been laying out in rent for a cramped little house in town. We could absorb the rest of the mortgage payment plus taxes and insurance, thanks to the generous arrangement Roger had worked out with Montpellier and the advance I'd just received for my first book.

"And we'll be saving money hand over fist," Elizabeth said, "even with the extra gas. We can grow our vegetables for the whole year, plus chickens, plus the apples. Is there room for us to put things in the fruit cellar?"

"We've never used it," I said. "You see what I mean about being wasted on us." I had never even taken the little Indian collection out of its niche. Somehow I liked the idea of the underground watcher there, all eyes and everlastingness. The kids, as children will, had made an idol of it at one time and then blocked it up with a piece of board and forgot it. Personally I enjoyed having a chthonic deity at hand.

"That's great!" Elizabeth said. "I want to do a *lot* of canning." She beamed at me. "I hope you enjoy the summer as much as I'm going to."

We had planned our sabbatical this way all along, with a three-month summer vacation up front rather than at the far end of it. Three months to settle comfortably into European mode and find living quarters we could relax in, rather than plunging into our work with residual jet lag, fussy children, and unpracticed language skills.

And we did think of it as *our* sabbatical, though we didn't refer to it that way in public. Even as it was, there was no lack of jokes about *this* Penelope not staying home while her husband took his Odyssey. I wouldn't be eligible for a sabbatical of my own for another two years. We had talked about waiting, but the Montpellier deal had been too good to pass up, and my textbook contract had come along at the right moment. I didn't have much trouble getting a year's leave without pay. "And this way," as Melanie had observed, "we can go twice." She had no notion, poor mite, of what a year in a foreign country involved, but she had picked up enthusiasm from Roger and me. Todd wasn't so sure. He'd had friends move away, and knew what it was to break contacts.

We aren't sightseers. We're so unsightseerly a bunch that in five previous trips to Europe I'd never seen Paris, and Roger, who's spent some time there almost every year for more than a decade, hadn't seen much else. Greece and Sicily are my thing; the Bibliothèque Nationale is his.

At the last minute we all had qualms. The children proposed taking the cats with us, and I was half-tempted to agree. You can't explain sabbaticals to cats. All they would know was that they had been abandoned by the humans they trusted. And Ajax would be seventeen years old this summer. The Bannermans were all fond of animals, besides being very responsible people; but what if Ajax needed some serious nursing? And it broke my heart to see tears in Melanie's eyes as she hugged Susie.

Fortunately Roger stood firm on that one. "They'd have to go through quarantine," he said. "And they'd be miserable. Ajax is a very old cat; the trip might kill him. Faraday, if we got him over there, would probably run away, and we'd never see him again." Faraday was the classically independent black cat, whose eyes, as Todd had pointed out, looked like solid orange juice.

"Couldn't we just take Susie?" Melanie asked.

Roger went down on his knees for an eye-to-eye. "Cats don't like new places. We'll be in a big city, where there are lots of cars and no grasshoppers to chase. Very dangerous for a little cat—very scary. We'd have to put her in a box to take her, and she wouldn't like that. You don't want to put Susie in a box, do you?"

"No. No box," Melanie agreed fiercely, and thrust her face into his shoulder. He closed his arms around her, and Susie escaped with an indignant mew.

But Roger had his own qualms. "You know, Pen," he said, looking at me over the car as we finished stowing the last suitcases, "this is the first time in about thirty years I've ever regretted leaving a place. People, yes. Libraries, yes. But place as place, not since I was a child." He slammed the trunk shut. "Remember when we went to Glacier and left the key with Sandy Sukovaty?"

"And the key wouldn't work, and he couldn't get in, all week long. I'll never forget. Lucky the cats were outside and the weather was nice."

"You're sure Elizabeth knows how to do it?"

"Elizabeth has practiced locking and unlocking every door. She has it down pat."

He looked back at the house, took a long breath, and let it out slowly. "Todd! Melanie! Come on, it's time to go!"

The kids have been used to camping since babyhood, so we rented a car in Brussels and camped our way to Montpellier. Not a totally stress-free experience, but it had its rejuvenating side. We laughed at the knowing looks of campground people who couldn't believe that Penelope Ross and Roger Deacon constituted a married couple.

"Maybe we should have gone for Ross-Deacon after all," I said ruefully.

"Deacon-Ross," Roger retorted, demonstrating one of the reasons why we hadn't.

In Montpellier we found a university-subsidized apartment in a new-but-not-too-new high rise, and began to settle in. Roger's job didn't start until September. Mine had already started.

Roger is History of Science, with a special interest in Nichole d'Oresme. I'm Greek Civilization, which is more specific than it sounds. I do get stuck with all sorts of classical history and art and literature and religion courses, and occasionally I find myself teaching Greek; but what interests me is what made people as far apart as Marseilles and Izmir, and as distant in time as two or three millennia, identify themselves as Greek. Roger's sabbatical was my chance to work on something I'd been wondering about—how Greek religion had changed outside of its homeland.

All this south coast, of course, was Roman long before it was anything that could be called French, and Greek long before it was Roman. Superficially, not much remains of the Greek occupation but a few names. The visible ruins are all Roman. The audible ones, too. Greek may have lingered in some of the urban centers for a century or two after the Romans took over, but Latin was the language that rooted itself here. Latin had mutated slowly into Provençal, and Provençal had been displaced only by French, another Roman ruin.

Still, the generations of Greeks that had lived and worked and worshiped here must have left traces. I was no archeologist, but I was an experienced peruser of museums. The Greek temples of Massalia and Antipolis and Agatha and Nicaea were long gone, but I was willing to bet that some of their worshipers' leavings could be found in the museums of Marseilles and Antibes and Agde and Nice. First though, I had a pilgrimage to make.

"Before you get too tied down," I said to Roger, "I want to go see some temples."

"Don't they have temples around here?"

"Not Greek temples. Roman just doesn't do it."

He squinted at me dubiously. "Do I have to see them, too?"

I've sometimes wished my children could have had a handsomer father, and played with the idea that I might have gone elsewhere for genes of pulchritude. Other than that, I've always thought I lucked out remarkably, considering the people I might have married.

"No, you don't have to see temples if you don't want to. I was thinking of just a few days. Just to"— I mimed a shudder of sensuality, snuggling more cozily into my skin—"you know, just to *feel* Greek temples again."

"Mmmm." He bobbed his eyebrows at me. Roger has nice eyebrows. "How's the drachma exchange rate?"

"I don't want to go to Greece. Sicily."

"You want to take the kids? It's all right with me if you want to leave one or two of them here, but I seem to recall you talking about showing them things."

"I don't know," I said.

"What's the problem?"

"No problem."

"You look grim, Pen."

"It's hell in Sicily. I'm not sure I want them to see that."

He looked suddenly grim himself. "Are you talking about the Mafia?"

"No." Though as I said the word, one of those little parental guilt alarms went off: *I don't worry about the right things. I should have been talking about the Mafia.* "No, it's driving down roads between three-foot drifts of trash and garbage. It's those instant slums—all the unfinished apartment buildings with people camped on every floor, with no electricity and no water. Not to mention the motorcycle purse-snatchers with the special knives for slashing shoulder straps. I guess I don't want the kids to see more nastiness than I can explain to them."

Roger gave me that look of his over the top of his glasses. "Isn't this the same island you've been bragging about for years?"

I sighed. "Oh, sure." There were so many things in Sicily I did want to show the children: not just the ruined temples, but Etna with its hot rocks and cinder geysers like the blowholes of infernal whales, the cactus orchards and centuries-old olive trees like arthritic giants, the cathedral clock in Syracuse with its marching mechanical figures, the pageants and puppets and decorated carriages, and the friendly, cynical people who would get a kick out of a pair of really rather well-behaved American children.

And maybe it was overprotective to try to shield them from the seamy side of southern Italian life. To shield them—let's be honest, Penelope—from the sight of poverty. Nobody has to cross an ocean to find massive misery and nastiness. Nastiness bubbles up everywhere.

He leaned over to bump the side of my head with the side of his. "Leave them here. We'll have fun. You need to be able to concentrate on your ruins."

Sicily, not Greece. I wanted to see Greek temples in a land where they were almost as alien as I; temples whose builders had plastered the native stone with gleaming white stucco in imitation of the brilliant marbles of their homeland—and, not incidentally, to protect against the searing wind laden with African sand and dust.

"I'll try to call every day," I told Roger. That was the least I could do, if *he* was thinking about the Mafia. "But if I don't get through, don't be surprised."

"I promise not to worry," he said. "Besides, the kids and I will be too busy."

I started at Palermo, partly for the museum and partly for the side trip to Segesta, where I could stroll through the best-preserved and perhaps the finest Greek temple in all Sicily. The powers that be have a sense of humor; it's a temple that was never finished, roofless not because its roof has collapsed but because it was never put on. Something wasn't quite right: politics, financing, maybe something invisibly wrong with the site. Not a place, perhaps, where gods had chosen to live. Whatever the reason, nobody's ever bothered to ruin it. The Sicilian sun baked and burned. Tourist children, unimpressed by weathered stone, ran among the windblown wildflowers, gathering fistfuls of red and blue. I stood soaking up Greekness with the sun.

My first call went through without a hitch. "We went to the beach," Roger said. "That's the last time I try that without help. Though I did meet a couple of very amiable young ladies. Small children are conducive to that."

"And here I am fending off the attentions of gorgeous young men, while you sport on the Riviera. Maybe I should stop fending."

"Count yourself lucky. I didn't get any attention—the kids got it all. You have a letter from Elizabeth."

"Already? You want to open it and read it to me?" Surely there wouldn't be a crisis yet, I thought. But Elizabeth was a nonstop talker. Maybe she wrote a lot of letters, too. Or just wanted to check in promptly at the start.

"*Dear Penny,*" Roger read. "*I'm sitting under the maple tree in your yard. Ajax just came out of the potting*

*shed where he's been spending most of his time and sat
down on my lap. Now he's purring.*"

"*That's* a relief," I said.

"Old Ajax is mellowing out," Roger said. "You know,
her handwriting is like a schoolgirl's.''

"You mean legible," I said. "Yes, I know. Go on."

"*The other cats are taking everything in their stride, even
Foxy.* Who's Foxy?"

"That's their little dachshund," I said. "She's about as
old as Ajax."

Roger read: "*We are settling in pretty well, with the
inevitible minor glitches.* She misspelled 'inevitable.' "

"Read me the glitches," I said.

"Hmmm. She doesn't specify. *We have tilled a 25 × 25
foot plot in the back and are getting the garden in. Mark
is working hard on the henhouse and hopes to install his
flock this week. George is being handyman to his heart's
content and more so. . . .*"

As he read, something inside me relaxed, reassured. The
house was all right. The cats were happy, or at least resigned. Elizabeth and her competent family would take care
of everything. "Let me talk to Melanie," I said. "I want
to ask her about the beach."

"Hey, this is great!" Roger said. "I haven't elicited
jealousy since I was a grad student."

"What makes you think it's jealousy? I'm just curious."

He made a kiss noise and laughed. "Take care. Here's
Melanie."

In Sicily, you can strike inland across the plains of Enna—
the once-fertile land whose grain had fed half the Roman
Empire—or you can trundle around the triangle of the coast.
I was sticking to the coast this trip. I didn't want to see
any unnecessary barrenness. Funny—sourly funny—that
Enna was Persephone's home, the site of the archetypal

rape of life by death, and life's irrepressible springing back. The irrepressible life of Sicily seemed to be on the coast now, and brutally shabby—at least if you stayed clear of the fancy new tourist motels. I took a bus, heading the long way, around two corners of the triangle, for Agrigento and its temples.

From the bus window you can see the rocks that Polyphemus, the blinded Cyclops, threw at the escaping Odysseus—sterile islets standing in the sea. Three of my fellow passengers pointed them out to me, with three different versions of the story. In Italy, as a bank teller once remarked while I changed my money, everybody is an archeologist. Or a mythographer.

There's a useful skill learned by people with work to do, especially parents of small children: how to listen and communicate and even enjoy with a piece of yourself, while another piece goes off alone. Alone on a crowded bus in Sicily, I thought about words. *Oikos* is Greek for *house.* Bastardized into Latin as *oecus* and then *ecus,* that gives us both *economy* and *ecology.* Even better is that wonderful Greek derivative *oikoumene,* the inhabited world, whence *ecumenical.* The world as house; humans, by definition, as inhabitants—it was a very Greek idea, at once civilized and natural. Like another Greek concept the modern world has never caught up with: Barbarians are ashamed to take off their clothes; only civilized people go naked.

Nature and civilization; it was Zeno the Stoic who had thought that relationship through. "You know," I told Roger on the phone from Taormina that night, "the next time I fill out a form that asks for my religious preference, I'm going to say 'Stoic.'"

I could almost hear his raised eyebrows. "You? I would have thought Epicurean."

"And you are clearly a Cynic," I said.

From the outside, I would have pegged myself as an Epicurean, too. In fact, there was a period in my undergraduate days when I claimed to be exactly that. One of my Epicurean pleasures was explaining to people how we Epicureans had been unjustly bad-mouthed for millennia. "It's not hedonism." *Hedonism* was a fashionable word in those days. "It's realism. Everything people do *is* for pleasure, or to avoid pain. Masochists do it one way, saints do it a little differently. Epicureans do it intelligently. After all, what's the most effective way to maximize pleasure and minimize pain? It's certainly not staying stoned and bloated and falling into bed with everybody who comes along." A good way, I had found, of halting unwanted sexual advances was to look the perpetrator in the eye and remark sweetly, "Do you mind? You're interfering with my pursuit of pleasure." Stoics, I had always assumed, were dull people.

But it was Epicureanism now that seemed dull, a sort of preindustrial Utilitarianism—the greatest pleasure for the greatest number. And Epicurus had taught, like so many benighted Christians after him, that the greatest pleasure came with unselfishness, forbearance, abstention. His big mistake, in my opinion. Whereas Stoics hold that pleasure and pain alike are superficial incidents, things to make the best of but not take seriously, and that the only morality is living in harmony with nature. If you're enjoying something, enjoy it; it will pass. If you're in pain, don't worry; it will pass.

I don't often dream about my children except when I'm away from them. An out-of-town conference is usually good for a sweet-anxious dream that often features them as infant savants. In Taormina, I dreamed that Melanie and I, with occasional help from Todd and Roger, were trying to rebuild a temple from its ruins. Todd's age seemed to be variable, sometimes much older than his actual eight years; Melanie was a diapered toddler. The temple was our house as well, with kitchen cabinets in the cella, and crushed bedrooms under the fallen architrave. I was explaining to the others, somewhat frantically, that the fruit cellar ("like other pre-Greek tombs in this area," I insisted) had been excavated in the bedrock without metal tools. "Stone can cut stone," Melanie asserted, foursquare in her diaper. "Break stone, break stone," I said; "not cut." A column fell, lightly as snow, behind us.

I had to come to Sicily to feel Greekness, and I did; but I also felt what I had missed before, the ancientness of the place. From my point of view, Greeks don't qualify as ancient. Neither do Carthaginians. But there were nations here before those latecomers, and politics and esthetics and theologies long before the Greeks invented those words. The stone-cut tombs that pocked the cliffs and crags were not only houses of the dead but wombs of the Goddess— the goddess most peculiarly and enduringly Sicilian. The Greeks had fused her worship with that of their own Demeter and her Girl, given her a human form and a Greek name—Persephone. But to think of her only as Demeter's daughter was to diminish her.

A Greek poet says that the great god Zeus gave Sicily outright to Persephone. It was she who provided those generous harvests for Greeks, and later for Romans. The Stoics, of course, had a sound ecological principle; as long as Sicilians had managed their island in harmony with nature, it had been rich. A less philosophical way to put it was that humans had angered Persephone by abusing her land.

I stood in the porch of the cathedral of Syracuse, looking up along a vast Doric column. It was easy to see why Christians had wanted to incorporate that power into their own version of the house of God. This had been Athena's temple once. Athena, Demeter, Artemis, Aphrodite—the Greeks had parceled out power in bits, focal points of the churning, meshing force that people have always prayed to. Not that Syracuse was unusual, except in the visibility of these columns. Many a cathedral has been built on a temple's foundation—faith belatedly plastered over practice. Place, it seems, is more important than theology. First we worship, then we think of a reason.

Plot all such churches on a sheet of graph paper, and you'd have a dot-matrix sketch of Europe—all the spots where people have found and commemorated nodes in whatever network it is they live in. Much the same, no doubt, in Africa and Asia and the parts of Latin America that were civilized before Columbus. (*Civilized*, as I always tell my students, isn't necessarily a term of praise. It just means "citified.") Things are different where there haven't been thousands of years of settled population. You don't find cathedrals like Syracuse's in North America or Australia. Does that mean the places aren't there, or simply that people haven't found them, or haven't built things on them? I didn't know.

"They don't keep it up too well, do they?" an American voice observed. "Did you see the dirt on that window?"

I put on a glacial expression (*I do not understand English or other barbarian tongues*) and glanced in the direction of the noise. A retired couple lagging behind their tour; I could see the tour guide motioning impatiently on the street below. The husband shifted his camera strap uncomfortably. "It's too bad they don't care enough about it to take care of it."

"Are you going to get a picture or not?"

"We don't have time. Anyway, we can get postcards of this." They hurried heavily down the worn steps, brushing through a Sicilian family as they might have brushed through a swarm of gnats.

If anybody had asked me, I would have said that "keeping a place up" doesn't have much to do with washing the windows. I laid my hand on the column. Maybe, I thought, the places *are* there, scattered across the continents, waiting for their people. They don't all have to be as obvious as the cathedral of Syracuse.

* * *

The hills of Sicily are nothing like the hills of the Palouse. Sicily's are blazing hills, strident hills, hills with a grudge. Good Greek hills, in other words. Sicily is full of natural acropolises. Agrigento is built on a steep-sided fortress of a hill. On the inland side, the grim ridge of the acropolis proper; facing the sea, a cliff battlemented with temples. I got there late in the afternoon, when sunlight lay flat and heavy across fallen stones, and the rock sanctuary just below the eastern corner of the cliff was all in shadow.

Agrigento is the Italian version of the Roman version of *Akragas,* which may well be the Greek version of a pre-Greek name. "Sanctuary of Demeter," the guidebooks call this holy place under the cliff, but so far as I know there's no evidence that it was exactly that. More cautious scholars call it simply a sanctuary of the chthonic deities—the Powers Underground. Sanctuary it certainly was. There were the caves into the cliff face, the round altars, the pits for pouring libations, and the trenches that had been filled with thousands of more solid offerings—little clay busts and figurines, all of women. But no inscriptions, no name tags. If this sanctuary is like anything, it's like another pre-Greek holy place, the sanctuary of Malaphoros at Selinunte, twenty miles farther along the south coast. The guidebooks call that a sanctuary of Demeter, too, but the only name there is Malaphoros. It means "Apple Carrier."

Along the top of the cliff, temples are strung like the jewels of a diadem. Some are shattered, some almost intact. Not one of the Greek temples in Sicily still has a roof—hardly surprising, since they've had to contend with the seasons of well over two thousand years, not to mention three or four changes of religion. But for the first time, pacing up the steps among the uncomprehending tourists, I wondered exactly what had brought down the roofs. A luxurious shudder ran up my spine. I didn't doubt that eventually beams and stones had gone into local cooking fires and pavements; but had they broken the backs of a few intruders first?

The last temple in the line, at the western corner, had been a marvel, planned to surpass anything in Sicily or in Greece. It was the temple of Olympian Zeus, and its architect must have had lofty ambitions. Everything about it was bigger, grander, more colossal. Instead of free-standing columns, there were to have been solid walls punctuated by half-columns, with stone giants between them holding up the roof. One of those giants lay on its back in the sunburnt grass, a broken limestone corpse with its elbows in the air, hands at head-level to receive the weight of a roofbeam. Carthaginians had sacked the temple before it was quite finished, and an earthquake had shaken it down. No one had ever worshiped there.

Just past its ruins, at the far west corner, is another ancient sanctuary, like the one at the east end but older. This one may go back to the Neolithic. The Fruit Carrier, the Powers Underground, had been in Sicily a lot longer than Zeus the Thunderer.

As the microwave flies, I was closer to Roger now than I had been in Taormina, but the connection was worse. Probably they didn't use microwaves. "I'm in Empedocles' home town," I told him.

"Whose home town?"

"Em-ped-o-cles. Empedocles."

"Oh, right! The four elements, the two forces. Very modern, if you take the elements as states of matter and the forces as attraction and repulsion. He called them love and strife, though." The line fizzed and crackled.

"What?" I said.

I thought he was probably laughing. "When will you get back here?"

"I want to spend some time in the museum tomorrow," I said.

"What? It's getting worse at this end."

"Day after tomorrow—Saturday. I'll be there Saturday."

"Good!" he shouted. This time I heard a definite laugh. "Another thing Empedocles said—" But after a minute's struggle we gave up. I dreamed of tangled phone lines and falling roofs. I hadn't even talked to the children.

My credentials were good enough—at least when supplemented by my amateur Italian and a lot of smiles—to get me into the storage section of the Museo Archeologico Nazionale. I didn't want to see the "best" specimens; I wanted to see the trash. Most of it had been all too biodegradable, but there were bins of chipped and battered terra-cottas from the temples' trash pits and most especially from those trenches at the chthonic sanctuaries. I hadn't tried to tell Roger through the static what it was I hoped to find at the museum. It was mediocrity.

Nobody uses the word *mediocre* except as an insult. All our children have got to be above average. A foreigner picking up English in middle-class America would surely conclude that to be mediocre is worse than to be flat-out bad. And yet mediocre is what we all are, almost by definition—with the obvious exception of the obvious exceptions. Why should we be ashamed of it? My own theory is that more marriages are destroyed by the pursuit of excellence than by lust, laziness, and spouse abuse put together. And for warping innocent children, it's right up there with fundamentalism.

The Greeks, of course, more or less invented the pursuit of excellence. The Doric temples were examples of excellence in practice. But once the expensive architects and sculptors and painters had finished their work and gone home, the temples, like the rest of the world, reverted to ordinary people. Ordinary manufacturers had made, and ordinary worshipers had dedicated, these thousands of little clay figures.

And it's little clay figures that outlast great stone temples, if only by unobtrusiveness and number, as ordinary people outlast royalty and rock stars. In the south of France I would find no Greek temples; but I thought I would find, in the back rooms of museums, the leavings of everyday Greek religion, and I wanted to establish some lines of comparison in Sicily.

At first they all looked alike, but they were all different. That in itself was impressive, because they were mass-produced from molds. For every one that had survived the millennia, dozens or hundreds of identical specimens must have ended up as Sicilian dust and mud.

Some of these battered figurines might represent a goddess, some a priestess, but there was nothing to indicate that most of them were anything but ordinary women. *I give a token of myself to the power that helps me.* Or were they surrogate slaves, handmaidens dedicated to the Goddess by both women and men? Or surrogate sacrifices? *I am not ready to die. Take this offering in my place.*

Thanks to the Greeks, that nameless Underground Power had a name: Persephone, Queen of the Dead. She was Demeter's Girl, too ("Maiden" is such a stilted translation of *Kore*) but in Sicily she was preeminently Queen of the Dead. Kore was always the slender, smiling girl whom Hades kidnapped—the crime that had stricken the rich fields of Enna with their first dormancy. Kore was the wheat reborn from its own grave, dancing green or golden in the sun. But Persephone had a stiller, graver power. Not everything is resurrected. She was queen of the part that is lost forever.

I was glad I hadn't brought the children. It was silly to have thought of doing so. With the connivance of the superintendent's assistant, I spent eight hours in the museum, not counting the two-hour interruption for lunch. I had to explain several times that I was both happily and faithfully married, but I did learn a good deal about the archeology of the Agrigentan area.

That night I couldn't get through to Montpellier at all. I went to bed at last dissatisfied and flustered, and dreamed a confused dream of sorting through endless broken figurines, some of whom I recognized. I was impatient to get home.

Melanie adored the marzipan pretties I brought back, but wouldn't consider eating them. Sicilian marzipan comes not just in the shapes of overcolored supermarket fruit but of flowers and nuts and beetles and prickly pears, so realistic that only a taste can convince you they're candy. Todd bravely took a bite of a green marzipan caterpillar and pronounced it "yuck," which confirmed their status as toys, not food. I was sorry when they got so messy they had to be confiscated. The puppet Saracen and the puppet Norman were more durable, and performed great feats all around the apartment.

The south of France is a different world from the south of Italy—a different room in the *oikoumene*. The language is a lot harder to pick up than Italian, but I had the head start of a reading knowledge and a willingness to try. I found out right away that the French, like most people, are generally very pleased with anybody who makes a serious and good-natured effort to speak their language. What they don't like are stuffy people who mouth strings of foreign-sounding syllables in the belief that they're speaking French and get annoyed when they're not understood.

"You're great," Roger said, and kissed me, almost knocking my glasses off. "You're absolutely great. Nine out of ten Americans in France at this moment are complaining about the French being hostile and rude and obstructionist, and you get along with them like old friends and neighbors. I love you."

"You didn't really think I'd be like *those* people, did you?" I said nettled.

"No, but—" His face went sober. "It's like lending someone you care about a book that's meant a lot to you. You're always afraid they won't like it—and *then* what happens to your relationship?"

I laughed. "What indeed? Or like the house. What if one of us had loved it and the other wasn't quite comfortable there?" I shuddered.

"You know," Roger said gravely, "I wonder if that isn't what's happening to Elizabeth and George?"

"What makes you think that?"

"I had a note from George." He rubbed his incipient bald spot, which with Roger is a sign of embarrassment. "I suspect he felt obliged to check in with me personally. The male-in-residence sort of thing. Definitely he's going to make *me* look like a duffer."

"What, in the male division?" I said indignantly. "George Bannerman is a macho wimp."

"Well, in the handyman division," Roger said, letting me pull his head around by the ears to plant a kiss on that spot. "But then, you always knew I was a klutz."

"Right. What's George doing? Don't let him mess up the house."

"I don't think we need to worry about that. We left enough real problems to keep him busy for at least the full year."

"Don't tell me he's fixing the garage door?"

"Well, he didn't mention that. But he has one or two more urgent things to cope with first." He made his rueful face.

"What's wrong?"

"Seems Elizabeth lost a contact lens down the upstairs bathroom sink; and when George tried to unscrew the trap, the pipe split—not the trap, I take it, but the pipe that goes into the wall, since he says he had to cut a piece of the wall out."

I was dismayed. "Our beautiful butterfly wallpaper!"

"He claims you can barely see the lines. If I'd cut it, the butterflies would be flying upside down. What worries me a lot more is that they've been having trouble with the electricity."

Nobody knew how old the wiring was. We had been expecting trouble since we moved in. "Tell him to get an electrician in and send us the bill," I said. "I don't want our house electrocuting anybody."

We found a retired schoolteacher in our building who liked to keep her British-style English in practice and was willing to tutor the children in French. "Madame is okay," Todd pronounced after the first few lessons. "She shows us good stuff." Madame's apartment was jammed with antique bric-a-brac, and the kids were acquiring an amazing vocabulary for old French trinkets and bibelots. As a useful antidote, she also took them to the playground behind the building, where, with her coaching, they joined in the intensely serious games of the local children. I breathed easier—another hurdle crossed—but at the same time I shook my head guiltily. I hadn't considered how awful it would be if Todd and Melanie didn't adapt; I had simply assumed they would. Well, luck is no accident.

In September, most of their playmates would be going back to school at the *école* a few blocks away. Roger had a talk with the superintendent, ending in the decision to enroll Todd with the eight-year-olds. Todd's birthday is in January, and most of his classmates have always been six months to a year older than he is, so in a way this was a step back for him. But given the realities of coping with a foreign curriculum and a foreign language, it made sense, even to Todd. "It's not like I flunked a grade," he observed philosophically. "Besides, I'll be in Gervais's class." Lucking out again; Gervais was the best friend he'd made so far.

For Melanie, there was a morning preschool operated

by the university, where she would get more serious French instruction and some minimal culture—singing songs and shaking a tambourine and splashing paint. Things looked as close to perfect as things get.

Elizabeth was an indefatigable correspondent. She wrote to me at least once a week, often more; and with the irregularity of overseas mail, her letters sometimes came in bunches. Part of this was her natural volubility; but part, I suspected, was a double diffidence—as caretaker to homeowner and as student to teacher. She wasn't my student now, of course, but that's a relationship almost as hard to shed as child-to-parent, and likely to be renewed by the very act of writing. I felt myself skidding into the same rut, answering her letters as if I were scribbling comments on a term paper.

Not that I tried to match her letter-writing pace. I used to love writing letters when I was an undergraduate, but not since I discovered work. Work is more entertaining and even better for the ego. It's the thing I most worry about for my children. How do you find your work, after all? Certainly not by planning ahead. I'm appalled by all these kids who select their careers in junior high on the basis of aptitude tests and anticipated earnings. No, you luck into it.

Elizabeth seemed to have found her work. She got excited about history. But her husband was still groping. Maybe he really was cut out to be a farmer—but not, I thought, a comfortable farmer.

Queen of the Dead, Queen of Underground. "You can't call it anything else without faking it," I said to Roger. "*Netherworld* is just too, too lit'ry, and besides, the meaning is wrong. *Underworld* ditto, and besides, it sounds like gangsters."

"And *Underground* is a British subway," Roger pointed out.

"Maybe not if you drop the definite article. Anyhow, I can't help it, that's what it means. Underground is where dead bodies go; underground is where plants sprout from; underground is what Persephone rules."

Conventional wisdom held that Sicily was Persephone's island because she had been the closest Greek match to the nameless ancient bisexual goddess (yes, exactly that) who had been worshiped there before the Greeks came. What I was finding—what I thought I was finding—was evidence that Persephone had been almost as important here, on the French coast. It was much too early to go leaping from branch to branch of the speculation tree; and I'm *not* an archeologist. The terra-cotta and limestone bits I was sifting through in the back rooms of museums were beyond my power either to identify or to date securely. I could only raise questions that somebody else would have to answer.

"It's lovely not to be on sabbatical," I said, giving Roger an impromptu hug. "This way, I can do all the things I'm not supposed to be qualified for."

"I wish I could do that," he said gloomily. "I'm beginning to feel sick of Nicole d'Oresme." But immediately he patted one of the volumes in the pile before him, as you might pat a dog you've just insulted. "Anyway, I thought you were getting at least one publication out of this."

"You bet I am. But I don't know how much it's going to do for my promotion chances. It may not fit the standard slot."

He reached to touch my arm with one finger. "You're unslottable, Penelope. The university will just have to accept that."

"How long are we going to stay here?" Melanie asked. She stood looking out the one window that came down to her level, holding her juice glass with its rim pressed against her chin. Not a fretful question, not complaining, not asking for anything. Just that terrible juvenile hopelessness that comes when children realize how totally the deck of power is stacked against them.

"Eight more months," I said. "I thought you liked it here."

She considered, sucking the rim of the glass. "I like it here," she said. "But it isn't home here."

"No, it isn't," I said, stricken—gratified, at the same time, that my children were so unlike that Hollywood version of middle-class American children, in whose unreal world such feelings did not exist. "But we *will* go home again, Melanie. Elizabeth's taking care of home for us."

"And she's taking care of Susie?"—the words forced out by need.

"Yes, sweetie, she's taking care of Susie for you. For all of us." I knelt to give her a serious hug, and we both got juice down our fronts.

Through the summer and into the fall Elizabeth's letters rolled in like the surf, regular except for the vagaries of postal weather. At first they blended into a litany that was half-humorous and half-apologetic. *I don't want you to think we're sabotaging your home, but . . . This week's minor catastrophe . . . George is keeping busy mending the steps. . . .* There was always some mishap to report—if not with the house or outbuildings, then with the Bannerman family. They had a round of summer flu, tripped on stairs, banged their heads on cabinet doors. *George is being such a handyman he's always covered with tape.* "Does that mean duct tape or bandages?" I wondered aloud; and Roger said, looking over his glasses, "Perhaps both."

I sympathized with Elizabeth's problems—after all, I had got her into this—but now and then I felt a smug little surge of superiority. George had turned out to be allergic to the attic dust—he had been up there trying to do something about a droopy spot in our roof that had him worried—and now he couldn't open the attic door without a sneezing fit. That didn't speak well for our housekeeping, but it made me smile. I remembered the first time I had seriously explored that attic. There I was on my knees under the slope of the roof, trying to move a partition that blocked off the last wedge of space above the eaves. I wanted to know if it was simply a space-waster, or another of the homemade storage compartments that were squeezed into all sorts of odd crannies. "It doesn't open," Roger announced, coming up the stairs with a load of boxes; "I already tried it. Maybe insulation behind it—" and at that moment a panel slid jerkily sideways under my pushing fingers and a torrent of treasure cascaded onto my thighs. I yelped and laughed. "What the hell is it?" Roger demanded, craning over his boxes.

"Nuts!" I cried. "Walnuts. Filberts." I scooped them by handfuls and let them pour around my knees.

Roger dropped the boxes with a thud and stooped to peer suspiciously over my shoulder. "I wonder how long they've been there. What happens to nuts? Do they turn rancid or just shrivel up?"

"Both, I think." I cracked a filbert against another one in my hand—it's what I've always liked about filberts, they're so easy to crack—and offered him the definitely unshriveled kernel. He munched it with the air of a connoisseur. "How is it?"

He grinned broadly. "Sweet as butter—or whatever it's supposed to be sweet as. Pen, this house has been waiting for you!"

I missed my house. Europe was wonderful, I didn't want to shorten the year; but I would be glad when it was over.

Gradually the tone of Elizabeth's letters grew more reserved and more somber. *I hope your work is going smoothly, and Roger's, too. I don't think I'll finish my dissertation this year after all. . . . We are all reasonably well. The cats are fine. . . . I'm sorry I have to send you*

another electrician's bill. We wish we were able to pay it
ourselves. At any rate we hope this will solve the problem.
. . . Thanks for the postcard from Arles. I envy you, Penny.

Elizabeth wasn't the only one with problems. "I don't
like school," Melanie said.

She had been accustomed to nursery school since she
was not quite three, and had always loved it. I remembered her silent, private tears on more than one vacation
day when there was no school to go to. "Oh, sweetie,
what's wrong with school?"

"I don't like it," she explained earnestly.

"Todd likes school."

"Todd's school is different."

"How do you suppose it's different?"

"He likes it," she said.

That seemed to cover it pretty accurately. Todd came in
almost every day in boisterous good spirits and so proud
of his French that he could hardly wait till after dinner to
do his homework. In Montpellier, Todd's homework was
a family affair—not because he needed so much parental
help, but because he had so much to show off. I was
pleased, Roger was delighted, Melanie seemed awed. It
wasn't until several weeks into the term that we found out
Melanie was supposed to be doing homework, too.

Roger happened to get the phone call; I had taken the
train to Marseilles on one of my museum jaunts. I got back
later than expected, excited over some fragments I'd found
at the Musée Borèly that looked to me like marble versions of Sicilian terra-cottas. Roger wasn't in a mood to
listen.

"I'd appreciate it if you'd try the maternal approach on
Melanie. She's stonewalling me."

"What's the problem?"

"Her teacher says all the children are given poems and

quotations to learn at home—and Melanie hasn't learned any of them."

"It's just a nursery school, for heaven's sake. She's not working on her Ph.D."

"Mademoiselle Whatshername sounded distinctly frosty. She says she's sent notes home with Melanie."

Melanie was waiting in her cubbyhole of a room, studiously looking at an Asterix comic book. I sat down on the bed beside her and gave her a hug that got no response. "Hi, Melanie."

"Hi."

"Do you have something that Mademoiselle gave you?"

She nodded slowly and slipped away from my arm to pull her private box from under the bed. Our children have always had private boxes into which no one, not even a parent, is allowed to peek on any excuse. We don't ask questions about the contents, and we don't even offer advice unless they're attracting ants. Melanie's was a cardboard boot box with one split corner. She rummaged for a minute, while I turned the pages of Asterix, and then mutely presented me with half a dozen folded papers.

I opened one. "*Il pleut, il pleut, bergère. Rentrez vos blancs moutons.* Oh, this is pretty, Melanie. Let's learn it, shall we?" We had been learning poems together since she was three.

She pulled it out of my hand, shaking her head.

"But why not, sweets?"

"Because Mademoiselle said to learn it *at home.*"

We worked that one out eventually, with linguistic explications by Roger, but we didn't touch the basic problem. It was true that we could have taken her out of school. I could have stayed with her while Roger was at work, which averaged about six hours a day, six days a week, or hired a baby-sitter for part of that time. But I needed my working time, too. I shouldered the appropriate guilt feelings almost deliberately—not because I considered myself guilty of anything, but to share Melanie's discomfort. Poor mite. I hadn't liked nursery school myself.

Almost three weeks went by without a letter from Elizabeth. "Don't worry about it," Roger said. "They're piling up in mid-Atlantic. Somewhere in the Azores there's a mailbag filled entirely with letters from Elizabeth Bannerman addressed to Penelope Ross."

"I'm not worrying," I said. "But it does set a new record."

Then came one of those write-your-own-message greeting cards, an idyllic scene of little-farm-girl-among-flowers, and in Elizabeth's round hand, *Just to let you know we're alive. Sorry I haven't written. More later.*

"What's the matter, Pen?" Roger said. "First you worry because she doesn't write, and then you worry because she does."

"I'm not worried," I said. "I'd just like to know what's worrying Elizabeth."

Melanie had started having bad dreams. "Maybe she's catching up on those nightmares that four-year-olds are supposed to have," Roger suggested.

"She did have a few of those on schedule. Anyway, I don't think there's a Bureau of Nightmares that keeps count."

"You think it's Too Long Away From Home beginning to tell on her?"

"Could be. I think it's telling on me a little."

Once the children were in bed, Roger and I would each take a slightly impatient breath and get down to work. We're both evening people, with our best ideas after dinner and a glass or two of wine—one reason we've never been heavy entertainers. At home we didn't have to wait for juvenile bedtime. We had worked downstairs, amicably sharing the dining table—the dining room had become a de facto joint office—while the kids played upstairs or outdoors or in the basement or in the attic. But in Montpellier, jammed into five small rooms on a single floor, with a foreign country just outside the door and not even a purring lap cat to relive tension, we had too much togetherness for concentration. We'd found that trying to do any serious study or writing before both Melanie and Todd were in bed only led to frayed tempers and hurt feelings.

We were still searching for the best allotment of working space. Our present compromise had Roger in the living-dining area and me in our bedroom. That meant I got wake-up duty—our term for being the designated parent to respond to bad dreams, attacks by monsters, sudden thirsts, and the like—until we ourselves sacked out, after which it was Roger's turn.

On the first whimper from Melanie's room—at least the first one audible through her closed door and the quiet racket of my lap computer—I hit "save" and got up; but in the time it took me to cross the narrow hall and open her door, it had blossomed into a desperate shriek. I lifted her bodily—this was no one-hug job—yanking covers away from her as if they were anacondas, and carried her back and forth, back and forth, hushing and hugging. After a while we could sit down on the bed, and I sang to her. She wouldn't let me sing any of the songs she'd learned in school, but the French lullabies that Roger had taught us were fine. She wouldn't or couldn't say what the dream had been. But at tucking in and last kiss she told me solemnly, "I don't want to go to school anymore. The ceiling came down."

We hadn't rushed into having our kids, like the get-it-over-with school of thought, and I admit there are moments when I look a little enviously at friends who have already finished with whatever stage of child development I'm coping with. But more often I'm feeling quite selfishly good about it, not only because Roger and I had time to get to know each other first and do a lot of Just Us things together, but because I shudder to think of what an inept parent I would have been in my twenties. I walked very thoughtfully into the living-dining area.

"Roger?"

"Mmm," he said—which is fairly gracious for an associate professor being interrupted while he's trying to revise a manuscript.

"Remember how we sneered at the Jacksons?"

He finished his sentence, put down his pen, and looked at me. "No. When was that?"

"When they were in Innsbruck, and we heard they'd taken Cheryl out of kindergarten because she couldn't understand German."

He nodded. "Right. I don't know whether I said it then, but I remember thinking, What the hell did they expect? *Kindergarten* is a German word."

"You did say it. And we were both saying how silly, what a wonderful opportunity lost, we'd never make that mistake with a kid of *ours*."

Roger tucked his chin down, leaned his forehead on one hand, and looked at me through his fingers. "Don't tell me."

I groaned. "What can I say? Todd is doing fine, but Melanie is miserable."

He ran the hand through his hair. "Yes, but how much of that is the school?"

"I really think that's the worst of it. She misses home, of course, but I think she could take that. There are lots of things here she likes."

"And she'll miss those when we get home again." His forehead wrinkled. "Damn it, it *is* a great opportunity. Children her age are supposed to pick up languages like little sponges. Couldn't she stick it out for a while? Don't you think she'll be glad later?"

"Oh, God, I don't know. No, Roger, I don't think so. She can still learn a lot of French. We'll be here for months yet, and she plays with French kids, and she talks to Madame. It's just the school; it's putting too many different pressures on her at once. The poor baby's hurting, Roger, really hurting."

He made noises—resentful, resigned, disappointed— but when I got up and put my arms over his shoulders from behind, he snuggled me around him like a comfortable jacket. "So what do you propose to do?" he asked grumpily.

"Take her out right away. Tomorrow. Then we can figure out what to do—home schooling, Madame again, snobby English kindergarten, whatever."

He picked up his pen. "All right. I'm sold." He laid it down again and pulled me a little tighter. "Hey, we've already broken the rhythm. Why don't we go to bed and think about it?"

I had hoped that Madame might be willing to take Melanie on every morning, but that was asking a little too much. We compromised on nine-thirty to twelve, Mondays, Wednesdays, and Fridays, which with a little extra help from Roger meant I could get away three mornings a week. Luckily he had no early classes. Melanie's bad dreams went away, but she was still given to wistful meditations with a juice glass.

Then came a letter from Elizabeth, the first since her uninformative greeting card. Melanie and I had gone downstairs together to look for mail; and when I saw the familiar schoolgirl handwriting, such a stillness came over me that Melanie had to tug at the tail of my blouse to bring me back. "Is that from Elizabeth?" she was asking. "Is it about Susie?"

It was not about Susie. *I might as well tell you,* Elizabeth began at once, *I've been really depressed. Just about everything that could have gone wrong this year, has. I won't bore you with details. I just wanted to explain why you aren't hearing from me the way you should. But the main thing for you to know is that WE ARE TAKING CARE OF YOUR HOUSE FOR YOU—underlined three times— and will continue to do so no matter what.*

The bits and pieces you mention about Persephone sound really interesting. I'm looking forward to reading your paper when it's published. But I hope we can talk about it before then.

Weather here is still nice, though we've had some pretty hard frosts. . . .

We had all agreed—"all" meaning Roger, me, Elizabeth, and especially George—that intercontinental telephone calls would be an unnecessary expense and bother except in cases of genuine emergency. But there are times when the written word is a very inadequate means of communication. I made sure that Melanie was well settled in her room, "writing a letter to Grandma Deacon," and then I came back to the living-dining area and stood beside the telephone, looking at my watch.

It's nine hours later in France than in the state of Washington. I had to count on my fingers—my brain seemed bemused—to figure out what time that made it for Elizabeth. Three-thirty P.M. here; the house would be just waking up, the birds making their morning statements outside, the cats wanting their breakfast, the furnace giving that little shrug as the thermostat was turned up. I ought to wait a little longer, give Elizabeth time to get her family fed and properly inserted into the day's routine—time to get George out of the house, was what I knew I really meant. But by that time she might have left the house, too. I wavered, my hand on the telephone. With the baby and the cats and the chickens, she couldn't be a late sleeper. But she'd be busy, half-awake, not in the mood or the position to talk.

I picked up the phone, quoting to myself the maxim Roger

and I had come up with years ago to justify our getting
married in uncertain circumstances: *When in doubt, don't
decide—just do it.*

I got through reasonably fast, for a French phone call,
and took that as a good omen. Elizabeth's voice answered—sounding, I thought, hesitant and apprehensive.

"Elizabeth—did I wake you up?" I could just hear the
baby crying in the background.

"No, I'm up." She sounded farther away than Washington. "Is this—it this Penny?" Incredulous.

"Yes!" I laughed at the absurdity of it.

Maybe she thought I was crying; her next words were
quick and anxious. "What's wrong, Penny? Are you all
right?"

"Yes, I'm fine. Everything's fine here. Are *you* all right?"

"Oh, golly, it's awfully early in the morning to answer
that." She laughed, evidently embarrassed. "Penny, could
you hold on *just* a minute? I think I have to do something
for the baby."

"Take your time. I'll hold."

Sounds of household business, George's voice, a child
complaining, the baby's cry rising shrilly and then fading
away. I tried to find it all reassuring. I would sound silly,
I hoped. Elizabeth would think me sweet and silly. George,
no doubt, would think me a nosy fool.

But Elizabeth's voice, when she returned, was definitely
strained. "Penny, you there?"

"Yes. All quiet now?"

"Listen, would it be all right if I called you back in just
a little while?"

"Of course," I said, chilled to the bone. "You have my
number?"

"Right here by the phone. Thanks. As soon as I can."

"What's the problem? Is the baby sick?" But she had
hung up, before I could tell her to call collect.

I tried to be annoyed—people who say they'll call back,
and you spend the rest of the day waiting by the phone! I

hoped guiltily that she would call before Roger came in. Not that Roger would give me any kind of a bad time; but if he arrived in the midst of this transaction, I'd have to explain everything to him, and that would make it real.

It was almost two hours later that the phone rang. I had shooed Todd and Melanie out into the playground and tried to settle down to work—unwilling to plan ahead, unwilling to speculate. I jumped, then waited carefully for two more rings before I picked up the phone. *Of your philosophy you make no use, If you give place to accidental evils.*

It was Elizabeth, laughing and hearty, profuse in apology. "I get these spells of being the overprotective mother. I wasn't so bad with the older kids, but somehow every time Molly cries a little bit different, I think she's got something ghastly. I had to rush her off to the doctor, and by the time we got in to see him, there was nothing wrong with her at all. Probably just a little tummy upset. George thinks I'm going crazy." She laughed boisterously. "So, anyway, here I am, and what can I do for you?"

"You can let me pay for this call, for one thing. Are you at the house now?" Somehow I couldn't say "at home." It wasn't Elizabeth's home.

"Yes." The heartiness washed out of her voice. "Is there something you want me to look for?"

"I just wanted to talk to you. Your last letter got me— well, scared."

There was a strange sound—a laugh or a sob or a shuddering breath, as if hands had touched her throat. "You, too? Oh, God, Penny. Thank you for calling. I didn't mean to scare you—I tried not to—"

"Tell me about it," I said firmly. Now that we had got past the horrible preliminaries, I was the teacher and she was the student. Whatever it was, *was* real, if only in Elizabeth's mind, and reality could be dealt with.

"This is going to sound ridiculous." I could hear the relief in her voice. "I know you love this house, Penny, but—" She stopped.

"But you don't."

A long breath. "It's more like it doesn't love me. That wouldn't be so bad, but it doesn't love any of my family, either." Her voice broke, and she covered the crack with a laugh. "I think it misses you, Penny. And it's taking it out on us. I'm kidding, you realize. I'm just a little worn down."

"I want to hear the whole thing," I said inexorably. "Come clean, Lizzie."

"Oh, God. Oh, golly. You don't know how glad I am to hear from you. I couldn't put this into a letter. It sounds so stupid, and besides, I hated to tell you—but I never had a good feeling about the house. You know, you talked about walking in and the baby stops crying; well, I walked in and Molly started whimpering. Not yowling or screaming, just whimpering like—oh, I don't know, just the most miserable little noise I ever heard out of her, like something was wrong inside. And you know she was never like that when you were here. And ever since then, everything's all wrong. I haven't written you half the things that have happened. Mark had to get rid of his hens; they just stopped laying, and a fox or a dog got in and killed three and mauled most of the rest. We've all been sick with this and that and the other and—" She swallowed so hard I heard it. "We just found out that Jane has toxoplasmosis." *

"What?" I said. Wasn't that one of the things people with AIDS died of? No, that was histo.

"Toxoplasmosis. I can't blame *that* on the house. It's endemic in the Midwest. You know, one of those things that everybody has, but usually nobody gets sick from. Cats carry it. You get it from changing litter boxes."

"Oh, my God," I said.

"No, no, not *your* cats. I'm sure she picked it up years ago in Illinois. Or got it from me. Pregnant women are the most susceptible. The thing is, you can carry it all your life and never know it, but once it gets activated—"

"Is it a virus?"

"No, it's a fungus. It attacks the central nervous system and the—the eyes—"

"But what *about* Jane? Is she all right?"

"She hasn't had to miss much school yet. The thing is—" She hesitated. "They don't have any cure for it. It's going to get worse."

Oh, God, Elizabeth! But I didn't say it aloud. The wise, supportive teacher, that's what I was. "So it's not acute, then," I said. "Have you seen a specialist yet?"

"Yes, we took her to Seattle last week. I hope you don't mind, Penny—we just put out two days' worth of food for the animals and took off, all of us. I thought it would do us good to get away from the house for a little while."

"Good idea. It sounds like you needed a vacation."

"Yes." She hesitated. "Oh, golly, I might as well say this. That wasn't the reason at all—the vacation thing. I had to drive because George's arm is in a sling—"

"What!"

"He fell down the fruit-cellar steps. He sprained his ankle too, but that doesn't slow him down. Penny, we have *all* fallen down stairs; every one of us. We've declared the fruit cellar off-limits. It's a death trap." Her voice shook. "The far end of it has started to cave in. The children are not allowed to go down in the basement alone, and I'm thinking seriously about laying mattresses in the dining room, so they won't have to go upstairs to bed." I heard her take a deep breath. "Anyway, I had to do the driving. And I would not, I would *not*, leave any of the kids here in my absence—or George, either. I think—" She mustered a laugh. "Well, if your house doesn't love any of our family, I think it hates George."

"Then for God's sake, Elizabeth, why don't you move out?"

She laughed hopelessly. "Because I promised to take care of your house for you. Besides, it's all nonsense. I don't actually believe the house is out to get us. I'm not *crazy*, Penny. Not yet, anyway."

"You don't have to be crazy to fall downstairs—just accident-prone. Whatever it is, if the house doesn't agree with you, there's no use making yourself miserable by staying there." My voice sounded so strong and reasonable, I felt reassured myself. "Just find yourself a place to rent and move out as fast as you can."

"Oh, Penny, thanks, but we can't do that. We made an agreement."

"Well, I'm nullifying the agreement. Move out, Lizzie."

"We can't *do* that. Somebody has to take care of the animals."

"I tell you what, Lizzie. I commission you to hire one of the neighbor kids to bicycle over and feed them every day—or every two days, that would be enough—" I was thinking rapidly about the feasibility of such a plan. We were on friendly terms with our neighbors, even though we testified on opposite sides at every public hearing on farm chemicals. But how would the cats take it? Faraday was likely to go exploring for a better home. Well, people were more important. But poor Ajax—

"And besides," Elizabeth said, "George would never agree. I barely got him to go to Seattle, and that was only because of Jane. I mean, he wanted to come, but he's dead set against being pushed around by my—my house paranoia. And besides again—that's a double 'besides'—if we're just accident-prone, we'll have accidents wherever we go; and if it's the house, then anybody who comes in here will be in trouble. Anybody but you and your family. So." Her voice had grown stronger, too. "I'm not going to run away from it. I'm really sorry I got you worried with all my craziness. I do want you to know that we're taking care of it. We'll fix the fruit cellar."

"Just leave the fruit cellar alone," I said. "Please."

"You know what I really think, Penny?" she said gravely. "There's nothing wrong with the house; it's just that we don't know how to live in it."

"Elizabeth," I said, "tell me one thing, truly. All right?"

"Yes, all right. What?"

"Has it been getting better, or worse?"

There was silence for a moment—the buzzing silence of an international phone connection. "Worse," she said.

I took a deep breath. "Just hang on, then. I'm coming home."

She burst into a flurry of protest. "Shut up," I said. "I'll be on the first plane I can get. And Elizabeth—" It was ridiculous, but I had to say it. "Just tell it I'm coming, all right?"

We both managed to laugh.

It didn't take as much explaining as I had thought. Roger shook his head resignedly. "Well, an irrational act for an irrational situation. That's perfectly reasonable."

"You don't think I'm crazy?"

"Of course you're crazy." He put his arms around me. "Do you want to take Melanie with you?"

"I can't imagine being there more than a few days. It would tear her up, going back and forth." I felt a double pang. Melanie needed me; but right now the house needed me more. I leaned against Roger. "Do you mind too much taking care of both kids? You'll have to hire a baby-sitter practically full time."

"Of course I mind taking care of the kids, and of course I mind the expense, and of course you should go." He kissed my nose. "And on top of all that, I'll probably miss you." Poor love, he did look exasperated. "Just don't blame me for whatever I mess up in your absence. And for God's sake—" He raised a hand and dropped it. "I don't know what to tell you. Do whatever you have to do with Elizabeth, but make sure the house and the cats don't suffer."

*   *   *

Outside the Pacific Northwest, most travel agents, like most other people, apparently believe there's only one city in the state of Washington. You're likely to end up flying three hundred miles past your destination, changing planes, and flying three hundred miles back. And if you're starting from Europe, don't mention the name of the state at all, or you'll be lucky not to end up in Washington, D.C.

"I don't want to go to Seattle," I repeated. "I want to go to Spokane."

The travel agent looked at me coldly. *Dummy,* was the message I received. *We are not talking about desires, we are talking about air routes.* What she said was, "You must go through Seattle to arrive at Spokane."

"Look," I said, drawing maps on the desktop with my fingers. "Here we are; here is Spokane; over there is Seattle, farther away. I want to get to Spokane the fastest way possible."

Dummy, her look said. *We are not talking about geography.* "The fastest way to Spokane is through Seattle," she told me.

I flung my hand up very Frenchly. "All right, all right! Get me the ticket."

Love and strife make the world go round. Attraction and repulsion. Empedocles was no dummy. From planets swinging in their orbits to little girls whimpering in their sleep, all we know of change and stability must be the product of those two forces, sucking and bumping and rearranging the universal raw materials. I don't believe—

"Pardon me?" said the businessman in the window seat beside me.

"Nothing," I said, and narrowed myself a little bit more. I don't like being stuck in the middle seat on a long flight, between a busy businessman and a sleepy grandfather. Evidently I had started my last sentence aloud. *Talking to yourself, Pen?* Roger would have said, and kissed me on some appropriate spot. Passion is nice, but the talking-to-yourself kisses are just as valuable. *Philia* and *neikos,* love and strife. I don't believe in gods, or demons either, but I do believe in focal points. Earth is unstable, what with all the bumping and sucking, but compared to ephemeral creatures like us it's pretty solid. *Philia* holds it together, *neikos* keeps it in the right shape—or, more likely, inter-action of the pair does both. And with all those forces pushing and pulling, there are bound to be focal points. Like the eddies you can see in a creek, stable in instabil-ity, holding more or less the same form and position even though they only exist as disturbances in a flow.

If you build a temple on a spot like that, probably you get results. The world is full of places where gods and saints and fairies have been doing cures and telling fortunes for thousands of years, and usually through several changes of religion. Believers are healed, regardless of what they believe. Opinion doesn't matter to a focal point. Attitude matters; compatibility matters. It's like a marriage.

Topology gets into it, too, no doubt. Do holes make fo-cal points, or do focal points make holes? Even the Rock of Gibraltar has a hole in it, one of those tomb-wombs that go back before the Romans, before the Greeks, before the Phoenicians. Before the Cro-Magnons, as a matter of fact; unless I was misremembering, the first Neanderthal skull was found in a cave at Gibraltar, though nobody knew what it was until after the German finds. But not all caves are shrines, even when people have lived around them for mil-lennia, and not all focal points have holes. Temples, when they aren't caves, tend to be built on high ground. But then again, there are vaults, cellars, crypts . . .

The flight attendants were passing out food and drinks again, and there was a general rattling of trays and maneu-vering of elbows. There would be major and minor focal points, of course—probably a wide range of discrete levels rather than a perfect continuum. (That's the way things work, according to Roger; everything comes in quanta.) In settled areas, the major ones would be discovered early. Those are the temples that last. But what if somebody built a house on a minor one?

It was a long way to Seattle. I ordered a gin and tonic, because I don't like gin and tonic, and concentrated on making it last. I hoped Elizabeth had given the house my message. When you go into a house in Sicily, you say hello. That's even if it's your own house, and even if you know there's nobody there. Old people say it's being polite to the spirits. It hadn't occurred to me before to think of it as courtesy to the house itself.

I would have half an hour in the Seattle-Tacoma airport—plenty of time to call Elizabeth. Perhaps we should have discussed what she would tell George about my spur-of-the-moment visit. George, I thought, was not a man who would take kindly to someone flying six thousand miles to examine his family's problems. The gin and tonic made my lips pucker.

I didn't have to worry about losing luggage; I'd brought nothing but one small carry-on bag. When I got off at Sea-Tac, the first thing I did was set my watch (still morning, as if the flight across an ocean and a continent were no more than a jaunt across France) and the next thing was to plop down my bag beside a public telephone. This might even be my best chance for a real talk with Elizabeth, unconstrained either by international phone rates or by family underfoot.

But with my hand on the phone I hesitated. What if George answered? I had nothing to say that he wouldn't consider idiotic. Besides, if I told Elizabeth what time I was arriving in Spokane, she'd want to drive up and meet me; but she'd be afraid to leave her family in the house, and George surely wouldn't come with her. George, I thought resentfully, might not even let her take the kids. He'd hide the car keys or something. More likely he'd give her a flat command, and I didn't know if Elizabeth would defy it. I didn't want to inflict that test on her. I turned away from the phone into the bar.

On the flight to Spokane I had a window seat, with an empty seat beside me. I started off with two aspirin. It was only a fifty-minute fight, but I knew that by the end of it my head would be throbbing. That's what happens when I have a couple of drinks in the middle of the day—not that this endless day had a middle to it. Small-scale instant hangover. We saluted Mount Rainier and banked eastward into an ocean of cloud.

Morality is a human concept. Neither gods nor animals ask themselves, "Is this right?" before they take action. What Zeno the Stoic figured out is that real civilization is achieved when citified humanity learns to live on the same harmonic principles as gods and animals. And plants—maybe especially plants. Zeno noticed that the only power really worth worshiping is the universe. By definition, the universe includes everything; there is nothing outside it. Deities are only parts of it; and, as another Greek pointed out, the whole is greater than any of its parts.

But *universe* is a Latinism. The Greek equivalent is *kosmos*. It means "order" and it means "beauty," which gives us both *cosmic* and *cosmetic* and tells a good deal about the Greek approach to things. If you live in harmony—*harmony*, that's another Greek word—with the cosmos, with nature, you get along pretty well with all the apparently battling powers that comprise it. Like life and death.

When it comes to the nitty-gritty, Persephone is the most important deity in the pantheon. Queen of the Dead, Queen of Underground, queen of all the fruits of the earth, Apple Carrier. Nature, of course, doesn't mean pretty greeting cards. Nature involves death and birth, neither of which is pretty.

I got off the plane congratulating myself on my lack of luggage and kicking myself for not having called from Seattle. Elementary courtesy, letting people know when to expect you. I checked perfunctorily with the local computer airline; as usual, the Pullman flights were full. Next step, to the nearest telephone.

One of my pet peeves is callers who hang up before you can get to the phone. I remembered joking about it once with Elizabeth. "So in the interest of universal harmony and communication," I'd said, "I always let it ring eight times."

She had agreed enthusiastically. "Oh, golly, yes! It takes at least four rings just to finish pinning a diaper."

But I understood why people hung up sooner. Eight rings is a long time when you're on the waiting end. Your mind can go through all kinds of elaborate fantasies between one ring and the next.

I let it ring seventeen times—twice eight, and one for just-in-case. Then I pulled the hook down with my finger and put the phone back quietly, as if I were afraid of disturbing someone. I picked up my carry-on bag and strode smartly to the nearest rent-a-car counter.

Between Spokane and Pullman, the highway cuts through the edge of what's called "the channeled scablands." That's got to be one of the most accurately descriptive geographical names ever coined. Picture a scab two hundred feet thick and a hundred miles across, split and furrowed in all directions by a network of cracks. Floodwaters tore those channels, as glacier melt piled up behind dams of ice and rubble and then broke through like the last deluge, time and again. Local fundamentalists who haven't thought it through sometimes give the credit to Noah's Flood.

But this has always been violent country. Long before the scabland soil was laid down to be channeled by water from a dying ice age, the whole southern half of what's now the state of Washington was inundated by flood after flood of molten rock—not spewed from volcanoes like Etna or Mount St. Helens, but poured like floodwater from cracks in the level plain. One of the things I like about this piece of Earth is the quietness of its power. Something like a Doric temple.

I don't like driving other people's cars—least of all everybody's rent-a-car. Driving isn't one of my easier skills, and having to cope with an unfamiliar personality at the same time, even if it's only a mechanical one, doesn't make for comfort. But today I hardly noticed. It was like that feeling of partial deafness when you're speaking a foreign language and the conversation gets so interesting you forget it's foreign. I wasn't thinking, exactly—certainly not planning ahead. I was feeling the countryside, feeling my way home.

South of the scablands, the landscape rounded. Not soft, not flimsy; but without angles, without straight lines, without roughness anywhere. Hills rolled around me like giant dunes, treeless, part the sandy gold of wheat stubble, part the brown-black of harrowed soil. Like rolling earth waves, like the rolling shoulders of enormous bears. I found myself slowing down and breathing easier. The Palouse was still here, and here was I on the Palouse. I made my foot a little heavier on the accelerator. If a car can have a personality—and any driver knows it can—then so can any other concatenation of forces and matter. Substitute *human being* for *car* in that sentence, and you don't change much.

Off to my left I could see Steptoe Butte silhouetted against the sky like a miniature Mount Fuji. And so it is: an ancient volcano, extinct before the later lava floods began, up to its neck in once-molten rock. Stroke after stroke of power from underground. Historical folklore has tagged that lonely little peak as the site of the Northwest's version of Custer's Last Stand—where handsome Colonel Steptoe and his soldiers were surrounded by a coalition of Indian tribes, and allowed to slip ignominiously away in the night, leaving their howitzers, their packhorses, and their supplies. As a matter of fact, it happened on a less impressive hill, already ten miles behind me to the north. But every hill has its history, and its prehistory.

You come over a certain rise and there's Pullman, instantaneously manifested out of the wheat fields: a little forest of houses and trees and university towers, color and roughness sprawled over four of those hills like a flowering vine.

Driving through town gave me a strange feeling. In Europe, Pullman would be unhesitatingly labeled a village. Once you've lived here a few years, the only strangers you're likely to see on the streets are students, who outnumber permanent residents five to one. I could have stopped the car almost anywhere, walked into a house or store, and yelled, "I'm home!" and people would have given me a hug or a handshake and started catching me up on the gossip I'd missed. But I didn't feel home yet. I felt like a spy, a ghost, a foreigner, slinking unseen through half-familiar streets.

Swinging past campus, I felt a more acute tug. Maybe I should stop just for a moment at the history office. I peered nostalgically at the students bolting through traffic. That bearded redhead had been in my ancient-history class last year. A hand-lettered paper banner was taped across the facade of one of the sororities: CONGRATS CANDY OUR GREEK GODDESS. Somebody had been elected to something.

I turned east down Farm Way, away from campus, away from town. Past the greenhouses, past the experimental feed-mixing tower like a Tinker Toy spacecraft on its launching pad, past the wildlife research field where a dozen bored-looking mountain sheep lay beside their bales of hay.

The whole Pullman summer was gone. I had missed the Hort Club plant sale, and the Garden Fair, and the St. James Episcopal Church's great August rummage sale. What did Etna and the Riviera matter in comparison?

I turned onto Airport Road, along the line of ancient willows. Antiquity had a different meaning here. Once past the Pullman-Moscow airport with its row of single-engined planes and its one runway tucked into a groove between low hills, it was hard to keep my eyes on the road. I kept looking up, ahead, to the left, straining for that first glimpse of the house. It would come into view suddenly, from behind a hill, and disappear again for a moment just before the gravel turnoff. That first sight had always been like undoing the first tight button—an immediate relaxation and a promise of comfort to come. The children might be squabbling in the backseat, the work in our briefcases might be pulling Roger and me in different dreary directions; but when we saw the house, we all responded with little comfortable noises. There was home.

Then where was it? I was edgy and uncomfortable with the car again. I'd been away too long; I'd spent too many hours on airplanes. For all the familiarity, nothing looked quite the way I thought I remembered it. Had I missed the house? Had I missed the turnoff?

Somebody honked behind me, and I realized I had suddenly slowed down. Luckily there was never much traffic on this road. Was there? I had a panicky feeling of alienation, of not knowing what country I was in. Jet lag, I told myself. This was what came of flying backward and forward across continents. I wasn't lost, and neither was the house. If I *had* missed the turnoff, I'd very soon come to the main highway, and I would simply turn around and come back to it.

No sooner had I made that steadying resolution than the house appeared, just where I was looking for it, and the world settled back into shape and position around it. The hills seemed more solid and the road more familiar. I felt, for the first time in over four months, the spiritual unbuttoning that meant coming home.

I pulled up beside George's secondhand pickup and got out. *We need to regravel this driveway,* I thought absently. The Bannermans' elderly dachshund—part dachshund, actually—waddled forward, industriously yapping.

There was a grit of dust on my teeth, something I might not have noticed if I hadn't been clenching them just a bit. That was homey, too—not the teeth-clenching, but the dust. The Palouse has the world's highest dryland wheat yield per acre, and one of the world's highest erosion rates. These hills look like dunes for good reason. They're windblown, like the loess hills of China—thousands of acres of somebody else's topsoil piled here ages past. In places, the topsoil goes down a hundred feet. I didn't have any clear idea of the timetable; Roger would know more about it. Perhaps these hills had been built just a few thousand years ago, while the Greeks, on the other side of the world, were deforesting their own hills for lumber and fuel and what we'd call development. Maybe some of the rich earth between my teeth had been stripped from the once-fertile landscape around Athens. Or, likelier—since Greece's erosion had been mostly runoff—from the overworked, overgrazed fields of Sicily. The wind that etched temples with dust from Africa could carry away the dust of Enna, and Palouse wheat might thrive in soil that had borne Persephone's flowers.

I stood with the dog yapping around my feet. As far as the dog was concerned, this was the Bannerman residence; I was on her turf. Something like shyness kept me from calling out the usual "Hello!" or "Anybody home?" If there were people here, they must have heard the car drive up or the dog barking. No other announcement should be necessary.

And somebody must be here. The family car stood in the open garage—that door still didn't work right, apparently—and here was George's pickup. "It's all right, Foxy,"

I said to the dog, remembering her name. "Where are the cats?" It seemed acceptable to ask that.

Hearing my own voice broke some lock that had held me motionless, and I walked past the car to the kitchen door. An enormous blob of fur, like a dingy yellow tabby brick, lay on the welcome mat. "Hello, Ajax," I said, and knelt to pet him. He opened his eyes and meowed fretfully, as much as to say, "You're late."

I'd had this cat longer than I'd had my professional degree. Telamonian Ajax, he had been christened, but in recent years he was as often called Schmoo or the Banana Slug. I had been afraid he wouldn't remember me. I had been afraid he would be dead.

Foxy yapped once or twice more and nosed at the door, ignoring Ajax. "It's all right, Foxy," I said strongly. "We'll get in." I gathered Ajax in my arms, and he twisted around to embrace me with his front paws, a trick he'd had since kittenhood. He was so light it startled me—a frail fur ghost of his old massiveness. His thunderous purr burst out, and I blinked hard, trying to keep my eyes dry enough for business. I stood up with him and disengaged one hand to knock on the door. No, my first knock wasn't firm enough. I tried again.

The door gave a little to my second knock; not quite latched. I pushed it open with my shoulder, sinking both my hands in Ajax's fur. "Anybody home?"

There was no answer. I stepped into the kitchen, and home descended on me like an echo. There were the signs of Other People here—the counters and stove and table were unwontedly clean and uncluttered, Other People's utensils hung from the wall hooks, and it would never have occurred to me to fill that barely accessible glass-fronted cupboard high on the west wall with bunches of dried flowers and herbs. But it was my kitchen nonetheless. "Hello," I said.

Foxy had gone straight to an empty food dish beside the refrigerator. After one sniff, she turned and waddled out the still-open door. "Elizabeth?" I called. "George?" I set Ajax down carefully, closed the door, and opened the bottom corner cabinet. Yes, they were still keeping the catfood there. I put a fistful of dry food into the bowl that Ajax was thoughtfully regarding and stroked his head.

There was a thump from the living room. I jumped defensively. Heck of a thing when I had to be defensive about walking into my own house. "It's not burglars," I called. "Come on and say hello."

Pat pat pat pat. I dropped my eyes from human to cat level in time to see Susie rounding the corner from the foyer into the kitchen. She stopped, surprised to see me. "Hello, little cat," I said, and knelt, holding out my hand to her. "Melanie says hi." It took a full minute of sniffings and hesitations before she was willing to brush past my knee and join Ajax at the food bowl. Would she be this shy of Melanie when Melanie came home? The year was less than half over.

I got up a little stiffly—all that time on the planes and in the car—and walked through the foyer into the living room. "Anybody?" It was almost a plea now. The middle sash of the bay window was up, and crooked—stuck, no doubt, as usual. George had installed the screens that Roger and I had never got around to—which in my opinion detracted from the whole room's appearance and definitely interfered with the view. On the Palouse, not enough bugs come in to make it worth bothering with screens, really, unless you have a bug phobia or a nearby barnyard. Of course, they *had* tried to keep chickens.

I knelt on the window seat and looked out. Nobody in the backyard, except Faraday stalking something among the golden maple leaves. Somebody had raked half the yard and leaned the rake against the maple's trunk. On the mountain-ash trees, clusters of bright red-orange berries hung so thick they dragged the slender branches downward like harvest festoons. Good news for the birds this winter, I thought. Faraday pounced.

"Hey, black cat!" I called. He startled so visibly I had to laugh, and jerked his head up, down, around. "Hearing voices, Faraday?" He stood in the grass and stared up at me with his orange-juice eyes.

I lifted my hands to the sash, trying to straighten it as I always did. It stuck for only an instant, then slid as smoothly as silk. "Hey!" I said, and laughed. "Welcome home." Faraday mewed plaintively.

On the evidence of the car and truck and the open kitchen door, they were here somewhere, and on the evidence of my unanswered knocks and calls, they weren't inside. The logical next step was to look for them outdoors, on the other side of the outbuildings or the other side of the lilacs. But now that I was in the house, I was reluctant to leave it without a good hello all around. I got up.

There was a new stain on the dining-room floor where one of the west windows must have leaked again. "Damn!" I said sincerely. From the kitchen came a series of high-pitched musical cheeps, Ajax's own anxiety call. I opened the dining-room door into the kitchen—something was wrong with one of the hinges—and picked him up. "Come on, Schmoo Cat," I said. "Show me around." He gave me the paw hug, laid his chin against my collarbone, and closed his eyes.

One of the treads halfway up the stairs was loose; I could feel it wobble under the carpeting. No wonder they'd been tripping. But hadn't one of Elizabeth's letters said that George had fixed the stairs? The banister was loose, too. I was surprised; George was supposed to be such a handyman.

The master-bedroom door was closed. From behind it came a trickle of sound—a sleeping baby on the teetery edge between slumber and serious crying. I opened the door, cradling Ajax with one arm.

Elizabeth was asleep on the bed, sprawled limply faceup on the covers. She looked like an oversized child—barefoot, dressed in shorts and sweatshirt, her face flushed and rounded and her hair tousled. A crib stood against the far side of the bed, and another of those half-waking whimpers came from it. "Elizabeth?" I said. She didn't respond, but the baby did. Definitely an awake cry now—awake and not happy.

Elizabeth didn't stir. She was breathing peacefully, her lips a little open. The corner of her mouth twitched spontaneously, like a sleeping child's. I eased Ajax down on the foot of the bed and went around it to the crib.

"Hey, punkin, what's the matter?" Molly must be almost two now. She was clambering to her feet, red-faced from crying, gripping the crib bars with solid little hands. She let me pick her up, but once in my arms she began to squall and struggle.

"What's wrong? What—? Who—?" Elizabeth, in a flood of disjointed noises, was sitting up clumsily. "Oh, my God— Penny! What's wrong?"

I plopped myself and the baby down beside her, jolting Ajax to a faint protest. "Nothing's wrong, except you're too sound asleep to hear people breaking and entering. Where are the diapers?"

She waved one hand vaguely. "Molly's room. No, wait— I put a few on the dresser. Oh, honey, *please* hush."

I found a diaper, but it was Elizabeth, groggy with weariness, who had to change it. Between Molly's fussing and her own confusion, it was hard to convince her that she hadn't waked in the midst of some catastrophe.

"I told you I was coming on the next plane. The door was unlocked and nobody answered, so I just walked in. Where are George and the big kids?"

"Where—?" Elizabeth cuddled Molly against her with one arm and reached for the alarm clock on the bedside table. She tilted the clock back and forth, staring at its face. "Two o'clock? Or is that twelve-ten?" She shook the clock. "What time is it really?"

I laughed. "You're asking somebody in a state of oscillating jet lag. It's Wednesday afternoon, I can promise you that much. Would you like me to fix a bottle or something?"

"She doesn't usually want a bottle after her nap. But she's been so fretful lately. . . . Are you hungry, Molly? You want a nice banana? Oh, God, I *think* we have bananas."

"Where are the big kids?" I asked again.

Elizabeth focused on me over her daughter's head. "Mark had this district 4-H thing to go to, and he wanted to stay over with his friend Jerry. And I just bundled Jane off to one of *her* friends in Pullman. They've been wanting to have a sleep-in for weeks, and I told them this was their chance." She hugged Molly tighter. "Penny . . ." She laughed helplessly. "Oh, golly, it's good to see you."

"I called from Spokane, but you didn't answer."

She made a pained grimace. "Oh, it's the phone. It does that sometimes. It *sounds* like it's ringing, but it doesn't. You can't call in or out when it's like that. George can't find anything wrong, and neither can the main office."

I gave one more stroke and pat to Ajax, who had settled into the rumples of the bedspread. "Come on, let's go look for bananas."

"Right. Just let me get my shoes on." She heaved herself up. "Be *really* careful on those stairs."

The bananas were rotten. Fruit flies danced around them. "Look at that," Elizabeth. "This is post-banana-bread stage. There's mold on all three of them. Yesterday—" She looked bemused. Molly wailed, reaching for the bananas.

"Bottle?" I suggested.

"Yes, bottle. Could you hold her a minute?" She put Molly into my arms and started measuring formula mix with a generous hand. "You didn't see George anywhere?"

"No, I didn't. I suppose he's outside being household-erly?" I had to suppress a momentary urge to laugh. George, with his sprained ankle and his arm in a sling, unable to go to work and limping around as he tried to set everything straight.

Elizabeth made a vague affirmative noise. Molly accepted the bottle fretfully. "Shall I put her in the high chair?" I asked.

"No, give her here. I don't trust that thing." She gathered Molly into her arms and kicked at the high chair's legs. "It's not stable. Let's go outside, all right?"

I followed her out into the mellow October sunlight. Just outside the door, she paused. "Where's Ajax? Didn't you have him with you?"

"We left him asleep on the bed. Poor old boy."

"You know, that's a funny thing," she said slowly. "He hasn't been willing to stay in the house at all. I've even had to feed him outside. I guess now you're here, it's all right again." She looked at me, humor struggling with other things. "Oh, golly, Penny. Me and Ajax both."

I gave her a crowded hug, with Molly and the bottle in the middle. "You and Ajax are absolutely right."

"I took you literally," she said, muffled. "I told the house you were coming."

I laughed, embarrassed now, and let them go. "Did it answer?"

"Not that I could tell. But I don't think I speak its language."

"Tell me about everything, Elizabeth."

"Let's find George," she said in a small voice.

We walked down the line of outbuildings. Foxy followed us a few paces and lay down with a sigh. Molly bounced on Elizabeth's hip, waving her bottle like a baton. "I had to get some sleep," Elizabeth said. "I was up all night."

"With Molly? With Jane?"

"We've all had trouble sleeping at night. And I've gotten to the point where I can't stand to leave Molly alone.

George thinks it's ridiculous. He won't humor me any-more—not that he ever did humor me all that much. But I knew I had to get some sleep while she took her nap, so I just wheeled her crib into our room."

"And what's George doing all day?" I asked, trying not to sound stuffy. Obviously he wasn't helping his wife and children.

"Oh, he's battening things down for winter." She shivered. "I probably shouldn't mention this, Penny—but when I told him you were coming—" She broke off.

"He didn't like it," I finished for her.

Molly had begun to squirm, and Elizabeth paused to set her down, keeping a firm grip on one little hand. "It's your house, Penny, you've got a right to be here anytime you want. What George doesn't like is the whole—" She gestured helplessly. "He thinks we're a couple of silly hysterical females. 'Feeding each other's superstitions.' He actually said that." She laughed, but her voice had an edge to it. "Of course, he didn't say it quite that way. He said we're beginning to sound like ignorant farm kids feeding each other's superstitions."

"I think our superstitions are too far apart for mutual nourishment," I said, and we laughed together.

Molly handed me her bottle, reaching up to thrust it imperiously at my hand, and turned back to beg a ride from her mother. I liked that. My babies had never been on such confiding terms with people they didn't know well. Elizabeth was a very open person.

She hugged Molly protectively. "He might have gone up to the orchard. But he said there was a lot of cleaning up to do in the henhouse. George? Are you there?"

He wasn't in the henhouse, or the potting shed, or the toolshed, and from here we could see what was left of the garden behind the lilacs, looking sad and empty. "The parsnips didn't even come up," Elizabeth said inconsequentially. Molly fretted and squirmed, dissatisfied in any position. "I should have checked in the basement," Elizabeth said. She was standing stock-still at the toolshed's open door, looking back at the house. Her voice was desperate with fear.

"He's got five acres to wander in, Lizzie," I said. "And we haven't looked at the fruit cellar."

"I don't want to look at the fruit cellar," she said tightly. "We keep away from your damned fruit cellar."

"Well, I'll just cast an eye on it," I said, "in the name of thoroughness." She needed a lot more sleep than she'd had. "You start back to the house, and I'll catch up with you."

She took a step toward the house, and I turned briskly around the corner of the toolshed.

The fruit cellar wasn't there. I stumbled hard, as if the ground had risen in the middle of my stride. Jet lag does funny things to you. My brain shook and bounced, flying through turbulence. Had I forgotten the layout of my own yard? Henhouse, potting shed, toolshed, and the fruit cellar behind the toolshed—a grassy mound like a giant's grave, four feet high and twice as long, with a sloping wooden door let into its blunt north end. I took another few steps, scanning left and right almost frantically.

Then I saw it, and dropped to my knees where I stood. The door had been open, and at least one of its hinges must have torn loose early on, so that it had escaped being buckled in the collapse. It lay flat now, straddling one end of the depression that had been a mound. Reaching forward, I could just touch it. Before our time, somebody had painted that door a dark gray-blue, and I thought, as I had thought so often before, that we really must get around to repainting it. But no, that was the wrong thought to be thinking.

Three beams like railroad ties had held up a solid two feet of earth. Maybe George was in the orchard. Maybe he was in the basement. But in that case, why would the fruit cellar have collapsed? No, that wasn't the right thought to think, either.

I knelt there for what seemed a long time, waiting for things to make some kind of sense that I was willing to live with; and Faraday, who had never been an affectionate cat, strolled up to me and pushed his nose into my slack hand. Suppose you had a faithful dog, I thought, a faithful dog that killed somebody. But that wasn't exactly it, was it? That wasn't it at all.

People survived the most astonishing things sometimes. I stood up, stumbling only a little. Elizabeth and I were both healthy young women, we could wield a spade and a shovel. It was convenient, after all, that the toolshed was so near.

Karl Edward Wagner is one of the finest craftsmen of short stories in the horror field. He has written many novels, primarily in the sword-and-sorcery category. He is a winner of the World Fantasy Award, and his stories have been collected in the volumes *In a Lonely Place* and *Why Not You and I?* He is the publisher of the small press Caracosa House, and the editor of the annual volume *The Year's Best Horror Stories.* He lives in Chapel Hill, North Carolina.

Like Sharon Baker's story in this volume, Karl Edward Wagner's "Cedar Lane" is set in the house where the author grew up. Here, a number of very different men are linked by the house on Cedar Lane and the boy who lives there—and his fate determines their own.

Cedar Lane

KARL EDWARD WAGNER

Dream is a shadow of something real.

—From the Peter Weir film *The Last Wave*

He was back at Cedar Lane again, in the big house where he had spent his childhood, growing up there until time to go away to college. He was the youngest, and his parents had sold the house then, moving into something smaller and more convenient in a newer and nicer suburban development.

A rite of passage, but for Garrett Larkin it truly reinforced the reality that he could never go home again. Except in dream. And dreams are what the world is made of.

At times it puzzled him that while he nightly dreamed of his boyhood home on Cedar Lane, he never dreamed about any of the houses he had lived in since.

Sometimes the dreams were scary.

Sometimes more so than others.

It was a big two-story house plus basement, built just before the war, the war in which he was born. It was very solid, faced with thick stones of pink-hued Tennessee marble from the local quarries. There were three dormer windows thrusting out from the roof in front, and Garrett liked to call it the House of the Three Gables because he always thought the Hawthorne book had a neat spooky title. He and his two brothers each had his private hideout in the little dormer rooms—just big enough for shelves, boxes of toys, a tiny desk for making models or working jigsaw puzzles. Homework was not to intrude here, relegated instead to the big desk in Dad's never-used study in the den downstairs.

Cedar Lane was an old country lane laid out probably at the beginning of the previous century along dirt farm roads. Now two narrow lanes of much-repaved blacktop twisted through a narrow gap curtained between rows of massive cedar trees. Garrett's house stood well back upon four acres of lawn, orchards, and vegetable garden—portioned off from farmland as the neighborhood shifted from rural to suburban just before the war.

It had been a wonderful house to grow up in—three boys upstairs and a sissy older sister with her own bedroom downstairs across the hall from Mom and Dad. There were two flights of stairs to run down—the other leading to the cavernous basement where Dad parked the new car and had all his shop tools and gardening equipment, and where dwelt the Molochian coal furnace named Fear and its nether realm, the monster-haunted coal cellar. The yard was bigger than any of his friends had, and until he grew old enough to have to mow the grass and cuss, it was a limitless playground to run and romp with the dogs, for ball games and playing cowboy or soldier, for climbing trees and building secret clubhouses out of boxes and scrap lumber.

Garrett loved the house on Cedar Lane. But he wished that he wouldn't dream about it *every* night. Sometimes he wondered if he might be haunted by the house. His shrink told him it was purely a fantasy-longing for his vanished childhood.

Only it wasn't. Some of the dreams disturbed him. Like the elusive fragrance of autumn leaves burning, and the fragmentary remembrance of carbonizing flesh.

*   *   *

Garrett Larkin was a very successful landscape architect, with his own offices and partnership in Chicago. He
had kept the same marvelous wife for going on thirty
years, was just now putting the youngest of their three
wonderful children through Antioch, was looking forward to a comfortable and placid fifth decade of life,
and had not slept in his bed at Cedar Lane since he was
seventeen.

Garrett Larkin awoke in his bed in the house on Cedar
Lane, feeling vaguely troubled. He groped over his head
for the black metal cowboy-silhouette wall lamp mounted
above his bed. He found the switch, but the lamp refused
to come on. He slipped out from beneath the covers, moved
through familiar darkness into the bathroom, thumbed the
light switch there.

He was filling the drinking glass with water when he noticed that his hands were those of an old man.

An old man's. Not his hands. Nor his the face in the
bathroom mirror. Lined with too many years, too many
cares. Hair gray and thinning. Nose bulbous and flecked
with red blotches. Left eyebrow missing the thin scar from
when he'd totaled the Volvo. Hands heavy with calluses
from manual labor. No wedding ring. None-too-clean flan-
nel pajamas, loose over a too-thin frame.

He swallowed the water slowly, studying the reflection.
It *could* have been him. Just another disturbing dream. He
waited for the awakening.

He walked down the hall to his brothers' room. There
were two young boys asleep there. Neither one was his
brother. They were probably between nine and thirteen
years in age, and somehow they reminded him of his
brothers—long ago, when they were all young together on
Cedar Lane.

One of them stirred suddenly and opened his eyes. He

looked up at the old man silhouetted by the distant bathroom light. He said sleepily, "What's wrong, Uncle Gary?"

"Nothing. I thought I heard one of you cry out. Go back to sleep now, Josh."

The voice was his, and the response came automatically. Garrett Larkin returned to his room and sat there on the edge of his bed, awaiting daylight.

Daylight came, and with the smell of coffee and frying bacon, and still the dream remained. Larkin found his clothes in the dimness, dragged on the familiar overalls, and made his way downstairs.

The carpet was new and much of the furniture was strange, but it was still the house on Cedar Lane. Only older.

His niece was bustling about the kitchen. She was pushing the limits of thirty and the seams of her housedress, and he had never seen her before in his life.

"Morning, Uncle Gary." She poured coffee into his cup. "Boys up yet?"

Garrett sat down in his chair at the kitchen table, blew cautiously over the coffee. "Dead to the world."

Lucille left the bacon for a moment and went around to the stairway. He could hear her voice echoing up the stairwell. "Dwayne! Josh! Rise and shine! Don't forget to bring down your dirty clothes when you come! Shake a leg now!"

Martin, his niece's husband, joined them in the kitchen, gave his wife a hug, and poured himself a cup of coffee. He stole a slice of bacon. "Morning, Gary. Sleep well?"

"I must have." Garrett stared at his cup.

Martin munched overcrisp bacon. "Need to get those boys working on the leaves after school."

Garrett thought of the smell of burning leaves and remembered the pain of vaporizing skin, and the coffee seared his throat like a rush of boiling blood, and he awoke.

Garrett Larkin gasped at the darkness and sat up in bed. He fumbled behind him for the cowboy-silhouette wall lamp, couldn't find it. Then there was light. A lamp on the nightstand from the opposite side of the king-size bed. His wife was staring at him in concern.

"Gar, are you okay?"

Garrett tried to compose his memory. "It's all right . . . Rachel. Just another bad dream is all."

"Another bad dream? *Yet* another bad dream, you mean. You sure you're telling your shrink about these?"

"He says it's just a nostalgic longing for childhood as I cope with advancing maturity."

"Must have been some happy childhood. Okay if I turn out the light now?"

And he was dreaming again, dreaming of Cedar Lane.

He was safe and snug in his own bed in his own room, burrowed beneath Mom's heirloom quilts against the October chill that penetrated the unheated upper story. Something pressed hard into his ribs, and he awoke to discover his Boy Scout flashlight was trapped beneath the covers—along with the forbidden E.C. horror comic books he'd been secretly reading after bedtime.

Gary thumbed on the light, turning it about his room. Its beam was sickly yellow because he needed fresh batteries, but it zigzagged reassuringly across the bedroom walls—made familiar by their airplane posters, blotchy paint-by-numbers oil paintings, and (a seasonal addition) cutout Halloween decorations of jack-o'-lanterns and black cats, broom-riding witches, and dancing skeletons. The beam probed into the dormer, picking out the shelved books and treasures, the half-completed B-36 "Flying Cigar" nuclear bomber rising above a desk strewn with plastic parts and tubes of glue.

The flashlight's fading beam shifted to the other side of his room and paused upon the face that looked down upon him from beside his bed. It was a grown-up's face, someone he'd never seen before, ghastly in the yellow light. At first Gary thought it must be one of his brothers in a Halloween mask, and then he knew it was really a demented killer with a butcher knife like he'd read about in the comics, and then the flesh began to peel away in blackened strips from the spotlit face, and bare bone and teeth charred and cracked apart into evaporating dust, and Gary's bladder exploded with a rush of steam.

Larkin muttered and stirred from drunken stupor, groping beneath the layers of tattered plastic for his crotch, thinking he had pissed himself in his sleep. He hadn't, but it really wouldn't have mattered to him if he had. Something was poking him in the ribs, and he retrieved the half-empty bottle of Thunderbird. He took a pull. The wine was warm with the heat of his body, and its fumes trickled up his nose.

Larkin scooted farther into his cardboard box, to where its back propped against the alley wall. It was cold this autumn night—another bad winter, for sure—and he wondered if he maybe ought to crawl out and join the others around the trash fire. He had another gulp of wine, letting it warm his throat and his guts.

When he could afford it, Larkin liked to drink Thunderbird. It was a link to his boyhood. "I learned to drive in my old man's brand-new 1961 Thunderbird," he often told whoever was crouched beside him. "White 1961 Thunderbird with turquoise-blue upholstery. Power everything and fast as shit. Girls back in high school would line up to date me for a ride in that brand-new Thunderbird. I was ass-deep in pussy!"

All of that was a lie, because his father had never trusted him to drive the Thunderbird, and Larkin instead had spent his teenage years burning out three clutches on the family hand-me-down Volkswagen Beetle. But none of that really mattered in the long run, because Larkin had been drafted right after college, and the best part of him never came back from Nam.

V.A. hospitals, treatment centers, halfway houses, too many jails to count. Why bother counting? Nobody else gave a damn. Larkin remembered that he had been dreaming about Cedar Lane again. Not even rotgut wine could kill those memories. Larkin shivered and wondered if he had anything left to eat. There'd been some spoiled produce from a dumpster, but that was gone now.

He decided to try his luck over at the trash fire. Crawling out of his cardboard box, he pocketed his wine bottle and tried to remember if he'd left anything worth stealing. Probably not. He remembered instead how he once had camped out in the huge box from their new refrigerator on Cedar Lane, before the rains melted the cardboard into mush.

There were half a dozen or so of them still up, silhouetted by the blaze flaring from the oil drum on the demolition site. They weren't supposed to be here, but then the site was supposed to have been cleared off two years ago. Larkin shuffled over toward them—an identical blob of tattered refuse at one with the urban wasteland.

"Wuz happnin', bro?" Pointman asked him.

"Too cold to sleep. Had dreams. Had bad dreams."

The black nodded understandingly and used his good arm to poke a stick into the fire. Sparks flew upward and vanished into the night. "About Nam?"

"Worse." Larkin dug out his bottle. "Dreamed I was a kid again. Back home. Cedar Lane."

Pointman took a long swallow and handed the bottle back. "Thought you told me you had a happy childhood."

"I did. As best I can remember." Larkin killed the bottle.

"That's it," Pointman advised. "Sometimes it's best to forget."

"Sometimes I can't remember who I am," Larkin told him.

"Sometimes that's the best thing, too."

Pointman hooked his fingers into an old shipping crate and heaved it into the oil drum. A rat had made a nest inside the packing material, and it all went up in a mushroom of bright sparks and thick black smoke.

Larkin listened to their frightened squeals and agonized

thrashing. It only lasted for a minute or two. Then he could smell the burning flesh, could hear the soft popping of exploding bodies. And he thought of autumn leaves burning at the curbside, and he remembered the soft popping of his eyeballs exploding.

Gary Blaze sucked in a lungful of crack fumes and fought to hold back a cough. He handed the pipe to Dr. Syn and exhaled. "It's like I keep having these dreams about back when I was a kid," he told his drummer. "And a lot of other shit. It gets really heavy some of the time, man."

Dr. Syn was the fourth drummer during the two-decades up-and-down career of Gary Blaze and the Craze. He had been with the band just over a year, and he hadn't heard Gary repeat his same old stories quite so many times as had the older survivors. Just now they were on a very hot worldwide tour, and Dr. Syn didn't want to go back to playing gigs in bars in Minnesota. He finished what was left of the pipe and said with sympathy, "Heavy shit."

"It's like some of the time I can't remember who I am," Gary Blaze confided, watching a groupie recharge the glass pipe. They had the air conditioner on full blast, and the hotel room felt cold.

"It's just all the years of being on the road," Dr. Syn reassured him. He was a tall kid half Gary's age, with the obligatory long blond hair and heavy-metal gear, and getting a big start with a fading rock superstar couldn't hurt his own rising career.

"You know"—Gary swallowed a lude with a vodka chaser—"you know, sometimes I get up onstage, and I can't really remember whether I can play this thing." He patted his vintage Strat. "And I've been playing ever since I bought my first Elvis forty-five."

"*Hound Dog* and *Don't Be Cruel,* back in 1956," Dr. Syn reminded him. "You were just a kid growing up in East Tennessee."

"And I keep dreaming about that. About the old family house on Cedar Lane."

Dr. Syn helped himself to another hit of Gary's crack. "It's all the years on the road," he coughed. "You keep thinking back to your roots."

"Maybe I ought to go back. Just once. You know—see the old place again. Wonder if it's still there?"

"Make it sort of a bad-rocker-comes-home gig?"

"Shit!" Gary shook his head. "I don't ever want to see the place again."

He inhaled forcefully, dragging the crack fumes deep into his lungs, and he remembered how his chest exploded in a great blast of superheated steam.

Garrett Larkin was dreaming again, dreaming of Cedar Lane.

His mother's voice awoke him, and that wasn't fair, because he knew before he fell asleep that today was Saturday.

"Gary! Rise and shine! Remember, you promised your father you'd have the leaves all raked before you watched that football game! Shake a leg now!"

"All right," he murmured down the stairs, and he whispered a couple swear words to himself. He threw his long legs over the side of his bed, yawned and stretched, struggled into blue jeans and high school sweatshirt, made it into the bathroom to wash up. A teenager's face looked back at him from the mirror. Gary explored a few incipient zits before brushing his teeth and applying fresh Butch Wax to his flattop.

He could smell the sausage frying and the pancakes turning golden-brown as he thumped down the stairs. Mom was in the kitchen, all business in her apron and housedress, already serving up his plate. Gary sat down at the table and chugged his orange juice.

"Your father gets back from Washington tomorrow after church," Mom reminded him. "He'll expect to see that lawn all raked clean."

"I'll get the front finished." Gary poured Karo syrup over each pancake in the stack.

"You said you'd do it all."

"But, Mom! The leaves are still falling down. It's only under those maples where they really need raking." Gary bolted a link of sausage.

"Chew your food," Mom nagged.

But it was a beautiful October morning, with the air cool and crisp, and the sky cloudless blue. His stomach comfortably full, Gary attacked the golden leaves, sweeping them up in swirling bunches with the rattling leafrake. Blackie, his aged white mutt, swayed over to a warm spot in the sun to oversee his work. She soon grew bored and fell asleep.

He started at the base of the pink marble front of the house, pulling leaves from under the shrubs and rolling them in windrows beneath the tall sugar maples and then onto the curb. Traffic was light this morning on Cedar Lane, and cars' occasional whizzing passages sent spirals of leaves briefly skyward from the pile. It was going faster than Gary had expected it to, and he might have time to start on the rest of the yard before lunch.

"There's really no point in this, Blackie," he told his dog. "There's just a lot more to come down."

Blackie thumped her tail in sympathy, and he paused to pat her head. He wondered how many years she had left in her, hoped it wouldn't happen until after he left for college.

Gary applied matches to the long row of leaves at the curbside. In a few minutes the pile was well ablaze, and the sweet smell of burning leaves filled the October day. Gary crossed to the front of the house and hooked up the garden hose to the faucet at the base of the wall, just in case. Already he'd worked up a good sweat, and he paused to drink from the rush of water.

Standing there before the pink marble wall, hose to his mouth, Gary suddenly looked up into the blue sky.

Of course, he never really saw the flash.

* * *

There are no cedars now on Cedar Lane, only rows of shattered and blackened stumps. No leaves to rake, only a sodden mush of dead ash. No blue October skies, only the dead gray of a long nuclear winter.

Although the house is only a memory preserved in charcoal, a section of the marble front wall still stands, and fused into the pink stone is the black silhouette of a teen-aged boy, looking confidently upward.

The gray wind blows fitfully across the dead wasteland, and the burned-out skeleton of the house on Cedar Lane still mourns the loss of those who loved it and those whom it loved.

Sleep well, Gary Larkin, and dream your dreams. Dream of all the men you might have become, dream of the world that might have been, dream of all the people who might have lived—had there never been that October day in 1962.

In life I could not spare you. In death I will shelter your soul and your dreams for as long as my wall shall stand.

> What we see,
>
> And what we seem,
>
> Are but a dream,
>
> A dream within a dream.

—From the Peter Weir film of Joan Lindsay's novel
Picnic at Hanging Rock